The Ballerina in the Ghetto

Book One: Invasion

By Terrance Williamson

Dedicated to:
My eternal sons,
My loving daughter,
And my patient wife.

"It's really a wonder that I haven't dropped all my ideals, because they seem so absurd and impossible to carry out. Yet I keep them, because in spite of everything, I still believe that people are really good at heart."

Anne Frank

Chapter One:
Melody Palace

"The harrowing of the soul can be like the harrowing of the soil;
to increase the yield, things are turned upside down."

Neal A. Maxwell

With a deep breath in and out, Franceska studied her pose in the standing mirror beside her bed in her little room. She held her arms in fourth position, making certain to display gracefulness, strength, and beauty — the holy trinity of ballet.

A small clock ticked patiently on her bedside table, and Franceska groaned with annoyance as she noted the time. Her friends were late, as usual, and she was already dressed for the highly anticipated evening adventures.

Switching to third position, she frowned at what she perceived as sloppiness. To the untrained eye, her movements were unparalleled in refinement, but she'd practiced those positions since she was five years old and readily recognized, and loathed, her imperfections.

Not that it was easy to study her movements with such poor lighting. It was late evening, and the only light in her room was a small table lamp so dim she felt it made no difference if it were on or off.

"Smile," a deep woman's voice startled her, and Franceska clutched her hands in fright.

Spinning around to face the door, Franceska spotted her mother shuffling in with a few garments thrown over her arm, ready to be put away.

"You scared me," Franceska responded, looking at herself again in the mirror.

"You should be prepared for anything," her mother continued, shuffling over to the closet to hang up a skirt. "Especially with that new hairdo of yours. I almost thought a man was wearing your clothes."

"I thought I looked rather smart." She inspected her wavy brown hair, now cut shorter and curled in the latest fashion. "I'm certain my friends will appreciate it as well."

"If they appreciate being shocked," her mother cackled, amusing herself.

"There are good shocks." Franceska grinned as her mother struggled to reach the hanger in her closet.

"I'm still shocked by your dress," her mother grumbled. "Or the fact that a man is trying on your clothes."

"Don't be facetious," she scoffed, returning to look in the mirror. "No man could pull off this dress."

"I'm sure some will try," her mother muttered.

"Pardon me?" Franceska looked at her mother in disbelief.

The dress in question was a black, bias-cut evening gown with a slit that showed her gorgeous legs when she walked or posed. Accessorized with black gloves, a white hat, and white necklace, she was certain she was the epitome of beauty and fashion.

Without responding, her mother continued to struggle and groan until she finally retrieved a hanger with a heavy huff. Her mother was a typical creature, she freely admitted, especially for a Jewish-Polish woman in her fifties. Outwardly, she was everything you would expect, but her character was often at odds with expectations levied against her. She was hunched over, wore a headscarf, and smoked like a chimney with her other elderly friends. She was heavyset from the sweets she often snuck from the pantry in the middle of the night, and she wore a permanent scowl.

While Franceska understood that this description wasn't unusual compared to most women her mother's age, it was curious, however, that she was an only child. Most other young men and women her age had at least four or five siblings. She knew that many looked upon her mother with a critical eye, but Franceska had yet to work up the courage to ask why. Then again, she knew her mother's response to such an improper question wouldn't be worth the reproach.

"Why do you make so much trouble for yourself?" Franceska crossed her arms, watching her mother's predictable routine.

"I'm aware of my daughter's habits."

"And what's that supposed to mean?" Franceska tilted her head, wondering.

"You'll leave the skirt on the bed, and it will get all wrinkled. Then my ironing will be all for naught."

"You think so little of me, don't you?" Franceska muttered to herself.

"I don't think little of you." Her mother waddled over to her daughter, reaching up to pinch her cheek. "To me you're still a young girl."

"I'm twenty-two years old." Franceska raised a jaded eyebrow.

"And still living with your parents." Her mother raised an eyebrow of her own.

"I'm married to dance; you know that," Franceska answered, resuming third position.

"You can do both, you know."

"I doubt that many pregnant ballerinas win competitions."

"Are you nervous?" Her mother stared at her in the mirror.

"About the competition in Brussels next month?" Franceska asked rhetorically before responding quickly, "Not in the slightest."

"If you're going to lie, make it convincing." Her mother rolled her eyes as she moved closer to help position Franceska's arms, adding, "I can't tell if your position is incorrect, or it looks wrong because you're wearing an evening dress."

"Do you like the dress, by the way?" Franceska spun on her toes.

"If dancing fails, you can always turn to prostitution."

"Mother!" Franceska's eyes bulged, astonished.

"Are you sure you won't be mistaken for a burlesque dancer showing that much leg?"

"I'll have you know this is quite decent, even modest!" Franceska threw her hands onto her hips.

"Do you see how I'm dressed?" her mother gestured to her clothing.

"I don't mean to insult you, Mother, but if I dress like you, no one will marry me."

"I dress with as many layers as an onion, and your father still won't leave me alone."

"Mother!" Franceska squeezed her eyes shut in disgust.

"Men don't need you to show them anything. They're attracted to the very idea of us, whether we show skin or not." Her mother attempted to fasten the slit on Franceska's dress.

"Maybe I'm not after a husband. Maybe I just want to look nice. Have you thought of that?" Franceska said, defending herself by batting her mother's hands away to stop interfering with the dress.

"Look nice for who?" Her mother stood upright, wincing and kneading her back in discomfort.

"For my friends and other people. There is such thing as merely enjoying attention."

"You're a foolish girl," Her mother shook her head in despair. "Your beauty will attract the attention of many, but men don't know where to draw the line. And even once they're aware, you still must spell it out for them; they think the line is meant to be crossed."

"Regardless, Mother, marriage and romance are entirely foreign concepts at the moment," Franceska glanced at her ballet tights. "I have bigger ambitions."

Her mother scoffed.

"What?" Franceska shrugged. "There are many successful ballerinas."

"I admire your passion, but do you really see yourself in this profession forever? What happens when you turn thirty? No one will want to marry you then."

"What about Mata Hari?" Franceska grimaced. "She danced for many years."

"Mata Hari was one step above a harlot with an unquenchable appetite for men and avarice. If she's your shining example, you're doomed." Her mother glared with indignation.

"Still, she danced." Franceska grinned.

"Danced her way into an early grave, I might add!" Her mother landed a swift backhand to her daughter's backside.

"Hey!"

"I'd hate to see you throw your life away is all."

"I'm not throwing anything away."

"Well, if—" her mother paused, wincing and grabbing her back.

"You really need to see a doctor." Franceska changed the subject. "Your back is clearly getting worse."

"Where are you going tonight?" Her mother asked, ignoring her daughter, although she was still in considerable pain.

"The Melody Palace," Franceska said quickly, bracing for her mother's reaction.

"The nightclub?!" Her mother clutched her chest in horror.

"It's perfectly respectable." Franceska attempted to reassure her mother.

"Respectable?" Her mother frowned sharply, shaking her head. "Establishments like that permit untold sins. You'll end up unmarried with a bastard child. Try dancing then! You'd best rethink living with us if you have a child out of wedlock!"

"Nothing of the sort will happen tonight." Franceska rolled her eyes. "We'll be chaperoned, anyway."

"And you trust these chaperones?"

"Jakub, Adam, and Jan will escort us."

"Oh …" Her mother softened a touch, nodding. "They're good boys, but I'm surprised that they also engage in degeneracy."

"You have a flair for the dramatic, Mother." Franceska smiled sweetly.

"You know you can't dance with any man at the club unless your chaperone approves it, yes?" Her mother eyed her closely.

"I'm well aware," Franceska replied patiently.

"And if this ballet phase doesn't work out, you won't end up dancing at one of those night clubs, will you?" Her mother asked, fretting.

"I wouldn't be caught dead dancing there." Franceska patted her mother's shoulder gently.

"That Jakub …" Mrs. Mann squinted. "He's easy on the eyes, isn't he?"

"On the eyes, yes, but on the ears, heart, and soul he's a plague." Franceska's countenance soured.

"He comes from privilege." Her mother hinted.

"And if I were his wife, I'd be the princess locked in the dragon's tower." Franceska raised a skeptical eyebrow.

"Now who's being dramatic?"

"There's nothing interesting about these men. They're all from the same mold straight out of the box, ready to go. Not one of them grabs my attention in the slightest."

"Fine. Die alone then." Her mother shuffled back to the door, shaking her head all the way, but stopped to add, "You would be prudent to remember that God laughs at the plans of men. Your determination is noble, but life is anything but kind. It would be smart to plan for the worst."

"God laughs at the plans of men, but what about the plans of women?"

"Even He doesn't understand them," her mother scoffed.

"As always, I appreciate your encouragement." Franceska smirked.

"You don't need encouragement. You need direction." Her mother left, muttering at her daughter but then said ironically, "Smile!"

Where is everyone? Franceska looked at the clock again. *They're ten minutes late.* She went to the small dresser by the mirror and took a silver bracelet from the drawer, wondering if she should add it to her evening outfit when a knock rattled against her door.

"Yes?" she called out.

"May I enter?" her father asked softly. He was usually so soft-spoken she had to strain to hear.

"I wish Mother would knock before bursting into my room," Franceska replied with a chuckle.

There was no response from her father.

"That means yes, Father," she added.

"Oh, sorry, I didn't know." Her tall father ducked and entered the room sheepishly. He seemed genuinely scared of his own shadow—almost.

He was a good foot taller than most men, and almost twice the height of his wife. He was handsome, but Franceska often felt that his lack of confidence likely convinced him that her mother was his best and only option.

Removing his hat, he fumbled with it awkwardly. He stood in her room like a boy summoned to the principal's office.

"Yes?" Franceska answered after a moment.

"Um, your friends are here."

"Oh, lovely!" Franceska grabbed her purse from the dresser. "Are they all here?"

"I didn't count, but the loud one is here."

"Stefania," Franceska nodded. "You should learn her name."

"That would take all the fun out of it," her father said quietly with his dry humor. "She gets all bothered when I pretend to forget her name."

"How do I look?" Franceska did a quick spin for him.

"Oh yes, nice … good." He cleared his throat as he inspected her as briefly as possible, being awkward with emotions or any displays of affection. He was not a man suited for having a daughter, and Franceska often wished that she had been born a boy for the sake of his discomfort.

"Can I ask you something?" Franceska studied him, ready to head out.

"Your friends are waiting." He nodded toward the stairs.

"Mother is convinced that I should pursue marriage rather than ballet, but what do you think?" Franceska asked, presenting the question matter-of-factly.

"Oh, that's not for me to decide." He placed his hat back on his head before opening the door and mentioning, "We shouldn't keep your friends waiting."

"I wouldn't dare think to make them wait," she said, glancing at the clock again.

Leaving her small bedroom, Franceska closed the door behind her and walked down the thin, dark hallway behind her father. Descending the narrow stairs, Franceska followed the sound of her friends' heartwarming conversation and laughter.

"There she is!" a young woman exclaimed, and Franceska spotted Stefania in the small living room. She wore a bright yellow dress almost as loud as her vibrant personality.

Stefania chatted with Wiera in the living room, another friend of Franceska's. Wiera was almost as quiet as

Franceska's father, thus appreciating Stefania's volume, which was about the same as Franceska's mother.

Accompanying Stefania in the living room was Franceska's other friend, Wiera, who was almost as quiet as her father and appreciated Stefania's volume about the same as well.

Standing with Wiera and Stefania in the living room were three male companions who Franceska had become recent acquaintances with. They were ready to escort and chaperone the girls to the nightclub, but Franceska found them, in their matching suits and hats, so dull and tiresome that she scarcely paid much attention to them. They were all handsome, she admitted, but still wearisome.

Not to mention, that the amount of cologne the men had doused themselves in led her to believe that they had emptied an entire bottle between the three of them. It was so overpowering that her eyes were watering before she had even arrived at the bottom of the stairs.

"You look ravishing!" Stefania squeezed Franceska's hands, inspecting her from head to toe, while the three men gawked, trying to look appear polished.

"I don't mean to rush you, but we're about to be late," one of the men, Jan, interjected as he peeked at his watch.

"Then you should have arrived on time, Jan," Franceska chastised.

"We've been here for ten minutes, waiting for you," Stefania added.

"She's lying. We've only just arrived," Wiera added dryly.

"Feels like ten minutes," Franceska's father muttered under his breath.

"In either case, we should be off." Jan nodded and the men proceeded to the door.

"I've set you up with Jakub," Stefania whispered, slinging her arm around Franceska's shoulder, but even with a hushed whisper she managed to draw attention, and Franceska spotted Jakub glancing over his shoulder as he headed out the door.

"I don't need you to set me up with anyone," Franceska looked at her friend with annoyance.

"But you need a husband!" Stefania insisted.

"Need?" Franceska raised an eyebrow. "What I need is someone interesting, and none of these men have any distinguishing qualities, including that Jakub you set me up with. They're all lumps of clay made from the same generic mold."

"You should get to know them." Stefania urged as they left the house and into the street where the three men were waiting.

"I'd rather suffer a painful illness." Franceska replied sarcastically.

"Stop! Don't be ridiculous!" Stefania laughed loudly.

"Alright," Jakub, the self-designated ringleader, began excitedly. "When we get to Melody Palace, let me do the talking. I know one of the mangers, and he has agreed to give us special seating."

"Really?" Stefania's jaw dropped in surprise as she grabbed roughly and eagerly onto Wiera and Franceska.

"You're pinching me," Wiera complained as she tried to wrench her arm free from Stefania.

"How did you manage that?" Stefania pressed for details.

"I have a few connections." Jakub shrugged, feigning nonchalance but thoroughly enjoying himself.

"Why can't you be more like Jakub?" Stefania abandoned the other two girls and claimed Jan's arm possessively.

"That wasn't entirely necessary to say," Jan muttered.

"We should hurry." Jakub glanced at his watch.

"Do we have to walk? Can't we take the tram?" Wiera groaned as they began the short trek.

"It's a twenty-minute walk," Jan called over his shoulder as he and Stefania began to lead the pack, and Wiera and Franceska walked together as Jakub and Adam walked just in front of them.

"That's twenty minutes more than I can stand in these heels." Wiera looked at her shoes regretfully.

"I can carry you if you'd like," Adam said politely, but a touch too eagerly.

"Absolutely not," Wiera replied callously, while Franceska smothered a smirk.

"Please be my friend now and always." Franceska wrapped her arm around Wiera.

"Do I have a choice?" Wiera grinned.

"None at all." Franceska smiled back.

"Good," Wiera nodded happily.

"The tram is right around the corner," Franceska added. "It takes us near the nightclub."

"A nice walk would be better," Jakub said as if his word were law.

With a few disappointed sighs, the company proceeded through the heart of Warsaw, and even though Franceska was raised there, she never tired of the scenery. She loved the beautiful old houses, churches, bridges, cobblestone roads, and clashing ancient structures mixing with modernity. Warsaw had its troubles like any other place in the world, but she couldn't imagine living in a more beautiful city.

The culture was vibrant and energetic with pubs, restaurants, and nightclubs always filled to capacity. The city also boasted a strong appreciation of the arts.

Franceska was well aware that the dance and nightlife opportunities she was afforded in Warsaw were scarce in many other cities. She was blessed, and for the most part, happy. Adding a man to her life now would likely ruin things, or so she was convinced.

But when they passed an anti-aircraft battery next to a church, she realized the potential for a darker future for the city. It was an ugly machine, she thought, pointing its long snout at the sky.

She wondered if they would ever need to use such a horrible and hateful weapon, but glad it existed in the event they ever came under attack.

"What do you guys think of Hitler?" Adam began rather abruptly, and Franceska assumed the weapon had also sparked his curiosity.

"Well…" Franceska hesitated as she glanced at Wiera awkwardly.

"You shouldn't ask ladies such things," Jakub scolded. "It's not polite."

"Not polite? We're not entitled to an opinion?" Franceska scowled at Jakub.

"Please tell me you're not one of those suffragettes?" Jakub walked backwards to look at Franceska. "I don't suppose they support your dancing profession?"

"You don't have to be part of the women's movement to realize that my gender shouldn't obstruct me from having an opinion, or at least a concern, over potential threats." Franceska tilted her head with frustration.

"Opinion?! Potential?!" Jakub scoffed. "That's why women shouldn't discuss politics. They're too emotional and there is no threat. It's just propaganda from the Western powers. They're scared of Hitler and their fearmongering is putting everyone on edge."

"What about the pogroms?" Adam asked cautiously. "The race laws are rather concerning. They're not part of any propaganda, either. The Nazi government isn't taking any pains to hide how they're treating people they deem inferior. As a Jewish man, this concerns me."

"Let's talk about happier subjects," Wiera chimed in, and Franceska noticed she was growing uncomfortable.

"You're Jewish, too?" Jakub asked Wiera, who nodded.

"As am I," Franceska added.

"Am I the only one who isn't Jewish?" Jakub laughed as he looked around at the group.

"Don't worry, we offer great interest rates," Wiera spoke sarcastically.

"Really?" Jakub asked genuinely as he looked at her. "As it happens—"

"She was being sarcastic." Adam slapped Jakub's chest.

"Ah, I see." Jakub held his finger in the air as he caught up to her mockery, but then looked at Franceska and stated, "You don't look Jewish."

"And how is a Jew supposed to look?" Franceska grew annoyed.

"Well, you have very light hair and fair skin." Jakub shrugged. "You could have fooled me."

"Well, if you want a brighter topic to discuss," Adam began cheerfully. "There's a new moving pictures theatre opening soon."

"That sounds lovely!" Franceska grew excited, having admired the pictures since she was a young girl.

"Quite incredible what some directors are able to do with film in our modern era," Jakub interjected.

"They could probably even turn you into a gentleman," Franceska quipped while Wiera snickered.

"I am a gentleman." Jakub frowned at Franceska.

"In what sense?" Franceska tested.

"I come from privilege." Jakub continued to frown. "I'm competent, capable, and able to care for any woman lucky enough to be courted by me."

"The very term *gentleman* is in and of itself an oxymoron," Franceska began with a little more ferocity than she knew was necessary, but she also loathed Jakub's arrogance. "The nature of man is barbaric, beastly, brutal, and for a man to be called gentle is, again, against his very character. So, you then, Jakub, are just a man."

"Well maybe I'm what this soft world needs," Jakub defended. "Too many weak men creating difficult times for Poland."

"What do you think, Adam?" Wiera asked sincerely while Franceska watched him closely.

"I…" Adam glanced at Jakub, who was also gazing intently at him, "I think the meek will inherit the Earth."

"Ah, you're a Christian Jew then, are you?" Jakub smirked.

"Ethnically Jewish, but my grandparents converted to Catholicism when my father was born," Adam replied softly.

"And what ancient and outdated religion do you resort to?" Jakub asked Franceska.

"My religious convictions are private," Franceska replied sharply.

"Which means you don't have any." Jakub raised a brow.

"You know very little, but somehow that has convinced you that you know everything." Franceska's nostrils flared with annoyance.

"Or maybe I'm perceptive and that bothers you?"

"You couldn't be further from the mark if you had shot straight into the air."

"I think you fancy me." Jakub grinned cockily. "You'll see; by the end of the night you'll be begging me to propose."

"If the proposal is that we never see each other again, then please, propose now." Franceska smiled wryly as she glanced at her friend.

"It would be best if you remained in my good graces," Jakub said with a veiled threat, and, by the look he was offering, Franceska knew she shouldn't test him further.

"If he had any good graces to begin with," Wiera whispered, and Franceska giggled.

"What did you say?" Jakub asked angrily.

"It's private," Franceska snickered.

"You're both immature." Jakub began to walk quickly. "Good luck getting into the club without me!"

"Don't leave," Wiera called out in a soft and mocking tone, and again Franceska laughed.

"If I haven't mentioned it lately, I do appreciate you, my friend." Franceska smiled at Wiera who offered a coy smile in response.

"Where are you going in such a hurry?!" Stefania grew concerned as Jakub passed by them.

"He's offended that women have opinions," Franceska yelled to Stefania.

"What did you do?!" Stefania glared at Franceska.

"Shared an opinion." Franceska shrugged.

"You're insufferable!" Stefania hiked up her skirt as she chased after Jakub while shouting, "Jakub! Wait! We need you!"

"Stefania!" Jan followed suit as he also gave chase.

"Do you really suppose we can't get into the club without him?" Wiera asked with a measure of concern.

"Don't let him discourage you. He just wants to sound important," Adam began nervously but stood between them, offering each an arm. "Take my arm. No club in the world would refuse you two."

"Then why do we need you?" Franceska frowned.

"There's no way in hell they're letting me in alone." Adam offered a pleading look to both Franceska and Wiera.

"The club won't permit women without a chaperon." Wiera took Adam's arm. "So, I suppose you should be grateful that we need each other."

"You have no idea." Adam exhaled nervously and Franceska found his unease endearing. She much preferred a man who was honest and kind to one who was overconfident.

"Finally," Wiera sighed her relief when they rounded the corner, and the nightclub came into view just a couple blocks down the street.

It was a modest club, which Franceska appreciated. It wasn't too flashy, the music was usually enjoyable, the men were normally respectable, and the drinks weren't overpriced.

"It's a long line." Adam grimaced, seeing a queue of about twenty couples waiting outside the club.

"Alright, Adam, you have one job tonight. No matter who asks me to dance, you must decline." Franceska looked at him sternly.

"What?!" Adam looked back at her with wide, frightful eyes. "Why would you do that to me?!"

"Because a woman can't dance with another man unless the man who brought her agrees to it."

"I know!" Adam glanced between the girls in a panic. "I'm very aware of our customs. But I'm not the sort of man who can say no."

"Tonight, young Adam, you are that sort of man." Franceska pinched his cheek.

"Ow!" Adam pulled away.

"Same for me, too." Wiera nodded.

"I have to decline all suitors for you, too?" Adam slouched as his face paled.

"There's Jakub." Wiera pointed, and Franceska spotted him arguing with the bouncer, who was not amused.

"He's livid," Franceska laughed.

"Stefania must already be inside." Wiera looked through the line of people.

"You want me to decline everyone? Everyone?!" Adam asked again, and Franceska spotted his pulse raging in his neck.

The thumping of the bass resonated into the street as they grew closer to the club, and Franceska could scarcely stand the anticipation. She couldn't wait to have a drink while listening to the lively Polish Tango and watch with amusement as Adam either drew upon his courage or crumbled.

"I'll tell you a secret, Adam." Wiera paused when they came to the back of the line. "I have affection for you."

"Affect—" the word stuck in Adam's throat, and he swallowed so loudly that the couple in front of them offered a disgusted look at him.

"But I like a man who can protect me, and who can be confident. Are you that man, Adam?" Wiera looked up at him sternly.

"Yeah…" Adam replied unconvincingly, and Franceska imagined he was fearing a long and uneasy night.

"Good." Wiera nodded decisively.

"You can prove yourself now by getting us into the club ahead of the line." Franceska nudged him.

Squeezing his eyes shut, Adam took a deep breath, puffed out his chest, then opened his eyes and marched confidently, with a girl on each arm, to the front of the line.

"Where does he think he's going?!" a woman asked in a hushed tone to her chaperone.

"Oh, good, you can vouch for me," Jakub spoke to Adam when he noticed him approaching.

"We would like entry, please," Adam spoke politely, but awkwardly, and the bouncer inspected them as his gaze lingered on Franceska before examining Wiera and then nodding for them to enter.

"Hey!" Jakub shouted as he pointed to his chest and added. "They're with me!"

"They don't look like they're with you." The bouncer shook his head.

"Franceska! Wiera! They won't let me in without a girl!" Jakub pleaded.

"Sorry, we don't have an opinion on the matter." Franceska offered a feigned apology as Adam led them down a small flight of stone steps toward a black steel door.

Franceska beamed with anticipation as the music became more defined, and the sound of lively chatter spilled through the door.

"Ready?" Adam asked with a smirk as he opened the door, and the music flooded out into the street.

Franceska's heart was filled to the brim as she walked into the club. The dim lighting, the smoke-filled air, the lively chatter, the drinks pouring liberally, and the dancers on stage brought a happy smile to her face.

But what tugged at Franceska's heart above all else was the music. A beautiful and soul-piercing female voice carried the energetic and moving Polish Tango that set Franceska's spirit aflame.

Studying the singer, Franceska admired her white sparkling dress accompanied by long grey gloves and a dainty tiara.

Flanking the singer on either side were dancers who were dressed to match the singer, and Franceska felt pity for them. She couldn't imagine the thought of desiring to be a dancer and then having to settle as some entertainment on the side of a stage.

"There's a spot over there!" Adam shouted above the music.

"There's a table open right here, though." Wiera pointed to a table beside them.

"The table over there will do," Adam replied decisively, and Franceska grinned as she guessed that he wanted to parade them through the club.

"Lead on!" Wiera patted his chest, and Franceska watched with amusement as Adam beamed with satisfaction as all eyes fell on him while he walked through the lively dance floor with a beautiful woman on each arm.

"Would you be so kind as to get us some drinks?" Wiera asked Adam as they sat in a booth that was on a slightly raised platform above the dance floor.

"What would you like?" Adam asked.

"Surprise us." Wiera fluttered her lashes. "I need a man who knows, anticipates I should say, my needs."

"Frankly, so do I," Adam said with a heavy and deflated sigh as a man approached their table.

The man's intentions were evident to all, and Franceska watched Adam intently, wondering how he would decline the man's request to dance with one of the ladies.

"No." Adam shook his head before the man even had a chance to make his request.

"No?" the man asked with surprise.

"N—" the word stuck in Adam's throat, and he coughed gently before replying as firmly as he was able as he shook like a leaf, "No."

"You don't even know what I'm about to ask." The man threw his hands out in frustration.

"You're about to ask what every other man who approaches this table is about to ask this evening." Adam continued to tremble while still unnerved, and Franceska found his courage moving.

"I was going to ask to danc—"

"And it's a no." Adam threw his hands into his pockets as he left toward the bar.

"You've got a problem with me or something?!" the man asked angrily as he trailed Adam.

"We should maybe ease off of him." Franceska smiled at Wiera.

"Maybe…but not yet." Wiera winked. "I think he's stronger than he supposes, and I want to see that side of him."

"You like him, don't you?" Franceska watched her friend closely.

"I do, but my father would never approve." Wiera twisted her mouth in disappointment. "Which I suppose makes him all that more appealing."

"Really? Why wouldn't your father approve?"

"Adam enlisted in the military."

"Adam?" Franceska threw her eyebrows up. "Our nation is doomed if that's who we have defending us. But why would your father oppose that?"

"He's a pacifist." Wiera shrugged. "He hates the military and any man who fights or resolves disagreements with violence, even in the most extreme cases."

"Do you suppose that it will come to war?"

"I don't like thinking about it." Wiera messaged her temples. "Especially with Adam being in the army."

"I hope Jakub is right and that it's just the western powers being paranoid." Franceska leaned back in the booth as she watched the dance floor nearly overflowing with happy couples, wondering if these days were numbered.

"There's Stefania." Wiera nodded. "She seems to be enjoying herself."

"That she does." Franceska grinned at her friend who was dancing awkwardly and wildly with Jan, who Franceska was surprised to notice was quite competent.

"Alright," Adam spoke with a huff as he returned to the table with a bottle of vodka and three glasses and asked, "Did any other potential suitors arrive without me to thwart them away?"

"None," Wiera replied with disappointment.

"Good," Adam sighed in relief. "That other gentleman threatened to beat me half to death."

"Don't worry, we wouldn't have let him hurt you." Franceska chuckled.

"Excuse me." A man tapped on Adam's shoulder.

"No," Adam replied quickly without even turning to look.

"No?" the man asked with equal abruptness as the previous man.

"They're not dancing with you," Adam spoke over his shoulder as he began pouring the vodka, and Francceska noticed that he was growing in confidence.

"Good. I'm not much of a dancer these days." The man raised his cane.

"Oh…" Adam swallowed as his cheeks flushed red with embarrassment

"I manage the girls." The man nodded to the dancers on stage, "But that's not why I'm here. There's a man outside, goes by the name Jakub, says that he knows you three and you can vouch for him."

"Jakub?" Franceska feigned ignorance as she squinted. "That name doesn't sound familiar."

"I've never heard of a Jakub before. Am I pronouncing it right? Jakub?" Wiera also played dumb.

"Enough." Adam shook his head in annoyance. "Yeah, we know him."

"Well, he's making quite the scene outside and I'd prefer to leave the authorities unbothered with this incident. Are you able to vouch for his conduct?"

"He's impolite but harmless." Adam nodded.

"That's most of the men in here." The man gestured toward someone standing at the door, signaling that Jakub could enter.

"I apologize about the confusion with…um…" Adam glanced down ashamedly at the man's cane.

"No need." The man shook his head as he took a step toward the table and looked at the girls closely before adding, "Although, having two beautiful ladies such as yourselves in here turning men away is going to be a problem."

"A lady isn't permitted an enjoyable evening of watching others dance?" Franceska tested the man who, she admitted, was quite handsome.

He was a good measure older than her, in his thirties she assumed, but he had a rather inquisitive and mischievous look that she appreciated. He seemed to be the sort of man that was saying one thing but thinking another, and she found him mysterious and alluring.

"Maybe you're scared to dance?" the man asked with a shrug before adding, "Nothing to be nervous about. Many men and women are mere amateurs. They dance for the enjoyment."

"My friend here is anything but an amateur," Wiera defended as she grew incensed.

"Oh?" The man asked as he narrowed his gaze.

"She's a prima ballerina who is competing in Brussels next month, and she was also in the short film, *Poles Are Famous*."

"Interesting." The man grinned before pointing at one of the women dancing on stage beside the band and mentioning, "She used to compete in Brussels as well. You two will have lots to discuss when you come to dance for me."

"I don't intend to offend you or this fine establishment, but my dancing is reserved for a more refined crowd," Franceska replied with as much tact as she could muster.

"You're a star of the moving pictures, and a famous prima ballerina, I wouldn't expect you to be jumping at the chance to dance here." The man looked back at her in such a manner that Franceska thought he was mocking her before he continued, "Problem with refined crowds, miss, is that they are fickle. They will love one day, and then suddenly hate you. When reality sinks in, come and find me. I'm Mr. Rosenberg." He extended his hand in greeting, but Franceska, enraged at his patronizing tone, turned away and refused to accept the gesture.

"Might be best to get back to your dancers," Adam added, and both Franceska and Wiera glanced at each other in shock at his boldness.

"As I said, I'm Mr. Rosenberg. If you ever change your mind, let me know." He nodded at both girls before departing.

"How dare he!" Wiera leaned over to Franceska. "I've seen you dance. You've got talent. They're good dancers too, but they're nothing compared to you."

"Thank you." Franceska smiled at her friend. "That is very kind of you to say."

"Here he comes." Adam braced, and Franceska spotted Jakub storming across the dance floor toward them.

"You're going to regret that!" Jakub pointed his finger in Adam's face before he turned to Franceska and added, "Someday you're going to be in a tough situation, and you'll turn to me for help. I'll remember what happened here tonight and laugh at you."

"It was just a bit of fun." Wiera shot her vodka back.

"This is mine now!" Jakub snatched the bottle of vodka off the table.

"Hey!" Adam reached for the bottle, but Jakub ripped of the lid and took a generous swig.

"Stop it both of you!" Franceska groaned. "We're all going to get kicked out of here."

"That wasn't a cheap bottle!" Adam griped.

"Maybe enjoying your company was a mistake, after all," Jakub began as he looked at the two women and added smugly, "Stefania is a divorcee."

Wiera shot Franceska a surprised glance, who assumed her friend was trying to decipher whether this information was factual.

"There were extenuating conditions." Franceska tilted her head in annoyance at Jakub but then explained to Wiera, "Her story is tragic."

"She's still divorced." Jakub took another sip of the vodka. "That's all that matters."

"Someday you'll be judged by the same standards you judge others," Franceska began cuttingly. "And I, for one, hope that I'm there when that happens."

With a mocking laugh, Jakub stumbled onto the dance floor while taking another sip.

"Go grab another bottle." Franceska patted Adam's arm tenderly as they watched Jakub making a fool of himself. "We'll pay for it."

"Really?" Adam shot his head back in surprise. "You'd do that?"

"Of course." Franceska nodded for him to go to the bar.

"That's very kind. Very kind indeed." Adam beamed happily as he left in the direction of more vodka.

"Did you bring any money?" Wiera whispered to Franceska.

"I don't have a penny to my name," Franceska whispered back as the two women howled at their own mischief.

"Well, when you win first place in Brussels, you'll be able to pay him."

"First place?!" Franceska laughed. "That's aiming a little high. I just don't want to embarrass myself in front of everyone."

"You'll do splendidly. I've seen you compete many times before. You're a natural."

"You're too kind." Franceska grinned. "But I'm too nervous to even think about it. Would you like to dance with me?"

"Where's Adam?" Wiera looked around in slight panic.

"Why?" Franceska also grew concerned.

"I need him to say no for me."

Franceska laughed.

Chapter Two:
Brussels

"The two most important days in your life are the day you were born and the day you find out why."

Mark Twain

Drawing a deep breath to calm her nerves, Franceska trembled as she sat in the chair before the mirror in her dressing room. The dim lights around the mirror made it difficult to determine if her makeup was done correctly, or if her costume was perfectly in place. Regardless, Franceska was more concerned with how she would perform in front of such a large audience.

She had danced many times before in public, but never at such a prestigious event, or in front of so many people. This competition could either serve to launch her international career or squander it altogether. She was about to compete against the best dancers from all over the world, and she knew her opponents would be fierce.

"You should smile," a coarse voice spoke from the doorway, and Franceska turned to see her instructor, Irena, looking intently at her.

Her instructor was a shorter woman, about the same height as Franceska's mother, and was dressed in the blandest fashion she could unearth. Her dress was beige with such an absence of body or shape that it appeared almost like a tarp. Her straight hair was cut abruptly at the shoulder, which Franceska felt made her head look like a square.

Still, what Irena lacked in fashion sense, she more than made up for in her ability to understand the finer movements of dance. She had trained many famous dancers over her decades of teaching, and Franceska hoped she would be able to include her name among them.

"Did my mother send you?" Franceska asked as she returned to inspect her makeup in the mirror.

"We both know that your mother terrifies me." Irena entered the dressing room and shut the door behind her.

The muffled roar of applause erupted from further within the building, and Franceska knew her time to perform was swiftly approaching.

Drawing another deep breath, Franceska failed to calm herself, and her leg bounced anxiously as she felt her arms quivering.

"Did you rehearse this morning?" Irena asked as she came to stand behind Franceska and began gingerly adjusting her hair.

"Three times." Franceska nodded.

"And how did you feel?" Irena asked as she placed her hands on Franceska's shoulders.

"Rusty," Franceska replied quickly.

"You would do well to remember that my reputation depends on you performing well today," Irena spoke without tact.

"I'm well aware." Franceska clenched her jaw, wishing Irena would have a little more emotional intelligence.

"Good." Irena patted Franceska's shoulders vigorously before adding, "Don't let me down."

"Thank you." Franceska squeezed her eyes shut.

"I've taught many girls how to dance over the years," Irena began as she headed for the door.

Franceska waited, hoping for a word of encouragement.

"And I've yet to be disappointed by how they perform at competitions. I pray that today you won't be the first," Irena spoke over her shoulder as she left the room and closed the door behind her.

"We forgive her because she is a genius," Franceska muttered to herself.

Then, looking at herself in the mirror, Franceska replayed the conversation in her mind and couldn't help letting a little chuckle escape.

"You're going to do well," Franceska said to herself in the mirror. *You're going to do well. Believe it. Mother and*

Father are here in the audience. Just pretend you're performing only for them. On second thought…maybe pretend they're not here at all. I'm still surprised Mother made the journey given the condition her back is in.

A knock rattled against the door before an assistant called in German, "You're on in five minutes!"

"Thank you!" Franceska called back in German.

After one last inspection of her makeup, hair, and outfit, Franceska left the room. Briskly, she walked through the corridors of dancers practicing or chatting liberally with each other while some sobbed in disappointment at their performance. Costumes on racks were being wheeled in one direction or another, agitated stagehands were frantically directing traffic and organizing the next performers, while ecstatic applause emanated from the audience.

"Name?" an attendant near the side stage asked in German when Franceska arrived to find a handful of other ballerinas preparing to perform.

"Franceska Mann," she replied quickly as her nerves rose.

"Franceska…Franceska…" The attendant ran his pen down the list. "Ah, there you are."

"I was concerned I wasn't on the list for a moment," Franceska said timidly as she scratched her arm.

"You're the last to dance tonight. You're third in line." The attendant pointed to two girls in front of her who were near the stage.

Smiling briefly at one of the girls as she took her place, Franceska turned her gaze to her feet as she tried to concentrate. She struggled to recall the movements of her performance as all she could think about was how horribly she was about to fail.

Regardless, she was distracted by the heated stares of the two girls in front of her. Breaking off her gaze from the floor, Franceska's eyes met theirs, and they were looking back at her with a sort of disgust and hatred that shocked her.

Wondering what was wrong, Franceska inspected her outfit, believing that something was out of place or that she had spilled food or ink on it.

"Your German isn't very good," one of the girls spoke coldly.

"Where are you from?" the other girl asked with equal hostility.

"Poland." Franceska swallowed as she looked back at them with wide eyes, still wondering why they were being so hostile toward her.

"Poland?" the first girl glanced at the second before asking Franceska, "You're Jewish? Odd, you don't look very Jewish. You have light skin and hair."

With a sigh of frustration, now understanding the root of their detestable opinion of her, Franceska nodded as she resumed staring at her feet, hoping that if she disengaged with them, they would leave her alone.

"What disease are you carrying?" the second girl asked. "Don't stand so close to us."

Franceska remained silent.

"You're going to fail out there." The first girl slapped Franceska roughly on the shoulder to get her attention before pointing to the stage and adding, "No impure race can win against a German. We are superior in every way."

Franceska remained silent as she struggled to focus on her performance that would take place in mere minutes.

"Don't you have anything to say? Or are you Jews to scared of a fight? You're all like sheep." The second girl snickered.

"I'll let my feet do the talking for me." Franceska tried to steady her nerves, but this confrontation was undermining her ability to think correctly.

She had experienced her fair share of prejudice in Warsaw, but the reports coming out of Nazi Germany were troubling at best. Meeting these two girls, and seeing the hatred they held without knowing her in the slightest, was frightening. The detestation and loathing they showed even in their gazes wasn't something Franceska believed she would readily overcome.

A round of applause emitted from the audience as the current dancer on stage took a polite bow before exiting.

With tears running down her face, the dancer bolted down the steps beside the stage and back toward the dressing rooms.

"She's Jewish, too," the second girl spoke to Franceska. "We told her she would fail, and she did."

"We voiced our objections to dancing beside subhuman creatures like you," the first girl added. "But we were told that no rat could possibly hope to win."

"Have you forgotten the 1936 Olympics?" Franceska asked as she drew courage from her annoyance with these two self-righteous dancers.

"Jessie Owens wasn't Jewish." The first girl stuck her nose in the air. "And that's beside the fact that he cheated."

"Keep moving!" The attendant beckoned the first girl to take her place on stage.

"Best of luck," Franceska muttered sarcastically.

"I don't need your support." She shook her head arrogantly.

With a strained sigh of impatience, Franceska watched as the first girl took her place on stage. The music began, and Franceska, with revulsion, watched as the girl danced majestically. Her movements were so natural and fluid that Franceska felt as if she was watching an instructional demonstration on proper form. It was majestic, entrancing, and perfect, which Franceska hated. She detested that someone so arrogant and hateful was so flawless in their craft.

The dance ended, and the first girl, with a polite bow of feigned humility, exited the stage.

Without so much as looking at Franceska, the girl descended the staircase to hefty praise from the other dancers who all sought her attention.

"Next!" the attendant called with waning patience.

Again, Franceska watched as the second conceited girl stole the stage with a mesmerizing performance. She wasn't as refined as the first girl, but still, Franceska knew that she would have to perform at the peak of her abilities if she had any hope of beating these two Germans.

Another round of applause erupted and the second girl, with equal disdain for Franceska, descended the stairs without so much as looking in her direction.

"Next!" The attendant waved at Franceska.

Her legs froze.

Franceska looked at the staircase in front of her, and then up at the awaiting stage, but she was unable to move.

Her heart pounded in her chest, and all she could hear was the snickering of the girls behind her, especially the two horrid girls who had danced before her.

"Next!" The attendant called again.

"I heard you!" Franceska barked back, and the attendant frowned sharply.

"Look, the poor thing is terrified," one of the girls began, which was all the motivation Franceska needed, and she immediately ascended the stairs and onto the empty stage.

Her legs felt like lead as she walked as gracefully as she was able to toward the middle of the stage. The bright lights blinded her from viewing the audience which, if she was honest, was a blessing.

The stage floor was surprisingly cold, considering that the heat from the lights made the atmosphere on the stage rather humid, and Franceska wondered how she would handle the rigid platform.

Taking her place, Franceska waited patiently for the music as she listened to the occasional coughing from the audience. She tried to peer through the lights to catch a glimpse of her parents or even Irena, but she couldn't discern anyone's face adequately.

A quick tap of the stick from the conductor offered the warning signal that the music would begin in three, two, one…

Franceska's mind went blank. She couldn't think, reason, feel, fear, or hope. She simply and automatically, without consciousness thought, performed the routine she had been practicing since she had been accepted to dance in this competition.

Suddenly, as soon as the performance had started, it ended, and Franceska, now fully returned to the present, bowed with a large smile as cheers and applause exploded liberally and without restraint. Whistles, accompanied by flowers thrown at the stage, gave Franceska every bit of confidence that she had somehow performed admirably.

Exiting the stage, Franceska's legs wobbled as she descended the stairs and was quick to notice the two girls glaring at her with menace.

With a graceful nod to the two girls, Franceska paid them no more attention as she was at once surrounded by other ballerinas eager to offer their congratulations and ask her all manner of questions.

"Slow down!" Franceska chuckled. "My German is not that good."

"Who taught you to dance like that?!" one ballerina asked as she tugged on Franceska's arm.

"I was instructed by Irena Prusicka." Franceska smiled proudly.

"I've never seen a routine like that before! Was that Irena's choreography or yours?!" another inquired eagerly.

"I like to think that it was a merger of talent." Franceska grinned proudly.

"I need everyone's attention!" the attendant shouted as he stood on a chair with his hand raised.

"He's rather pleasant, isn't he?" Franceska whispered sarcastically to a dancer beside her who giggled.

"The awards will be given out shortly. The judges have already made their decisions. Would everyone please, and in a timely fashion, make their way onto the stage in the order that you performed." The attendant pointed directions.

At once the room exploded into a frenzied chit chat as the girls tried to organize themselves into the order of their performances.

Lost to the ecstasy of the moment, and thoroughly enjoying the energy in the room, Franceska retreated to the back of the line that was a craze of organized chaos.

But her cheer quickly faded when she spotted the two German girls who had danced before her, and realized she would have to stand in line with them. If she did manage to win a prize, or be awarded with any sort of prestige, the two girls would be thoroughly disappointed at best, and vengeful at worst.

By their flaring nostrils, clenched jaws, and hateful gazes, Franceska imagined they would likely take revenge on her in a horrible manner should she win a higher position than them.

Regardless, Franceska held her head high and confidently as she took her place at the back of the line, not allowing the two girls' prejudice to soil a proud moment.

More applause emanated from the audience as the ballerinas began to filter onto the stage, and Franceska shuffled slowly behind the line that was sluggishly moving forward.

The two German girls were keen to throw sullied looks over their shoulder at Franceska, and she took this as a good indication that she had, in fact, performed admirably.

With an enthusiastic wave and a kiss to the audience as she climbed onto the stage, Franceska took her place beside the two girls who were now forcing polite smiles toward the judges.

"Thank you to all the competitors," an announcer began in German, but Franceska, thanks to her nerves, struggled to concentrate properly.

"Which judge are you having an affair with?" the first German girl whispered from the corner of her mouth while still smiling garishly.

Franceska, while offended, didn't reply as she tried to distract herself by peering as best as she was able into the crowd to spot her parents or her instructor.

"Because that is the only explanation if you win. I watched your performance. It was pitiful."

"It's not a crime to be afraid," Franceska began, also feigning a polite smile as she continued, "But it does look terrible on you."

"I'm not afraid," she replied coarsely.

"We will now begin with the results," the announcer resumed the program. "Only ten prizes will be awarded this evening."

The announcer opened a sealed envelope that was handed to him by an attendant, and Franceska felt her heart drop into her stomach.

She prayed that her name was on the list of awards. What it would mean for her to bring a prestigious medal back with her to Warsaw, and to win something of this magnitude for Irena's dance school. She knew it was an honor to even be competing on the world stage, and

Franceska prayed that she had performed more than adequately for the judges.

"Beginning with tenth place, Maria Berkowicz," the announcer began, and a cheer of excitement escaped a younger girl who quickly walked to the front of the stage where she graciously accepted her award with an apathetic round of applause from the audience.

Franceska's hopes of being awarded a prize dwindled as the ninth, eighth, seventh, and sixth place were presented without her name being called.

"Fifth place is awarded to a very special dancer indeed who I would argue has captured the heart of everyone here, especially given her dedication to the Nazi Party and their ideals for a greater Germany." The announcer looked especially pleased as he read out the name, "Lily Muller."

The German girl beside Franceska gasped with excitement, and took extra pleasure in brushing rudely past Franceska as she made her way to the front of the stage to accept her prize. The applause was louder for her than any other prize awarded yet, and Franceska wondered if the judges were basing their decisions on popularity.

"What did I tell you?" Lily asked when she returned to standing beside Franceska. "A Jew will never beat a true German."

"The judges have been so kind as to advise me that fourth place and third place were incredibly hard to discern between," the announcer began with anticipation building in his voice.

Franceska struggled to hold back the tears as she stood beside the gloating Lily. Her disappointment at not being able to provide her trophy to Irena, or show her friends how well she performed, merely served to reinforce her mother's remarks about the futility of her career choice.

Maybe mother was right all along, and I should've found a husband and settled down. At least then I wouldn't be feeling the heat of this humiliation. Not to mention how much I hate that Lily is radiating with pride. If her nose was pointed any higher in the air, she'd drown when it rains. I hate that my family is here to witness me fail this way.

A girl in front of Franceska turned around to look at her, and then another, and another, and Franceska noticed the rageful expression on Lily's face.

"What's wrong?" Franceska asked with panic.

"He announced your name," a dancer with a sweet smile replied.

"My name?" Franceska asked as she choked and struggled to contain her emotions.

"Franceska Mann?" the announcer asked as he peered into the crowd of ballerinas. "Are you among us?"

"Yes! Sorry!" Franceska replied quickly in German as she scurried to the front of the stage.

"Daydreaming were we?" the announcer asked rhetorically as the crowd chuckled.

Then, placing his hand on her lower back, he handed her the fourth-place plaque as they posed for a quick photograph.

"Thank you." Franceska curtseyed graciously as the crowd applauded loudly and emphatically.

With happy tears that couldn't be thwarted, Franceska held her plaque tightly against her chest as she walked back to her place in line where she noticed Lily's face was red with humiliation and rage.

"What position did you get again?" Franceska asked Lily, giving in to cattiness.

"My father will hear about this!" Lily griped through gritted teeth as she stormed off the stage and Franceska smiled brightly.

Chapter Three:
The Beginning of the End

"Germany has concluded a Non-Aggression Pact with Poland. We shall adhere to it unconditionally. We recognize Poland as the home of a great and nationally conscious people."

Adolph Hitler

With a yawn and a stretch, Franceska sat upright in bed to the pleasant sound of birds chirping brightly outside her window.

Glancing over at the nightstand, Franceska spotted her plaque which proudly displayed her fourth-place achievement at the world competition, and she could scarcely contain a delighted smile.

Grabbing the plaque as she swung her legs over the side of the bed, Franceska studied it with mesmerization, still in disbelief that she had achieved such an amazing rank. It felt like a dream, and she toyed with the thought that it was, in fact, all fiction. A part of her wondered if she would wake up and realize she still had to perform in Brussels.

Setting the plaque back on the nightstand, and rubbing her tired eyes, Franceska began to prepare for the day. Her dance instructor, Irena, was not content to permit even a single day of respite. The next competition was just around the corner, and Irena wanted to begin preparations.

Not that Franceska minded as she was eager to see what new dance Irena had choreographed. She imagined her instructor would increase the difficulty substantially now that Franceska had achieved a measure of success.

Throwing on her robe, Franceska left her room to prepare a light breakfast. She found it uncomfortable to eat too much before enduring Irena's demanding hours where she pushed the limits of physical ability.

Arriving in the living room, Franceska spotted her mother and father huddled by the radio. They seemed rather perturbed by whatever solemn news was being broadcast, but this was not entirely abnormal. Her parents were prime targets for any sort of propaganda, and they believed nearly anything if it was stated over the radio.

"Would either of you care for some breakfast?" Franceska asked politely as she stopped to wait for their reply.

Neither her mother nor father responded as their attention was stolen by the broadcast.

"Thank you again for coming to watch me perform in Brussels." Franceska smiled coyly. "I only wish that you could've seen that German girl's face from a closer vantage point."

Still, neither of them responded.

"I'm making something light if either of you—"

"Shhh!" Her father waved with a frown as he turned his ear to the radio.

"I hardly think that was necessary," Franceska muttered as she began walking toward the kitchen, surprised that her father would behave in such a manner.

"I repeat, take shelter immediately!" the announcer beckoned.

Franceska spun back to face the radio as she felt her pulse race, hoping that her parents were merely listening to a dramatic reading of a book or a play.

Slowly, and cautiously, Franceska walked toward the radio, straining to hear the announcer better.

"The invasion of our glorious nation began in the early hours," the announcer continued, and Franceska stifled a gasp with her hand as she felt her legs growing weak when he added, "German forces have launched an invasion into Poland. Reports of large groups of Luftwaffe, including bombers and fighters, have been flooding in. Take shelter if you can. Thus, we are at war."

A tear escaped Franceska's eye and ran down her cheek as she listened to the harrowing report.

Silence.

No sound emanated from the radio, and no one dared to utter a word. Franceska felt as if she simply imagined the announcement, but by the stunned looks on her parents' faces, she knew that this was all too real.

Unable to speak, or barely breathe properly, Franceska sat on the couch and stared at the rose pattern on the wallpaper.

The clock ticked steadily as Franceska felt like she had been shocked into numbness. Her parents, too, simply sat and stared with terror at each other. There was nothing to be said that would ease the dread of what they had just heard over the radio, especially considering their Jewish heritage and the reports of how the Nazis were treating Jews in Germany.

"Our army is prepared, aren't they?" Franceska's voice quivered.

She knew it was a ridiculous question, but it was all she could think to ask. She needed some reassurance, even if it was false, that this was not the end. Regardless, in her heart she knew Warsaw, and the whole of Poland, were at the mercy of a madman.

"Our boys will do their best," her father replied softly. "I have no doubt that they'll make their families proud."

"Is there anything that can be done to stop this?" Franceska asked as she began to panic. "Can't we—"

"Don't be absurd," her father interrupted with a touch of annoyance, and Franceska understood that he was also terrified.

A knock sounded against the front door, and Franceska, along with her parents, all startled and stared at the door.

Franceska's mind ran wild with visions of Nazi soldiers going door to door, killing and looting at will. She had heard stories of how the Jews were being mistreated in Germany, but she wanted to believe that they were mere fabrications. In her heart, she knew the truth, and she felt silly for all the time she spent focusing on trivial matters like dance instead of obtaining skills that would be useful at a time like this.

The knock sounded again.

"Answer it!" her mother whispered harshly to her father.

With a groan of frustration mixed with fear, Mr. Mann stood slowly from his chair, and Franceska noticed that he was stiff with anxiety.

Franceska's breathing labored as her father walked cautiously toward the door before opening it a crack and peeking out into the street.

From her position, Franceska couldn't see who he was talking with, but she could faintly make out the tone of a younger woman's voice which instantly put her at ease.

"Please, come in!" Mr. Mann stood back from the door and Franceska watched as Stefania burst inside the property with tears running down her face.

"What's wrong?!" Franceska asked as she stood and embraced her friend who buried her face into Franceska's shoulder.

She knew it was a ridiculous question given the gravity of recent events, but it was an almost automatic response to seeing her friend in distress.

"I can't find him!" Stefania mumbled through sobs.

"Who?" Franceska asked. "Jan?"

"I've been calling him all morning with no answer!"

"Oh, you sweet thing, it's best not to jump to conclusions." Franceska rubbed Stefania's arms as she stepped back.

"He's dead! I just know it!" Stefania continued in her hysteria.

"He's not dead! Come, sit!" Franceska led Stefania over to the couch.

"I'll put the kettle on," Mrs. Mann spoke quietly as she stood, and the look of dread painted on her face haunted Franceska.

Franceska watched her mother with a heavy heart as she shuffled toward the kitchen, and she wished with all her might and soul that she could take this burden from her. She hated the thought of anything terrible happening to such sweet people, but Franceska knew she had to be brave and banish such thoughts from her mind.

The state of her mother's back was also troubling to Franceska, as she knew that Mrs. Mann wouldn't be able to travel for long periods of time if they needed to leave the city, or even the country.

"He probably went to see his parents," Franceska spoke softly to Stefania as she sat beside her.

"His parents have a farm a few miles away." Stefania sniffled.

"Maybe he went to go collect them?" Franceska shrugged.

"If he went without me, then I'll kill him myself." Stefania raised her eyebrows. "Either way, he's dead. If the Nazis haven't killed him, I will."

"I'm sure he'll be in contact with you shortly." Franceska rubbed Stefania's back.

"You're right." Stefania retrieved a handkerchief from her skirt pocket and dabbed her eyes. "Sometimes I let my imagination get the best of me. I won't keep you any longer. I should get back home in case he calls."

"Stay as long as you'd like," Mr. Mann spoke quietly as he again sat by the radio, and Franceska knew how terrified of the invasion he truly was if he appreciated Stefania's company.

"When do you think it will happen?" Stefania shivered with anxiety as she stared at the radio. "The Germans invading, that is."

"Happen?" Mr. Mann raised his eyebrows. "It's happening right now as we speak."

"What are we supposed to do?" Stefania looked at Franceska with fearful, teary eyes.

"There are shelters set up around the city," Mr. Mann replied with equal trepidation. "I'm sure that we'll be notified once we're supposed to evacuate to one of them."

"Didn't the radio already mention that we're supposed to seek shelter?" Franceska frowned.

"Yes, well, I think they were merely preparing us. I don't think they were literally telling us to find shelter at this very moment."

"That is a relief, yet—" Stefania began, but was interrupted by a horrifying, gut-wrenching sound.

It started slowly but built into a petrifying crescendo. The air raid siren was so loud and piercing that Franceska felt her legs growing wobbly. She had heard the siren plenty of times during drills and practices, but to hear its shrill scream, signifying that they were about to be subjected to bombing, caused such a terror within her that she wished she could close her eyes and enter into a cocoon of some sort.

Finding her strength, Franceska rushed over to the living room window and threw open the curtains, but she couldn't see anything in the overcast sky.

"Stay away from the window!" Mr. Mann barked.

"What do we do?!" Mrs. Mann panicked as she shuffled as best as she was able back to the living room while carrying a rattling tray with the kettle, cups, tea bags, cream, and sugar.

"Where is the nearest shelter?" Stefania asked as she also stood near the window.

"Get away from the window I said!" Mr. Mann waved frantically for them to move away.

"The closest shelter is about a mile away," Mrs. Mann spoke with a trembling voice.

"What do we do?!" Stefania held her hand over her mouth as she stared up at the sky, searching for any signs of the enemy.

"Nobody listens to me!" Mr. Mann griped as he headed toward the door. "Stay by the window all you want!"

"Where are you going?!" Mrs. Mann asked with fright.

"To see what everyone else is doing!" Mr. Mann shouted back at his wife as he ripped the door open.

"I've never heard your father yell before," Stefania whispered to Franceska with a look of terror that signified she understood the implication of Mr. Mann's demeanor.

There were only two times in her life where Franceska had seen her father raise his voice. The first was when her grandfather had passed away. She was a younger girl, about five, and didn't understand the gravity of a funeral. She was misbehaving, as five-year-olds often do, and Mr. Mann rebuked her loudly and publicly.

The second instance was at this very moment, and Franceska spiraled further into panic knowing how dire the situation was.

"We're going to be fine." Franceska took her friend's hand in hers. "Let's follow my father. He'll know a place for us to take shelter."

"And leave me all alone?!" Mrs. Mann scoffed.

"We're all going." Franceska nodded.

"I'll slow you down." Mrs. Mann waved to dismiss the invite.

"Nonsense." Franceska held her hand out to her mother.

"Leave me here." Mrs. Mann set the tray down on the coffee table, and Franceska watched with a broken heart as her hands shook while she tried to pour herself a cup.

"I'm not leaving you alone." Franceska walked over to her mother and gently took her by the arm.

Franceska tried to concentrate on her mother's mental and emotional state, but the terror from the blaring air raid sirens was difficult to suppress. Her heart seemed to surge with the rise and fall of the siren, and she felt her stomach churning with worry. She prayed for the moment when the sirens would cease, and all would return to normal.

"Leave me!" Her mother swiped at Franceska's hand.

"Mother," Franceska pleaded while trying to show her respect but also compelled to hurry her along.

"I'm not leaving my home!" Mrs. Mann plumped a tea bag into a cup before adding, "Not to mention, my back is killing me. I can barely walk to the kitchen and back without requiring a rest."

Franceska's heart nearly stopped when she heard the dim but steadily growing drone of airplanes. She knew that they would be upon them within minutes, and they had no choice but to seek shelter immediately.

"Let's go!" Franceska nearly shouted as she roughly grabbed her mother's arm and pulled her along to the front door.

"You're going too fast!" Mrs. Mann grumbled loudly as she placed a hand to her back and moaned, "My back! My back!"

"We have to hurry!" Franceska panicked as Stefania grabbed Mrs. Mann's other arm to assist her.

The deafening shriek of the siren struck deep into Franceska's soul as they walked out to the street, and she felt her legs nearly giving out under her. If she didn't have her mother to care for, Franceska believed she would've collapsed right then and there.

"I can walk by myself!" Mrs. Mann yelled, but neither Franceska nor Stefania relented.

They both understood that time was of the essence, and both were also too afraid to even listen. They clung to Mrs. Mann as they hurried her along into the street where Mr. Mann was talking with a soldier who was wildly pointing directions and talking excitedly.

The streets were filled with families, policemen, soldiers, and all manner of people running in every direction.

Some families were frantically packing their belongings onto horse drawn carts, others were throwing bedding and heirlooms into strollers, trollies, or anything that could be used to carry their possessions.

Policemen were busy diverting vehicles to park on the side of the road to make way for the military trucks that were either packed with soldiers or supplies being shipped to various strategic areas of the city.

"There's a shelter about a mile away from here!" Mr. Mann called to his family and Stefania as he pointed in the direction and added, "But we have to hurry! There's limited capacity!"

"It's hopeless!" Mrs. Mann yelled above the noise and chaos. "You go on without me! I can't hurry along with the state my back is in!"

"I'm not leaving without you!" Mr. Mann shook his head adamantly.

"Because you're a fool!" Mrs. Mann gazed at her husband with tears in her eyes.

"What happens to you, happens to me." Mr. Mann took Stefania's place as he grabbed his wife's arm.

BOOM! BOOM! BOOM!

A sudden burst of gunfire from an anti-aircraft gun further up the street erupted, and Franceska covered her ear with her free hand at the near-constant thundering.

Within seconds, other anti-aircraft guns nearby opened fire, and Franceska made the terrible mistake of looking up.

Hundreds of enemy aircraft were blotting the sky like large black dots. Dozens of larger aircraft, which Franceska assumed were bombers, were flanked by smaller fighters. The drone of their engines could be heard even above the flak explosions in the sky from the guns on the ground, and Franceska could feel the earth shaking under her feet.

"We have to go!" Mr. Mann shouted, and Franceska helped her father hurry their mother along the street while Stefania followed closely behind.

"Look!" Stefania pointed up the street, and Franceska looked in the direction to see that Adam, with Wiera sitting beside him, was speeding toward them in a horse-drawn cart.

Without a word, Adam brought the cart to a stop as he jumped down to assist Mr. Mann and Franceska with hoisting Mrs. Mann into the back.

"Get out of the street!" a soldier shouted at them.

"We are!" Adam shouted back as he led Mr. and Mrs. Mann to the back of the cart.

"Now!" the soldier screamed as he pointed his rifle at them.

"Give us a minute for pity's sake!" Adam yelled as he and Mr. Mann shoved Mrs. Mann roughly into the back of the cart.

Franceska's heart shattered as her mother screamed in agony, and she knew that the motion had severely injured her. She prayed that the injury was minor.

"Get in!" Mr. Mann yelled as he held out his hand to Franceska while Stefania scrambled to climb in, and Adam jumped to the front of the cart to take the reins.

"Move!" the soldier waved emphatically.

"We're moving! We're moving!" Adam barked back as he spurred the horse to a trot before continuing into a gallop.

"Are you alright?" Franceska asked as she knelt beside her mother who was moaning in discomfort.

Before Mrs. Mann had the chance to respond, high-pitched whistles came from the sky, and Franceska looked up in horror as shell upon shell upon shell were being emptied from the bombers over their heads.

"Faster!" Mr. Mann shouted in his panic.

"I can't push the horses any harder!" Adam shouted back.

"We have to take the chance!" Mr. Mann urged.

"Come on!" Adam's face flushed red with rage as he beckoned the horses onward.

Yet as Franceska looked again at the sky, she knew that speed now counted for nothing. Bombs were hurtling toward the earth on every side of them. There was nowhere now that would be safe, and Franceska knew that pure luck was their only hope.

"Cover your heads!" Mr. Mann shouted as he himself ducked down.

Stefania, who was now screaming and balling in fear, covered her head as she huddled beside Franceska in the middle of the cart. Mrs. Mann continued to moan loudly in pain, and Franceska hoped that a bomb would land squarely on them and end this nightmare.

The whistle of the bombs grew louder and fiercer as they dove callously toward their targets, and Franceska covered her ears and squeezed her eyes shut. She wished to silence the death approaching from above, the moaning of her mother, the wailing of Stefania, and the screams of terror from the innocents all around them.

Within seconds, loud explosions shook the earth, causing untold and unprejudiced destruction. Even with her ears covered, Franceska's eardrums rang from the detonations that were louder than anything she could've possibly imagined.

The heat from the incendiary bombs was so intense that Franceska believed her clothing was on fire and she opened her eyes, fully expecting to see her clothes were on fire. Yet how she wished she had kept her eyes closed as the sight of the city around her was hellish.

She watched helplessly as a bomb landed squarely on a transport of soldiers, flaying body pieces into the air, painting the walls of the houses and buildings nearby with a ghastly coat of red. A family's cry from a recently bombed house was snuffed out when the structure collapsed on itself, forever silencing their pleas. A man carrying his recently severed arm was stumbling through the street, looking half-drunk as blood poured from his wound.

Everywhere Franceska looked she witnessed these scenes, and she knew that Hell itself had ascended into Warsaw in the form of a cruel and merciless enemy bent on the destruction of everything and everyone she held dear.

Chapter Four: Siege

"You ask what is our aim? I can answer in one word: Victory. Victory at all costs. Victory in spite of all terror. Victory however long and hard the road may be. For without victory there is no survival."

Winston Churchill

Suddenly, the anti-aircraft guns ceased firing, and Franceska looked around in confusion, wondering if the attack was already over.

"Look!" Wiera pointed to the sky excitedly.

Glancing in the direction, Franceska wasn't sure if she could permit herself to hope. Yet what she saw gave her a glimmer of courage, even though she knew it was a desperate attempt.

Charging rapidly toward the enemy fighters and bombers were Polish fighter planes. Even from a distance, Franceska recognized that their own tactics were not nearly as refined as the Luftwaffe, and the Polish formations were untidy and a disorganized.

Still, armed with courage, the Polish fighter planes engaged their enemy, setting the sky ablaze. The heavens became a battleground as bullets either pierced opposing aircraft or hurtled harmlessly through the air. Explosions, followed by large puffs of white or black smoke, trailed aircraft as they screamed helplessly toward the earth.

It was difficult to tell who had the advantage, and in the ensuing dogfights, Franceska found it impossible to tell which fighter was the enemy and which was an ally. Regardless, the objective of the Polish fighters had been met as the enemy bombers had ceased their attack run and were disengaging.

"Quickly! Get to cover!" an officer shouted to civilians in the street. "Find a shelter or else stay out of the open, and stay away from windows or anything that could shatter!"

"The shelter isn't far from here!" Adam called over his shoulder as he continued to spur his horse onwards.

"How is she?" Mr. Mann asked Franceska worriedly.

"Are you able to sit up?" Franceska asked her mother, who was still in so much pain she was covering her face with her hands.

Her mother didn't reply but simply moaned quietly as she tried to manage the anguish. Franceska wished that she could do something to help her, but she was powerless to assist her mother while they were all jostled in the bumpy cart.

"Hold on, dear!" Mr. Mann called out to his wife. "We're almost at the shel—"

The carriage came to a sudden stop, and, curious at the disruption, Franceska looked up to find a harrowing sight.

The entrance to the bomb shelter had collapsed in on itself, and Franceska could hear the heart-wrenching cries of those now trapped within. They had entered the shelter hoping to find sanctuary, but instead found themselves sealed within a tomb.

"You there!" A soldier pointed toward their carriage.

"Me?" Adam asked sheepishly.

"We need assistance." The soldier waved for Adam to help him remove blocks away from the shelter entrance.

"I need to get my family to safety." Adam pointed to the others in the carriage, hoping to excuse himself.

"If we don't get the entrance opened, they'll all suffocate." The soldier spoke in such a manner that Franceska knew he would not accept another refusal.

"I'll take them," Mr. Mann spoke softly to Adam as he grabbed the reins.

"How will I find you?" Adam asked as he climbed down from the carriage.

"I…" Mr. Mann shook his head, not sure how to answer.

"I'll find you." Wiera leaned out of the cart and offered him her hand. "I promise. There's nothing in this world that would stop me from finding you."

"I love you," Adam spoke with a tearful voice, and in that moment, Franceska almost forgot about the battle raging above their heads. Theirs was a true and beautiful love, and Franceska regarded Wiera in a new light.

With that, Adam left to help a group of men that were hacking, pulling, and prying at the rocks which had enclosed an untold number of innocents inside the shelter.

Mr. Mann, showing a degree of confidence that Franceska had never witnessed in her father before, spurred the carriage deeper into the heart of Warsaw, away from the outskirts of the city that were prone to bombing.

"Where are we going?" Wiera asked Mr. Mann as she looked back in the direction of Adam.

"There's another shelter a handful of blocks from here." Mr. Mann pointed in the direction as he drove the carriage around craters and raging fires.

"If they're targeting the city, shouldn't we try to leave?" Franceska asked. "What about leaving Warsaw?"

"And where would we go?" Mr. Mann asked with a scoff. "We left without grabbing any money or food, and your mother needs to see a physician."

"There's no point staying here!" Wiera agreed with Franceska.

"I believe in our men." Mr. Mann's voice wavered. "They'll be able to repel these godless hordes."

Franceska glanced at Wiera and Stefania, discouraged by the skeptical tone in her father's voice.

"What if we end up trapped in a shelter like those other poor souls?" Wiera whispered to Franceska and Stefania.

"My father is convinced that this is the right direction." Franceska shook her head before adding, "Unless you can think of a better solution?"

Wiera thought for a moment as she glanced between a cautiously optimistic Franceska and Stefania.

The explosions in the sky continued to startle Franceska, and each boom or pop felt as though it would be the last sound she would hear.

But the most distressing thing Franceska noticed about the bombardment was the smell. The toxic fumes from melting and burning wallpaper or paint on residential properties, or the horrid and unmistakable smell of burning flesh from innocents and animals, or the ghastly scent of burning metal and oil from cars that were now blocks of flame.

"Mr. Mann," Wiera began as an idea popped into her head.

"What is it?" Mr. Mann asked impatiently.

"We should go to my residence."

"What?! Why?"

"The enemy priority is the military targets," Wiera explained. "Our residence is far removed, but the shelters are much too close to our defensive positions."

"They told us to get to shelter." Mr. Mann shook his head as he steered the cart around another crater in the pavement.

"And look how it helped out those others."

Mr. Mann rubbed his face quickly in frustration, and Franceska understood that it was difficult for him to think straight.

"We live near a physician's office," Wiera pressed. "My family knows the doctor quite well. We'll call him immediately to assist Mrs. Mann."

With a reluctant nod of agreement, Mr. Mann spurred the cart back in the direction that they had come. Franceska knew it was risky to go back through the areas that had been bombed, but the Polish fighter plans were giving them a much-needed moment of reprieve.

"Thank you," Franceska whispered to Wiera.

"Don't thank me yet," Wiera replied with a look of worry. "Hopefully I'm right, and that our area will be free from bombing."

Franceska watched her friend closely, knowing that she was worried. They all were. And as they drove back through the city, Franceska was stunned at the level of destruction. It was so painful to see the city that she loved given over to such heartlessness.

But what truly tore at her spirit were the lives that had been destroyed. Parents wept as they held the lifeless bodies of their children, men bound their arms together to act as stretches as they rushed the wounded this way and that in the hopes they could find reprieve, and the blood in the sidewalks and streets from victims was something Franceska would not soon forget.

After a few minutes, the cart came to a stop, and Franceska looked at her father to see that his face was pale, and he was staring at a pile of rubble.

"Why have we stopped?!" Franceska looked around at the rubble, wondering why her father had halted and asked, "What is it?!"

"My sweet friend," Stefania began tenderly as she took Franceska's hand in hers and explained, "This is your street."

"What?!" Franceska scoffed as she looked back at her friend with incredulity. "Don't be ridiculous. Our street is back…"

At once, Franceska recognized the location, and a pit formed in her stomach as she gazed at a pile of rubble that she now understood was once her home.

In a state of utter shock and disbelief, Franceska simply sat in the cart and stared at the debris. She couldn't believe that the home she had grown up in, where she had spent her whole life with her parents, had been, in an instant, reduced to nothing more than a pile of bricks. Nothing was left. It had been entirely destroyed, and Franceska struggled to comprehend the reality that was before her.

"God in Heaven." Mr. Mann removed his hat as he stepped down from the cart before walking hopelessly toward the heap of bricks.

"We have to keep moving!" Wiera grew nervous as she looked up at the sky.

"Father?" Franceska's trance broke as she left the car and chased after Mr. Mann.

"It's gone." Mr. Mann shook his head in disbelief as he kicked a brick with his feet, raising a small plume of concrete dust. "Everything is gone."

"We'll come back." Franceska grabbed his arm to bring him to the cart, but he wouldn't budge. "We'll come back when it's safe."

"Come back for what?" Mr. Mann kicked another brick angrily. "Everything is gone!"

"Please! Mother is hurting!"

"What's the point?" Mr. Mann shrugged as he continued in raw shock.

"You still have your wife and daughter." Franceska urged. "But that won't be for long if we don't get to safety! Please! Mother is in pain."

"Leave me here." Mr. Mann swallowed as his eyes welled. "Everything I had, everything I owned, is now dirt."

"I'm not leaving you!" Franceska frowned angrily at him before demanding. "Now, come!"

"Everything I worked for is—"

"Enough of your self-pity!" Franceska stood in front of her father and pointed a finger in his face. "Show us that you're worthy to be the man of this family! Your wife is in incredible pain, and your daughter is terrified. Show some backbone!"

"Self-pity?" Mr. Mann scoffed as an explosion erupted about a block away, but he didn't even so much as flinch.

"Pity is a limited resource, if you use it all on yourself, no one will have any left for you." Franceska spun his shoulders back toward the cart.

"Wait! Wait!" Mr. Mann wrestled free as he turned back to the house and moved aside some bricks to free something underneath.

"What is it?" Franceska asked.

Slowly, Mr. Mann knelt beside the demolished house and began moving bricks aside.

"We don't have time for this! We'll come back! I promise."

"This is yours." Mr. Mann held up the plaque.

Surprised, Franceska took the plaque from her father and examined the perfectly intact fourth place commemoration from Brussels. Mere moments earlier she was examining it on her bedside table, delighting in an accomplishment that now seemed insignificant.

"Franceska!" Wiera called.

"We have to go!" Franceska clamped the plaque under her arm as she grabbed her father's hand and sped him back toward the cart.

"I can't do it." Mr. Mann shook his head as he stared at his feet, seemingly unable to move.

"You don't get that option!" Franceska stared deep into her father's eyes. "We need you! Do you understand?! Your wife and daughter need you! I know you have it in you!"

Glancing at Wiera and Stefania, Mr. Mann grew acutely aware of his poor behavior and offered a slight nod of understanding to his daughter before climbing woodenly into the cart.

"I'll sit up there with you." Wiera climbed to the front of the cart.

"I'm so sorry." Stefania looked at Franceska sympathetically.

"The only thing that survived was my plaque." Franceska looked back at Stefania before bursting into tears, and mentioning through sobs, "My entire childhood was wiped out in an instant, and for what? Why are they doing this?"

"I'm sorry." Stefania held Franceska close.

The only comfort Franceska retained in those bitter moments was the calm that seemed to envelop them the further they traveled into the city. The horrid drone of the planes diminished to a low hum while Franceska imagined the explosions to be the happy sound of fireworks instead of the terror they inflicted upon thousands of guiltless citizens.

"We need to get her to a doctor," Stefania spoke quietly, but with worry, and Franceska looked over at her mother to find that she had stopped moaning and looked pale.

"Mother?" Franceska placed a gentle hand to her mother's shoulder.

No response.

"Mother?!" Franceska asked with greater urgency, and she noticed her father glancing over his shoulder with worry.

"She's still breathing," Stefania reported, her hand supporting Mrs. Mann's back.

Franceska copied Stefania as she felt the shallow, but noticeable, inhale and exhale from her mother.

"She doesn't look good." Franceska sat back as she studied her mother's face with distress.

"We're almost there!" Wiera called over her shoulder.

"What about your family?" Mr. Mann asked Stefania. "Do we need to collect them?"

"No." Stefania shook her head quickly, and Franceska glanced out the corner of her eye, understanding her friend's apprehension.

"No?" Mr. Mann asked with concern. "Why not?"

"It's difficult to explain, sir," Stefania spoke politely, but Franceska understood that she didn't want to dwell on the subject.

"The city is being bombed! How can you not—"

"My family is in Berlin," Stefania interrupted as she explained.

Mr. Mann's expression morphed from unease into suspicion as he eyed Stefania curiously.

"I thought I detected an accent." Mr. Mann tilted his head as he pointed up to the sky and muttered, "The work of your countrymen."

"They may be my countrymen, but they hate me as much as they hate you." Stefania looked down at her hands nervously.

"I see," Mr. Mann spoke softly, realizing that she was also Jewish.

The cart grew silent as everyone reflected on what had happened to them and their city. No conversation, apart from what was necessary, seemed appropriate given the circumstances.

"What will happen to us if our defenses fail?" Stefania asked as she broke the silence.

"Our boys are valiant." Mr. Mann nodded adamantly. "We once boasted the greatest cavalry in all of Europe. The winged hussars were a formidable opponent to anyone who tried to overthrow us."

"I'm not sure what good cavalry will do against tanks," Franceska muttered.

"It's the spirit that lives on!" Mr. Mann grew animated at Franceska's dismissal. "That same spirit of determination, resilience, and fighting to the bitter end is still part of our Polish pride and history!"

Franceska eyed her father questionably for his sudden shift in character. Only minutes ago she had to convince him to take his family to safety, and now he was proudly boasting of the Polish spirit.

"France and England have signed a defensive pact with us," Wiera spoke over her shoulder as she tried to restore some calm.

"But will they honor it?" Stefania asked.

"They'll honor it." Mr. Mann nodded repeatedly as he seemed to be trying to convince himself.

"They have to." Stefania crossed her arms as she looked at the sky with tears in her eyes.

"Look!" Mr. Mann pointed, and Franceska glanced in the direction to find a field hospital was being erected in a nearby park.

"But we're almost at my residence!" Wiera panicked. "We should keep moving."

"I'm not overlooking an opportunity like this." Mr. Mann shook his head.

A large canvas tent was being raised near some wealthier residential buildings with a bright red cross on each side. Doctors, nurses, and volunteers were running in every which direction trying to get the makeshift hospital operational and to accept the wounded that were already pouring in.

It was then that Franceska noticed the flood of ambulance sirens echoing throughout the city, and she wondered how she had been able to block out the noise. In either case, the sirens grew louder as they sped toward the hospital, and Franceska watched as dozens of injured stumbled, or were carried on stretchers, toward the promise of relief.

"Quickly! We need to get her in before the hospital is inundated with patients!" Franceska shouted as she jumped down from the cart.

"We need a stretcher," Stefania added. "She's unconscious."

"Can we carry her?" Mr. Mann asked as he jumped down from the cart and tied up the reins to a nearby lamp post.

"Depends on what the injury to her back is." Stefania shrugged. "What condition does she have?"

"The doctors can't quite figure it out." Mr. Mann shook his head in frustration. "Her lower back has always been an issue, but it's been terrible these last couple of years."

"I'll collect a stretcher!" Franceska called as she ran toward the hospital while waving her arms frantically to anyone who would pay attention and yelling, "Help! We need help!"

"Where?" a nurse asked calmly but earnestly when she took note of Franceska's distress.

"My mother." Franceska pointed back toward the cart. "We need a stretcher."

"The whole city needs a stretcher," the nurse replied tiredly as she looked around hopelessly.

"Please! My mother is unconscious!" Franceska pleaded.

"Take theirs when they're done." The nurse pointed to a couple of soldiers rushing into the tent with an injured companion on a stretcher.

Without wasting any time, Franceska ran into the tent after the soldiers, and, without explaining herself, snatched the stretcher after they had laid it on the ground and placed the injured soldier on a cot.

"Hey! We need that stretcher!" one of the soldiers called after Franceska.

"I'll bring it right back!" Franceska shouted over her shoulder as she rushed out of the tent.

"Oh, thank goodness!" Mr. Mann breathed a heavy sigh of relief when Franceska returned.

"Let's get her into position." Wiera jumped into the back of the cart as she added, "I need someone to help me support her head."

Then, abruptly, the vile screech of an air raid siren began to fill the air with its dreadful warning, and

Franceska looked to the sky to see it was darkening with another wave of enemy bombers and fighters. The anti-aircraft guns began to unleash their arsenal, shaking the earth with their attempts at thwarting the enemy.

"Raise the stretcher as high as you can," Mr. Mann ordered Franceska and Stefania as they held it open.

"I'll try—" Wiera paused as she looked toward the sky, distracted by the sound of an incoming plane.

Looking in the direction, Franceska's heart fell into her stomach when she saw a single plane diving directly at the medical tent.

In utter disbelief and bewilderment, Franceska shuddered when the enemy fighter unloaded its machine gun fire upon the tent. With callous, heartless, and shameless hatred, the enemy fighter plane fired upon countless injured civilians, doctors, nurses, and soldiers. Horrifying, gut-wrenching screams came from within the tent as those who had previously thought to have found relief now experienced a new hell.

Pulling up at the last minute, the fighter turned the nose of his plane back toward the heavens, and Franceska knew this was not a solitary pass.

"We can't stay here!" Stefania climbed back into the cart, followed swiftly by Franceska and Wiera as Mr. Mann quickly untied the reins.

"How could they?!" Franceska asked rhetorically as she couldn't believe such a horrid reality.

With a shout, Mr. Mann spurred the cart onward, and Franceska watched the solo enemy fighter making another run at his helpless victims. It was so unkind, cruel, and merciless that Franceska struggled to comprehend what she had witnessed.

"Where do we go now?" Franceska asked in a state of shock as she knelt beside her mother and inspected her carefully.

Her breathing was beginning to labor, and she looked so pale that Franceska feared the worst.

"Halt!" a shout came from the street ahead of them, and Franceska peeked her head up to see a handful of soldiers, and an officer, with their hands raised to stop the cart.

"We seek medical attention!" Mr. Mann spoke eagerly. "My wife is—"

"No carts or vehicles other than military or emergency," the officer replied sternly. "Every able-bodied man is required to assist."

"We can't carry my wife in her condition," Mr. Mann argued grumpily. "She's unable to walk, and we'll need the cart to take her to medical care."

"I'll have a couple of my younger medics take her to the army hospital." The officer snapped his fingers at two young medical soldiers, who were little more than boys, Franceska thought, and ordered, "Bring the stretcher."

"I need to be with her." Mr. Mann stepped down from the cart.

"We need you to assist us with the defenses." The officer pointed down the street and Franceska spotted a group of civilians and soldiers assembling anti-tank barriers and rolling out barbed wire.

"I can't leave these women alone, they're—"

"We need them too." The officer waved for the women to exit the cart.

Glancing at each other awkwardly, Franceska, Stefania, and Wiera weren't entirely sure how to respond. Franceska, for her part, was adamant not to leave her mother, especially in the hands of these two medics barely out of adolescence.

"Now!" the officer shouted. "Everyone out!"

At once, the women obeyed and quickly descended from the cart.

Hurrying, although awkwardly, the two young medics arrived with a stretcher at the back of the cart.

"Please be careful with her! Please!" Mr. Mann urged the medics as they gingerly lifted Mrs. Mann into the stretcher, and it bothered Franceska greatly that her mother made no noise. She wanted her to respond, or to show some signs of life. Mrs. Mann was such a resilient woman, and for Franceska to see her mother in this vulnerable state was nerve shattering.

"Let's move!" the officer waved impatiently for Mr. Mann and the three young women to attend to their newly conscripted duties.

Glancing over her shoulder, Franceska watched her mother for as long as possible as the two young medics, while thankfully competent, turned a corner and disappeared with Mrs. Mann down a street.

A sinking feeling formed in Franceska's gut that she had seen her mother for the last time. *Don't you dare think like that!* Franceska shook her head to rid herself of such horrid thoughts.

"She'll be well taken care of," the officer spoke with a measure of kindness as he took sympathy on their concerns.

I'll see her soon. Franceska nodded adamantly to herself.

"Report to the man with the black hat." The officer pointed to the end of the street where another officer was shouting orders at the civilians and soldiers preparing the defenses.

Nodding as he accepted his charge, Mr. Mann led the three women toward the group. And while Franceska was happy to do her part in bolstering the defenses, she was not skilled in practical means. She could dance professionally, sing beautifully, and, to a degree, considered herself on the higher end of her class. She wondered what use she would be in constructing defenses.

"I promise your mother will be fine." Stefania gently squeezed the back of Franceska's arm as they joined the group organizing the defenses.

"Thank you," Franceska replied loudly, appreciating her friend's perception of the situation and her emotional state.

"Reporting for duty," Mr. Mann spoke quietly to the officer in the black hat.

"Are you fit for digging?" The officer in the black hat asked Mr. Mann.

"Yes, sir," Mr. Mann replied.

"Good, I need you to help those men down there." The officer grabbed a shovel that was leaning against a cart and handed it to Mr. Mann who at once took his place and began digging a trench.

"You three." The man looked at the three girls as he squinted and then looked over his shoulder before adding. "Help with the barbed wire."

"Let's go!" Franceska latched onto Stefania's hand as the three girls sped over to the men rolling out the barbed wire.

She knew that her part to play in the defense of her city was small, but Franceska felt a measure of pride that she was performing an active part rather than hunkering down in some shelter underground. Although, she understood that these defenses were to protect Warsaw from a ground assault, and the very idea of coming face to face with these brutish Nazi soldiers was not a thought she relished. She merely hoped that whatever she did, however small, would buy her mother some time to recover.

That was all that mattered. All she cared about now, above everything, was seeing and speaking with her mother again. Her only aim, her only goal, was to ensure that her mother survived this hell.

Chapter Five: Night

"Jakoś to będzie (It will all work out somehow)"

Polish saying

"Here, love," a sweet elderly voice spoke from behind Franceska, and she turned around to find a woman holding a pot with a ladle and some bowls.

"Thank you!" Franceska gratefully accepted the gift of soup as she set down her roll of barbed wire.

Yet when she grabbed the warm bowl, it stung her hands, and she found it difficult to grip the spoon. Glancing down at the palms of her hands, Franceska noticed they were red, and blisters were already forming. She, along with Stefania and Wiera, had worked for hours on end late into the evening, holding the wooden spools while unrolling the barbed wire.

"Allow me," the sweet woman spoke tenderly as she scooped out some more soup for Franceska to make sure her bowl was full.

"You're very kind," Stefania also spoke with appreciation and the three girls took a minute to sit on a bolder and rest from their labors.

In exhaustion, and content to scarf down their meals, the three girls sat in silence as they ate. Franceska watched as the older woman made her rounds to the other soldiers and civilians nearby and they happily accepted her warm gesture. It was a simple, yet sweet act of kindness, and Franceska felt a sense of comfort in knowing that caring women like her existed in this dark world.

"It's still overcast," Wiera spoke after a moment as she stared up at the darkening sky.

"I wonder how well our fighters fared against the Nazis?" Stefania also looked up at the gloomy heavens. "Or if tomorrow will be much the same?"

"We took heavy losses," Mr. Mann chimed in as he sat on the pavement near the girls. "At least that is what the men are saying."

"Any word on mother?" Franceska asked, and Mr. Mann shook his head solemnly.

"Warning!" a soldier announced from a loudspeaker on the back of a truck that was slowly driving through the city. "Turn off all lights. The use of electricity, or candles, is prohibited. All lights must be turned off during the night."

"So the bombers can't spot us?" Stefania asked quickly.

"That would be my assumption." Franceska nodded.

"Will that actually work?" Wiera asked skeptically.

"Anything is worth a shot at this point." Mr. Mann shrugged.

The company returned to silence, and Franceska knew that everyone was fearing and hoping for the same outcomes. What would happen to them should the Nazi invasion be successful? Can their soldiers repel the might of Germany? What will happen to them should the Nazis take over the city? Where will they sleep tonight? How will they collect money to eat or buy clothing?

After a few moments, an elderly man sat on a bolder across from Franceska. He was looking intently at Wiera, who was invested in her bowl of soup and not paying him any attention.

He looked kind, Franceska thought, with a neatly trimmed beard and gray, wavy hair. He was also dressed well with a navy-blue suit, and it was evident he took pride in his appearance.

"Can we help you?" Mr. Mann asked, and Franceska thought he sounded nervous.

"What I would give to hear you sing right now," the man spoke to Wiera with a warm voice.

"Papa!" Wiera quickly set her bowl down as she ran over to the man and wrapped her arms around him.

Both Franceska and Stefania glanced at each other, surprised at Wiera's emotional outburst.

"How did you find us?" Wiera broke off her embrace as she sat beside her father.

"Purely by chance." Wiera's father placed a gentle hand on her back.

"I was worried about you!"

"Nonsense." Wiera's father waved to dismiss the idea as he looked at the other two women and Mr. Mann before asking his daughter, "Why don't you tell me about your companions?"

"This is Franceska Mann, and her father Mr. Mann, and this is Stefania Grodzieńska. Everyone, this is my father, Mr. Gran," Wiera introduced.

"I wish we were meeting under kinder circumstances." Mr. Mann nodded his greeting.

"Indeed." Mr. Gran nodded back.

"I was worried about you." Wiera returned to her reserved demeanor.

"Same." Mr. Gran looked back at his daughter tenderly before stating with a kind gesture, "Why don't you serenade us?"

"I don't think that's appropriate." Wiera shook her head with a mixture of annoyance and embarrassment.

"Oh, would be so kind?" Mr. Mann pressed, and Franceska still found it difficult to reconcile the quiet man she had grown up with to this person who had moments of confidence and excitability. "I've heard your voice was truly remarkable."

"My father embellishes." Wiera waved to dismiss the compliment.

"And my daughter is coy." Her father smirked.

"This isn't the time." Wiera remained adamant. "It's not appropriate when so many have lost their lives and their homes."

"My dear, your light is exactly what we need in these dark times. Please, raise us out our mirey pit." Wiera's father pressed.

"Oh, go on!" Stefania gave Wiera a kind, yet generous, shove to stand her to her feet. "Everyone is taking a break right now. They would love to hear you sing while they eat."

"Fine." Wiera slapped her hand against her thigh as she looked around at everyone before asking, "What would you like to hear? I don't believe the Polish Tango is suitable for this environment."

"That's not all you sing." Mr. Gran looked at her with a wry grin.

"No, I'm not singing that." Wiera shook her head quickly. "Besides, I'm not confident that I'll remember the lyrics."

"Fortunate that I brought a copy, then." Wiera's father reached into his shirt and retrieved a folded letter which he then handed to his daughter.

"Convenient," Wiera muttered as she unfolded it and looked over the lyrics quickly.

"Well?" Stefania urged.

With a deep breath, Wiera closed her eyes and cleared her throat before singing a tune that struck Franceska in the deepest places of her soul.

"I am a poor wayfaring stranger
I'm travelling through this world with woe
Yet there's no sickness, toil, nor danger
In that bright land to which I go
    I'm going there to see my father
I'm going there no more to roam
I'm only going over Jordan
I'm only going over home
    I know dark clouds will gather round me
I know my way is rough and steep
But golden fields lie just before me
Where God's redeemed shall ever sleep
    I'm going home to see my mother
And all my loved ones who've gone on
I'm only going over Jordan
I'm only going over home

I am a poor wayfaring stranger
I'm travelling through this world of woe
Yet there's no sickness, toil, nor danger
In that bright land to which I go
    I'm going there to see my father
I'm going there, no more to roam
I'm only going over Jordan
I'm only going over home."

Not a dry eye remained, and when Wiera opened her eyes she looked almost startled to realize that her song had drawn a crowd of soldiers, civilians, and children, who were either holding back tears or sobbing liberally at the beautiful tune. Many, Franceska knew, were Jews like herself. Some were practicing Christians, while others kept to their Judaic roots, and still, others were secular. Regardless of their religious or cultural orientation, the song carried the courage they all needed to hear that this was not the end; they were merely strangers in this land, and their true home was far removed from the hell of this one.

"Thank you," Wiera's father spoke sincerely as he looked at his daughter with the great pride. Everyone, including Franceska, knew that each and every moment was now suddenly dear and precious.

And while Franceska would never wish or be thankful that this was happening to so many innocents, she did, at least, perceive that many people, who would otherwise never speak to each other, were holding hands, hugging, and coming together in a way that only tragedy can induce. Jews wrapped their arms around Gentiles, Protestants held the hands of Catholics, and enemies laid aside petty grievances. They were all united in a common purpose: they were all proud to call Poland their home, and they were all determined to defend Warsaw to their last breath.

Yet there was one man, Franceska noticed, who had not stopped working. Even with a cane in one hand, he held a shovel in the other and dug as best as he was able. It was then that Franceska noticed it was one of the managers, Mr. Rosenberg, from The Melody Palace. She felt horrible for how rude she had been to him the other night, but assumed that he didn't remember her.

"Another song?" a man in the crowd asked Wiera hopefully.

"Any requests?" Wiera asked with a shy smile, and Franceska felt a sense of pride for having a friend with such talent.

A few songs were requested from the crowd, and Franceska grew excited when she spotted a couple bottles of vodka being passed around. She knew they had a lot of work left to be ready for the ground assault, but it was too dark now with all the lights in the city turned off to even see a few feet in front of them.

Wiera began to sing another beautiful song, but this one was more upbeat and uplifting. Still, Franceska was distracted by Mr. Rosenberg, who she could vaguely make out his silhouette while he continued to shovel.

Squeezing her way through the crowd, Franceska came to stand above Mr. Rosenberg in the ditch as she called down to him, "There's vodka and soup being passed around."

"No thanks," he replied quickly.

"It's much too dark to be doing this sort of work." Franceska pressed.

"Is that the excuse you'll tell yourself when the Nazis invade and overrun us?"

"Pardon me?" Franceska shot her head back in shock. "I'll have you know that I worked all day constructing defenses."

"And now you're enjoying revelry and good company." Mr. Rosenberg stopped and looked up at her grumpily. "Not me. I'll know, when the time comes, and it will, that I did everything I could and poured out every ounce of strength I had to hold the barbarians back."

Fuming, Franceska stormed back toward the crowd, snatched a half empty bottle of vodka, and returned to the pit before climbing down, rolling up her sleeves, and squaring up with Mr. Roseberg.

"What are you doing?" Mr. Rosenberg demanded.

"One drink together, then I'll help you dig." Franceska handed him the bottle.

Slowly, Mr. Rosenberg took the bottle and looked at it with what Franceska perceived as unease before he handed the bottle back to her and mentioned with what sounded like regret, "I don't partake."

"I'll drink double then." Franceska took a generous sip from the bottle as she felt the burning in her throat.

"You look familiar." Mr. Rosenberg squinted at her in the dark before he chuckled softly and mentioned, "You're the dancer from the other night. The one who preferred to dance for, what was the word you used? Oh, right, *refined crowds*."

"Give me a shovel." Franceska held out her hand.

"Do you think you can keep up with me?" Mr. Rosenberg challenged as he lifted his cane in salute, and Franceska thought the quip at his own disability was endearing.

"I understand your point about working to keep the invaders out, but what they're doing now is of equal importance," Franceska began as she dug her shovel into the earth.

"Yeah? How so?" Mr. Rosenberg asked cynically.

"She's reminding them of why they're fighting," Franceska replied quickly, and Mr. Rosenberg paused.

"And what's that?" he asked, and Franceska noticed his tone soften a touch.

"Love, friendship, family." Franceska shrugged as she also stopped to look at him.

"Well, all of that will mean nothing if the Nazis get their way," he retorted callously as he resumed shoveling, and Franceska found it admirable how he worked so hard while at a significant handicap.

"Need some help?" Stefania asked as she also climbed into the pit.

"Here's a shovel." Mr. Rosenberg handed one to Stefania as she began to dig beside Franceska.

"I forgot to ask Wiera, but I thought Adam enlisted?" Franceska asked Stefania. "Why wasn't he with the army when he rescued us with the cart? Thank goodness he did, by the way. We scarcely left our house before it was destroyed. I shudder to think what would've happened had we stayed."

"Apparently he failed the physical exam," Stefania explained.

"He failed?" Franceska frowned. "How?"

"I didn't get the details. Wiera only told me last night. She was relieved, and I imagine she's more than relieved now knowing that he's not in danger fighting right now."

"That's shocking to me." Franceska remained baffled.

"It's hard to believe for sure, but—"

The gut-wrenching sound of the air raid siren began, and Franceska didn't believe she would ever become accustomed to that loathsome noise.

"Do they have no mercy?!" Stefania shouted.

"Where do we go?!" Franceska panicked.

"Everyone! Find shelter!" an officer shouted as he blew his whistle and pointed directions which Franceska could scarcely make out in the dark.

"Come!" Franceska grabbed Stefania's hand as they left the ditch and ran back to her father.

Franceska bumped into shoulders and elbows as she and Stefania pushed through the crowd while under the cover of darkness. Soldiers and civilians were running in every which direction, and most, Franceska assumed, were as ignorant as she was about where to find shelter. Without any light to guide their way, it was easy to lose direction.

"Franceska!" Mr. Mann's voice was faintly heard above the roar of the panicked crowd and shrieking sirens.

"Over here!" Franceska shouted, hoping he would call out again so that she could pinpoint his location.

"Franceska!" Mr. Mann yelled, and Franceska knew he was close by.

"Get out of the way!" a soldier screamed as a squad of soldiers, with flashlights lighting their path, rushed by Franceska.

"Mommy!" a young voice called, and Franceska's heart shattered as she watched a young girl standing in the middle of a crowd and balling.

"I'm here!" a woman replied as she scooped up the little girl into her arms, and Franceska sighed her relief.

"Franceska!" Mr. Mann's call came again, and she could hear the panic in his voice.

"I'm here!" Franceska yelled as she waved her arms, not that it would do any good in the dark, but it was instinctual to try and get his attention.

"There you are!" Mr. Mann reached out and latched onto Franceska's arm.

"Where's Wiera?!" Stefania asked as she peered into the darkness.

"I'm here!" Wiera replied from a few feet behind Mr. Mann as she arrived while holding her father's hand.

"Where do we go?!" Franceska asked as the drone of the bombers grew louder.

"Follow me!" Mr. Gran demanded, and Franceska appreciated his confidence.

Latching onto each other as best as they were able while they were jostled and pushed by the crowd, the group came to what Franceska believed were some previously bombed houses.

"Get in!" Mr. Gran pointed, and Mr. Mann stepped over a pile of bricks blown out of the wall of a house which still had a roof overhead.

Following closely behind, Franceska entered the house, and, even in the darkness, discovered that almost everything inside the property had been obliterated. Furniture, photographs, clothing, toys, and most of the walls were stained in black soot from the explosion.

Still, in the corner of the house, where the chimney was intact, they found some shelter, and Franceska cowered on the floor near her father as the screech of the bombs falling to earth caused her to tremble.

"Is everyone accounted for?" Mr. Gran asked as he also joined them in the corner.

"We're all here." Mr. Mann replied quietly.

The company drew silent as they all huddled together and waited for the bombs to strike their targets indiscriminately. Franceska didn't know why, but she found that if they remained quiet, somehow the Nazis wouldn't know where they were hiding. It was foolish, she understood, but with everyone else remaining quiet, she assumed they were thinking the same.

The explosions began in the distance, like thunder or fireworks, and Franceska felt a sort of relief wash over her as she knew that the bombers were not targeting their area. At least, that is, for now.

"Is this still functional?" Stefania asked quietly as she inspected the chimney.

"Even if it was, we're not permitted to start a fire," Mr. Mann whispered as he shook his head.

"You'll have to keep me warm then." Stefania squeezed tightly against Franceska.

"I hope mother is alright," Franceska mentioned to her father.

"She's fine!" Mr. Mann griped.

"I'm allowed to be worried about her!" Franceska lost her patience.

"And how is that going to help?!" Mr. Mann nearly shouted.

"I want her to—"

"Stop talking about it!" Mr. Mann's voice wavered, but he cleared his throat to hide his emotions, and Franceska knew he was masking his grief. Still, she felt it unjust of him to forbid her from expressing her fears.

"Your leg is so cold!" Wiera shifted the subject.

"Who's leg?" Mr. Gran asked.

"Well, yours, clearly."

"What do you mean?" Mr. Gran grew concerned.

"I mean, why is your leg so—" Wiera paused before she let out a little shriek.

"What is it?!" Franceska asked as Wiera scurried away.

"There's a body!" Wiera covered her mouth with her hands as she tried to stifle her outburst.

"A body?!" Stefania nearly squealed.

"Beside me! I thought my leg was resting against my father's." Wiera rubbed her arms as her skin crawled with disgust.

"Help me with this." Mr. Gran stood swiftly as he consulted with Mr. Mann.

"You three stay here," Mr. Mann added as he grabbed the arms of a deceased elderly man.

With a heave, the two men lifted the body, and Franceska studied the face of the dead man. Dried blood was caked on the side of his face, and Franceska felt a loneliness she didn't know how to explain. This poor man had died while isolated in his own home. She wondered about his wife, children, or even grandchildren, and what his last conversation with them had been.

She hated the feeling of loneliness from seeing his body being taken out of his house. She hated knowing the fear he probably felt while secluded in his property, and that his life was extinguished because of a tyrannical maniac. What did this man do to Hitler, or to the pilots in the bombers above his head? It was unjust, cruel, and Franceska grew resentment in her heart toward the enemy that was trying to eradicate them.

"It's too dangerous to take the body now!" Wiera tried to stop her father and Mr. Mann from leaving.

"We'll be right back," Mr. Mann called over his shoulder, and Franceska caught the emotional inflection in his voice. She pondered that he may have seen himself in this elderly man, and knew that, if it were his body, he would want it disposed of properly.

Boom! Crack!

The explosions that were once rattling off in the distance grew closer, and Franceska offered a worried look to Stefania and Wiera, wondering if someone would soon be collecting their bodies like they had this elderly man.

"What did we do to deserve this?" Stefania sniffled as she leaned her head on Franceska's shoulder.

"Nothing," Wiera replied as she sat on the other side of Franceska, and the three huddled together for warmth and safety.

"Did I not pray enough? Is God punish—"

"Don't think like that." Wiera looked sternly at Stefania. "It does no one any good to think about what ifs or should haves. We must deal with what is."

"How do we do that?" Stefania pressed.

"To start, by keeping each other close. Surviving the bombing will be one thing, but surviving what comes next, that will be the true test."

"And what does come next?" Stefania asked with wide eyes.

"Get some sleep if you can," Wiera replied. "We need our strength to help the men tomorrow."

"I'm not sure how I'm going to sleep on a pile of bricks." Stefania kicked a loose brick with her foot.

"I feel bad for that man who lived here." Franceska looked around the destroyed house, but it was still too dark to see much of anything.

"You can't do that, either." Wiera shook her head.

"Do what?" Franceska asked for clarification.

"Feel bad." Wiera glanced at Franceska and then away before adding, "It's going to get a lot worse before it gets better, if it gets better at all. You'll weep from morning until night if you allow yourself to feel. It would be best if you save yourself some grief by turning off empathy and sympathy."

"I think it's important to feel," Franceska retorted. "Feeling is what keeps me close to you and Stefania. Compassion is what will save us."

"Compassion is what will drown us. What will save us is having bigger guns than our enemies."

"And since we don't have bigger guns?" Franceska pressed.

"Let's talk about something else, please." Stefania chewed her nails.

"Maybe we should try and sleep, actually." Wiera rubbed her eyes.

"How can you be so callous?" Franceska frowned at her friend.

"What you perceive as heartless is actually kindness. You might not realize that now, but maybe someday you will. In order to survive, you'll have to become ruthless."

"I'll never become ruthless." Franceska shook her head adamantly.

"The only survivors will be those who abandon principle." Wiera looked sternly at the two girls with her.

"You can keep your moral code, and lose your life, or lose your ethics and keep your life. The choice is yours."

"You're wrong." Franceska shook her head.

"Can we please discuss something else?!" Stefania nearly shouted.

"I'm worried about Adam," Wiera began.

"Do feelings for your significant other fit within your uncaring worldview?" Franceska asked with a hint of sarcasm.

"That I can't help." Wiera stared out the gaping hole on the side of the house before turning to Stefania and asking, "What about Jan?"

"I haven't heard from him." Stefania looked down at the floor with worry. "I tried calling him all morning, but then the invasion started."

"As long as we have each other, we'll be fine." Wiera looked at them kindly, but Franceska still found her insensitive attitude distasteful.

"You two have been excellent friends to me since I moved to Warsaw," Stefania spoke caringly. "I don't know where I would be without you girls. The divorce was harsh, and I lost many friends. Friends that I was convinced I would grow old with, but they cared more about appearances than the truth."

"I never did ask you about the divorce," Wiera spoke quietly as she looked at her friend.

"And I appreciate that you didn't need to know all the details before accepting me as your companion." Stefania smiled back at her. "The truth of the matter is not so complicated. He beat me, terribly, and I felt I was worth more than that. I lost my home, my family. When I came to Warsaw, I was worried that I would be alone forever, but now I know that I found friends of much higher caliber."

"I'm certain that Wiera would agree that we're the fortunate ones to have you." Franceska pinched Stefania's arm gently.

"I heard about your dance competition." Stefania forced a smile as she shifted the subject. "You came in fourth place? That's so wonderful!"

"Feels trivial to think about something as silly as dancing right now." Franceska grew embarrassed.

"It's anything but trivial. You're what this horrid world needs." Stefania pressed as she grabbed Franceska's hand. "You're the bright light shining in the darkness."

"That's a little too kind." Franceska smiled coyly.

The partially destroyed house grew silent as the three girls listened to the distant explosions, knowing that the Nazis were making many more houses piles of rubble like the one they were sheltering in.

Sirens, ambulances, alarms, crying, yelling, shrieking and shouting filled the air, and Franceska understood that a night like this was only one of many to come. They would have to be vigilant, crafty, and alert if they wanted to survive, but still, her mind dwelt on her mother, and she prayed that she was alright and being taken care of sufficiently. How she wished to be by her side again.

Chapter Six:
Maternity

"The mind is its own place, and in itself can make a heaven of hell, a hell of heaven."

John Milton

Franceska peeked out from heavy eyelids, but her sleepiness was disorientating, and she could scarcely recall where she was or why. All she could discern was that it was morning, and that a radio was playing nearby. She couldn't make out what the announcer was saying, but it sounded solemn.

Opening her eyelids wider, Franceska realized that she was sitting upright, and that Stefania was lying next to her while Wiera was still sleeping close by, curled up in a ball on the hard floor.

Yet when Franceska tried to move, she winced at a terrible stiffness in her lower back. She recognized that falling asleep in that position, after a day of manual labor, was ill advised, to say the least, but she was also surprised that she had fallen asleep that quickly.

Looking down at her hands, Franceska inspected them in the light and was surprised at how blistered they were. She regretted not using gloves while she was handling the rolls of barbed wire, but arrangements for such items were scarce given the emergency of the situation. Still, she took a measure of pride in the callouses developing on her hands. She felt as if she had participated in the defense of the city. She knew her contribution would likely be ineffective against the German war machine, but she believed that whatever time she could afford her mother was well spent.

Brushing herself off, Franceska stood and gingerly walked over to Mr. Mann and Mr. Gran, who were sitting in front of the radio and looking downcast. They had managed to salvage a few chairs and a coffee table where they had placed a portable radio.

It was a surreal image, Franceska thought, of the two men sitting on sad wooden chairs in front of a radio. The gaping hole in the side of the house served as a backdrop that looked into the damaged city with black smoke rising to heaven.

She was still struggling to wake up, but the announcement over the radio felt like a splash of cold water in her face.

"I repeat, the police forces, fire brigades, and city administration have evacuated the city," the announcer continued. "All young, able-bodied men are hereby also ordered to evacuate the city."

"Why are they ordering the young men out?" Franceska shot her father a confused glance. "Don't they want them to fight? And why are the police and fire brigades leaving? Why would they leave us so vulnerable?"

"They also withdrew most of the garrison," Mr. Mann added solemnly. "There are only four battalions left to defend the city."

"I…" Franceska was lost for words.

"Our task is great, our enemy is fierce, but Poland will remain as long as we keep fighting. We call upon every civilian to take it upon themselves to assist in the construction, assembly, and placement of barricades and anti-tank barriers. Long live Poland."

The Polish national anthem began to play over the static, and Franceska sat dumbfounded beside her father and Mr. Gran.

"He orders us to fight, yet tells all the young men to leave?" Mr. Mann shook his head in wonder.

"It's likely that they want to keep a reserve of men for future fighting." Mr. Gran suggested. "It's sad to think of how many men in our current army will perish."

"As long as Britain and France uphold their obligations and attack Germany, we stand a chance." Mr. Mann rubbed the stubble growing on his chin, and Franceska realized that this was the first time she had ever seen him with any facial hair longer than a 'five o'clock shadow'.

"Do you think that they will?" Franceska asked nervously.

"As far as I'm aware, the English don't even have a standing army, but they are known for their navy. If they can at least harass German supply boats or destroyers, then I…I don't know." Mr. Gran rubbed the back of his neck with frustration.

"Have either of you slept?" Franceska asked as she studied their long faces and bloodshot eyes.

Mr. Mann shook his head quickly as he stared at the radio, listening to the Polish National Anthem that was intended to invoke patriotism.

"Have you heard from mother?" Franceska asked.

"Give me a moment, please, without your persistent questions." Mr. Mann looked sternly at his daughter.

Glancing away with crimson cheeks, Franceska did not appreciate being spoken to as if she were a pestering child.

"No," Mr. Mann began with a sigh and added, "I haven't heard from her."

"I'll see what I can find out today," Franceska muttered as her stomach rumbled loudly.

"And I'll make it my mission to gather food and supplies." Mr. Gran glanced over at her. "And coffee. I'd kill for a hot cup of coffee."

"Might be difficult to locate anything with the administration evacuating the city. Not to mention, without police, this could get ugly, and quickly." Mr. Mann shook his head with dismay.

"Why don't you get some sleep?" Franceska looked at him with a measure of sympathy. "I'll find out what I can about mother and come right back."

Without another word, Mr. Mann nodded and walked over to the corner of the house where the other two girls were still sleeping. Finding a spot at a respectable distance from them, Mr. Mann lay on his back, folded his hands across his chest, and covered his face with his cap as he attempted to sleep.

"Would you like me to accompany you?" Mr. Gran asked.

"I'll be alright, but thank you." Franceska smiled politely. "You should get some sleep as well."

"I'll sleep when I'm dead." Mr. Gran waved to dismiss her. "Be careful out there. Trust no one. Wicked men will be happy to take advantage of the chaos."

"I appreciate the advice." Franceska nodded, but in the back of her mind she wondered if it would be all that different from how she usually ventured out alone in the city as a young woman.

"I'll see if I can find some food." Mr. Gran stood and left the property through the hole in the front of the house.

"It's cold." Stefania shivered as she came to sit beside Franceska.

"Yeah, it is." Franceska frowned as she looked down at her arms to find that they were covered in goosebumps. She found it odd that she hadn't noticed how chilly it was, but she was preoccupied with the announcement and worried about her mother's condition.

"Your father is still sleeping." Stefania nodded in the direction.

"He only just lied down now." Franceska looked back in the direction of her father to see that he was already snoring.

"I wonder how long we slept," Stefania pondered aloud. "I'm starving."

"Mr. Gran went to look for food."

"Good." Stefania nodded as she looked sleepily at the radio that was still playing music in an attempt to lift spirits. "I half hoped that I would wake up this morning to discover this was all a terrible dream."

"Still doesn't feel quite real." Franceska nodded in agreement. "I'm going to see if I can find where they took my mother."

"Want some company?" Stefania asked, but Franceska felt that she was merely being polite.

"I'll be alright, but I appreciate the offer."

"Please!" Stefania pressed. "Don't leave me alone with Wiera."

"What's wrong with Wiera?" Franceska frowned, but her stomach growled angrily, and she lost most interest in the subject.

"Nothing at all apart from the fact that she and I don't really have a relationship. You're the glue to our friendship, my dear Franceska." Stefania reached out and took Franceska's hand in hers.

"That's very kind." Franceska grinned bashfully.

"So, let's go find your mother."

"Wiera will be upset that we left her." Franceska looked back at her friend still sleeping on the hard floor.

"She'll be fine. She's a tough girl."

"That she is." Franceska nodded as she added, "If you're sincere then I would appreciate your company."

"Good." Stefania stood with some enthusiasm, but her expression immediately turned sour.

"What's wrong?" Franceska asked as she also stood.

"A little dizzy is all." Stefania drew a deep breath. "Hard work and little sleep are a poor combination for stability."

"I think the hard work is far from over." Franceska looked regretfully at her friend as they both left the property, carefully stepping over bricks and debris.

"What do you mean?" Stefania asked with concern.

"They've ordered all the young men to evacuate the city."

"What?!" Stefania's eyes bulged with surprise. "Whatever for?"

"They didn't mention, but the assumption is so that they can use them for future fighting."

"I don't understand that." Stefania shook her head as they climbed over a heap of rubble in the middle of the street.

"Hey…" Franceska spoke in a hushed tone to her friend when she looked down the street and spotted Mr. Rosenberg still working in the same trench that he had been last night. "Do you remember him from last night?"

"Yeah, he's a manager at The Melody Palace. Why? How do you know him?" Stefania glanced in the direction of Mr. Rosenberg.

"When we went dancing the other night, he asked if I would be interested in performing."

"Really? What did you say?" Stefania watched her friend closely.

"I regret it now, but I was a little high-browed when I told him that his club was, in other words, beneath me."

"I imagine he didn't take that well?"

"He didn't forget it, either."

"Oh dear." Stefania grimaced.

"Feels rather ridiculous to dwell on such things, especially given the much worse situation many others are facing now, but I can't help admitting that I feel foolish around him." Franceska watched a cart brimming with clothes, bedding, and a chair being wheeled past them by an elderly couple and an adolescent boy.

They seemed downcast, as one would imagine, and in quietness accompanied by dismal countenances, they navigated through the once smoothly paved streets that had been upturned by the Nazi bombs.

Franceska's heart ached for their troubles, and she wished that she could alleviate their sorrows. She wondered if the parents had perished, and now the son was left alone with the grandparents. She knew, by their expression, that they had experienced significant trauma, and she wished that the enemy could see their faces. Maybe then, being moved by the images of these lonely and dejected people, they would realize the error of their ways.

But as Franceska and Stefania moved further into the city, the more these carts became familiar. Thousands of people were fleeing, carrying whatever they could on their backs, in carts or carriages, heaped in piles that were tied together with rope, away from the approaching Germans.

Some of the items that people chose to save seemed rather odd to Franceska. A man, while holding his young daughter's hand, carried a large painting tied to his back. She wondered if he believed it would be worth selling, or if it was some sort of family heirloom. In either case, she found it unusual that he would save such an item and yet no clothing or bedding. Still, she knew that the shock of the bombings was creating some rather rash feelings in people, and she knew it wasn't right for her to judge his position.

She was also surprised to see the level of destruction that had occurred overnight. Hundreds of houses, businesses, statues, and buildings were either nothing more than their frames, or a heap of rubble. She knew she had walked down these streets dozens, if not hundreds, of times before in her daily journeys about the city, but with such destruction, she felt as if she was walking in a foreign land.

"What are they doing?" Stefania pointed down a main street that they passed by, and Franceska noticed a group of men, under military supervision, tearing up the tracks of a tram car.

"I believe they're turning them into tank traps." Franceska nodded to another area of the main street where the men were driving long pieces of the torn-up tracks into the ground.

"You!" an officer called out to the girls as they were passing by a trench.

"Us?" Franceska pointed to herself as she wasn't entirely sure who he was calling to on the busy street.

"We need help digging." The officer waved for them to take the shovels near the ditch.

"I'm trying to find my mother," Franceska explained.

"Your mother can wait. We need everyone to pitch in." The officer pointed sternly at the shovels, and Franceska knew he wasn't going to budge on the matter.

"Then why did we evacuate half the men?" Stefania muttered under her breath.

"I really need to know if she's alright," Franceska also muttered as she picked up the shovel and joined the ranks of civilians digging trenches and raising the defenses.

"I could use something to eat," Stefania grumbled. "They should be providing food if they're going to be forcing us to work."

"If it wasn't for that soup from the sweet lady last night, I don't think I'd be able to stand." Franceska grunted as she dug her shovel into the earth. She knew it was wrong to complain, but she also understood that hunger affected her better judgment.

"Stop bickering," a man near them moaned. "We're all hungry. Doesn't ease the hunger pains with you constantly mentioning it."

"When do we get food?" a younger boy, about the age of ten, quietly asked his mother as he continued to dig.

"See?" the man frowned at Stefania and Franceska. "He didn't mention a word until you reminded him."

"You think he forgot?" Stefania angrily dug her shovel into the earth.

"Listen!" the man threw his shovel down as he stormed over to the girls.

"Hey! Hey!" an officer blew his whistle aggressively to put a swift end to the fight before it got out of control.

"You're fortunate he's here." The man pointed a finger in Stefania's face as he returned to digging.

"What a terrible man!" Stefania fumed as she dug furiously.

"Conserve your energy." Franceska tried to calm her friend. "We're all hungry, scared, and tired. It's important that we remain united."

"Tell that to him," Stefania mumbled as she remained stubborn in her outrage.

"Who knows what he lost yesterday." Franceska looked over at the man who was again at his assigned duties.

"When did you suddenly become so altruistic?" Stefania growled at Franceska. "You were complaining with me only moments ago, and now you're the meek peacemaker? Don't take his side."

"There are only two sides: us and the Nazis. We'd do well to remember that." Franceska raised an eyebrow to drive home the point.

"Stop making sense and be angry with me." Stefania shook her head in annoyance.

Franceska chuckled before changing the subject and asked, "When you get the chance, try and contact Jan. I'm sure you're worried about him. You two seemed rather close at the dance."

"Maybe it's for the best, anyway. His wife was becoming suspicious."

"His wife?!" Franceska's mouth fell open in shock.

"He hid that fact well." Stefania shook her head in mesmerization. "Even his friends were unaware that he was married. Apparently, his marriage wasn't entirely of his choosing, but the fact that he hid that detail from me was unacceptable."

"Did his parents arrange his marriage?" Franceska watched her friend curiously.

"In a way, but he married because he thought it was what he was supposed to do. He was merely going through the motions only to discover that he didn't love her as much as a husband should."

"So, you're going to break it off with him?" Franceska grunted as she began digging.

"Oh, goodness no."

"What?!" Franceska paused. "You're going to—"

"I'm not letting a marriage get in the way of my happiness." Stefania shook her head. "Besides, he's going to divorce her."

"And you believed him?" Franceska frowned.

"Why wouldn't I?" Stefania also paused as she stood up straight and looked at Franceska before asking, "Do you suppose I was tricked?"

"The unhappily married man who promises his mistress that he will divorce his wife for her sake?" Franceska's countenance turned sympathetic as she studied her friend. "That's a tale as old as time itself."

"I believe him," Stefania spoke with confidence as she returned to shoveling.

"For your sake, and I mean this sincerely, I hope you're right."

"Glad you're so—"

The air raid siren began to blare again, dropping Franceska's heart into her stomach.

"I hate that noise!" Stefania shouted angrily at the sky.

"Get to shelter!" the officer yelled as he blew his whistle and ordered the civilians to exit the ditch.

"Where?!" Franceska asked in a panic as she frantically climbed out of the ditch.

"There's no shelter nearby!" another civilian called to the officer in a panic.

"Get into houses, stores, sheds!" the officer grew frantic as he waved for everyone to depart.

"Should we go back to the house?" Stefania asked as she clung to Franceska.

"It's too far." Franceska shook her head. "Besides, we need to find my mother. She's probably terrified during these raids and supposing we abandoned her."

"Let's take shelter in that shop then!" Stefania pointed at a local grocer, and, without wasting a further moment, took Franceska's hand and the two ran over to the store for cover.

To Franceska's dismay, many others had the same idea, and the store was now packed full of women and children desperate to escape the coming devastation.

"Get away from the window!" the store clerk yelled.

"There's nowhere else to go!" a woman yelled back in fright.

"We can't stay here." Stefania again took Franceska's hand, and the two left the store in a hurry.

Glancing up at the sky, Franceska was relieved, in part, to find that the enemy bombers were targeting another area of the city, and they were, for now, safe.

"We should hurry before they start focusing on this area," Stefania mentioned as she also looked up at the sky.

"Agreed!" Franceska replied as she still eagerly clung to her friend's hand. "But I'm not sure where to even start searching for my mother."

"Let's start with the nearest hospital, then we'll go from there." Stefania glanced again up at the sky to ensure it was still safe to be out in the open.

The drone of the bombers and fighters overhead combined with the thudding of distant explosions and the anti-aircraft guns unleashing their arsenal, began to weaken Franceska's resolve. She didn't know if she could handle much more of the constant noise, or the inhumanity of dropping explosives onto innocents, and she wished with all her heart to simply disappear.

As they walked through the city, they spotted countless citizens, again carrying whatever they could, trying to escape the city. Franceska knew that as soon as they found her mother, it would be best to leave as well. Regardless of money or even a direction for them to head in, anything was better, she believed, than simply hoping that the constant shelling wouldn't take their lives as well.

"My God!" Franceska stopped short in her tracks when the two girls spotted a maternity hospital at the end of the street.

Hundreds of injured were limping, walking, or being carried on stretchers toward the hospital. Children and elderly were missing limbs and screaming in pain as parents or caretakers yelled for help, many were bleeding profusely from other wounds, and others limped or were assisted to the hospital to deal with their injuries.

Franceska felt as though she was observing a scene out of *Dante's Inferno* where souls were suffering intensely with little hope of relief.

"Out of the way!" a man shouted from behind Franceska, and she turned to see a teary-eyed father rushing toward the hospital with a girl in his arms. The girl, about five or six, Franceska assumed, was entirely limp. Dried, dark red blood had run out of her ears and down her neck.

It was clear to Franceska, and likely everyone else, that there was no hope for her. Still, she understood the urgency of the father not to give up hope, and she watched him with a broken heart.

The sight of the girl sank deep into Franceska's spirit, and she felt a pain that she didn't believe possible. She couldn't imagine what that father was enduring, and Franceska couldn't understand what he or his daughter had done to deserve this torment.

She wasn't necessarily a religious person, but still, Franceska found herself praying in her heart that God would show mercy to them. She didn't know if anyone would listen to her prayer, but it was almost instinctual to utter the words in her heart.

"Let's find your mother quickly," Stefania spoke quietly, and Franceska knew that she was also shaken by the harrowing scene.

"This is a maternity hospital, though." Franceska glanced at her friend with concern.

"It appears that they've converted it for the general public as well." Stefania looked around before adding, "I wouldn't overlook it."

"I'm glad you're with me," Franceska spoke softly to Stefania as they approached the doors of the hospital, which were packed tightly with the injured who were trying to obtain some relief.

"I need ten cots along that wall, and another ten along that wall," a nurse commanded some volunteers as they began to organize beds along the outside of the hospital.

"They're overrun." Franceska felt a lump forming in her throat, worried about the care her mother was receiving in these conditions.

The two girls pushed their way into the hospital, being as careful as possible to avoid the seriously injured. Yet when they entered the building, they found that they had only descended further into another level of horror.

The hallways were filled with the injured and wounded with many being forced to lay on the floor. The groans and moans of agony were distressing to even the hardest of hearts, but what Franceska couldn't stomach was witnessing surgery out in the open. Without privacy, and in some cases without anesthesia, the operations were conducted in a hasty attempt to save lives.

Stepping over bodies of those either sleeping, groaning in pain, or moments away from death, the two girls made sure to get out of the way of the frantic nurses and doctors.

"What floor would she be on?" Stefania asked as they came to a hallway with a placard stating the location of each ward.

"I haven't the faintest idea." Franceska could scarcely handle her stress as she began to read the signs, but the words seemed to be jumbled and mixed around with each other. She knew it was a biproduct of the pressure she was under, and she tried desperately to clear her mind with little success.

"Who are you looking for?" a nurse asked quickly as she walked by them with her arms full of bed sheets.

"My mother," Franceska responded as the nurse continued to walk down the hallway. "She had a back injury."

"Second floor. Take the stairs to your right, then turn left as soon as you arrive."

"Thank you!" Franceska yelled as the two girls sped to the stairs and followed her directions.

When they arrived at the second floor, Franceska was thankful, at least, to find that the patients had been, to an extent, successfully triaged. Not that she blamed the staff for what was occurring in the slightest, but she hoped that if her mother was at this hospital she wasn't left stranded in a hallway.

Still, the ward was a level of chaos that Franceska found disconcerting. While there were no patients stranded in the hallway, doctors and nurses were running in and out of rooms, hurriedly checking over charts, and shouting orders and codes to each other that Franceska didn't understand.

"Let's go room by room," Franceska said to Stefania.

Taking advantage of the chaos, the two girls began searching each and every room, unchecked by the staff as to the reason for their intrusion.

Yet Franceska's heart began to sink further and further as her mother was absent from each room they checked.

Men, women, and children of every age were bandaged or recovering from some injury sustained in the bombing, but none of them were Mrs. Mann.

"To the cellar!" a voice demanded over the loudspeaker, followed shortly by the horrifying sound of the air raid siren.

At once, everyone, including doctors and nurses, stopped and waited, hoping beyond hope, that they merely imagined the voice. No one, Franceska assumed, believed that the Nazis would be so bold as to deliberately bomb a hospital.

"To the cellar!" the voice demanded again.

Immediately, the entire ward sprang into action, and nurses, with newborns in their arms, or pushing mothers in wheelchairs after just giving birth, made their way to the cellar.

The sound of babies wailing cut deep into Franceska's heart. How she wished to scoop each and every one into her arms and comfort them. The lamentation of the mothers who desperately wanted to hold their child or bitterly complained of their pains was also difficult for Franceska to digest.

"What are you two doing?!" a nurse asked abruptly to Franceska and Stefania.

"Looking for my mother," Franceska replied quickly.

"Make yourself useful in the meantime." She snapped her fingers toward a couple of beds where some mothers who clearly had just given birth were lying. "Help them into the cellar."

"Us?" Stefania placed a limp hand to her chest in confusion.

The nurse didn't reply as she busied herself with assisting other patients.

Not wasting anymore time trying to discern their role, Franceska and Stefania entered the room and each took upon themselves the task of assisting a mother.

"Slowly!" one of the mothers barked as she winced in pain while trying to sit upright.

"Are there anymore wheelchairs?" Franceska asked aloud as she looked around the room.

"I don't see any." Stefania also checked the room.

"How are we going to assist them down the stairs?" Franceska asked quietly as she threw the patient's arm around her shoulder.

"I can't take the stairs," the patient with Stefania moaned in pain.

"I don't believe we have any other option." Franceska shook her head.

"Where's my baby?" the mother with Franceska asked.

"Everyone is being moved to the cellar," Franceska explained. "I'm sure your baby is down there."

"I'm not leaving until I'm sure she's safe!" the patient replied angrily.

"Nurse?!" Franceska called out to a nurse passing by the room.

"What?!" the nurse asked hurriedly.

"Are all the newborns accounted for?" Franceska asked as she led her patient gingerly to the door.

"I checked myself." The nurse nodded before vanishing to assist others.

"I need to hold her!" the patient with Franceska began to cry.

"You will! I promise! We'll get down to the cellar and you will hold your baby!"

As briskly as they were able, Franceska and Stefania led their new charges down the stairs and to the cellar.

For her part, Franceska couldn't understand the inhumanity of their enemy. Targeting civilians, especially those in such precarious and delicate circumstances, was an evil Franceska didn't know if she could comprehend.

The wailing of the newborns, the cries of the mothers for their children, and the moans and groans of those in bitter pains, was horrific.

This, Franceska understood, was Hell.

Chapter Seven:
The Cellar

"Waste no more time arguing what a good man should be. Be one."

Marcus Aurelius

"You're safe here," a nurse consoled a weeping mother as she breastfed her child that was born mere hours earlier.

"*Are* we safe down here?" Franceska whispered to Stefania.

The cellar was beneath the hospital, and Franceska felt as though it was more of a tomb than a shelter. It was dark with the only light coming from dim bulbs hanging down from the ceiling, the smell of must and mold was palpable, and the only place to sit was on the concrete floor.

Still, all the mothers and babies from the ward had been transported safely to the cellar. Not a single one was unaccounted for as the bombs began to fall against the building, and Franceska and Stefania had been able to transport their new charges safely.

The only thing that Franceska appreciated about the cellar was how it muffled the explosions. They sounded like nothing more than distant thunder; a storm on the horizon that posed no threat.

"We're fine." Stefania patted Franceska's shoulder to reassure her.

"Here's some bread," a nurse further in the cellar broke off a piece from a loaf and handed it to a hungry mother.

At the mere mention of food, Franceska's gaze locked onto the basket in the nurse's arm. All she could think about was food, and her stomach growled loudly in anticipation.

"Will they give us some?" Stefania asked loudly enough to be heard but not too loud as to be thought of as obnoxious.

"The bread is reserved for patients and volunteers," a mother nearby interjected as she rocked her child. "I'm sure they would be happy for the help of a couple young girls like yourselves."

"How do we volunteer?" Stefania nearly shot to her feet with the promise of food in exchange for services rendered.

"Talk to the nurse at the end there with the clipboard." The mother pointed, and at once Franceska and Stefania sped over to the nurse while being careful not to disturb any of the patients,

"No," the nurse spoke flatly with her head down and working on the clipboard.

"No?" Franceska shot her head back in surprise.

"Sound travels in this cellar. I heard your conversation," the nurse explained. "There's barely enough bread for the patients. We can't afford to feed you as well."

"If I—" Stefania began angrily, but Franceska put her hand out to stop her from saying anything rash.

"We will volunteer for free, then." Franceska nodded.

"For free?" the nurse asked as she offered them an incredulous look.

"It would be better than merely sitting here." Franceska shrugged. "Help pass the time and keep our mind off our hunger and fear."

"If that's the case, I won't stop you." The nurse's expression softened a little. "If you're willing, there are a couple of mothers who are in desperate need of rest. Their babies need to be held, fed, changed, and everything else that comes with motherhood."

"We can handle that." Franceska nodded firmly.

"Good." The nurse watched them warily before looking over her chart and pointing at a mother near the door with a bandage on her leg and stated, "That's Maria. She was shot hours before going into labor."

"Shot by the Germans?" Franceska asked aloud.

"We didn't have time to uncover the truth, but I'm certain that's the case," the nurse replied callously before adding with a strict tone, "And it's not your business, either. Care for her child and let her get some rest. That's all."

With a nod at each other, Stefania and Franceska approached the woman and noticed that she was quite pale. The bandage on her leg was still bright red which Franceska assumed meant she was still bleeding.

She was a younger girl, and quite lean, even after being nine months pregnant. She wore a brown head scarf which was tattered and faded, giving Franceska the impression that she was often in the sun and likely a farmer or a peasant.

Her baby girl cried softly as she laid across her chest, and seemed to be in some general discomfort. Franceska didn't have much experience with babies or attending to younger children, but she had a nurturing spirit and didn't perceive that she would have too much difficulty with this task.

"Maria?" Stefania asked tenderly as she knelt in front of the mother.

Without replying, Maria looked back at them with a tired and dazed stare before offering a faint nod.

"Can we watch your baby while you get some rest?" Franceska asked as she also knelt.

Looking down at her child, Maria looked back at them before shaking her head.

"I think it would be best if you rested," Franceska pressed, growing concerned with Maria's condition.

"I'll rest forever soon," Maria replied with a weak voice.

"Don't say that." Stefania gently touched Maria's uninjured leg.

"I'm losing blood." Maria's lips trembled as she kissed her baby's head. "These are my last moments with her. Don't take that from me."

"You're going to be fine," Franceska encouraged, but doubted every word as she continued to inspect Maria.

"What will happen to her after I'm gone?" Maria closed her eyes as the tears streamed down her cheeks. "Who will watch over my baby? We were so happy when we found out I was pregnant. If I had known then what would happen, I…"

"Where is the baby's father?" Franceska asked. "We could locate him for you?"

"He's lying dead in the fields." Maria shook her head as she gestured to her legs. "The German planes flew low, gunning us down with their machine guns. Eight men and women died yesterday. If we don't harvest the fields, we starve, if we do harvest the fields, we're slaughtered by the Germans. There is no hope."

"Hope is coming." Stefania rubbed Maria's arm.

"Hope is coming?" Maria chuckled ironically.

"I thought I told you to let her rest?" the nurse asked grumpily as she came to stand over the women.

"She would like to stay with her child," Franceska defended.

"Those were not your orders." The nurse threw her hands onto her hips. "If I tell you to do something, you do it. Is that understood?"

"Yes, ma'am," Stefania replied sheepishly.

"Since her child is now sleeping, it would be best to move on to a child that is awake so the mother can also sleep." The nurse looked over her clipboard before glancing around the room and then in frustration mentioned, "Just pick a child, any child, and give the mother some rest."

Feeling rather out of her element, Franceska, with a grumbling stomach, walked with Stefania through the crowded cellar looking for other mothers to assist. Still, her mind dwelt on Maria and what she had been through.

"Excuse me, ma'am, but I'd be happy to give you a moment to rest." Franceska held out her hand to take a baby from a weary mother.

"Thank you," the mother replied tiredly as she gently transferred the baby into Franceska's arms.

"What's her name?" Franceska asked the mother.

"Julia."

"Hello Julia," Franceska spoke quietly and with a large smile as she looked down at the infant who was indifferently inspecting the world around her.

Finding a spot at a respectful distance from the mother, Franceska sat on the cold concrete as she held the sweet child in her arms.

While she found the moment beautiful and loving, Franceska couldn't help but feeling the bitterness of a child being born at such a time as this. The words of Maria rang in her ears, and Franceska found herself agreeing with the harsh judgement.

She didn't know how a mother would care for a child without a home to reside in, or how they would collect food for the family if the Nazis were gunning them down in their fields, or how they could possibly hope to provide them with a happy childhood.

Franceska began to appreciate her upbringing the more she contemplated the current state of her country. She had a father when many others were fatherless due to the last war they had endured, she had opportunities many wouldn't even be able to dream of when all they could think about is surviving, and she wondered if she had wasted her time doing something trivial rather than something important like becoming a nurse.

Julia yawned, and Franceska's heart melted. Despite all the horrors surrounding them, despite all the death and destruction, Franceska was looking into the face of new life, and that, she thought, was encouraging.

"Quickly," the nurse with the basket full of bread whispered to Franceska.

Looking at the basket, and then back at the head nurse who was momentarily distracted, Franceska understood the gesture and swiftly snatched a piece of bread out of the basket before shoving it into her mouth. Disregarding convention or manners, Franceska chewed rapidly as she offered the nurse a look of gratitude.

A knock came to the cellar door, and the head nurse hustled over to look through the peephole.

From her position in the cellar, Franceska couldn't hear what was being discussed with the party on the other side, but after what seemed to be a heated debate, the head nurse opened the door and announced, "The raid has ended. You will be escorted back to the ward."

A collective sigh mixed with groaning erupted in the cellar as mothers who had only just become comfortable in their new environment were now required to move again, while others were desperate to leave the basement, and likely the hospital altogether.

"Thank you for letting me hold her," Franceska spoke politely to the mother as she gingerly handed Julia back.

"How long was I out?" the mother asked groggily.

"Only a few minutes I'm afraid. The bombing run has already passed and it's safe to return to the ward."

"For now." The mother raised an unimpressed eyebrow. "Might as well keep us down here. There'll be another raid shortly."

"I hate to say it, but I think you're right." Franceska looked gloomily back at the mother.

"We should leave." Stefania tapped Franceska's shoulder.

"Agreed." Franceska nodded and the two followed the slow-moving train of new mothers waddling or being assisted out of the cellar.

Yet Franceska's heart shattered when she walked past Maria and noticed that a white sheet was being placed over her body.

"Wait! Wait!" Franceska panicked. "She's still alive."

"She passed a minute ago," a nurse replied tenderly yet firmly as she looked at her watch.

"That can't be, I spoke with her only—"

"Keep moving!" the head nurse commanded from the back of the line.

"What's going to happen to her baby?" Franceska continued in her alarm as she looked around for Maria's daughter.

"Like many children, she'll be sent to an orphanage." The nurse left Maria's body and began to inspect other patients.

"I don't understand." Franceska looked at Stefania with teary eyes while they exited the cellar. "We spoke with her minutes ago."

"Which makes me wonder if Wiera was right after all."

"What do you mean?" Franceska asked as they climbed the stairs to the main floor and were once again enveloped into the chaotic scene.

"A calloused temperament is best for survival." Stefania's lips trembled. "It's impossible to look at what everyone is enduring and keep your heart intact."

"I still think she's wrong." Franceska shook her head, but couldn't ignore her own self-doubt.

Making their way through the overcrowded entrance, Franceska and Stefania spotted areas of the hospital that had been struck by shrapnel. Many windows were shattered, and some of the beds along the wall were charred and bent, but the structure of the hospital had proven strong and was intact. Still, Franceska knew that if a direct hit had struck the hospital, it may have been a different outcome.

"Should we continue to look for your mother?" Stefania asked as she looked around at the destruction outside the hospital.

"No, let's reconvene with my father." Franceska rubbed the back of her neck with exhaustion.

"Did that nice nurse give you some bread?" Stefania whispered, still afraid of the head nurse overhearing.

"She did." Franceska smiled. "Although I'm still famished. One little piece of bread didn't quite cut it."

"Hopefully Wiera's father found some food."

"That would be nice." Franceska felt herself growing faint from fatigue and hunger.

"Let's go a different way back." Stefania held a hand out to Franceska to stop her as she looked down the street.

"Good idea." Franceska nodded as she also looked down the street and noticed an officer stopping civilians to assist with removing rubble or constructing defenses.

"I think I'd collapse if I did any more physical labor without having something decent to eat."

"All I can think about is food." Franceska shook her head in wonder. "Every second thought is where I can find food and what will be available."

Without another word, Franceska and Stefania walked through the city, taking the longer route back to the property they had commandeered, and finding that few places had been spared from the bombing.

Civilians, carrying whatever they could afford, trudged toward the edges of the city, hoping to find relief from the Nazi war machine that was not only content, but seemingly pleased, to kill simple peasants gathering food. It was clear to everyone that they would find no mercy should the Germans occupy the city.

"For the sake of all that is good," Stefania muttered when they turned the corner to another street, and they spotted a dead horse in the middle of the road.

Flies were busy making their homes in a wound on the horse's belly, and Franceska's heart broke for the poor creature. Nobody deserved the fate that many of the civilians were facing, but least deserving of all, Franceska believed, were harmless and unassuming creatures.

"Poor thing," Franceska added as they walked by the horse, and she stared into its big lifeless eyes.

"I wish there was someone to take him away." Stefania turned her gaze, unable to bear the sight any longer.

"It's not fair. None of this is fair."

With the terrible image stuck in their minds, Franceska and Stefania walked quietly toward their destination, both silently hoping that there would be some good news about food.

As they walked through the city, Franceska began to realize that the horrors of this siege were only in their infancy.

Young men, numbering in the thousands, were beginning their mass exodus from the city. Weeping mothers kissed or clung to their sons, knowing that it was unlikely they would meet again. Young families accompanied young husbands out of the city, and Franceska's heart was heavy as she spotted the looks of dejection and despair, not knowing where they would end up.

Further cutting into whatever sense of hope Franceska still clung to was the sight of policemen and firemen leaving in droves. The civilians remaining in Warsaw were now entirely isolated, and Franceska feared the men of ill repute who had remained in the city. She imagined that robberies, assaults, and all other sorts of unrestrained behaviors would run rampant in short time. She prayed that the men who remained would have the decency to fight the common enemy, and not look to their own selfish desires or wants.

"What are they doing there?" Stefania asked as they walked down a street closer to the edge of the city.

"They're…painting the street?" Franceska frowned as she watched a group of women with buckets filled with some sort of sticky liquid and using brushes to spread it all over the road.

She couldn't understand what the purpose of them painting the street would accomplish, especially with the substance they were choosing. All that it appeared to achieve was making the roads shiny.

"Ah, it's turpentine." Stefania sniffed when they came closer to the women.

"Turpentine?" Franceska tilted her head. "Why?"

"It's incredibly flammable." Stefania nodded excitedly. "And ingenious if it works."

"I'm not following." Franceska remained lost.

"If I'm correct, they're going to use it against the ground assault." Stefania grew proud of herself for deciphering.

"I'm happy for anything that works." Franceska raised an eyebrow before asking, "When do you think the Germans will approach?"

"Everything they've done seems unpredictable to date." Stefania shook her head. "It would probably be best for us to move to a side of the city that is furthest from their battalions."

"Oh dear." Franceska grimaced when they turned the corner to where their 'shelter' was, and Franceska spotted Mr. Mann and Wiera engaged in some sort of heated debate.

"I wonder what that's about?" Stefania asked under her breath as the two girls hurried to defuse the situation.

"Why not?!" Wiera asked angrily with her hands on her hips.

"Because it's suicide!" Mr. Mann threw his hands out in frustration.

"But we can have food!" Wiera countered.

"What's going on?!" Franceska asked with a mixture of concern and curiosity as she arrived near her father.

"I found a place for us to live," Wiera replied cuttingly as she glared at Mr. Mann.

"You found a place for us to become target practice!" Mr. Mann countered.

"Where is it?" Stefania asked, holding her conclusion in reserve.

"There's a park about five minutes from here." Wiera pointed in the direction. "A community has formed to share food, bedding, and other necessities."

"And what's the problem?" Franceska frowned at her father.

"It's in a wide-open park." Mr. Mann rubbed the back of his neck and Franceska noticed that his shoulders were raised and tight. "One bomb from the enemy, and hundreds of people are wiped out! It's stupidity!"

"What's the alternative?" Franceska asked.

"What do you mean?" Mr. Mann looked at her crossly, before glancing away.

"Where else can we stay?" Franceska shrugged. "Where else can we get food?"

Mr. Mann sighed with frustration before adding, "Her father hasn't returned yet, so I don't know."

"Why don't we stay here until he returns, and then we can all vote?" Stefania asked politely.

"You can all do whatever the hell you like." Mr. Mann shook his head. "I'm not voting. I'll do as I see fit."

"Fair enough." Stefania nodded as she glanced at Franceska, knowing that Mr. Mann's behavior was entirely out of the ordinary.

"Did you find her?" Mr. Mann asked Franceska.

Franceska shook her head.

"Of course you didn't." Mr. Mann gritted his teeth as he began to pace.

"You need to take a minute." Franceska placed a gentle hand to her father's arm, but he pulled away sharply.

"I need to find my wife! You were supposed to find her!" Mr. Mann's eyes bulged as he glared at Franceska.

"I'm sorry." Franceska looked back at her father with a broken heart. She hated seeing him in this panicked and irate state. He wasn't thinking clearly, and she understood that he was hungry and afraid which was a potent mix at any time, but especially in war during a siege.

"We can't do anything until my father returns," Wiera spoke softly to try and achieve a level of calm. "I'm sure he'll show up shortly. In the meantime, let's sit and think about the best route forward."

"How can you ask me to sit while my wife is out there by herself?" Mr. Mann lost his composure, and he turned away to hide his emotions.

Franceska, Stefania, and Wiera all looked at each other cluelessly. Franceska assumed that they felt as helpless as she did for how to help Mr. Mann. Franceska couldn't remember a time where her mother and father had spent more than a minute apart, and she knew that his anxiety at their forced separation was becoming impossible for him to manage.

"She's dead." Mr. Mann turned back to them as he shook his head hopelessly.

"Don't speak such evil!" Franceska barked at her father, unable to control her temper at his pity.

"What's the point in going on?" Mr. Mann couldn't contain the tears, and they poured down his cheek.

"We're going to find her!" Franceska barked grumpily.

"We're going to find her dead somewhere. She died alone. If I had known that was the last time I saw her, I would've—"

"Get a hold of yourself!" Franceska lost her patience as she grabbed his shoulders and shook him. "Be a man! I need you! We're going to stick together and we're going to find her! But I can't do this alone!"

"There's my father!" Wiera pointed toward the end of the street.

Turning in the direction, Franceska's hopes took another dive when she noticed that Mr. Gran was returning to them empty handed and his shirt was covered in blood.

Chapter Eight:
Sitting Ducks

"…we shall fight on the beaches, we shall fight on the landing grounds, we shall fight in the fields and in the streets, we shall fight in the hills; we shall never surrender…"

Winston Churchill

"What happened to you?!" Wiera asked with distress as she rushed over to her father.

"Nothing to concern yourself with." He shook his head, but his worried expression revealed the truth.

"Who did this to you?" Wiera pressed as her father walked past them and toward the house that they had been using for shelter.

"Did you find food?" Franceska asked. She knew it was an insensitive question given the circumstances, but the words almost fell out of her mouth.

"I did…" Mr. Gran stopped in his tracks and looked at her solemnly before continuing, "Unfortunately, that made me a target."

"Who did this to you?!" Wiera demanded.

"Don't worry about them. The world will take care of selfish people like that." Mr. Gran waved to dismiss her concerns, and Franceska understood that he had been robbed. She couldn't believe that under such circumstances, people could be so heartless and selfish, but given the absence of police, she wasn't that surprised either.

"Are we able to purchase more food? We can all go with you for protection," Wiera pressed.

"That was all I had." Mr. Gran patted his pockets to reveal they were empty before he nodded toward Mr. Mann.

"Every penny I had was in the house." Mr. Mann shook his head.

"We could try the farms?" Mr. Gran shrugged.

"We can't steal from peasants." Mr. Mann shook his head.

"Regardless, the Germans are gunning them down in the field," Stefania added, and Franceska remembered Maria, the sweet mother in the cellar.

"Then we are doomed to die of starvation." Mr. Gran looked solemnly at his feet.

"About that…" Mr. Mann began sheepishly. "Your daughter may have a solution…"

"Oh?" Mr. Gran frowned, and Wiera shot Mr. Mann a surprised look.

"There's a community, not far from here, that have set themselves up in a park," Wiera explained. "They're sharing food, clothing, bedding, and anything that can be used for the collective."

"What do they want in return?" Mr. Gran remained skeptical.

"Nothing." Wiera shook her head.

"It's never nothing." Mr. Gran looked at his daughter with disappointment for her ignorance.

"Well, our options are to stay here and starve or join this community." Wiera shrugged. "I vote we take a chance on not starving."

"I'm so hungry." Stefania squeezed her eyes shut as she held her belly.

"How far away did you say it was?" Mr. Gran asked wearily.

"About a five-minute walk." Wiera pointed in the direction.

"Alright." Mr. Gran conceded, and Mr. Mann, with no choice left, also agreed.

Exhausted and famished, the company trudged in the direction that Wiera was now leading them. Franceska's feet ached, and she wished that she was able to switch her shoes for a pair of boots like the soldiers had. Walking over the rubble and the little jagged bricks and stones was starting to wear out her shoes. She could feel the blisters forming on her feet, and the aching in her legs was gnawing away at whatever determination was left.

Francesa stayed her complaints, however, knowing that there were much bigger issues to contend with. She thought of her mother, and hoped that she was being cared for. She refused to let her father's damning words drown her resolve. Franceska knew her mother was still alive, and she couldn't wait to hold her hands again. She also knew that if anything had happened to her mother, it would be the end of Mr. Mann, and Franceska refused to entertain such a depressing thought.

"Have you heard from Adam?" Stefania asked Wiera.

"No." Wiera shook her head. "I imagine he's heading out of the city."

"Would he leave without saying goodbye?" Franceska asked as she studied her friend closely.

Wiera didn't reply as she stared at the ground while they walked, and Franceska knew she was trying to mask her emotions. Still, Franceska wished that Wiera would speak freely. She also knew how impossible it would be to reach him. All communication had been disrupted, and even if they could find a telephone or send a telegram, who knew if it would reach him.

Glancing over her shoulder, Franceska checked on her father to find that he was walking a few paces behind them while whispering with Mr. Gran. She wondered what they would be discussing in private and hated the thought of being excluded from something important.

Mr. Mann, despite his admirable qualities, was rather antiquated in his valuing of women's opinions. Franceska often thought that, if her father had enough courage, he would have overruled his wife on many occasions. Yet because of his fear of Mrs. Mann, her father often stayed quiet or else muttered his opinion under his breath.

As promised by Wiera, after a quick five-minute walk, they arrived at the park. Beds, tents, tables, couches, dressers, and cabinets were spread out in chaotic organization. White sheets were raised in some places to offer a degree of privacy between families, but Franceska was startled to see how some had abandoned propriety, although she understood that option no longer existed.

"I see why your father was so concerned," Stefania spoke under her breath to Franceska when they came to the park. "One bomb and hundreds of families would be obliterated."

Men and women, in little more than their undergarments, were washing themselves in bowls set beside their beds. Others were sitting on the ground and eating food like wild creatures, stuffing their mouths with as much as they could, and Franceska knew that they were likely as hungry as she was.

Groups of children had organized activities while other adults were engaging in card games. Music was playing from different sectors as some had brought their accordions or guitars. Mothers and fathers wept for their losses, orphaned children wailed unconsolably, and many bemoaned their sorrows. It was unlike anything Franceska had ever seen before. Everyone had arrived with a story to tell. Some accounts were more horrific than others, but Franceska knew that everyone in this little park had experienced horrors that they would never wish upon anyone else.

But her attention was interrupted by a line of hungry people at a table where a nun was serving soup from a large pot. Without mentioning where she was heading or why, Franceska started to walk toward the table as if her legs were on some sort of track, and she couldn't control where she was walking. Her hunger, she understood, was entirely in control.

Trying to remain as patient and polite as possible, Franceska stood at the back of the line where she was joined by her father and friends.

The line moved at a gradual pace, and it took everything within Franceska not to scream and shout for them to hurry.

A child in front of Franceska began crying up at her mother, and Franceska was almost startled to see the child. She had been so focused on the pacing of the line that she didn't realize a child was standing right in front of her.

"Thank you, Sister," a woman a few places in front of Franceska offered her gratitude to the nun serving soup.

"God bless you," the nun replied softly.

She was a sweet, older lady, yet Franceska perceived that this nun had a spirited side to her, much like Mrs. Mann.

"Take this," a younger nun spoke to Franceska as she handed her a cheap wooden bowl and added, "Make sure not to lose it. We have limited supplies."

"Thank…" the words stuck in Franceska's mouth as her tongue ran dry. "Thank you."

"Here you are, love." The older nun scooped out a serving into Franceska's bowl, yet she was so hungry that she walked away from the table without a word of appreciation.

Absent of decorum or caring who should witness her in such a primal state, Franceska tipped the bowl back and poured the lukewarm broth into her mouth. She gulped the soup back like it was water, and didn't care at all whether the flavor was lacking or that the temperature was not quite right.

"How much?" Mr. Mann asked quietly, and Franceska turned to see him speaking with the young nun handing him a bowl and knew that he was still skeptical.

"It's free, sir." The young nun smiled at him as she also handed a bowl to Wiera.

"Nothing is free." Mr. Mann shook his head.

"How right you are, but for you this meal is free." The young nun nodded for him to continue along the line.

"Nothing is free," Mr. Mann muttered as he reluctantly accepted the gift of soup.

"Who can we inquire with about obtaining a spot for us to use?" Wiera asked the older nun. "Our homes were lost."

"Where are your belongings?" the nun asked as she looked behind them, and Franceska assumed she was checking for bags or a cart.

"We're wearing them, Sister."

"Father Kolbe?" the nun called to a priest that was visiting with a distraught family, but then added, "He's busy now, but go see him. He'll find somewhere for you."

"At the price of our conversion, I'm sure," Mr. Mann whispered cynically to Franceska.

"Wait here," Franceska spoke to her father and friends as they were now huddled in a circle near the table and eating their soup. "I'll speak with the priest."

"Be careful," Mr. Mann warned.

"When am I ever not careful?" Franceska frowned at her father with confusion.

Walking slowly over to the priest, and careful to keep her distance as he spoke with the family, Franceska waited patiently for him to finish. She tried her best not to pry, but her curiosity urged her to listen.

"There's nothing we can do but to trust God in this moment," the priest spoke softly to the family.

Despite her lack of knowledge of religious institutions, Franceska believed that the priest was of the Franciscan order. He wore a dark brown robe with a small rope tied around his waist. His hair was shorter, but his beard was long yet tidy.

"Will God be fighting our enemies?" the mother of the family asked cynically.

"It is difficult, I know, but there is a greater conflict happening than the one which we can see in the sky." The priest looked around at the family with a measure of compassion. "The conflict happening within you, within each of us, is where we must triumph. There are two irreconcilable enemies in the depth of every soul: good and evil, sin and love. If we can conquer these, no weapon, no threat, not even death itself, can be used by the Germans against us."

Franceska watched Father Kolbe with growing interest. While she didn't appreciate that his words of comfort seemed without relief, she did appreciate the sentiment.

"How can I help you, dear?" Father Kolbe turned his attention to Franceska when he noticed she was waiting for him.

"My family…" Franceska pointed toward her father and friends. "We've lost everything, and we have nowhere to turn. We were told you—"

"There's a couple of beds at the end there." Father Kolbe pointed before adding with a sympathetic grimace, "They're yours for as long as you need them."

"That's very kind of you, Father, thank you." Franceska nodded her appreciation.

"Father Kolbe!" a man half-ran toward the priest before latching onto his arm and demanding, "My son is sick! Please! Come pray for him."

"Of course." Father Kolbe nodded but then spoke to Franceska over his shoulder, "I would like to speak with you and your family later."

I'm sure my father would love that, Franceska thought as she began walking back toward the group.

"I promise you," Mr. Mann spoke softly yet with warning to the others as Franceska returned, "They're going to use this tragedy to try and convert us. Just watch!"

"Is it possible they're simply following through with their religious obligations?" Mr. Gran asked tenderly, and it was clear to Franceska that the much-needed relief from food was already calming some tempers.

"I found us some beds," Franceska announced softly, understanding that this was hardly and upgrade from the house that they were using as shelter.

"Did you have to sell your soul?" Mr. Mann asked grumpily.

"Not yet." Franceska replied with a slight smirk.

"Lead on, then." Mr. Gran nodded.

Walking through the harrowing landscape of families, many of which she had seen during her passing through the city or at grocery stores or cafés, Franceska noticed that they had all be reduced to equals. Both the wealthy and the impoverished were almost indistinguishable. Rich merchants laid on beds beside beggars who, for all things considered, experienced little difference in their way of life. The only thing separating families was a thin bed sheet hung on a clothesline to bring some semblance of privacy.

Arriving at their assigned quarters, Franceska immediately realized the logistical issue. There were only a couple of beds remaining, and looking at the surrounding area, Franceska knew there was no chance of them securing another bed or place for them to sleep or shelter.

The beds in question, Franceska noticed, seemed to be recently used. The sheets were messy, a pair of shoes lay at the foot of one bed, and a newspaper was unfolded on the other.

"Did the priest make a mistake?" Mr. Mann asked, noticing Franceska's concern. "These beds look like they're already spoken for."

"They *were* spoken for," an elderly man sitting on a bed near them interjected after hearing their conversation and added, "The whole family was gunned down in the fields by German planes."

"That's terrible." Mr. Mann ran his tongue along his cheek, and Franceska thought he possibly felt embarrassed about his complaint.

Not that she blamed him, and felt that it was rather unnerving to simply move in where another family had once taken temporary shelter. She knew that they had likely been as afraid and hungry as she had, and wondered if they had family elsewhere in the city as well. Being gunned down in the fields when you simply wanted to collect food for yourself or your family was a cruelty Franceska felt was unparalleled to anything she had ever witnessed.

"Not much for privacy," Wiera muttered as their elderly neighbor gawked at them in the manner that is privileged to those advanced in years.

"Are we all supposed to sleep here?" Stefania asked warily as she looked at the two small beds and then at the five of them.

"I'll sleep on the ground." Mr. Mann inspected the grassy area beside one of the beds.

"You'll do no such thing." Franceska waved to dismiss his preposterous idea. "If anyone is sleeping on the ground, it's me."

"What would people think if they saw me on the bed while you're lying on the grass?" Mr. Mann tilted his head.

Without responding, Franceska sat on the edge of the bed and held her head in her hands as she felt the exhaustion overpowering her.

"Let's see what they're reporting about the front," Mr. Gran spoke softly as he sat on the other bed and opened the newspaper.

"Hopefully some good news," Mr. Mann mentioned softly as he stood near Franceska.

"Well, yes, actually," Mr. Gran spoke with a measure of suspicion.

"Really?" Mr. Mann's voice resounded with hope.

"The paper is reporting victory after victory." Mr. Gran stood as he grew excited.

"By our army?" Stefania asked as she also allowed herself to cling to good news.

"It's all lies," the elderly neighbor beside them interjected.

"You know more than the papers, do you?" Stefania asked defiantly.

"I know when I'm being lied to," the neighbor retorted. "It's propaganda to keep our spirits up."

"What do you think?" Franceska asked her father quietly.

"Doesn't matter." Mr. Mann scratched the back of his neck. "Time will tell the truth, I suppose. All that we need to worry about now is finding your mother."

"Settling in?" Father Kolbe spoke warmly as he approached Franceska and company.

"We appreciate your generosity," Mr. Mann spoke politely to the priest, but Franceska perceived he wanted to wrap up the conversation quickly.

"I only wish I could do more." Father Kolbe tilted his head with sorrow. "There is a church nearby that I would offer as shelter, but the roof caved in after a bomb. I fear that it's not much better than what you have here."

"Not even churches are safe." Mr. Gran shook his head in dismay.

"I'm afraid not." Father Kolbe threw his hands behind his back as he studied Franceska, and she felt that there was a question burning on his mind that he was trying to articulate.

"I apologize if you're expecting some sort of payment or donation," Mr. Mann began as he patted his pockets to show that they were empty.

"Heavens no!" Father Kolbe shook his head. "I wouldn't dare demand anything after what you've been through."

"That's kind," Mr. Mann replied slowly, and Franceska knew that he remained skeptical.

"You're not Catholic, are you?" Father Kolbe squinted at Franceska as he held his hands gently in front of him.

"He wants the payment of our souls," Mr. Mann muttered under his breath as he sat on the bed, displeased with what he observed as a cheap conversion attempt in exchange for lodging.

Franceska shook her head as she feared her father was correct.

"What faith are you, then?" Father Kolbe continued his investigation, and, if it were not for his generosity, Franceska would've likely found occasion to retort rudely.

"My faith is a private matter," Franceska replied with as much tact as she could summon.

"That means you're either of no faith, or of a faith which you sense will displease me." Father Kolbe raised his eyebrows. "You're Jewish?"

"Will that be a problem?" Wiera asked while distrustful.

"Not at all." Father Kolbe smiled brightly. "Everyone is my brother and sister. I only wish I had more to offer apart from some soup, but with the administration evacuating the city we're left to our own devices."

"I still don't understand how they could order them out?" Mr. Gran shook his head in wonder.

"Turn out the lights!" a voice over a loudspeaker announced from a truck driving by. "No candles or fires are permitted. All lights must be turned off."

"Not sure what the point of a blackout is when half the city is burning." Wiera's father looked up at the sky and Franceska also looked up to see an orange hue bleeding into the starry black from the fires raging around the city.

Franceska grew resentful at the lack of light or not being allowed to warm oneself by the fire. The darkness made the proximity of their enemies feel so much closer and more menacing.

"I will leave you to rest now," Father Kolbe spoke politely as he looked at them with a mixture of sympathy and pity.

"We appreciate everything you've done for us, and I'm sure many others are appreciative as well." Stefania looked around at the park that was full of people who were now fed and had a place to at least sleep that wasn't a pile of rubble.

With a nod of thanks, Father Kolbe turned to another family nearby and began to speak with them.

While she was still skeptical of the priest, Franceska didn't detect that any insincerity. She perceived that he was just as he appeared. He was a man of faith and simply wanted to help in any capacity that he could.

"I wonder where Adam is," Wiera spoke with a touch of emotion as she sat on the edge of the bed.

"I'm sure he would've returned to you if he could've." Franceska squeezed Wiera's shoulder as she sat beside her. "With the order for young men to evacuate, he likely didn't have a chance to try and find you."

"I imagine that you miss him terribly." Stefania asked as she also came to sit beside Wiera.

"I can't afford such nonsense." Wiera shook her head quickly, and both Franceska and Stefania looked at each other knowingly.

"I think I understand what you meant earlier about turning off feeling sorrowful or pitiful about the horrible things happening around us," Franceska began as she looked up at the starry sky before continuing, "But with us, you should permit yourself a moment of vulnerability."

Wiera didn't reply as she stared at the grass at her feet. Then, after a moment, she reached out and took Franceska and Stefania's hands in hers.

"No matter what happens, we need to stay together." Wiera glanced at Stefania and then at Franceska before adding, "Promise me that!"

"We promise." Franceska leaned her head on Wiera's shoulder.

In the darkness, and in the open field, the three girls took comfort in each other, and Franceska knew that no matter what came to pass, she would be alright.

"Let's try and get some sleep." Mr. Mann kicked off his shoes as he sat on the other bed. "We'll look for Mother tomorrow."

"I'm exhausted, but I don't think I'll be able to sleep." Stefania sighed. "It's so loud here."

And, as if on cue, the air raid siren began to blare.

"What's the point of even using the siren if they're always bombing us?" Wiera grumbled. "We should merely assume that bombs are continually falling."

"Everyone!" Father Kolbe stood on a table as he waved his hands in the air for their attention. "There are three shelters nearby. Please make your way to one that is closest to you and proceed in good order."

"Who needs sleep anyway?" Mr. Mann grumbled as he put his shoes back on.

"Don't worry, things will be set right soon enough. You'll see." Franceska tried to comfort her father as she repeated to herself, *You'll see.*

Chapter Nine:
Winged Hussars

"Matka Boska (Mother of God)"

Battle cry of the Winged Hussars

With tired eyes, Franceska stared up at the beautiful orange and pink morning sky from the flat of her back. In between dogs howling, babies crying, drunks laughing or arguing, musicians playing, or her father's snoring, Franceska believed that she only slept a couple of hours during the night.

All she could contemplate through the long stretches of insomnia was her mother's condition. She wondered if she was alright, if she was being fed, or if she was in terrible pain while alone, wondering why her family had abandoned her.

The one consolation Franceska felt was the kindness of her father to provide her with the thin mattress sheet and pillow. It saved her dress from getting even dirtier than it already was, and Franceska wished with all her heart that she could slip into new clothes or at least wash herself.

"Morning," Stefania spoke softly as she sat beside Franceska with a cup of coffee.

Without replying, Franceska studied Stefania suspiciously.

"Don't worry, I brought you a cup, too." Stefania grinned as she handed a white cup in a white saucer to Franceska.

"You're an angel from heaven!" Franceska nearly yanked the cup out of Stefania's hands as she held its warmth tenderly in her hands before taking a generous sip.

"Careful, it's still quite hot." Stefania urged caution with her gaze.

"Let it burn me." Franceska closed her eyes as she inhaled the energizing fragrance.

"It's early, but I think it would be best if we set out to search for your mother as soon as possible." Stefania sipped from her cup as she tried to appear respectable.

"You really shouldn't feel any obligation to assist me." Franceska looked warmly, yet tiredly, at her friend.

"I have no family of my own to search for, but I know, that if I did, I would appreciate all the help that I could get."

"You're my family." Franceska forced a grin in exhaustion.

"Besides, it helps take my mind of Jan." Stefania shrugged.

"I'm sure he's fine." Franceska looked back at Stefania with sympathy.

"If he's not…"

"You'll kill him." Franceska grinned.

"Why does it feel like weeks have passed?" Stefania glanced at Franceska.

"Since the invasion started?" Franceska asked rhetorically before she added, "The life we once had feels so distant. Dancing, nightclubs, socializing…"

"Do you miss it?"

"I miss feeling like what I was doing held some importance." Franceska stared into her coffee cup. "Dancing, at times, felt like nothing else in the world mattered."

"You're an exceptional dancer."

"Doesn't mean anything now." Franceska shrugged. "Dancing won't save my mother or help us find food and shelter."

"But you learned strength; you were taught how to push your body to extreme limits. That aspect will likely come in handy."

"I never thought of it that way." Franceska studied Stefania with a fresh perspective.

The two girls sat for a moment in silence as Wiera and the two men continued to sleep. Franceska longed for the day when she could curl up under her own bed sheets again, and wondered when life would return to normal or if it ever would.

"Everyone!" A shout came from further within the encampment, and both Franceska and Stefania looked in the direction, fearing the worst. "Turn on your radios!"

"Do we have a radio?" Stefania asked eagerly.

"What do you think?" Franceska replied grumpily as they both stood quickly, hoping to catch whatever important news this was.

"Come here." The elderly neighbor waved them over, and both girls nearly ran to his side as he flicked on the little handheld radio beside his bed.

He was still dressed in his clothes from the previous day, and he smelled awful, although Franceska recognized that she likely smelled just as unpleasant and it would be imprudent to judge him so harshly.

"I speak to you now as the newly appointed president of Warsaw," a commanding voice came over the radio, and Franceska noticed everyone in the park was turning their ear as they took courage from his commanding tone.

"Who is that?" Stefania whispered.

"Stefan Starzyński," the neighbor replied quickly.

"England and France have declared war on Germany," Stefan continued.

At once, cheering erupted throughout the camp, and Franceska and Stefania embraced as they cried and laughed in their relief that their struggles would likely soon be over.

"What does this mean?!" Stefania tried to contain her appreciative laugh but failed miserably.

"It means nothing," the elderly neighbor spoke bitterly, but Franceska ignored him in her elation.

"Warsaw is burning," Stefan continued over the radio, and Franceska didn't detect any glimmer of hope in his voice. He was determined, resolute, and she knew that the neighbor was likely right in his assertion that the declaration was an empty gesture. "But we will fight our enemy in a mortal battle of mettle and resolve. We will have our revenge upon the barbarian. We call upon everyone, whether they be child or elderly, help us strengthen our defenses, construct anti-tank barricades, dig trenches, whatever capacity you can afford, give more. This war will require everything from us."

"Different perspective than what the papers are stating," Stefania muttered to Franceska.

"Quiet!" The neighbor hushed them.

"I have ordered the administration to return to their posts. Food, water, and supplies will be distributed to everyone at allocated stations."

A collective sigh of relief could be heard throughout the entire encampment, and Franceska didn't believe that richer words existed.

"I have established the Civil Guard to replace the dispersed police force. Many people from the east are flooding into Warsaw from towns and cities overrun by the enemy. We will ensure that shelter is prepared for them. We are in a war of which there is little hope of success, but we will give the enemy as much difficulty as possible, allowing time for our allies to come to our aid. Matka Boska!"

"Matka Boska!" a few others resounded.

"Mother of God?" Stefania frowned in her confusion.

"It's the battle cry of the winged hussars," the neighbor smiled.

"I read about them when I was younger, but I don't remember much." Franceska tilted her head as she waited for the man to continue.

"They were the bane of every empire that sought to overthrow us." The old man smiled with pride. "The Ottomans and Russians were all turned away tucking their tails between their legs after they met our winged hussars in battle. Imagine the terror our enemies felt when they beheld what they believed to be angels or Valkyrie charging at them with fury."

"God knows we could use them now," Franceska sighed.

"Their spirit is still very much a part of us." The old man looked solemnly at Franceska. "That undying will to fight is still in every Pole who calls this land home."

"I imagine it won't be long before we don't have a choice," Stefania spoke under her breath as she looked sadly at Franceska.

"At least we know our newly appointed president is honest." The neighbor turned off the radio and lay down in bed.

"How so?" Franceska asked.

"The papers are telling us of resolute victories to keep our spirits up, but he's the only one with the guts to tell us the truth. We're losing this battle, and he knows that no help is coming to our aid. We're alone. Utterly."

Franceska and Stefania looked at each other with a sense of hopelessness, both fearing the worst, especially due to their Jewish heritage. Their enemy took no pains in hiding their disdain of what they perceived were subhuman peoples, and Franceska knew that if they were gunning down innocent peasants in the field, they would show little to no clemency for her.

"Let's make the best use of today." Franceska looked resolutely at Stefania. "If you're still content to help me, that is?"

"God knows I could use the distraction." Stefania looked worriedly at the radio.

"I should tell my father, but he's still sleeping." Franceska looked over at Mr. Mann. "He needs all the rest he can get."

"Let's go quickly then, and hopefully we'll return with good news for him."

Agreeing, Franceska and Stefania walked briskly through the camp, which they both noticed had swollen with numbers throughout the night. Families, which mostly consisted of mothers and children, were washing in bowls unashamedly out in the open. Franceska grieved for those who had children in such a terrible time, and she recalled Maria at the maternity ward. She couldn't imagine how difficult it would be to raise young kids, who didn't understand what was happening, in such extreme conditions.

In silence, the girls walked through the city, still shocked at the level of devastation. Hundreds of men, women, and children had taken to heart their newly appointed president's words, and they were making strong the defenses.

"Is…is The Melody Palace still open?" Stefania asked with shock.

Looking in the direction, Franceska was initially surprised to realize what end of the city they were in. The destruction around them was so vast that it had entirely reshaped her understanding of the city's layout. She was also astonished to find that Stefania was correct.

A singer, along with a few dancers and some other musicians, were exiting the club after having performed all night. Mr. Rosenberg, the manager, was standing near the exit and paying each performer as they left.

"How could they possibly be so selfish?" Stefania asked a little too loudly for Franceska's liking.

Catching their heated gazes, Mr. Rosenberg tipped his hat in greeting, but neither girl returned the gesture. Lighting a cigarette, Mr. Rosenberg leaned against the door as the two girls walked by on the opposite side of the street, still offering him steely glares.

"Every interaction I've had with that man leaves a terrible taste in my mouth," Franceska muttered under her breath when they were well out of earshot.

"I hope you don't mean me," a man called from behind them, and a startled Franceska spun around to find Father Kolbe.

"How long have you been trailing us?" Franceska asked abruptly, still unnerved, and noticed that the priest was carrying a few books in a sack slung over his shoulder and using a walking staff.

"Not long." Father Kolbe chuckled at her panicked state before adding, "I do apologize, I didn't intend to give you such a fright. And, no, I wasn't trailing you. I merely happened to spot you along my path. I have a monastery outside of the city that we converted into a hospital. I'm worried it will fall into German hands shortly and wanted to see how I can help prevent that from happening."

"I see." Franceska nodded.

"Where are you heading?" Father Kolbe asked as he caught up to their pace and walked beside Franceska.

"To be honest, we're not entirely sure." Franceska glanced at Stefania, realizing that both wished to have the holy man absent. He was nice, of course, but Franceska had inherited her father's skepticism and feared a conversion attempt at any moment.

"'If one does not know to which port he is sailing, no wind is favorable'," Father Kolbe quoted.

"Plato?" Stefania tilted her head.

"Seneca," Father Kolbe replied before adding, "But that's a good guess. What are you searching for? Maybe I can assist you?"

"My mother," Franceska replied as she studied the priest. "She was injured during the first day of the invasion. She was taken to receive care, but we don't know where."

"I've been to many of the hospitals around the city. Describe her to me and I'll see if something comes to mind."

"Well, she's a short Jewish woman with an even shorter temper," Franceska began.

"You just described half the city." Father Kolbe grinned at his own quip, but, due to the circumstances, Franceska did not find it amusing.

"She injured her back," Stefania interjected. "We had to lift her into the cart quickly which caused her considerable pain."

"And she's alone?" Father Kolbe narrowed his gaze, and Franceska hoped that he was recalling her mother.

"She is." Franceska remained wary.

"I can't promise anything, but there was a woman who I visited that was alone. She could barely open her eyes she was in so much agony."

"That could be anyone," Franceska replied cautiously. "Did she give you her name?"

"She refused to speak to me. She thought I was trying to convert her and mentioned that I could return when she was actually dying."

"That does sound like her," Stefania whispered to Franceska.

"I don't want to give you false hope, but I would love to take you to this woman."

Franceska shot Stefania a curious glance, wondering if they should take the risk.

"We have no leads. It could we worth the shot, even if it is a vague description." Stefania shrugged.

"Only if that is not too out of your way," Franceska spoke kindly to Father Kolbe. "I know you have many under your charge."

"It's a bit of a walk." He looked between them warily.

"That's alright," Franceska replied eagerly before glancing down at her shoes, which were not made for this uneven terrain, and noticed that they were continuing to deteriorate.

"Well, I am happy to have company this morning." Father Kolbe smiled.

"We're not interrupting your visit to the monastery?" Franceska asked politely, although she didn't know if it was wise to remind him as she needed his guidance.

"I discovered, many years ago in Japan, that God rarely, if ever, allows my plans to continue as intended."

"You were in Japan?" Stefania asked as her interest piqued. "What was it like?"

"The views were beautiful." Father Kolbe looked off into the distance as he grew reflective. "One felt as though they were living in a painting. The people were kind, but severe. Honor means everything to the Japanese. I arrived in Japan full of hope and optimism that I would plant a church. I tried, for some time, but I had difficulty converting anyone. The villages and cities I attended had been abused by wolves in sheep's clothing, if you understand me. Previous priests had left a rather bitter taste in their mouths. But then I moved to a place called Nagasaki and was able to establish a beautiful monastery there. I plan to revisit someday, God willing this invasion is brought to a swift halt."

"What was the food like?" Stefania pressed. "I've often thought about travelling out east."

"The food, if I'm to be honest, was rather shocking to my pallet." Father Kolbe grimaced as he glanced at them. "It took me considerable time to adjust from the comforts of Polish food which, when I described to the native Japanese what we ate, they turned their noses up in disgust."

"Really?"

"It is another world in almost every sense." Father Kolbe smiled.

"What books are those?" Franceska asked as she nodded to the sack around his shoulder.

"Some of my writings." Father Kolbe patted the books. "I thought it was time to document my life and my convictions."

"May I ask, when did you enter the priesthood?" Stefania asked, entirely enthralled by this man.

"As soon as I could." He looked at them with a coy grin. "When I was nine, I had a vision of the Virgin Mary."

"A vision?" Franceska remained skeptical.

"I was in the middle of prayer when she visited me. I asked what was to become of my life, and she offered me two crowns, one white for purity, the other red for martyrdom. She asked me if I was willing to accept either of these crowns. I said that I would accept them both."

Franceska felt the hair on her arm stand on edge as the priest spoke with conviction.

"And now I feel that time is drawing near." Father Kolbe looked up at the sky. "I will lay down my life for God and for Poland."

"Will you fight?" Stefania asked quietly.

"Never." He shook his head adamantly. "My father fought with the Polish Legions for an independent Poland. He was hung as a traitor by our oppressors. No, my young friend, I will never take the life of another, even at the peril of my own."

"That's rather admirable." Stefania stared at her feet contemplatively as they continued to walk.

"But it all means nothing when the time comes if I don't follow through with such bold statements." Father Kolbe raised an eyebrow. "I pray when the day comes I can meet God knowing that I followed through with my convictions and didn't bend under the pressure. That's why we must prepare, each and every day, to meet our end, so that when it comes, we may give the best accounting of ourselves to both God and men."

Franceska pondered his statement, but found his ideals rather extreme. She much preferred the comprehension of God in simple living, and found Father Kolbe to be too zealous. He appeared rather humble in his behavior, and Franceska didn't quite know how to reconcile how he spoke and how he acted. In either case, she didn't dare say anything to upset him when he was potentially leading them to her mother.

"Ah, excellent, the President is already making good on his promise of food and supplies." Father Kolbe pointed when they rounded the corner of a street.

Looking in the direction, Franceska spotted a long line of people waiting for bread, and she wondered if there really were enough provisions for so many. The line stretched down the street and even rounded the corner beyond Franceska's view. Hundreds of women and children waited patiently in the slow but steady queue. Most looked like Franceska felt: exhausted, famished, and terrified. No one spoke apart from mothers either shushing or comforting their children. They were already defeated, Franceska thought, and wondered how they would stomach the coming days or even weeks.

A younger girl, about the age of three or four, stood in line while holding her mother's hand. She had a bright red jacket and was clutching a teddy bear so tightly Franceska was certain the head was about to pop off. She was adorable, Franceska thought, but knew how stressful it would be to raise children in these perilous times. She counted herself fortunate that she was still childless and unattached to any man.

"Should I get in line?" Stefania asked. "Then you can meet me on your way back?"

"Might as well." Franceska nodded. "The announcement was only just made on the radio. I'm sure the line will only swell."

"I'm not sure how much they can give me, but I'll grab all that I can," Stefania called over her shoulder as she left Franceska alone with Father Kolbe.

"She's a good friend to you," Father Kolbe commented with a cheerfulness in his voice that unnerved Franceska.

Franceska didn't reply apart from a hum of agreement. She wished that Stefania had stayed with them and begrudged being alone with the priest. Although she was Jewish by ethnicity, her parents were not practicing, and she spent most of her childhood surrounded by nuns and priests in school. For the most part she resented the religious instructions, not entirely because of the content, but rather the method it was delivered. She never understood why left-handed people were deemed wicked, or why people who professed to serve a loving God behaved so inhumanely at times.

"What's on your mind?" Father Kolbe probed.

"Contemplating the state of my mother," Franceska replied quickly.

"I understand," Father Kolbe replied softly, and Franceska knew that her grumpiness had seeped through.

She regretted her behavior, but she couldn't stand his cheery disposition in such grim times. Even when he was talking zealously about visions and ideals of martyrdom he appeared happy.

"Oh dear," Father Kolbe spoke with sorrow as he stopped in the middle of the street.

"What is it?" Franceska asked with a touch of panic.

Then, slowly, Father Kolbe knelt on one knee in the middle of the road and looked down a dark alleyway. Wondering if anyone was watching this unusual behavior, Franceska checked over her shoulder as she stood in the middle of the road with the priest, curious if he had gone mad.

"Come on out," Father Kolbe spoke gently as he beckoned with an open hand, and, cautiously but desperately, a sweet, older dog limped out of the shadows toward the priest.

The dog's back right leg seemed to have been injured, and Franceska imagined it had been broken or sprained during the bombings.

"I don't have much," Father Kolbe began as he reached into his bag. "But I have a smidgeon of bread."

Tearing off a piece of the bread, Father Kolbe held it out to the dog who remained wary of the gesture.

"If you're too nervous, I understand." Father Kolbe slowly stood, careful not to startle the dog, before tossing the bread toward him.

Sniffing the food eagerly, while keeping an eye on the priest, the dog gratefully took the food and retreated back to the shadows.

"Mother of God, have mercy on us," Father Kolbe prayed as he watched the dog with sorrow, and Franceska couldn't help but remember the battle cry of the winged hussars.

Suddenly, and still as startling as ever, the air raid sirens began to bellow.

"We should hurry!" Father Kolbe clutched his bag tightly to his chest and the two rushed in the direction where, Franceska hoped, they would find her mother.

Chapter Ten:
Matka

"What society does to its children, so will its children do to society."

Cicero

"Thank God!" Father Kolbe exclaimed when they drew near to a hospital, still running from the bombs.

"Thank God?" Franceska griped. She didn't mean to blurt her thoughts out loud, but she had had enough of the holy man's piety.

"You take offense at giving thanks?" Father Kolbe asked as he panted.

"When children are dying, when dogs are starving to death, when families are being torn apart? Yes, I take offense," Franceska replied coarsely.

"Do you want to know a secret about life?" Father Kolbe slowed his pace to a walk.

"A secret?" Franceska panted as she looked up at the sky, double checking that no bombers were overhead as she also slowed to a walk.

"Give God thanks for Hell and watch what happens to your spirit."

"I don't understand." Franceska squinted at him.

"God uses the weak things of this world to shame the strong, and the foolish to shame the wise. Whether you believe in God or not, my young friend, give Him thanks, and see what happens." Father Kolbe continued to pant as they approached the hospital.

"Is that what you tell the mothers and fathers who lost their children? Give thanks?" Franceska couldn't believe what she was hearing.

"There are two languages the devil doesn't understand: gratitude and love. We must be better than our enemy, otherwise why should we struggle? Who are we to condemn others when we have wickedness within our own hearts?"

"We are wicked?" Franceska narrowed her gaze defensively. "Are you saying we deserve this?"

"I don't mean to lecture you with a sermon," Father Kolbe relented as he understood Franceska's frustration. "But is it possible that this suffering has always existed and you're only noticing it now because it is on a scale that can't be ignored?"

"Well…" Franceska tried to defend herself but found his words convicting.

"I've consoled many grieving parents, buried many who never knew love, and seen the worst that humanity and nature have to offer. This suffering was always around you. Always. I wrestled with resentment for many years, decades really, and I would caution you to uproot it while you still have your youth."

"I don't understand why you care so strongly about my opinion?" Franceska watched him suspiciously out the corner of her eye as they drew closer to the hospital. "We've only just met. I don't understand why you are singling me out."

"I know value when I see it." Father Kolbe leaned heavily on his walking stick. "And maybe your impact to this world is more important than you realize."

Franceska didn't reply as she stared at her feet, pondering his statement.

"Resentment starts small," he continued his lecture. "But it eats away at the soul like a plague. Resentment is what caused this war. A man imagined an aggrievance, and has convinced the whole of Germany that they, too, have reason to be bitter."

"That bitterness is imagined." Franceska watched his reaction.

"And yet he's convinced himself that it's real." Father Koble tilted his head. "And he's excellent at persuading his followers that they can blame others for their troubles. Resentment shifts the fault."

"You want me to forgive the Germans? Is that it?" Franceska furrowed her eyebrows with indignation.

"Like I said, resentment is akin to a plague. A good surgeon cuts out the infection before it spreads to the rest of the host. I'm a surgeon of souls, and I want to uproot your resentment before it has a chance to take your spirit, and the spirits of those you hold so dearly. So, again, forgive me for my sermon, but give thanks for even the worst of the worst, and watch what it does to your soul."

Suddenly, an ambulance rounded the corner quickly and sped towards the hospital. It was heavily damaged by shrapnel with one of the tires punctured, causing it to thump, thump, thump, along the street.

Swiftly moving out of the way, Franceska and Father Kolbe stood back as they watched the ambulance arrive at the hospital.

At once, the doors to the ambulance swung open, and two medics jumped out of the back, carrying a younger boy on a blood-stained stretcher. The boy was unconscious, and a young woman, whom Franceska assumed was his mother, also leapt out of the back of the ambulance, following closely behind the stretcher and weeping.

"How am I to give thanks for that?" Franceska asked genuinely, and was surprised to see tears in the priest's eyes as he watched the child being carried quickly into the hospital.

"I don't know." Father Kolbe shook his head dejectedly. "But someday maybe you'll find a way. Guard your heart, my friend. Guard your heart."

"I appreciate you leading me here. I hope my mother is inside," Franceska spoke softly as she nodded her goodbye to the priest before leaving him in the street and entering the hospital.

She was relieved, at least, to find that the conditions in this hospital were far improved from the maternity hospital. Not that they were ideal, and the foyer was still overcrowded, but there were no emergency surgeries commencing in the hallways and most of the injuries appeared to be minor.

Looking at the placards on the wall, Franceska felt lost. This was a much larger hospital than the maternity hospital, and she had no clue where to start. It would take her all day to search every ward and room.

The hollow clicking of a wooden staff against the marble floor approached from behind Franceska, and she knew that the priest had followed her into the hospital.

"Shall I lead the way?" Father Kolbe asked quietly when he came to stand beside her.

"I haven't scared you away yet?" Franceska rubbed her arm, feeling a touch embarrassed by her behavior.

"Don't insult my fortitude." Father Kolbe grew a cheeky grin as he winked at Franceska.

Grinning slightly, Franceska followed the priest as he walked through the hospital. The smell of blood was intense, and Franceska struggled to withhold the urge to cover her nose. The groans and moans of the patients in pain was difficult to bear, and Franceska wondered if she would ever become accustomed to this hell.

"Father Kolbe! Pray for me!" a man in a room called out when he recognized the priest.

"I will, my son!" Father Kolbe shouted back.

"Bless us, Father!" a woman cried as she carried her toddler who had a cast on his arm.

"May Jesus be your friend now and always." Father Kolbe gently patted the boy's head.

"Thank you, Father! Thank you!" The mother looked back at the priest with tears in her eyes.

The two continued through the hospital in silence as they ascended the stairs to the third level, but Franceska couldn't help from feeling that they would once again come up empty-handed. She prayed that Father Kolbe was leading her to her mother, but also knew how unlikely it would be that they would be reunited.

“I do sincerely hope that I have not led you astray.” Father Kolbe paused when they arrived at the top of the stairs.

“You’ve been kind to me.” Franceska smiled politely. “That I will remember.”

With a nod of understanding, Father Kolbe pushed the door open to the third floor and they began looking room by room for Mrs. Mann.

“She’s impossible to deal with!” a nurse griped to a fellow nurse as she exited a room further down the hall.

“She still won’t take her meds?” the other nurse asked.

“She swears that I’m trying to sedate her.”

“Sedate her for what?”

“I don’t know! She’s paranoid.”

“But she’s in substantial pain.”

“Her stubbornness is greater I guess.” The nurse shrugged.

“They’re talking about my mother.” Franceska nodded at the priest.

“How can you be so sure?”

“A stubborn woman lost to paranoia?”

“Again, you’ve described half the city.” Father Kolbe raised a brow.

“Excuse me,” Franceska asked the grumbling nurse.

“Yes?” The nurse studied Franceska and then the priest.

“The woman you were talking about, which room is she in?”

“Room five.” The nurse pointed before leaving to assist other patients.

“I can see why my mother doesn’t like her.”

“Why is that?” Father Kolbe chuckled.

“She doesn’t trust pretty girls.”

“Forgive me for being so forward, but you yourself are rather attractive.” Father Kolbe tilted his head. “How does that factor into her relationship with you?”

"Oh, she doesn't trust me in the slightest." Franceska grinned.

"Father?" a woman in another room called out to him.

"Yes, my dear?" Father Kolbe asked as he left to attend to her concerns.

Franceska's heart pounded in her chest as she peeked her head into room five and found that it was crowded with four women. Dressed in hospital gowns, they were all donning headscarves and a couple were smoking liberally.

"Mother?!" Franceska asked when she spotted one of the women on her side with her back toward them.

No reply.

Walking further into the room, with her heart still racing, Franceska walked slowly over to the woman, certain that it was her mother but unsure if she should allow herself to hope.

"Your father had better be with you as well," Mrs. Mann spoke with irritation as she turned her head slightly and spotted her daughter.

"It is you! Thank God!" Franceska shouted as she fell to her knees beside the bed and embraced her mother.

With tears streaming down her cheeks, Franceska took her mother's hand in hers and squeezed tightly. Mrs. Mann's hand was warm, and Franceska rested her forehead against the back of her mother's hand as she allowed herself to release the long-stifled emotions.

Looking up at her mother, Franceska noticed that her condition, while seemingly stable, also revealed that she was still in considerable pain.

Peeking through heavy eyelids, Mrs. Mann looked at her daughter with a touch of brightness in her eyes, but Franceska could still see they were riddled with agony.

"You look awful!" Mrs. Mann studied her daughter with disgust. "Your hair is all knotted!"

"I'm so glad I found you!" Franceska ignored her mother's comments as she stood and kissed her mother's cheek generously.

"Enough of that!" Mrs. Mann grumbled as she waved to stop her daughter's outpouring of affection. "You smell terrible."

"Why aren't you taking your meds?" Franceska sniffled happily as she offered a light, playful slap against her mother's arm.

"You see these fools?" Mrs. Mann pointed over her shoulder to the other women in the room. "They're taking the meds and look what's happening to them."

"They seem happy." Franceska grew confused.

"Happiness is for fools."

"And yet you're the fool." Franceska shook her head in disbelief as she wiped away the tears.

"What took you so long?" Mrs. Mann asked with annoyance. "Weren't you worried about your poor mother all alone on this ward with doctors and nurses who only want to sedate me? Who knows what they have planned once I'm unconscious?"

"I was worried sick. I could barely sleep." Franceska knew that nothing would change her mother's opinion.

"Barely sleep? That's more than I could do." Mrs. Mann winced suddenly.

"You're in pain!" Franceska griped. "You should take the medicine!"

"Then who would look after your father if I lose my wits?" Mrs. Mann asked as she tried to sit up.

"What are you doing?" Franceska held her hands out to stop her mother.

"Get off me!" Mrs. Mann barked as she swatted at Franceska's hands.

"Nurse?!" Franceska shouted as Mrs. Mann continued her attempt to sit upright.

"Mrs. Mann, I told you that you must take it easy," the nurse argued as she came to the bedside.

"All I've been doing is taking it easy, and I'm no better for it."

"We still don't know what's wrong with your back." The nurse glanced at Franceska with worry.

"You don't?" Franceska shot her head back in surprise.

"We weren't able to run any tests." The nurse shrugged. "We're being overrun, and the equipment hasn't been available. We've tried to medicate her while we wait for an opening, but—"

"May I speak with the doctor?" Franceska grew animated with worry.

"Of course." The nurse left quickly to track down a physician.

"Why are you being so stubborn?" Franceska asked her mother angrily.

"You left me alone here!" Mrs. Mann nearly shouted.

"We spent days looking for you!" Franceska yelled back.

"What?" Mrs. Mann paused as she studied her daughter intently.

"They didn't tell us which hospital they took you to." Franceska continued to defend herself.

"You should've asked before they took me!" Mrs. Mann frowned sharply at Franceska.

"They didn't even know where they were taking you!" Franceska threw her hands out in frustration. "But I promise you that I didn't stop looking!"

"Get me out of here." Mrs. Mann reached out for Franceska's hand to help her sit up.

"Mrs. Mann, I would strongly encourage you to remain in bed," the doctor said as he arrived at her side with a clipboard in hand.

"The nurse mentioned that you don't know what's wrong with her?" Franceska asked.

"Without doing an x-ray its anyone's guess." The doctor looked lost.

"She's in incredible pain," Franceska pleaded. "Surely that gives her some priority status."

"Her pain, from what I can tell, is positional." The doctor pointed to Mrs. Mann's lower back. "If she remains in place, the pain is manageable."

"And what does that indicate?" Franceska pressed.

"It could be a compression fracture, or it could be osteoporosis, or it could merely be a strain. I'm taking a shot in the dark here until we can get an x-ray."

"I'm not waiting around here!" Mrs. Mann argued as she finally sat upright, but continued to wince at even the slightest of movements.

"I know it's frustrating, but we need to understand the state of the hospital given the circumstances." The doctor drew a deep breath. "We were overrun and understaffed even before the invasion. Some of these nurses haven't seen their families in days. They've been working around the clock, barely eating or taking even a moment for themselves."

"Then I'll be one less burden for them," Mrs. Mann grunted as she tried to stand.

"Is there any possibility of having her examined? I can maybe convince her to stay if that is the case." Franceska looked hopefully at the doctor.

"I'm sorry." The doctor shook his head. "The list of people needing the machines is shocking, and more severe cases, which come in every day, push back people like your mother."

Franceska nodded in her understanding as her heart sank into her stomach.

"What is the danger of her leaving in this condition?" the nurse asked the doctor quietly.

"Without being properly diagnosed, it's impossible to say, but there is a chance she will always be in pain." The doctor looked at Franceska with sympathy as he continued, "I know you want to do the right thing for your mother, and, at this time, patience is your best option."

"She's being fed," the nurse interjected. "Or, at least, she's being given the option of food. That's better than what most are experiencing outside of these walls."

"That is true." Franceska looked at her mother to drive home the point.

"She has a bed, she has someone to look after her, she—"

"We get it!" Mrs. Mann interrupted rudely as she began to lie back down, surrendering.

"Incoming!" a nurse from outside the room shouted into the ward. "Ten patients! All with severe fractures!"

"Prepare the beds!" The doctor called back as he immediately left the room, trailed by the nurse.

"We don't have ten beds!" another nurse called out.

"I know it's not ideal, but they're right," Franceska argued to Mrs. Mann.

"I want to go home." Mrs. Mann's lips trembled and seeing her in this state shocked Franceska.

"I'm sorry," Franceska choked as she looked back at her mother, but couldn't bring herself to tell her that their home was gone.

"I want to go home," Mrs. Mann continued as she closed her eyes.

"We'll go…we'll leave soon, I promise." Franceska kissed her mother's forehead.

"How did you find me, by the way?" Mrs. Mann looked up at her daughter.

"A priest, Father Kolbe, was helping me."

"Did he try to convert you?" Mrs. Mann smirked.

"He probably would've been less annoying if he had tried."

"How's your father?" Mrs. Mann winced. "Why didn't he come to see me?"

"He was still sleeping when I left this morning."

"Still sleeping?!" Mrs. Mann scowled. "He's sleeping while I'm suffering here in the hospital?! I swear to God Almighty when I get out of this prison, I'm going to send him here with so many broken bones it will take a month just to x-ray him."

"He was up all night looking for you and for food," Franceska defended her father.

"Looking for food?" Mrs. Mann squinted. "What's wrong with the food in the cupboard?"

"Well…" Franceska paused, not sure if she should break the news to her mother.

"All visitors need to leave!" a nurse called out.

"I'll be back! I promise!" Franceska squeezed her mother's hand tightly.

"If you say so," Mrs. Mann grumbled, but then added, "Brush your hair and wash yourself before you come back."

"Please take the pain meds!" Franceska called as she ran out of the room.

To her shock, Franceska noticed that Father Kolbe was standing near the entrance to the ward.

"You waited?" Franceska asked him with surprise.

"I wanted to make sure everything was alright." Father Kolbe smiled gently.

"Well, it is and it isn't." Franceska looked over her shoulder at her mother's room. "I'm glad I found her, but she's in rough condition."

"What's the issue?"

"They don't know for sure." Franceska shook her head as they began to walk down the stairs.

"That's unfortunate," Father Kolbe sighed.

"I appreciate your assistance today." Franceska looked kindly at the priest.

"It wasn't me." Father Kolbe looked solemnly back at her. "I was merely the vessel. Thank God that he sent me to assist you."

"Do we really want to start this conversation again?" Franceska's aversion to religious conversation returned.

"I've yet to meet a single embittered person who has made this world a better place by being aggrieved." Father Kolbe raised a brow. "Be the light in this world, Franceska. Be the dancer, be the good daughter, be the good friend, even to your enemies. I promise, it's not for their sake, but yours."

"You're condoning selfishness then, are you?" Franceska quipped.

"With every fiber of my being." Father Kolbe also grinned as they exited the hospital and into the street.

Then, tapping his walking stick on the ground, he mentioned, "I am off the monastery now. Hopefully the Germans will leave it alone. If we meet again, in this life or the next, I want to hear what you're thankful for."

I'm thankful for this conversation to end, Franceska wished to retort. Instead, Franceska merely nodded in agreement and watched the friar priest walk contentedly in the direction of the monastery.

Drawing a deep breath, Franceska trekked away from the hospital and back toward her father and company. She was excited to tell him that his wife was alive, and, despite her pain, still had enough wits about her. She felt it was unkind of her not to tell her mother about their destroyed home, but she also didn't want to strip away that hope.

Regardless, Franceska knew how fortunate they were. She had assumed, like her father, that it was unlikely they would ever be reunited with Mrs. Mann, yet her chance interaction with the priest had led her directly to her mother. She began to contemplate if such an event was entirely random, or if some other force was at work.

In either case, Franceska could scarcely contain her smile that was mixed with tears. She had found her mother, and now her focus was entirely centered on how to assist her mother in leaving the hospital and being reunited with her and her father.

Walking back through the city, Franceska spotted the fresh new fires started by the incendiary bombs, the newly destroyed houses, and the bodies that were being cleared by weeping relatives or medical personnel.

She wondered if there ever would come a day where she could be, as Wiera stated, unattached. She prayed that day would never come. It was painful to watch the family members mourning, knowing that she would be lucky indeed if her family escaped unscathed.

I wonder if Stefania is still in the food line? Franceska thought as she drew close to where she and her friend had parted.

But Franceska's heart was ripped out of her chest when she turned the corner to see eight bodies of women and children scattered near where the bread line had been. Blood had pooled around their bodies, and it was evident that they were all dead.

Among the bodies was a sight that Franceska didn't believe she would ever forget. The young girl she had spotted earlier in the line with the bright red jacket and teddy bear, was lying face down on the ground, still clutching her stuffed animal.

Franceska collapsed to her knees. She couldn't pry her eyes away from the horrific destruction. It was so cruel and inhumane, and she couldn't understand why their enemies were so hateful. What had these women and children done to deserve this fate that they should die while collecting bread?

The sight of the little girl in the red jacket haunted Franceska severely. She had only seen her in passing mere hours ago, but this little girl had stuck in her mind. Seeing that innocence and that beauty wiped out needlessly was horrific.

"He risked his life to kill them," a voice spoke from beside her, and Franceska looked up to see a tear-stained Stefania standing with her hands clenched into fists.

"I…" Franceska squeezed her eyes shut as she tried to find the words or anything to say that would help make sense of what she was seeing.

"The anti-aircraft guns were firing, trying to stop his approach." Stefania knelt beside Franceska. "He was the only fighter plane in this quadrant, but instead of aiming for a military target, he made significant maneuvers, at great risk to his life, to gun down women and children lining up for bread."

Franceska didn't respond as she stared at the little girl with her face in the dirt. It didn't make sense, and the priest's caution of thankfulness rang dead in her ears. She allowed resentment to dig its roots in her heart, and she hated their enemy deeply and truly,.

"He risked his life to kill innocents," Stefania repeated as if she herself didn't believe the words.

"I hate them." Franceska gritted her teeth. "I've never wanted to kill anyone before, but if I ever get the chance, I'll kill as many Nazis as I can."

Chapter Eleven:
Uncivil

"Warsaw is burning. Warsaw is fighting its enemy in this last mortal battle. All the promises let us down, the help did not arrive. Lack of food and lack of potable water paralyzes and weakens. Yet we fight: with the enemy, with the fire and with the epidemics. Everyone is fighting. Whole city is tied in this mortal struggle. You send us letters of compliments and best wishes from London and Paris. We don't want wishes any more, nor do we await your help. It's too late for help. Before it arrives there will be only rubble here, a corpses-covered, leveled terrain. What we await is revenge. We expect that you will start fighting one day, just like Warsaw is… A day will come when Berlin will be set on flames, when German women and children will die just like ours are dying. I hope all of you will understand then that there is God's justice."

Stefan Starzyński (President of Warsaw)

"How was your mother?" Stefania asked Franceska as the two walked back through the city.

"Stubborn," Franceska replied quickly, still disturbed by the sight of the innocent people slaughtered for the simple act of lining up for bread.

"I'm glad you found her," Stefania continued, but Franceska could hear the shock in her voice and knew that her mind was also captive to the recent tragedy.

Without another word, Franceska and Stefania walked through the city, sickened by what they were experiencing and understanding that no words would soothe what they had just witnessed.

And as they walked through the city, Franceska spotted a row of apartment housing with dozens of families crowding around a man standing on a small wooden box. The man was holding up a sign, but from her distance, Franceska couldn't read it.

Many of the family members appeared to be angry with the man on the box who was also apparently upset with them as he shouted while shaking his fist.

But as Franceska and Stefania drew closer, they could hear racial slurs and insults being flung between the man on the box and the crowd.

"We have nowhere else to go!" a father from the crowd, with two children beside him, shouted at the man on the box.

"I simply can't give away apartments for free." The man on the box defended, and Franceska discerned that he was a landlord eager to rent out the recently vacated units.

"We will pay you once we have money!" the father shouted louder, and his sentiment was echoed by the other families in the crowd.

"And who is going to pay for your rent if you can't?" the landlord retorted angrily. "I have a family, too! I need to provide for them!"

"You're a Nazi lover!" a woman in the crowd shook her fist at the landlord.

"I resent that!" the landlord stepped down and came face-to-face with the woman.

"Resent it all you like, it's the truth!" the woman shoved the landlord's shoulder.

"How dare you!" The landlord shoved the woman back, and at once the crowd became a frenzy of a few protecting the landlord while most were eager to tear him limb from limb.

"Let's keep moving," Stefania whispered to Franceska, and the two girls hurried along before they were caught up in a scuffle.

"I hope the tram becomes functional again soon," Franceska muttered as she looked down at her dirty shoes and weary feet.

"I hope everything returns to normal soon," Stefania added. "But I agree. It would be nice to make our way around the city without having to walk everywhere."

"I don't know if I can handle this much longer." Franceska shook her head in mesmerization. "I hope France and England will make good on their declarations and put an end to this nightmare."

"My father fought in the Great War."

"Really?" Franceska glanced at her friend.

"He said it was the war to end all wars."

The two girls returned to silence as their hunger added another layer to the exhaustion, and Franceska hoped that they would be provided with some more bread and soup at the shelter.

"What on Earth is he doing?!" Franceska almost laughed when they arrived back at the encampment and spotted Mr. Mann, along with Wiera's father, standing at attention with a group of men, women, and children.

A civilian was pacing in front of this group, giving what Franceska believed to be a rousing speech. He seemed impassioned, but she was too far away to hear exactly what he was saying. In either case, she was still too stunned to see her father involved.

Then, and more surprising still, the civilian leader began handing out riffles to the men, women, and even children.

"I'm confused." Stefania concurred as they slowly approached this group, and Franceska was worried that they were somehow about to be roped into whatever organization this was.

"Meet back here in exactly one hour!" the leader announced, and the group immediately burst into excited chatter with the younger boys looking over their weapons eagerly while their mothers grew increasingly worried.

"What is going on?" Franceska asked her father as he and Mr. Gran approached them while brandishing proud smiles.

"We've volunteered to fight in the Civil Guard," Mr. Mann replied softly and with about as much confidence as Franceska could expect from him.

"Have you ever shot a rifle?" Stefania asked, and Franceska wondered if she had meant to ask that question out loud.

Mr. Mann didn't reply as he looked over his weapon, but Franceska knew her father was quite offended by Stefania, and she would likely hear him muttering under his breath later.

"Any news on your mother?" Mr. Gran asked with a measure of concern that Franceska appreciated.

"Oh, of course!" Franceska shook her head in wonder that she hadn't already spilled the news to Mr. Mann, but the sight of him in the Civil Guard had stunned her. "I found her!"

"You did?!" Mr. Mann's eyes flew wide open as he stared back at his daughter, and he almost seemed scared to hear her answer.

"The priest took me to the hospital where she was being cared for. She's still in pain but refusing to take her medication, and—"

"Which hospital?!" Mr. Mann pressed.

"It's on the—"

"Why is she refusing medication?" Mr. Mann frowned as he didn't wait to hear her response. "Is she alright?! How does she look?!"

"She suspects they're trying to sedate her for some reason that I'm still not sure about."

"That stubborn woman!" Mr. Mann closed his eyes as he turned his face toward heaven and sighed, "This is horrible news!"

"I thought you'd be relieved?" Franceska studied her father.

"Relieved?!" He looked at her with incredulity. "How could I be comforted knowing that she's suffering without me there to help her?!"

"She has a bed, food, and I made her promise that she would take the pain medication," Franceska pressed. "She's in a much more fortunate situation than we are."

"Did she ask about me?" Mr. Mann looked sheepishly at his feet.

"In a way." Franceska bit her lip.

"She's upset with me?" Mr. Mann looked up at her in surprise. "How?"

"She thought that we were aware of the hospital she was taken to and that we were merely ignoring her." Franceska shrugged.

"How could we possibly have known?" Mr. Mann's composure dwindled into frustration.

"I tried to explain, but you know mother."

"That I do." Mr. Mann rubbed his eyes in exhaustion. "How did she take the news of the house being destroyed? I bet she was devastated to learn that her spoon collection is gone."

“I may have hidden that information from her.” Franceska braced for her father’s reaction.

“You…” Mr. Mann was about to become indignant, but then relaxed his shoulders and mentioned, “That was probably wise. She’s likely under enough stress as it is.”

“I can take you to see her if you’d like?” Franceska offered, but she hoped that he would decline as she was anxious to have a moment to rest and recover.

“That may have to wait,” Mr. Gran interjected as he slung his rifle around his shoulder. “We will be assigned our duties in the Civil Guard shortly. We’ve resolved to fight to defend our city.”

“If it comes to that, yes, but I have a feeling we’re mostly going to be used for free labor.” Mr. Mann again looked over his rifle nervously. “They’ll make us busy constructing defenses, I’m sure.”

“In any case, the Germans would know best to avoid you.” Franceska tried to encourage her father, but knew how unconvincing she sounded.

She was absolutely terrified at the idea of her father fighting. He was a gentle and kind man who, not counting recent episodes of him shouting during the bombings, could barely be heard over a whisper.

“I thought I would be reassured hearing that she was alive and being taken care of, but now I’m somehow more anxious than before.” Mr. Mann bit his lip as he looked worriedly at his daughter. “We need to make a plan to get your mother home.”

“She can’t come here.” Franceska looked out over the encampment. “She needs something stable, and away from these crowds.”

“Where else can we go?” Mr. Mann shook his head.

“We saw some apartments for rent on our way back from the hospital.” Franceska clicked her tongue as she thought. “But the landlord is turning away people who can’t afford to pay upfront.”

"Well, there's the problem." Mr. Mann chuckled ironically. "We don't have a penny to our name."

"I will look for employment." Franceska nodded.

"You? What skills do you have?" Stefania asked with a patronizing tone that Franceska did not appreciate.

"Well…I…" Franceska paused as she stared at her feet. "All I know is dance."

"I don't imagine there's much use for that right now," Mr. Gran added, further twisting the knife.

"Actually…" Franceska looked at her father and Stefania before continuing, "There is one place."

"Where?" Stefania shook her head.

"The Melody Palace."

"The night club?!" Mr. Mann nearly dropped his rifle in shock at her statement.

"Yes." Franceska swallowed.

"No daughter of mine is going to be parading herself on stage for other men to ogle at!" Mr. Mann's eyes bulged.

"What other choice do we have?!" Franceska threw her arms out in sheer frustration. "I certainly have no interest in that sort of entertainment but it's an option."

"Entertainment?" Mr. Mann scoffed.

"Where else can I earn some money?!" Franceska continued in her frustration.

"Why don't we look for other places of employment first?" Stefania interjected, taking the odd moment to be calm as the group hummed with concern. "I need to find employment as well. I'll help you search."

"We'll find another way. I promise." Mr. Mann drew a deep breath to calm his nerves. "I doubt anyone is hiring at the moment. We'll find some other way to obtain the apartment or at least somewhere more suitable to live."

"There you are," Wiera added as she came to stand with the group. "Did you find your mother?"

"I did." Franceska smiled politely.

"And?! How is she?!"

"She's in considerable pain, and refusing to take her medication, but we need to find somewhere suitable to live so that we can get her out of the hospital."

"They killed them all!" a shout rang out in the crowd.

Everyone's attention turned to see what the commotion was about, and Franceska grew nervous that something sinister had happened. She didn't know if she could handle any further heartbreak today.

"They killed them all!" the shout came again.

"What's happening?" Mr. Gran asked as the company moved toward the commotion where they noticed a younger woman hysterically shouting.

"They killed them all!" the young woman fell to her knees.

"Killed who?" a woman nearby asked as she knelt beside the young woman.

"The people!" The young woman sobbed. "The Germans killed all of them!"

"Where?" Mr. Gran asked.

"The train! The German fighters gunned down the train! They killed everyone! Hundreds of people. Women, children, everyone!" The young woman screamed with hateful rage, and Franceska wondered if this woman's family had perished on that train.

Murmurs began to circulate throughout the swelling crowd, and Franceska's shoulders tightened with worry. She knew that they were fighting an enemy who was hellbent on killing everyone. Whether it was peasants in the field collecting food, or a passenger train full of women and children, the Germans were not fighting for conquest, but annihilation.

"This is madness!" Mr. Gran looked at Mr. Mann. "Where is our help? Where is France and England? Where are our allies? They're killing us with impunity."

Mr. Mann didn't reply as he looked hopelessly back at Mr. Gran, and Franceska knew, even by his expression, that they were entirely alone. She had been convinced of that truth for a while, and she was certain her father was as well.

"How are the French going to help us?!" a man near Mr. Gran asked angrily. "They'll have to go through Germany to get to us!"

"They can at least put pressure on Germany's western front, show the enemy that they're serious about their guarantee to come to our aid!" Mr. Gran defended. "Not only so, but it will give our boys some courage knowing that the enemy is pinned in on both sides."

"And how long do you think that will last?" the man squared up with Mr. Gran. "Even if the French launch an offensive, Hitler won't stop trying to achieve his grisly objectives in Poland."

"You know the mind of Hitler?" Mr. Gran challenged, and Franceska feared that a fight was about to break out.

Everyone was hungry, scared, grieving, angry, resentful, bitter, and experiencing the height of human emotions that come with the horrors of war. Franceska knew that these arguments were akin to lighting a match and throwing it into a tank of gasoline.

"We have no one coming to our aid!" the man shouted.

"What about England?!" a young woman asked sincerely. "They've declared war on Germany as well!"

"Good luck to them breaking through Germany's battleships!" another man in the crowd cast his opinion into the ring.

"We're alone!" Mr. Gran shouted, startling Franceska.

Many in the crowd turned to look at him, waiting for him to continue. Franceska, like many others she assumed, was anxiously waiting for some words of wisdom or hope, and she prayed he would deliver.

"A house divided cannot stand," Mr. Gran continued. "We must be as one. We have one goal, one purpose, one reason for our existence: to beat back the invading Germans."

A few heads nodded in agreement while others remained skeptical.

"We should surrender," someone in the crowd interjected. "Maybe then they will show mercy, or at least stop butchering civilians."

"Or make it easier for them to kill us at will!" another in the crowd shouted.

"We can't be ignorant and believe that victory on the battlefield is possible." Mr. Gran looked out over the crowd with a countenance that revealed his troubled heart. "But for every square inch that they take of our sacred Poland, we will give them hell. One day, they will take over this city. That is inevitable. And when they do, we will make their existence here as terrible as we possibly can."

"How?" someone from the crowd asked.

"We'll use their greatest weakness against them."

"Which is?!" Another from the crowd pressed.

"Arrogance." Mr. Gran nodded firmly. "They believe they are superior to us in every way. This will lead them to disregard our intelligence, our passion for this sacred land, and our willingness to preserve every syllable of our glorious language and culture, even at the cost of our lives."

"None of that will help us fire a bullet or sink battleships," another man in the crowd complained.

"No, it won't." Mr. Gran shook his head in agreement. "But we don't fight for today, we fight for tomorrow. We fight for our children and their grandchildren. If everything we've feared about the Nazis and Hitler is true, then it is likely many of us will perish and never see Poland free from his grip. All they know is hate. They hate us for our race, whether you're Jewish, like myself, or Polish like many of you here. But we have a love for this sacred ground that they will never understand. We have a love for each other that will never be snuffed out. Hold onto that. We must stand united."

The crowd looked at each other with mixed reactions. Some seemed to be impressed with his words while others, Franceska noted, were of a more cynical nature.

Not that she blamed them, either. What they needed were more fighters, planes, and battleships. When the Germans inevitably conquer the city, Franceska knew that there would be nowhere for them to hide. She needed to get her mother healthy so that they could escape. That was her only priority.

Chapter Twelve: Disharmony

"It was pride that changed angels into devils; it is humility that makes men as angels."

St. Augustine

"You really didn't have to come with me," Franceska spoke to Stefania and Wiera as they waited for the tram to arrive.

"Oh, I wouldn't miss this for the world," Stefania replied with a smirk.

"Thankfully the trams are up and running again," Wiera glanced down at her feet. "I don't think I'd brave the journey otherwise."

Franceska chuckled slightly as she took note of a handful of other people also anxiously waiting for the tram. She felt a sense of relief that a portion of her life was returning to normal. Walking everywhere was becoming a serious strain on her joints and, not to mention, her only pair of shoes.

"When is the tram coming?" an impatient young girl, about the age of five Franceska thought, tugged on the sleeve of her mother's arm.

"I told you before, it goes slower every time you ask," the mother replied bluntly, and Franceska noted how weary and exhausted she appeared.

And it wasn't just this mother, either. The whole city appeared tired and fatigued. The daily and nightly bombings continued to weaken morale, and few were fortunate enough to get a full night's rest during the nocturnal barrages.

"I could use a drink," Wiera muttered under her breath.

"It's not even three o'clock in the afternoon." Stefania peeked at her watch.

"And maybe a gentleman at The Melody Palace will buy us a free drink while Franceska conducts her business?" Wiera shrugged.

"The club isn't even open yet." Stefania glanced at her friend with a frown. "And we're not there to mingle. We're joining Franceska for moral support."

"Is that why you're joining?" Franceska asked with a sarcastic grin.

"Why else?" Stefania looked offended at Franceska.

"There isn't a side of you that hopes to see me embarrass myself publicly?" Franceska tilted her chin up as she looked down her nose at her friend, judging her reaction.

"I resent that you think I have such a side to me!" Stefania frowned sharply as she turned away.

"That's not why I'm joining, but now that you mention it, that does sound entertaining," Wiera added with a chuckle.

"None of that now!" Stefania offered a stern warning to Wiera.

"Don't worry, I'm still focused on my free drink. The club will have some men working there preparing for the night." Wiera defended. "Maybe one of them needs a break?"

"Have you forgotten Adam already?" Franceska studied her friend.

"It's Adam who forgot me, I'm sure." Wiera glanced away.

"I doubt anyone could forget you," Stefania encouraged Wiera.

"I really wonder where he is." Wiera began to chew her bottom lip nervously.

"I'm sure he's more than fine," Franceska spoke tenderly to Wiera. "In fact, I'm positive that he's doing well. He will return when he's able. You'll see."

"In either case, I'm glad the tram is working again," Stefania spoke with excitement as they heard the bell before it rounded the corner.

"Only in the areas of the city where they didn't tear up the tracks I suppose," Franceska added.

With a piercing squeak, the boxy red streetcar stopped in front of the group waiting to board. Franceska grinned as she scanned the little tram with excitement. She didn't imagine that she would ever be so thrilled to engage in something that was once considered ordinary. But the little red tram, with its golden trimmed windows, provoked a sense of hope within Franceska that the world, or at least a portion of it, was about to return to normal.

"Hello Henryk!" Franceska spoke cheerfully to the tram operator as she beamed with delight to see a familiar face.

"Hello," Henryk replied, absent of the same enthusiasm as he inspected Franceska with a look that indicated her recognized her but couldn't quite remember where from.

Henryk, a stout aging man with strikingly white hair and beard, had been a tram operator for as long as Franceska could remember. He seemed, to Franceska, to carry a permanent look of confusion as if he had just been awoken from a dream or a pressing thought had been interrupted.

"Thank you," Henryk spoke plainly as he accepted the fare from Stefania who had graciously paid for all three girls to board.

"That's very kind of you to pay," Franceska thanked Stefania as the three girls squished into a booth near the back of the almost empty tram.

"Would the little one like a treat?" Henryk asked the young girl as she boarded with her mother, invoking Franceska's recollection of the many times he had offered her the same gesture during her younger years.

"That would be wonderful, thank you!" the mother exclaimed with relief.

Without a second thought, the young girl snatched the sweet out of Henryk's hand.

"What do you say?" the mother prodded her daughter to be polite.

"Do you want some?" the young girl asked Henryk.

"No, but thank you," Henryk chuckled.

"Say 'thank you'," the mother reminded the young girl.

"Why? He already said thank you!" the young girl defended.

"Never mind," the mother sighed as she forsook the lesson in politeness while they took their seat.

"Does your elbow need to rest in my ribcage?" Wiera griped at Stefania as the tram jolted to a start and they began their journey to the nightclub.

"How are my elbows the problem?!" Stefania grew incensed. "I'm the one squished into the middle and my arms are forward."

"Everything about you is bony." Wiera tried to shuffle closer to the window.

"I've barely eaten in weeks," Stefania defended.

Franceska laughed at her two friends, and it felt good to have a moment of something seemingly ordinary. She missed the laughs and petty squabbles between her friends, and felt like the three of them going back to the nightclub was stepping back in time.

It was only a handful of nights ago that they had arrived with their partners at the night club, having offended Jakub with their feminine opinions. Franceska smiled as she recalled Adam bravely shooing away men desperate to dance with either herself or Wiera.

But her recollection turned sour when she remembered how she had spoken to Mr. Rosenberg. Not to mention their previous interaction while shoveling in the ditch together was not all that encouraging, either. She wondered if he would still be of the opinion to provide her with employment.

The tram came to another stop, and Franceska watched as two younger women, about the same age as her, climbed aboard. They were neatly dressed, and Franceska immediately grew self-conscious of her own attire.

She had worn the same dress for days on end, her shoes were nearly worn out and looking tattered, and her hair was styled as best as she was able given the circumstances. Still, she knew how she appeared, and she hoped this wouldn't sour Mr. Rosenberg's attitude toward her.

"How do I look?" Franceska asked the two girls.

"Better than I do," Stefania grumbled.

"You look dashing." Wiera winked.

"I hope Mr. Rosenberg thinks so, too." Franceska stared out the window at the city passing them by.

Regardless of her appearance, Franceska was resolved to make a better second impression on Mr. Rosenberg and hopefully secure a position dancing. She still loathed the idea of dancing in that fashion for others to gawk at, but Franceska would do nearly anything to earn money so that they could move into an apartment.

Besides, Franceska was craving the opportunity to dance and prayed that she would at least have an opening to showcase her talents. Maybe, she pondered, this would lead to her securing a greater position in another, more respectable establishment.

"What are you going to tell your father? If you get the position that is?" Stefania asked with a wry smile.

"That I became a clerk for an accountant."

"He'll believe that?" Wiera frowned. "What if he decides to investigate?"

"Of course he'll believe it!" Franceska frowned back. "I'm smart."

"If you say so." Stefania grinned.

"Besides, he loathes accountants or anyone in a position that deals with money."

"Really? Why?" Wiera asked.

"He's convinced they're all corrupt." Franceska smiled as she recalled the many comments her father made under his breath.

"He might not be too far from the mark on that one." Wiera raised a brow.

"What are you going to say to the manager?" Wiera asked.

"I haven't thought that far ahead yet." Franceska grimaced.

"Do you think—" Stefania stopped herself short when she spotted something outside the tram that caught her attention.

Others within the tram began to whisper with each other as the tram came to a halt, and Franceska grew worried that something foul was occurring.

Standing, Franceska rushed to the front of the tram where she spotted hundreds, if not thousands, of Polish soldiers walking through the city. She assumed that they were retreating from the front lines as they walked with shoulders slouched and gazes at their feet. Many of them were bandaged with injuries on their arms, legs, and heads. Mud and dirt was caked on their faces and arms, and she knew they likely had gone just as long as she had without adequate bathing.

She appreciated that there would be more men within the city to help them fight the invasion in a more concentrated effort, but their expressions concerned her gravely. These men were defeated, utterly. Their spirits were broken, and Franceska feared that the enemy would take advantage of their low morale.

The train of men continued further into the city, and Franceska returned to her seat as the tram resumed its trek as if nothing significant had just occurred. Everyone in the tram remained silent, and the rest of the journey was eerie as no one dared to utter a word.

"Thank you, Henryk," Franceska spoke politely to the operator as they exited at their stop.

"Yep," Henryk replied casually, and the bell rang as the tram resumed its loop.

"Are you ready?" Stefania asked as they approached the nightclub.

"I don't have a choice otherwise," Franceska replied briskly, trying to convince herself to be courageous.

She didn't know what she would do if Mr. Rosenberg refused. She needed the money so that they could have a place for her mother. That was all that mattered to Franceska, and she didn't care how she achieved that result.

"Is the club even open?" Stefania asked with concern.

"Only one way to find out," Franceska replied as she grabbed onto the door handle, and she was slightly disappointed to find that it was unlocked. A part of her wished that the doors were, in fact, locked and she would be forced to seek employment elsewhere.

"We'll be close by if you need us." Wiera patted Franceska's shoulder as they all walked into the club.

Yet when Franceska was inside, she almost thought that she had entered the wrong property. With the lights on, the absence of a haze of smoke, and the dance floor free from happy couples, the nightclub appeared like an entirely different place.

"He's over at the bar." Stefania nudged Franceska with her elbow before pointing at Mr. Rosenberg.

Glancing in the direction, Franceska spotted Mr. Rosenberg standing at the bar looking over what she believed was an inventory list. He seemed to be perturbed by whatever he was viewing, and she imagined that his supplies had been seriously depleted by the invasion.

"Wait here," Franceska spoke over her shoulder as she began walking toward the manager.

"What about our drinks?" Wiera whined.

"You can drink after she's rejected," Stefania whispered to Wiera.

"Excuse me," Franceska spoke softly as she stood behind Mr. Rosenberg, and it was then that she noticed he wasn't using a cane. She found this unusual, given that she assumed he had some sort of disability and required the use of a cane.

"No thank you," Mr. Rosenberg replied without turning toward her.

"You don't even know what I'm about to ask." Franceska frowned.

"This sounds like the beginning of a conversation we had the other night," Mr. Rosenberg replied, still with his back toward her, and Franceska found it baffling how he knew it was her.

"About that conversation…" Franceska cleared her throat.

"You've changed your mind, and you want to dance?" Mr. Rosenberg scribbled some notes on the inventory list before placing it down and turning toward her as he leaned against the bar.

He appeared charming, Franceska thought, as he leaned against the bar and carried a casualness that she appreciated.

"Please," Franceska felt her shoulders relaxing, sensing the reassurance in his voice.

"Well, go on, ask me." He rolled his hand for her to proceed.

"Alright, Mr. Rosenberg, I would—"

"Marek, please."

"Marek." Franceska swallowed as she held her hands politely in front of her, again quite mindful of her tattered appearance. "I would like to dance at The Melody Palace."

"Are you alright dancing in front of, how did you put it again, a 'less refined crowd'?"

"I do apologize for my inconsiderate remarks." Franceska's cheeks turned crimson with embarrassment.

"But you're alright with it now?" Marek held his conclusion in reserve.

I don't have any other choice, Franceska wished to say, but knew that would not be prudent in landing her the position. Instead, she stated, "I would be delighted to have the opportunity to dance, in any capacity."

"You really were a ballerina?" Marek pressed as he crossed his arms.

"Yes." Franceska smiled proudly. "I won fourth place in Brussels."

"Brussels?" Marek raised his eyebrows.

"Yes, Brussels," Franceska replied, hoping her achievement would help her secure the position.

"And you would like to dance here now?"

"Yes, very much so."

"No," Marek blurted quickly as he brushed past her.

"No?" Franceska turned as she watched him walking to the back of the nightclub where she assumed the offices were.

Marek didn't reply as he dug into his pocket before retrieving a set of keys and stopping before a door with his name painted in black letters.

"What do you mean, no?" Franceska asked indignantly as she began trailing him. "You were eager to employ me when we first met."

"Eager?" Marek scoffed and unlocked his office door.

"You practically begged me!" Franceska shot her head back in surprise at his poor recollection.

"It was a ploy," Marek sighed as he turned to look at her.

"A ploy?" Franceska frowned, but then the realization hit her, and she looked back at him with a scowl.

"I tell a woman she's pretty, that she could dance or sing, and they get so caught up in their own ambition that it's easy to—"

"I get it!" Franceska interrupted. "You're a pig."

"Is that any way to talk to a perspective employer?" Marek smirked.

"You find this amusing?" Franceska continued to scowl at him.

"Your reaction is amusing." Marek crossed his arms as he leaned against the doorpost.

"If you hire me, I could amuse you all day." Franceska's eyes lit up.

"Oh?" Marek's smile grew.

"Not in that sense!" Franceska's scowl returned. "Maybe I don't want to work for you."

"Sweetheart, if you can't handle this conversation, how will you handle the comments the men will hurl at you on stage?" Marek looked at her in a patronizing manner that she loathed.

Franceska didn't reply as she looked back in the direction of the stage. She longed to dance, this much was true, but hated the idea of her becoming some sexual object that lonely men ogled.

"Truth be told, I would love to hire you," Marek continued as he placed his hand to the doorknob, signaling that the conversation was coming to an end. "But I can barely pay the staff we have due to the current state of affairs. All the young men are out of the city, leaving old perverts like me to fill the clubs, and that does not draw young women in. Without young women, there are no young men, and without young men buying the young women drinks, the whole enterprise unravels."

With a polite nod of farewell, Marek began to close the door.

"What if I can help with that?" Franceska put her hand out to stop the door.

Marek shook his head as he smirked with derision before attempting to close the door again.

"Please!" Franceska insisted as she put her foot against the door.

"How?" Marek studied her with incredulity.

"If I tell you, you'll steal my idea and then there's no need to hire me."

"You have an idea to help me bring young men and women to this nightclub?" Marek remained unconvinced.

"I do!" Franceska nodded adamantly. "If I bring five men and women, do I have a job?"

Marek studied her pensively for a moment before bartering, "Twenty men and women."

"Ten."

"Fifteen."

"Ten." Franceska remained resolute.

With a heavy sigh, Marek held out his hand to cement the deal.

"Done." Franceska shook his hand vigorously.

"By tomorrow night." Marek continued to hold her hand as he tilted his head, furthering the constraints of the deal.

"I can do better." Franceska nodded. "I'll have them here tonight."

"I appreciate your drive, but we will find out if that amounts to anything." Marek continued to look at her suspiciously, but Franceska knew he couldn't relinquish the chance.

"You won't be disappointed." Franceska smiled confidently.

"Tonight, it is then." Marek closed the door slowly as he continued to offer her a curious glare.

How in Heaven's name am I going to pull this off? Franceska began to panic as she turned toward her friends who she spotted talking with a young bartender. Stefania was giggling while she chatted away and Wiera was more than content to enjoy her drink.

"Stefania! Wiera!" Franceska called as she headed toward the exit.

"We have to go! We'll be back soon!" Stefania blew a kiss to the bartender as she and Wiera sped after Franceska.

"Are you a dancer now?" Wiera asked plainly as they all left the nightclub.

"You two wasted no time on the drinks I see." Franceska frowned in disbelief.

"I had a couple," Wiera replied casually.

"I told you that men love buying us drinks." Stefania bobbled her head smugly.

"I have an idea…" Franceska bit her lip in thought.

"I hope it involves more booze?" Stefania laughed.

"Actually…it does…" Franceska grinned. "But I'm going to need your help."

Chapter Thirteen:
The Plans of Women

"Even a fool, when he holdeth his peace, is counted wise."

Proverbs 17:28

"Excuse me," Franceska asked a passing waiter in the nightclub that was now brimming with soldiers dancing and drinking with young women. "Where is Marek?"

"Marek?" the waiter asked with confusion.

"Sorry, Mr. Rosenberg."

"I haven't seen him all afternoon, but I would suggest, for your sake, that you be absent when he arrives. He's going to kill you when he finds out what you've done." The waiter shook his head as he walked by briskly with a tray of drinks.

"What's the point of all this if Marek isn't even here to see it?" Franceska chewed her nails and bounced her leg as she watched the door anxiously.

"I'm having fun." Stefania shrugged as she shot back her drink before returning to the dance floor.

"That's a relief," Franceska added sarcastically.

"Strange to think, isn't it?" Wiera asked as she slurred her words while she leaned on Franceska.

"What is?" Franceska asked, half paying attention as her eyes were glued to the door.

"Not long ago, we were sitting right here, in this very spot, at this very club." Wiera rested her head on the table before adding, "Everything is spinning."

"You should drink some water," Franceska added.

"Where is my Adam?" Wiera asked mournfully. "Why didn't he come back for me?"

"He probably doesn't even know where we are." Franceska tried to console her friend.

"He's probably with some other girl already."

"I doubt that." Franceska scoffed.

"Why?" Wiera glanced up at her with a frown.

"Well…because…I mean…he couldn't possibly do better than you."

"You're kind." Wiera dropped her forehead to the edge of the table before adding, "I think I'm going to be sick."

"If you're going to be sick, do it outside." Franceska growled. "Last thing I need is for you to make a mess when Marek returns. I'm risking enough as it is."

"It paid off." Wiera lifted her head and pointed to the dance floor. "You got exactly what you wanted."

"Not on the terms Marek wanted, though." Franceska bit her cheek. "Do you think he'll be mad?"

"Yes."

"I appreciate your support." Franceska shuffled her jaw in exasperation.

"I'll always be here for you." Wiera raised her drink with her head still planted on the table. "You may not like it, but I'll always be here."

"Can I buy you lovely ladies a drink?" a soldier asked eagerly as he arrived at their table.

"Yes!" Wiera nearly shouted.

"She's had enough." Franceska waved for them to move along.

The door opened, and Franceska searched nervously for Marek, but it was only a couple of soldiers seeking a good night.

"Where is he?" Franceska muttered under her breath.

"He didn't mention anything to you?" Wiera asked.

"The bargain was for tonight." Franceska tried to release the tension in her shoulders, but the anxiety of how he might react sent her into a near panic.

"That could mean anytime."

"I realize that now." Franceska looked around the nightclub for a clock but couldn't see one anywhere.

Returning her attention to the dance floor, Franceska tried to distract herself by being amused with Stefania's antics. It was good for Franceska to see her friend in such a happy state and enjoying the night.

Then, and to Franceska's horror, the air raid siren began faintly. It was so faint, in fact, that Franceska thought she had imagined it. No one on the dance floor, or anyone in the club for that matter, seemed to notice. It wasn't until the doors were opened and more soldiers came in that Franceska knew recognized the attack was real.

"Everyone! May I have your attention please?" the singer asked loudly in the microphone as the musicians ceased playing. "We've just heard the air raid sirens. We're going to stop playing until the bombing raid is over."

The crowd groaned in annoyance, less so at the music stopping and more so at the fact that there was yet another bombing run. Most knew, however, that this area of the city had been almost entirely free from bombings, and the practice of taking cover was mostly routine.

"Please take shelter under tables until it is safe to come out."

"Lot of good this will do if a bomb lands right on our heads," Wiera spoke a little louder than Franceska appreciated as she helped her friend climb under the table.

While the music and dancing had stopped, and most people were now under tables, the nightclub was still a frenzy of lively chattering with soldiers flirting with women, drunken men laughing loudly at some off color joke, and the waiting staff taking a much-deserved break.

"Feels so strange that we're trying to get back to normal," Wiera began as she struggled to keep her eyes open.

"That it does." Franceska nodded as she grew reflective.

She knew how unusual this appeared or seemed, but she also understood that this was their new normal, their new way of living. Bombings happened daily, and often a few times during the day. Life had to go on regardless, and Franceska knew she needed this job so that she could secure a place for them to stay. She needed to get her mother out of the hospital and back into a normal living space.

"Not to shift focus away from your pressing concerns, but I have some good news to share." Wiera tried to contain her smile but failed.

"Oh?" Franceska looked at her curiously.

"Remember the other night when I sang in front of the crowd?" Wiera asked.

"I do…" Franceska held her conclusion in reserve.

"Well it turns out that the theatre manager was among the crowd. He was impressed with my voice and wants me to sing at the theatre!" Wiera beamed with pride.

"That's amazing!" Franceska grew excited for her friend.

Suddenly, the doors to the nightclub opened, and Marek, looking downcast with his gaze at his feet, walked straight toward his office, seemingly ignoring the club full of soldiers and women hiding under tables.

Franceska watched him eagerly, wondering if he would be impressed with how many people were in the club, but he seemed disinterested in anything, even the air raid.

Unlocking the door, Marek entered his office and closed the door behind him, leaving a thoroughly perplexed Franceska to wonder what could've caused him to be so distraught that he didn't even notice what was happening in the club.

"I should go talk to him." Franceska stood and brushed herself off.

"I wouldn't if I were you," one of the waiters nearby spoke up. "I've never seen him that angry before."

"Might be best to get it over with now then." Franceska drew a deep breath as she walked through the nightclub that was eager to resume dancing.

It was a surreal moment, she thought, as she walked past a table with a couple passionately kissing underneath, soldiers who were mocking the kissing couple, and a couple engaged in a heated argument. All the while she could hear bombs dropping in the distance. War had become the new normal, and they were adapting to this abnormality, as people often do.

Knocking on the office door, Franceska cleared her throat before adding, "It's me, Franceska."

No response.

"I held up my end of the bargain," Franceska pressed as she moved closer to the door.

Footsteps approached the door from the other side, and Franceska stood back. The door unlocked, and the footsteps retreated in the direction that they had come.

Opening the door, Franceska peeked her head inside the office to find Marek sitting behind a desk with an open bottle of vodka in front of him.

"Close the door," Marek spoke softly.

Slowly, and nervously, Franceska obeyed and closed the door.

"Sit." Marek nodded to a chair in front of the desk.

Holding her hands politely in front of her, Franceska inspected the office as she accepted the offer to sit.

It was a dark room without windows or much lighting at all apart from a dim lamp on the desk. Stacks of paper were scattered on a table in the corner or else on filing cabinets. The organization of the club was chaotic at best, Franceska thought, and she wondered how he managed to make The Melody Palace appear so well-ordered.

But what surprised Franceska the most in the office were the books. There were at least four bookshelves, about seven or eight feet tall, bursting with books of every variety and genre. She was shocked that the man sitting in front of her with the open, yet untouched bottle of vodka, was so well-read.

It seemed, to Franceska, that the genre he loved the most was poetry. Five books of poetry, with the corners of certain pages folded over, were scattered on his desk. They appeared to have been read multiple times as they were tattered and the corners of the books were creased.

Glancing at Marek, who was sitting back in his chair and staring at the wall, Franceska didn't quite know how to proceed. If he was already upset, she knew it was best not to prod him further.

The silence in the room grew more uncomfortable by the second for Franceska, and all she could hear was the muffled explosions of distant bombs, the chatter from outside leaking through the door, and Marek's heavy breathing.

"Why don't you have any clocks in the nightclub?" Franceska asked, feeling as though the words fell out of her mouth without much conscious effort.

"Clocks?" Marek frowned as he glanced over at her.

"I noticed there were none."

"This bothers you?" Marek raised an eyebrow.

"I wouldn't say it bothers me. I merely found it…interesting."

"I'll get you a clock then." Marek looked at the bottle of vodka.

"So…" Franceska swallowed.

"I heard what you did." Marek began rubbing his chin.

"And?" Franceska braced for his response.

Marek continued to stare at the bottle without offering another word.

"And?" Franceska pressed.

"Tell Piotr to come here." Marek pointed at the door.

"I don't know who—"

"Open the door and call him in here!" Marek barked.

Flushing red with embarrassment, Franceska opened the door and called out, "Piotr?"

"What?" a handful of men replied.

Of course it's the most popular name in all of Poland, Franceska rolled her eyes before continuing, "Mr. Rosenberg wants to see you."

Closing the door, Franceska returned to the chair in front of Marek's desk and crossed her arms as she glared at him.

"You're upset?" Marek asked with disbelief as he pointed to his chest. "With me?"

The door opened, and one of the waiters that Franceska had spotted earlier poked his head inside and asked, "You wanted to see me?"

"Come in." Marek pointed to the chair beside Franceska.

"Mr. Rosenberg, I didn't know she was going to—"

"It's alright." Marek waved for Piotr to hurry.

"She told us that you hired her and that you wanted to do something special tonight. I should've known that—"

"I know, I know." Marek drew a deep breath as he sat upright and folded his hands as he looked intently at Piotr.

"I should've known." Piotr remained nervous.

"How much did we lose?" Marek asked as he closed his eyes, and Franceska knew he was expecting a terrible result.

"Lose?" Piotr asked.

"Money, Piotr!" Marek lost his patience. "How much money did we lose?!"

"Well…uh…none."

"What?" Marek frowned in confusion. "How is that possible?"

"This is the best night we've had since the invasion began."

"You're telling me that this…" Marek glanced at Franceska as he bit his tongue and continued, "This creature and her little gang of friends went all over the city, telling the soldiers that their first two drinks were free at our club, and we *made* money?!"

"They're spending all their money on the women." Piotr shrugged. "Usually, a guy will buy a girl a drink or two, but now that their drinks are free, they're spending every penny on helping the women get drunk, hoping it will improve their chances."

With a dumfounded look of disbelief, Marek reached into his drawer, grabbed two shot glasses, and poured some vodka into each glass for Franceska and Piotr.

"To your health." Piotr clinked his glass with Franceska's.

"What about you?" Franceska asked as she gestured to his drink.

"I don't drink." Marek shook his head as he put the cap back on the bottle before shoving it into a drawer.

"To your health then." Franceska clinked her glass with Piotr's and they both drank.

"What about Mrs. Judtowa?" Piotr asked nervously.

"Who?" Franceska frowned.

"The owner of this club," Marek explained with a great deal of apprehension. "She will bite my head off for allowing you to pull this stunt."

"But we made money?" Franceska grew confused.

"It's *we* already is it?" Marek smirked before adding, "We did make some money, but this is a respectable club and not some vending machine where you can use a free voucher. The fact that I went rogue and allowed you to conjure up this event will not bode well for me."

"You did give me your blessing." Franceska tilted her head.

"Blessing?!" Marek nearly laughed. "I merely agreed to your wager that you could convince ten men and ten women to come to the club. Nothing more!"

"I admit that I took liberties." Franceska bit her lip.

"Liberties with my employment!" Marek tapped his chest with annoyance.

"Would you like me to speak with Mrs. Judtowa?"

"No!" Both Marek and Piotr shouted, startling Franceska.

"I will advise Mrs. Judtowa that this was my idea," Marek continued with a bit more restraint.

"You're going to take credit for my success?" Franceska narrowed her gaze.

"Credit?" Marek chuckled ironically. "The day that Mrs. Judtowa hands out praise will be the day that I grow wings. No, I'm sparing you from her wrath."

"And what do I get out of this?" Franceska grew annoyed.

"Are you able to start tomorrow?" Marek leaned back in his chair as he appeared to be on the fence about this arrangement.

"Start?"

"Dancing." Marek shrugged. "You held up your end. I'll hold up mine."

"I will need an advance on my pay," Franceska spoke commandingly as she stood.

"You're already making demands?" Marek threw his hands out in shock. "You're fortunate that I'm even offering you a position with the liberties you've taken."

"My liberties are already making this club money." Franceska leaned on the back of her chair as she glared at Marek. "I expect my advance tomorrow."

Chapter Fourteen: Invasion

"If you're going through hell, keep going."

Winston Churchill

"Remember, she hasn't seen you in a while," Franceska warned her father when she brought him to the hospital where her mother was recovering. "She's also hopefully taking the pain meds, so she may be a little loopy."

"I'm nervous." Mr. Mann straightened out his shirt.

"I'm not sure why you had to bring the rifle with you." Franceska rolled her eyes at her father.

"She won't believe I'm in the Civil Guard if I don't have proof," Mr. Mann defended.

"Sir, you can't bring a weapon into the hospital," an exhausted nurse from behind a desk stated as she walked over to him with her hand out.

"I'm part of the Civil Guard," Mr. Mann replied proudly.

"You can guard the President of Warsaw for all I care," the nurse retorted as she continued to hold her hand out to Mr. Mann. "You're not bringing a rifle into a hospital with patients who are suffering from bullet wounds."

"Fair point." Mr. Mann grudgingly handed over his rifle to the nurse as she turned and placed it behind the desk.

"I'll support anything you tell mother about your new duties." Franceska patted her father's shoulder in reassurance.

"You think she'll believe you?" Mr. Mann scoffed.

"I'm not sure what she'll believe while she's on her pain meds." Franceska glanced at her father with worry.

"How do I look?" Mr. Mann asked nervously as they climbed the stairs to the second floor.

"You look dashing." Franceska smiled at him, although a part of her wished for a measure of revenge. She recalled the countless times she would ask her father for an opinion on her appearance, and he would simply get embarrassed and mumble something to dismiss the subject.

"I'm sure your mother will find something to complain about." Mr. Mann continued to inspect himself.

"One of the few guarantees in life is that mother will find some issue to complain about. I imagine, in many years, when she arrives in Heaven, she'll find it too peaceful."

"Or too nice." Mr. Mann grinned.

"Too many angels and not enough people."

"The food was better on Earth."

"She'll miss her back pain."

"She'll complain about the lack of doctors."

"That mother of mine." Franceska chuckled.

Mr. Mann offered a nervous chuckle of his own as they arrived at the second floor and Franceska led him to the room where she last met her mother.

Franceska's heart broke when she spotted her mother, still seemingly in lots of pain, lying on her side and rubbing her back with her hand.

"Where have you been?!" Mrs. Mann barked at her husband when she spotted him entering the room.

"Searching all of Warsaw for you," Mr. Mann spoke softly as he sat on a chair beside his wife's bed.

"All of Warsaw knows I'm here," Mrs. Mann retorted.

"How are you feeling?" Mr. Mann examined his wife with concern.

"How do you think I'm feeling?!" Mrs. Mann barked but then turned her attention to Franceska while demanding, "Why are you wearing the same dress as last time? Did you lose your vanity? At least you did your hair this time and don't smell nearly as bad."

"Are you taking your medication?" Franceska asked with concern as her mother still seemed to be in intolerable discomfort.

"She's still refusing," a nurse, who walked into the room behind Franceska, added as she arrived with medication and a cup of water.

"I don't trust them," Mrs. Mann whispered to Mr. Mann.

"They're trying to help you," Mr. Mann replied.

"They're in league with the Germans." Mrs. Mann looked out the corner of her eye at the nurse.

"What a ridiculous thing to say," Mr. Mann whispered, and Franceska noticed he was embarrassed by his wife's accusation of the nurse.

"People are dying here, daily," Mrs. Mann continued in a hushed tone. "They're not inspecting anyone. They're giving them pills and saying that's all they can do."

"That is all they can do." Franceska knelt in front of her mother. "I talked to the doctor last time I was here. He mentioned that with the invasion the equipment is in constant use."

"Last time you were here was ages ago."

"It was two days ago." Franceska tilted her head.

"You didn't bother to come see me yesterday. Am I some old woman that you can put into a facility when you're no longer interested in dealing with? And you can't just visit me when you're feeling guilty about all you've put me through."

"Nothing about this visit eases our guilt," Mr. Mann muttered under his breath.

"I was looking for employment so that we can find an apartment for us," Franceska pressed, but immediately regretted telling her mother, realizing that she was not aware their house had been destroyed.

"An apartment?" Mrs. Mann frowned. "Why would we need an apartment?"

Mr. Mann and Franceska glanced at each other, both unsure of how to inform Mrs. Mann about the tragedy.

"Why do we need an apartment?!" Mrs. Mann grew upset as she glared at her husband. "Did you lose it gambling?!"

"Gambling?!" Mr. Mann shot his head back in surprise. "I've never gambled a day in my life!"

"I leave you in charge for one moment, and you lose —"

"The house was destroyed in a bombing run," Franceska blurted, and Mrs. Mann's countenance morphed from rage into shock.

"I told you we bought that house in a poor location." Mrs. Mann returned to glaring at her husband. "I liked the houses on the east side of Warsaw, but you decided on the west. Now look where we're at. Homeless, locked in an insane asylum, and surrounded by incompetence. Did you save anything from the property?"

"The house was entirely destroyed. The only thing that withstood the bomb was Franceska's plaque from Brussels."

"That is important." Mrs. Mann nodded genuinely, which surprised Franceska.

"You found a job then?" Mr. Mann asked his daughter softly.

"I did, and I'm going to the office today to collect an advance."

"Where?" Mrs. Mann asked.

"Accounting."

Mr. and Mrs. Mann looked at each other quickly before erupting into laughter, and Franceska glared at them in disgust for their mockery.

"Which firm?" Mrs. Mann asked. "I'll tell everyone to avoid it."

"Doesn't matter," Franceska mumbled in her embarrassment.

"Why didn't you seek employment?" Mrs. Mann shot a dagger at her husband. "Why is our daughter working while you're sitting around? Where are you living then if the house is destroyed?"

"We found a field." Mr. Mann shook his head in disbelief at his own statement. "Some churches placed beds and such in a field. We were fortunate enough to secure a spot for us to sleep."

"And the reason he's not working is because he joined the Civil Guard." Franceska beamed with pride at her father.

"What's that? Some social club?" Mrs. Mann remained unimpressed. "You couldn't come see your wife because you have social commitments?"

"It's the civilian police outfit. They're going to maintain the security of Warsaw and, if it comes to it, assist with thwarting the invading Germans."

Mrs. Mann burst into a cackle and wiped the tears from her eyes as she stated, "I needed a good laugh."

"I'm not sure why that's so amusing." Mr. Mann frowned in annoyance mixed with embarrassment.

"You? Fighting? Policing?" Mrs. Mann continued to laugh hysterically until, suddenly, her face contorted with pain.

"Mother, you need to take your medication," Franceska pressed. "It's ridiculous to allow yourself to be in so much discomfort."

"Get me out of here, and I'll take all the medication you want. But I'm not taking anything under their watch." Mrs. Mann looked around the room suspiciously.

"I'll collect the money today and find an apartment." Franceska patted her mother's hand. "But only if you take the medication. It's too difficult for me knowing that you're in pain."

"I'll take them." Mrs. Mann nodded reluctantly.

"Nope. I want to see you take them." Franceska stood and walked to the bedside table where the nurse had left the medication and water.

"I'm not a child," Mrs. Mann growled.

"Good, then I won't have to force you to take this." Franceska held the two cups in her hand as she spoke to her father, "Are you able to help her sit upright so she can take these?"

"Do you get a uniform in the Civil Guard?" Mrs. Mann asked with a smirk as her husband slowly, and with great pain to Mrs. Mann, sat her upright.

"Unfortunately, no."

"Unfortunate, indeed." Mrs. Mann winked at her husband before adding, "I do like a man in uniform."

"Take these, please." Franceska held medication out to her mother.

"You don't believe I can take these medications on my own?" Mrs. Mann asked.

"I asked you to take them a couple of days ago, and yet here we are."

"How dare you speak to your own mother that way!" Mrs. Mann yelled at Franceska. "I didn't raise you to be so disrespectful."

"Take them." Franceska ignored her mother's deflecting tactics as she nodded to the medication.

Without further debate, Mrs. Mann swallowed the pills quickly before crumpling up the paper cup and tossing it onto the floor.

"There's no need to be rude." Franceska bent down to pick up the cup.

"On the contrary, there's every need." Mrs. Mann grew a wry grin. "It amuses me, and being in good spirits helps heal the body, or so I'm told."

"At least don't be rude to the people who are trying to help you." Franceska tossed the cup into a wastebasket.

Mrs. Mann grew thoughtful for a moment before asking her husband sincerely, "Everything really is gone?"

Mr. Mann nodded as he shot his gaze down at his feet as if it were his fault.

"Our house was one of the first to be hit," Franceska added.

"All our savings?" Mrs. Mann continued in her disbelief.

"Every penny was wiped out." Mr. Mann waved his hand to mimic something disappearing into thin air.

"How is that possible?" Mrs. Mann asked quietly, and Franceska allowed her mother a moment for the reality to sink in.

"All our clothes, photographs, personal items, gone." Mr. Mann returned his gaze to his feet.

"But all three of us are still here," Franceska added. "And that is something many others can't boast of."

"I think I'd rather have my favorite dress than your father." Mrs. Mann winked at her husband, who responded with a chuckle at her jest.

"Your favorite dress would likely be more competent at fighting off the Germans than I am," Mr. Mann added with a smirk.

"Oh, turn that up!" Mrs. Mann pointed frantically at the radio in the middle of the room. "I love his morning addresses. He has such a nice voice."

"How quickly do those pain meds work?" Mr. Mann whispered to Franceska.

Walking over to the radio, Franceska turned up the volume and stood back as she listened to the newly-appointed President of Warsaw's daily address.

"I wanted Warsaw to be great," Stefan began in his quiet and warm voice. "I was convinced that it would be. But it became great sooner than I thought. Not in fifty years, not in one hundred, but today, as I speak to you. I see it through the window in all its size and glory, surrounded by clouds of smoke, red from the fires, magnificent, indescribable: Warsaw fighting! This morning I have learned the terrible news that many suburbs have been taken by the Germans. Warsaw now stands alone. We must fight to protect this city, this sacred land, and our people!"

Franceska felt the hair on her arms standing on edge as her heart burst with pride for her city and people. This patriotic spirit was contagious, and she knew that their cause was righteous.

"I was ordered to leave the city," President Starzyński continued. "But I cannot leave the people of Warsaw. I will be with you, and I will stay with you. We must remain calm. Merchants, open up your shops. Cafés, restaurants, vendors, sell your wares. We must return to a society under control. We cannot permit the Germans to gain any moral victories. We cannot control what areas they bomb, or who they choose to target, but we can choose how we respond. We will give them no victory over our minds, over our hearts."

Suddenly, a nurse burst into the room and announced loudly and in a panic, "The Germans are trying to break into the city. Everyone who is not staff or a patient must evacuate immediately. The hospital is about to be overrun with the injured."

"I'll collect my rifle." Mr. Mann stood as quickly as his old age would allow him.

"We'll come back for you." Franceska kissed her mother's forehead. "Tomorrow. I promise."

"Don't leave me," Mrs. Mann spoke with a sorrow Franceska had never heard from her mother.

"Everyone out! Now!" the nurse shouted as she went room by room, ordering anyone who wasn't vital to leave the hospital.

"We don't have a choice." Franceska looked back at her mother with heartbreak, and yet, somehow, she knew that her mother would blame Franceska for abandoning her.

"Out! Out! Out!" The nurse waved for them to hurry.

"They better not have misplaced my rifle," Mr. Mann spoke softly.

Returning to the foyer, Mr. Mann nearly ran toward his rifle when he spotted it behind the desk, and slung it around his shoulder before the two of them exited the hospital.

Yet as soon as they left the hospital, Franceska and Mr. Mann were immediately engulfed in a flurry of pamphlets.

Glancing up at the sky, Franceska noticed that a German plane was pouring thousands of these pamphlets over the city.

Stooping down to pick one up, Franceska discovered that they were propaganda leaflets.

"You have no more…no more…" Mr. Mann squinted as he tried to read the pamphlet. "I can't read that last word."

"They're riddled with spelling mistakes." Franceska also grew confused. "Surely they could've found someone who was fluent in Polish?"

"Ah! Airforce, that's what they're trying to say." Mr. Mann finally deciphered the wording. "You have no more Airforce. Your leaders have abandoned you. Surrender."

"Compelling argument…" Franceska glanced at her father. "If it wasn't for the spelling mistake, I think I'd surrender."

"They're right about our Airforce." Mr. Mann studied the sky. "I haven't seen one of our fighters in some time."

"There's smoke over there!" Franceska pointed to the horizon.

In the distance, machine gun fire and explosions could be heard. Franceska's legs felt unsteady as she listened to the horrifying noise, signifying the approaching enemy.

"Let's get a better vantage point." Mr. Mann tapped Franceska's elbow as he pointed to a bridge where a where a cluster of people had gathered, looking in the direction of the smoke.

Joining the others on the small bridge, which was slightly elevated and provided a great view of the city, Franceska spotted the battle scene on the outskirts of Warsaw. It was dreadful to watch, but she couldn't pry her eyes away.

Dozens of enemy tanks, thousands of infantry, and many large pieces of artillery, flanked the city. It was a scene of utter chaos. Explosions tore up the fields outside the city and the outskirts where the defenders were valiantly holding their positions.

"The Germans are losing so many tanks!" Franceska tugged on her father's arm, hoping that this would be good news for them.

"Yet they're still advancing." Mr. Mann shook his head in disappointment. "The enemy is well trained. They have high morale. They won't break easy."

Confirming Mr. Mann's observation, Franceska watched as a couple of German takes broke through the lines and entered the city. She feared the worst and held her breath, watching them proceed into the city, seemingly unimpeded.

Then, suddenly, the tanks that had entered the city burst into flames. Franceska let out a loud cheer, and noticed that more people had joined the crowded bridge to inspect the scene. A few people nearby began clapping as well when they realized that the Germans were suffering major losses to their tanks.

Franceska recalled watching the defenders and civilians painting the roads with turpentine, and knew that their ingenuity had caused them a great measure of success. Almost every tank that had entered the city had fallen into the trap of the turpentine, which was now blazing and burning anyone or anything who dared to trespass.

After what felt like hours, the Germans broke off their attack and retreated to their lines.

Loud cheers, applause, and shouts of joy came from those on the bridge. With a chuckle of relief, Franceska felt a pinch of hope, but this faded quickly when she noticed that her father was not sharing in the revelry.

"What's wrong? Are you not happy with the victory?" Franceska asked.

"That was just a taste." Mr. Mann looked back at Franceska warily. "The Germans will try again, and soon. Our defenses took heavy losses. If the Germans cannot take the city by force, they'll resort to starving us out. Our supplies are low, meaning it will be a short siege. I fear that the horrors of this war are only in their infancy, and we're about to see a terror which has never been unleashed upon the earth."

Chapter Fifteen:
Lola

"Your task will not be an easy one. Your enemy is well-trained, well-equipped and battle-hardened. He will fight savagely."

General Dwight Eisenhower

"What do you think?" Franceska asked when her and her father arrived at the first-floor rental apartment.

"It's not me you have to convince," Mr. Mann replied quietly.

"Well, mother isn't here to choose, and we don't have much in the way of options, either." Franceska threw her hands onto her hips as she looked around the room.

It was a dimly lit, one-bedroom apartment with little in the way of attraction. The wooden floors were old with obvious signs of wear and tear from the previous inhabitants, the kitchen was equipped with a single, rusted stove, and the bedroom was incredibly small.

"You have enough to cover the rent?" Mr. Mann glanced curiously at his daughter.

"And some furniture." Franceska nodded. "We'll need a good bed for mother."

"And a good chair."

"And a decent couch for me to sleep on while I save up for a bed of my own."

"You can't sleep on a couch." Mr. Man offered his daughter a sympathetic gaze.

"I'm currently sleeping on the ground in a field." Franceska raised a brow. "A couch is a considerable upgrade. Not to mention that I'm anxious to bathe properly and with some privacy."

"I'm not sure how we'll collect your mother." Mr. Mann rubbed the back of his neck with worry. "It bothers me that they haven't been able to assess her properly, but I also don't want her to wait in the hospital for days, or even weeks, until the equipment becomes available."

"I think the appropriate thing to do is bring her to our new home."

"I still have trouble believing it," Mr. Mann spoke softly as he scratched his chin while peeking out the small window in the living room.

"Believing what?" Franceska watched him closely.

"Our house, everything we owned, gone in an instant. A single bomb obliterated our entire lives. All trace of our existent was eradicated in a flash." Mr. Mann continued to look out the window, but Franceska was certain that he was growing emotional.

"I should make my way to work," Franceska began after a moment. "Will you visit mother?"

"I'll go and see her now." Mr. Mann nodded. "When will you be back?"

"Not until quite late." Franceska ran her tongue along her teeth as she continued the fabrication, "I want to make a good impression. I'll work as long as I can before hopefully getting a chance to visit with Stefania and Wiera."

"They're good girls those two." Mr. Mann drew a deep breath. "Annoying, but honest and considerate."

"Here's some money to buy furniture." Franceska handed a few bills to her father who seemed embarrassed to be taking them from his daughter. "I included some extra to pay for transportation."

"It feels wrong taking this from you." Mr. Mann held the money sheepishly down by his side. "I should be the one providing for you, not the other way around."

"You provided for me for years." Franceska offered her father a kiss on the cheek. "I'm happy to repay it."

"Speaking of repayment, I'll pay every last penny back." Mr. Mann folded the bills before placing them in his pocket, and Franceska knew he was still mortified by the arrangement, but there was also no other choice.

"I'd prefer that you didn't. Also, be careful out there. Many unsavory characters are still taking advantage of the situation."

"I'm glad I have my rifle with me. I've heard the reports of thieves running around unchecked. Make sure you stay safe. Would you like me to walk with you to work? I could be your personal escort?"

"That's kind, but I'll be alright." Franceska smiled politely, understanding that her father would disown her if he knew her real place of employment was the nightclub.

"If you insist." Mr. Mann began walking toward the door. "I'll buy some furniture and see where the nearest bread line is."

"I'm glad you approve of the place." Franceska took the key out of her pocket and locked the door behind them.

"I'm not sure approve is the word I'd use," Mr. Mann muttered. "But we are on the end of the city that I doubt will see much conflict, so that is encouraging, and it is a roof over our head which will be a welcome change."

"Tell mother I say hello."

"If she stops berating me, I'll make sure to include it." Mr. Mann left the building and walked in the direction of the hospital and Franceska watched him for a minute with a slight smile.

Walking toward the nightclub, Franceska could hear machine gun fire and explosions in the distance, and she knew the Germans were making another attempt to enter the city. It felt odd, she thought, to be walking to work while her city was being invaded.

The abnormal had become normal, the unusual had become mundane. Sorrow, tragedy, destruction, and death had all become so ordinary and part of everyday life, that Franceska found her heart becoming hard.

And as she walked, Franceska experienced a phenomenon that had become an all too familiar aspect of the invasion. The street she was currently walking down was untouched by bombs, and with the tall apartments and other commercial buildings, it would almost appear as if there was no invasion at all. But when she turned the corner, Franceska came face to face with rubble and devastation.

Nearly every house and building on the street she turned onto had been entirely leveled. Only a few frames of buildings were left standing, and the damage was evidently recent with some of the rubble still smoldering.

Civilian and military crews were working feverishly to remove bricks and wood to be employed in either creating shelters or bolstering the defenses.

But then something caught Franceska's eye, and she stopped in her tracks.

On one pile of rubble sat a young boy, about ten years old, and his face and hands were encrusted in soot and dust. A tear track ran down his face, but he appeared sullen and grim. He simply sat on the pile of rubble staring at a twisted and broken toy plane at his feet. Behind him was a bent and burnt bed frame, which was all that survived the bombing.

"Do you need any help?" Franceska asked softly as she approached him. She didn't know how she could assist, but knew she couldn't possibly leave him alone.

Without responding, the boy looked back at her with startling blue eyes. The black soot coating his face accentuated the bright and stunning color of his eyes, but there was no life behind them, and Franceska felt a lump in her throat as she studied him.

She wondered about his family, and where they were or if he was the only survivor. She felt such a pity for the young boy having become so bitter at life at such a tender age.

"Ezekiel?" a voice behind Franceska asked, and she turned to find that Father Kolbe was approaching them.

"You know this boy, Father?" Franceska asked hopefully.

"I know his parents," Father Kolbe replied solemnly as he surveyed the ruins.

The boy looked coldly over at the priest before he returned his attention to the toy plane.

"Are your parents dead?" Father Kolbe asked bluntly, and Franceska was taken aback at his lack of tact.

The boy nodded.

"And your sister?"

The boy nodded again.

"Come with me." Father Kolbe held out his hand to the boy.

The boy didn't budge.

"Your parents and sister are dead," Father Kolbe continued, again with such bluntness that stunned Franceska, and she wondered why the priest was being so cruel.

"Do you really feel it's necessary to remind him of his sorrows?" Franceska frowned at the priest.

"He hasn't forgotten." Father Kolbe offered a stern stare at Franceska before adding, "You believe I'm being rude?"

"Can you help him?" Franceska asked as she looked back at the boy.

"I can give him food and shelter, but only God can heal his soul." Father Kolbe took another step toward Ezekiel and took his hand.

Ezekiel withdrew and turned away from the priest.

"My child, we cannot dwell."

"He needs a moment to reflect," Franceska pressed.

"He's not reflecting," Father Kolbe replied as he added softly, "I believe he's blaming himself."

Ezekiel shot the priest a surprised glance.

"How could you have possibly known that?" Franceska frowned.

"Because, unfortunately, there are way too many young boys and girls under my care from this invasion. In some way or another, most children, especially of his tender age, somehow feel that this is a result of something bad they did. They're convinced, and maybe due to some incorrect teachings by the church, that God punishes evil and rewards good. They see this as a punishment from God."

Franceska's heart shattered as she studied Ezekiel in a new light.

"My son," Father Kolbe began as he knelt. "You did nothing wrong."

At this, the boy erupted into tears and buried his face in the priest's shoulder.

"It's alright." Father Kolbe patted Ezekiel's back. "This happened because other men, wicked men, did something bad. Do you understand?"

Ezekiel sniffled loudly as he tried to regain his composure.

"I have a chocolate for you." Father Kolbe dug into his satchel and retrieved the sweet for Ezekiel.

"What brought you into the city?" Franceska asked when Ezekiel calmed a little and ate his chocolate in silence.

"This morning, I didn't know why I was coming into the city, but now I do." Father Kolbe nodded to Ezekiel.

"I admire your faith." Franceska studied the priest closely.

"And yet all I have are doubts." Father Kolbe looked back at her with a heavy gaze.

"How many children are under your care now?" Franceska asked, wondering if she truly wanted to hear his reply.

"There's a few boys and girls at the monastery, but it's not a great place for them. We're using it as a hospital as well, and the children are constantly exposed to trauma. There's an orphanage not far from here. I'll see if they can take Ezekiel, but they are overrun and have little money to accommodate the children they already care for. I have no money of my own, but I hope they'll take him on account of our friendship."

"I have some money," Franceska said, but every word felt as heavy as lead, knowing that she was taking food out of her own mouth.

"Are you sure?" Father Kolbe looked at her curiously.

"Yes," Franceska replied feebly as she dug into her pocket to retrieve the bills, but her hand seemed to grow heavy as she handed the money to Father Kolbe.

"This will help considerably." Father Kolbe nodded excitedly as he placed the money into his satchel. "They will be able to take him and pay for some food for the others as well. Before the invasion, the nuns would take every child without question, but with so many children being orphaned lately, they cannot accept anyone without payment, otherwise they can't feed them."

"I'm glad I was able to help." Franceska forced a smile as all she could think about was her own hunger.

"This wasn't a chance meeting." Father Kolbe shook his head as he looked intently at Franceska.

"I struggle to follow that logic." Franceska looked back at the priest regretfully. "If God played by those rules, his parents would still be alive."

"Maybe." Father Kolbe tilted his head before continuing, "But maybe someone was hurting, and maybe you, today, were put into a position to help that person."

"I think you're looking for meaning where there is none."

"It will be meaningful to him." Father Kolbe patted Ezekiel's shoulder. "He's all that matters right now. Meaning or no meaning, I would help him all the same, but I take courage in thinking that, despite the horror, there is still some good in this world."

Franceska didn't reply as Father Kolbe and Ezekiel began walking away. She didn't understand the priest's view of the world, and thought, perhaps, that she never would. Although, despite her theological differences with Father Kolbe, Franceska was jealous of his convictions. He lived a more meaningful existence, and she couldn't deny that if more people were like him, it would be a much better world.

I should make my way to the club, Franceska thought as she began to walk toward The Melody Palace. It was then, though, that she realized she could still hear the gunfire and explosions and that she had drowned them out. Again, the realization that this hell was now becoming normal was a terrifying reality for her.

Weighed down with worry for her mother, and wondering if her father would buy appropriate furniture, Franceska made her way to the club where she noticed there was already a lineup of patrons. She was, however, happy to see there were no soldiers today, and she hoped they were doing their duty to defend the city.

Skipping the line, Franceska was ushered inside by the bouncer, and found that the scene in the club was utter chaos.

Waiters were hurriedly setting tables and arranging the dance floor, the musicians and singer were rehearsing, and the bartender was frantically stocking the bar.

"Piotr, what's going on?" Franceska asked as the young waiter walked by her quickly with a case of vodka.

"Mr. Rosenberg is in a craze! He's waiting for you in the office."

He is? Franceska grew worried as she began to walk toward his office, wondering what could have possibly sent him into a frenzy.

Yet as she walked toward the office, Franceska did a double take seeing a clock recently installed behind the bar.

Hmm, Franceska pondered as she recalled complaining to Marek previously about the odd absence of clocks in the nightclub.

Proceeding with little caution, Franceska knocked on Marek's office door before entering.

"What the hell?!" Marek shouted as he pulled up his trousers while standing in the middle of the office

"Why are you—"

"Usually, when one knocks, one waits for a reply before opening the door!" Marek barked at her, and she spotted a thin mattress behind his desk.

"Are you sleeping here?" Franceska frowned.

"And? What of it?" Marek growled as he stood the mattress on its side and slid it behind a wall of filing cabinets.

"I should've waited." Franceska shook her head, trying to rid herself of the embarrassment.

"It's fine!" Marek sat behind his desk and lit a cigarette before asking grumpily. "What do you want?!"

"I wanted to discuss my schedule and some of the particulars."

"What sort of particulars?"

"When will I be fitted for my dance costume? What sort of—"

"Fitted?" Marek smirked.

"I'm assuming the tailor will make an outfit to accommodate my measurements."

"Tailor?" Marek burst into a laugh before walking over to the door, throwing it open and yelling, "Hey, Piotr?"

"What?" Piotr shouted back, and Franceska sat in the chair before Marek's desk with a clenched jaw as she awaited the inevitable mockery.

"Miss…uh…" Marek paused and turned to Franceska and asked, "What is your last name again?"

"Mann," Franceska replied as she tried to hide her displeasure, continually reminding herself of how dire she needed the employment.

"Miss Mann here was asking when we're going to tailor her dance outfit?!" Marek laughed loudly, and Franceska could hear Piotr snickering in response.

"Was that necessary?" Franceska asked as Marek closed the door and returned to sitting behind his desk.

"In these trying times, sweetheart, we need all the brightness we can obtain." Marek puffed his cigarette as he stared at the ceiling and continued to chuckle.

"I see there's a lineup of patrons outside." Franceska tried to shift the subject.

"Yeah, and, if our men can successfully defend this city again, they will be running to our club for their first free drink." Marek offered Franceska a quick glance.

"The first two-drink deal was only for that one night." Franceska frowned.

"Did you tell them that?" Marek tilted his head.

"I…" Franceska clicked her tongue in thought as her cheeks flushed crimson.

"I can answer that for you: you didn't." Marek put out his cigarette in the ash tray. "But I really should be thanking you. Business has never been better."

"Until the Germans take over, that is."

"*If* they take over." Marek shot a glance at Franceska. "Are you not a patriot?"

"I love Poland more than anyone I know," Franceska defended. "But I'm also a realist. We do not have the manpower or equipment. If France and England can't help us, then we are facing an enemy we can't defeat."

"Well, if you're right, then we will pivot and offer the first drink to our noble conquerors." Marek mockingly raised an imaginary glass in the air.

"You'd serve the Germans who conquered you?" Franceska watched him closely, wondering if he could be trusted.

"I serve whoever will pay me." Marek shrugged. "German money, Polish money — doesn't matter. Money is money."

"I'm not sure if I respect that opinion." Franceska narrowed her gaze.

"Then you don't need to work here." Marek sat upright as he retrieved another cigarette. "But tell me one thing, *if* the Germans break through our defenses before the English or French come to our aid, will you still need money?"

"Yes," Franceska replied reluctantly.

"You'll still need to eat, pay for rent, buy pretty dresses, hire a tailor, or whatever it is that you do with your money." Marek took a puff of his cigarette as he continued, "Piotr will still need employment as well. Should I kick you, and him, and all the rest of the staff, to the curb in the name of patriotism? Do you think the Germans would allow this club to exist if I don't serve them?"

"I get your point." Franceska stood and snatched the cigarette out of Marek's hand.

"Hey!" Marek looked at her indignantly.

"You've mocked me relentlessly since I helped to turn this establishment around." Franceska took a puff of the cigarette. "I would think that you'd be thanking me with much greater enthusiasm."

Marek studied her for a moment with a slight look of contrition before asking, "Did you see the clock?"

"I did." Franceska handed the cigarette back to Marek.

"You're welcome." Marek nodded.

"I'll make my way to the dressing room. I assume you've advised the dancers and musicians as to my involvement? I do hope they can accommodate my dance style."

"Miss Mann, you've come down a fair way in the world," Marek began as he stood and looked at her with a measure of compassion. "You're not a prima ballerina anymore. Those days are behind us, at least for now. Tonight, you're a dancer on stage at a night club."

Feeling severely humbled, Franceska shuffled her jaw before offering Marek a forced nod of appreciation and left the office.

"Backstage you'll find the dressing rooms," Marek called behind her. "Third door on the left is where the dancers change."

"Third door on the left," Franceska repeated as she walked past the stage where the musicians were tuning their instruments, and the singer hummed a song, following notes on the music sheet.

Opening the door beside the stage, Franceska entered a long hallway with many rooms. One room was labeled with a name, which Franceska assumed was the singer that serenaded the club each night, and others were labeled with more generic terms like *Musician* or *Staff*.

Arriving at the third door on the left, Franceska read the sign on the door which read *Dancers*.

Opening the door slowly, Franceska peeked her head inside to find two other women in varying stages of undress. One was almost entirely nude with only tights and smoking a cigarette while applying makeup in the large well-lit mirror. The other woman was still in pedestrian clothing but about to shed her layers and don her costume.

"Close the door before Piotr sneaks a peek," the woman with the cigarette spoke to Franceska as she looked at her in the mirror.

"He likes to pretend that he walks into the wrong room by mistake," the other woman added.

"We've asked Mr. Rosenberg for locks on the doors, but he keeps forgetting." The woman with the cigarette rolled her eyes. "Or so he says."

"What can we do for you?" the other woman asked as she removed her shoes.

"I'm the new dancer." Franceska looked between them nervously.

"New dancer?" the woman puffed her cigarette as she glanced at the other woman with confusion.

They were kind enough women, Franceska assessed, but they were a little rougher around the edges than she was accustomed to, and Franceska felt like she had stepped into a different world.

The woman with the cigarette was, Franceska thought, much prettier than herself. She had bright blonde hair with stunning blue eyes and a figure that anyone would kill for. The other woman, while still tremendously pretty, seemed to have a permanent scowl, which severely impacted her appearance, and Franceska couldn't help but be reminded of her mother.

"Marek didn't inform you?" Franceska asked rhetorically.

"Marek?" the woman with the cigarette glanced at the other dancer. "You're on a first name basis already? You work quickly!"

"Sorry, Mr. Rosenberg." Franceska grew embarrassed for the slip.

"Wait, are you the same girl who organized the free drink night?"

"That would be me." Franceska looked at them sheepishly.

"Now I get it." The woman with the cigarette smirked.

"Get what?" Franceska frowned.

"Why he fell on his sword for you."

"What do you mean?" Franceska frowned.

"With the owner, Mrs. Judtowa." The woman took a puff. "She yelled at him for ten straight minutes in his office. He took the fall for your little stunt."

"Took the fall?" Franceska tilted her head. "I think he should rather be thanking me profusely. I turned the club around in one night!"

"You're not one for subtlety, are you?" the woman with the cigarette asked as she narrowed her gaze.

"It's not your fault Mr. Rosenberg didn't tell us about you," the other dancer spoke to Franceska from the mirror. "I think he's quite scared of us. He only talks to us when he needs to, and even then, he usually avoids it."

"Well, I'm Franceska." She offered a polite smile.

"I'm Angelica," the woman with the cigarette pointed to herself before pointing to the other woman and adding, "That's Celina."

"Nice to meet you both." Franceska drew a deep breath and asked, "Is there an outfit for me?"

"Lena likes us to match her outfit."

"Lena?" Franceska grew confused.

"The singer." Angelica nodded toward the stage. "She's as rude as anyone can be. Don't talk to her unless you enjoy having your head bitten off."

"Problem is, there are only two good outfits left for tonight, and the spare one is, well…" Celina gestured to a clothes rack where some outfits were hung up.

The silver outfit on the rack, which matched the outfits the other two were changing into, was stained, had a tear near the left shoulder, and was fading in color.

"Maybe I can use the outfit once you change out of—"

"Sorry, sweety," Angelica stamped out her cigarette in an ash tray. "Mr. Rosenberg pays us for how long we dance. We don't take breaks or stop until the night is over."

"He didn't tell you about the pay, either?" Celina squinted at Franceska.

"He seems to be tight lipped about a good number of details." Franceska ran her tongue along her teeth as she found herself regretting her decisions.

This is for Mother, this is for Mother, this is for Mother, Franceska reminded herself.

"You didn't bring makeup either, did you?" Celina asked as she returned to inspecting herself in the mirror.

Franceska shook her head. She didn't want them to think less of her for having no possessions. It was foolish, she knew, seeing as most of the city was being bombed in an invasion, but still, she wanted to make a good impression with these women.

"You can use mine tonight. Make sure you bring your own set tomorrow."

"Thank you." Franceska swallowed as she walked over to an open mirror with a chair, pulled it out, and sat in front of it with a heavy heart.

Then, slowly, Franceska returned to the clothes rack, and reluctantly removed her outfit from the hanger. How she missed her form fitting tights and proper ballet costume. How she missed performing for 'refined crowds' as art instead of some object of entertainment.

Sheepishly, Franceska began removing her dress when the door behind her popped open and she spotted Piotr's head peek inside.

"You're on in five minutes," Piotr announced.

"Get out of here!" Celina grabbed a shoe beside her and threw it in his direction but Piotr quickly closed the door.

Unsatisfied with a mere chasing away, Celina ran over to the door, threw it open, and shouted into the hallway, "Next time you open the door without knocking, it'll be the last time you eat without a straw!"

"If he ever gives you trouble, let us know," Angelica spoke kindly to Franceska.

"I think I can handle boys like him, but thank you."

"He's a little pervert," Celina fumed as she returned to her mirror and angrily applied the last bit of makeup.

"Are you married?" Angelica asked as she slipped into her outfit.

"No." Franceska shook her head.

"Really?" Celina frowned as she examined Franceska. "What's wrong with you?"

"Did your husband die?" Angelica asked bluntly.

"Angelica!" Celina looked at her dancing partner with annoyance.

"What?!" Angelica threw her hands out in defense. "It's a genuine question. We're under siege with bombs killing lots of people."

"No, I've never been married, and, quite frankly, I'm not sure I ever will." Franceska grudgingly put on her outfit.

"You want to dance forever?" Angelica raised an eyebrow.

"Yes, actually." Franceska smiled brightly. "I was a prima ballerina. I came in fourth place in Brussels."

"In Brussels? What's in Brussels?" Celina looked warily at Franceska.

"It's the world dance competition!" Angelica smacked Celina's arm. "I told you that I competed there!"

"And now we're both here," Franceska quipped.

Neither Angelica nor Celina replied, but both glanced at each other in such a manner that Franceska had already guessed their thoughts and that she had offended them severely.

"Don't be late," Celina warned as she and Angelica left the dressing room.

Alone, and in front of her mirror, Franceska felt a rotting feeling festering in her heart. She knew it was wrong to despise this opportunity, but she hated the ugly costume and having to dance for this crowd. She knew that she would make her way back to the top somehow, and, if not for the invasion, she would've been well on her way to achieving status that she could've only dreamed of. Still, she wasn't going to give up quite yet.

With the lingering sting in her fall from glory and prestige, Franceska wished that she could look upon her predicament as an opportunity. She knew that there were many people in the city that were suffering far worse fates than her own, and she should be thankful, but still, she found this hurtful.

For Mother, Franceska reminded herself as she slipped into the costume.

A knock came to the door of the dressing room.

"Go away, Piotr!" Franceska barked as she hurried to get ready and join Angelica and Celina on stage.

"It's me," Marek replied. "Piotr would've opened the door already."

"I've noticed," Franceska muttered before adding, "Come in."

Opening the door, Marek stared at Franceska in the mirror as the glowing lights illuminated the sorrow etched on her face.

"See how I waited for you to tell me to come into the room after I knocked?"

"I already apologized." Franceska shot him a heated glance before demanding, "We need a lock on the door."

"Piotr is harmless." Marek waved to dismiss his concerns.

"How would you feel if he was purposefully peeking in on you while you changed?" Franceska raised a brow.

"I'd bash his teeth in."

"Well, if you prefer your staff to have all their teeth, then put a lock on the door, otherwise he'll be serving drinks with—"

"I get it, I get it!"

"I should make my way onto stage." Franceska stood and inspected her outfit one last time.

"You look…nice…" Marek cleared his throat as he grew uncomfortable.

"Was that a compliment?" Franceska looked at him with disbelief.

"What's your stage name?" Marek asked as he took out a pen and a pad of paper.

"Stage name?" Franceska frowned.

"Believe me when I tell you that you don't want any of those gentlemen out there knowing your real name." Marek alluded to the patrons packing the nightclub.

"That's encouraging," Franceska replied sarcastically. "I'll go by the name Lola. Lola Horowitz."

"Any particular reason?" Marek asked as he scribbled the name on his pad.

"Does there need to be a reason?"

"No, just curious." Marek shrugged as he returned the pen and pad to his pocket. "I'll escort you."

"I'm more than capable of walking by myself, thank you," Franceska grew incensed as she left the room and marched confidently toward the stage.

"Wrong way," Marek called after her.

Spinning on her heels, Franceska refused to permit any humiliation as she added grumpily, "I'm still capable of walking by myself."

"Hold up!" Marek chuckled as he sped after her. "I want to introduce you first."

"Introduce me?" Franceska frowned at him as they walked.

"You're our new star dancer." Marek smirked. "You have quite the credentials. I thought it would help stir some interest."

"That would be appreciated." Franceska returned a shy smirk, feeling elevated by his kind words.

The bass began thumping, and the singer's beautiful yet strong voice cut through Franceska's heart again, although she was worried about the repercussions from Celina and Angelica for being late.

Nearing the back of the stage, Marek held up his hand to stop Franceska as he peeked through the door.

"Wait until the song finishes," Marek explained. "Then I'll introduce you."

Agreeing, Franceska stood with Marek in the dark hallway as he continued to peek through the door. Yet as he stood before her, Franceska took a moment to inspect him properly. He seemed to be a competent man, but Franceska noticed there was no wedding ring. She appreciated that when he looked at her, he did so respectfully and didn't press an advantage.

Still, there was much to this man that Franceska was curious about. He seemed withdrawn at times, as though he was hiding some sort of secret.

The music suddenly ceased, followed by an ecstatic round of applause, and Franceska could tell that the nightclub was already briming with patrons. She began to feel nervous about performing again, and especially with a style of dance she had never executed previously.

"Stay here until I call your name," Marek spoke quickly to Franceska before rushing onto the stage.

The door closed on Franceska as she listened patiently for Marek to call her name.

"Good evening, ladies and gentlemen," Marek began in the microphone and his voice was so full of confidence and energy that Franceska almost thought it was someone else speaking. It was only when she opened the door a touch that she confirmed it was, in fact, Marek.

"We have a special treat for everyone tonight. A prima ballerina has joined the cohorts of our lovely dancers."

Some whistles and clapping erupted, and Franceska smiled with happy anticipation.

"She recently won fourth place in the world dance competition in Brussels. Please put your hands together for the lovely Lola Horowitz."

The crowd again erupted into applause and cheers, and Franceska opened the door as she walked confidently onto the stage over to Marek who was holding out his hand to her.

Taking his hand, Franceska curtseyed to the crowd before taking her place on stage beside Celina and

Angelica, who, she noticed, were both eyeing her enviously.

"Thank you, Mr. Rosenberg," the singer, Lena, said warmly and smiled politely at him as he left the stage, but Franceska caught the look of disdain the singer offered to the bassist. She wondered about the secret rivalries between performers in this nightclub world.

"One, two, three, four," the guitarist counted them in, and another song began.

Drawing a quick breath to steady her nerves, Franceska followed along with the movements of Celina and Angelica. It was not a difficult dance to participate in, and even from viewing these two women a handful of times while sitting in the club, Franceska was able to keep pace.

Once again, Franceska was thankful for the bright lights illuminating the stage as it made it difficult for her to view who was on the dance floor. She found herself less worried about the men ogling her, or the women judging her outfit, or from others recognizing her if she couldn't see them.

She was simply able to dance and became lost in the music. Her worries for her mother or how they would survive the invasion seemed to lessen the more the night progressed. Her only focus was the intricate movements of her feet and hands while keeping in step with her two dancing companions.

It was therapeutic to free herself from the constraints of consciousness, and Franceska was already looking forward to the next time she could take the stage.

As the night wore on, Franceska noticed that the crowd, from what she could hear, wasn't dissipating. They seemed as energetic and as eager as they had when the night began. Franceska wondered how much longer she could dance without falling over, but didn't want to be too obvious by looking at the clock behind the bar.

"Thank you, ladies and gentlemen," Lena finally announced the closing of the show. "You've been an excellent audience. And to our brave heroes, may you defend sacred Poland admirably and without fear."

With wobbly legs, Franceska exited the stage, followed by Celina and Angelica, feeling happy and confident in her performance.

Entering the dressing room, Franceska held the door open for Celina and Angelica who, she noticed, both seemed to be harboring some resentment against her.

But then Franceska smirked when she closed the door and realized that a bolt lock had been installed. Happily, she locked the door behind her, but didn't want to mention anything to the other two women quite yet as they both still seemed on edge.

With exhaustion, Franceska sat on the chair and began to undress when, suddenly, a thud sounded against the door.

"Ow!" Piotr cried.

"It's locked!" Franceska shouted.

"Did you ask Mr. Rosenberg to put a lock on the door?" Celina studied Franceska curiously.

Franceska nodded as she waited for their reaction.

"We've been asking him for years, and tonight, when you show up, he agrees?" Angelica remained skeptical. "Are you two romantically involved?"

"Heaven's no." Franceska shook her head in disgust.

Marek was a handsome man, Franceska freely admitted, but when it came to romance, she couldn't see anything developing in that realm.

"He's in love with you," Celina added.

"Why is the door locked?" Piotr asked from the other side.

"Why do you think? Scram!" Franceska barked.

"I like you." Celina smiled in such a way as if she only just realized that she was fond of Franceska.

"You can dance well," Angelica agreed.

"I think you're already in his good books, but if you want to impress Mr. Rosenberg, buying him a drink would go a long way." Celina looked at Franceska softly.

"I appreciate that." Franceska nodded her thanks.

Quietly, and exhaustedly, Celina and Angelica returned to their regular clothes before departing for the night.

Sitting alone in the dressing room, Franceska took a moment to reflect on how drastically life had changed only days ago. They had lost all their belongings, money, home, and possessions, but Franceska was thankful she could still pursue dancing, even if it was in a manner she would've never foreseen for herself.

Wasting no more time reminiscing, Franceska changed back into the only dress she had, hung the tattered outfit back on the rack, grabbed her purse and jacket, and marched toward the bar where she spotted a busy Piotr organizing some boxes.

"Piotr!" Franceska demanded, and the young man looked up at her, startled.

"Ye…yes?" Piotr stumbled on his words as he stared at her with wide eyes.

"Vodka." Franceska nodded to a bottle.

"At once!" Piotr grabbed a glass.

"No, I want the whole bottle." Franceska held out her hand.

"The…what?" Piotr hesitated.

"The whole bottle." Franceska looked at him sternly. "Quickly!"

"Yes, ma'am." Piotr swallowed as he swiftly placed the bottle in her hands.

"You're a good kid." Franceska grinned as she walked toward Marek's office feeling elated and proud of herself.

"Franceska!" a happy cry came from a booth nearby and she turned to see an ecstatic Stefania and Wiera charging toward her.

"Don't tell me you were here the whole night?" Franceska panicked as the two girls crashed into her with an embrace.

"Why would we miss it?" Stefania looked cheerfully at Franceska.

"It's not my usual dancing I suppose." Franceska shrugged.

"You were excellent," Wiera added in her usual calm manner.

"That's very kind." Franceska studied her friends with admiration.

"I heard you found a place to rent?!" Stefania bubbled with excitement.

"We did!" Franceska tried to match Stefania's energy but found that level too difficult to achieve. "It's not much, but it's something."

"We also found a place," Wiera added. "I spoke to your father earlier this evening and it turns out we're almost neighbors."

"You spoke to my father?" Franceska asked nervously as she turned pale. "Did you mention The Melody Palace?"

"We mentioned he was welcome to join us, but he said he was going to check in on your mother again."

"You told him?!" Franceska grimaced before asking, "Did he seem upset?"

"About your mother?" Wiera asked with confusion.

"No, about me dancing here." Franceska looked back at them with worry.

"I forgot that he didn't know!" Stefania held her hands over her face in shock before turning to Wiera and asking, "What have you done?!"

"Me?!" Wiera shot her head back in surprise at the allegation. "I'm lucky if I can get a word in with you around. You blabbed to her father about this place, not I!"

"I told him I was working at an accounting firm," Franceska sighed as she hung her head low, feeling awful for lying to her parents.

"I'm so sorry!" Stefania glanced at Franceska with guilt.

"He would've found out sooner or later." Franceska waved to dismiss their concerns.

"We have to be off now, but we wanted to be sure to tell you how wonderful you were and that we love you." Stefania offered Franceska a warm embrace.

Franceska smiled at her friends as they quickly left the nightclub, and she felt blessed to have them in her life.

Then, with the bottle of vodka still in her hand, Franceska marched over to Marek's office and banged on the door loudly.

"I'm busy!" Marek shouted back.

Undeterred, Franceska burst into Marek's office to find him setting up his mattress.

"At this rate, why do you even bother knocking?" Marek asked grumpily.

"This is what you're busy with?" Franceska asked as she closed the door behind her.

"You shouldn't be in here." Marek glanced at the door.

"Why? Are you afraid that they're going to talk about us?" Franceska asked as she placed the bottle of vodka on the desk and sat in the chair.

"Well, yes, actually." Marek eyed the vodka intently.

"They're already talking." Franceska tilted her head.

"What do you mean?" Marek frowned as he lit a cigarette and sat down behind the desk.

"You have to stop doing things for me," Franceska replied quickly as she unscrewed the cap on the bottle of vodka.

"Things? What things?" Marek remained confused.

"The clock, the lock on the door." Franceska took a generous sip from the bottle.

"You noticed, did you?" Marek stared at the ceiling.

"And so did Celina and Angelica." Franceska tilted her head. "I'm the new girl, and you're making them jealous."

"They're not the jealous type." Marek shook his head.

"Then why did they tell me to buy you a drink?" Franceska shook the bottle of vodka.

"What do you mean?" Marek glanced at the bottle and Franccska noticed he had difficulty diverting his gaze.

"You mentioned that you don't partake, and I'm guessing this is no secret?" Franceska asked. "They told me to buy you a drink to embarrass me. You do see that, don't you?"

"I'll talk to them tomorrow." Marek puffed his smoke.

"You'll do no such thing." Franceska shook her head.

"Excuse me?" Marek glared at her. "I'm still the manager here!"

"And sometimes, sticking your nose into problems only makes them worse. They need to respect me. If you demand that they treat me right, they'll only think of me as your pet."

"Maybe you are my pet." Marek grinned.

"I need to impress them with my skills in dance, and—"

Marek chuckled.

"What's so amusing?" Franceska frowned.

"I'm sure you're a wonderful ballerina, but if you want to impress Celina and Angelica, you need to put some serious effort into this style of dance."

"I don't understand." Franceska pulled back in surprise. "Celina and Angelica complimented my dancing, and even my friends—"

"You danced like a ballerina," Marek interrupted.

"Thank you," Franceska replied quickly, stubbornly choosing to see his remarks as a compliment.

"You're too graceful." Marek shrugged. "Tango is about feeling the music and moving your body sensually."

"Excuse me?" Franceska grew indignant. "I'm not here to be an object."

"I'm not keep you here against your will. The door is right there. You're free to leave whenever you choose." Marek pointed.

Franceska crossed her arms as she glared at Marek.

"I thought as much." Marek stubbed his cigarette out before extending his hand to her.

"What are you doing?" Franceska looked at his hand suspiciously.

"I'm going to show you how to dance."

"I—"

"Come on!" Marek waved. "Don't be shy!"

Warily, Franceska took Marek's hand, and the two took their dancing positions in the office with his hand on her waist and his other hand holding hers loosely.

"How is—" Franceska's voice stuck in her throat. "How is us dancing together going to teach me how to dance on stage?"

"I want to show you the rhythm," Marek explained as he began the movements slowly while humming the familiar Polish Tango tune.

He was confident, poised, and gentle in his dancing, and Franceska was stunned by his cadence and demeanor.

As they danced something happened that Franceska didn't expected. With his strong hand down by her waist, and feeling the warmth of his chest against hers, Franceska's heart began to awaken to sensations she never knew were possible.

Her breathing began to labor, her hands began to tingle, and an almost painful commotion erupted within her.

She studied his thin yet alluring lips, his strong jawline with thick stubble, and his light brown eyes that hinted at hidden secrets.

"You're staring," Marek whispered with a smirk, and Franceska immediately turned her gaze away as her cheeks flushed crimson.

In that moment she finally understood Wiera and Stefania's obsession with love. Marck was not a man that Franceska would've ever considered as a romantic interest, yet in his small office, with the two of them dancing closely together, and his confidence radiating, Franceska was smitten.

"There! You're getting it!" Marek grew excited, and Franceska, for once in her life, couldn't think of a witty remark, and instead blushed with a smile.

"I think that's good enough for one evening," Franceska blurted as she broke away from Marek.

"Fair enough." Marek glanced at his watch. "May I escort you home?"

"I'm perfectly capable of walking," Franceska retorted angrily.

"I'm aware." Marek leaned against the edge of his desk.

Terrified at how she was feeling toward Marek, Franceska was about to leave his office when she spotted the bottle of vodka still on his desk.

"You can take it." Marek nodded.

"I'm going to ask you a question, and I want you to tell me the truth." Franceska crossed her arms as she tested Marek.

"I've never lied to you." Marek shrugged.

"All you've done is lie to me."

"I wouldn't say all I've done is—"

"Why do you have trouble with liquor?"

Marek didn't respond as he looked back at Franceska with a calculating gaze.

"I want to know why," Franceska grabbed the bottle.

"Well…as for the why?" Marek stared at the bottle before adding, "That I, nor anyone else I know, can answer correctly. Other people seem to be able to have a drink or two and then call it a night. I, on the other hand, when I take a drink, or even a sip for that matter, don't seem to know how to stop."

Franceska watched him for a moment as she judged his sincerity.

"I've lost a lot in my life because I'm unable to handle my liquor as others can." Marek looked at her with shame in his eyes. "I've never understood why."

"Thank you for telling me the truth." Franceska examined him thoroughly before asking, "Why do you keep a bottle in your desk, then?"

"That's a story for another time." Marek looked back at her regretfully.

"Another question…" Franceska narrowed her gaze.

"Really?" Marek again glanced at his watch. "It's very late and—"

"When we met, you had a cane. Why?"

"Twisted my ankle." Marek chuckled. "There's really nothing more to the story than that."

"Hmm." Franceska remained unconvinced.

"Did you suppose I was a cripple?" Marek frowned.

"It's not important." Franceska twisted her lips.

"Are you sure I can't walk you home? It is late at night, we're in the middle of an invasion, and half the police force have left."

"I'll see you tomorrow." Franceska opened the door and left the office, knowing that if she spent another minute with Marek, she would fall in love with him.

While she did suddenly and unexpectedly find his character alluring, Franceska knew that being involved with him was nothing but bad news. He was her employer, he had trouble with liquor, and he was a good measure older than her. Besides, she needed to focus on her mother. That was, and should be, she understood, her only priority.

Still, as she left the nightclub and began the journey back to her new apartment, Franceska's mind dwelt on Marek and Marek only.

Chapter Sixteen:
Soviet

"A single death is a tragedy; a million deaths is a statistic."

Joseph Stalin

<u>September 17, 1939</u>

"Tea?" Franceska asked her father as he sat in his chair in the living room during the early morning hours while reading over the paper.

Mr. Mann didn't reply as he turned the page.

"Are you still not talking to me?" Franceska asked as she sat on the couch and swirled her tea to help it cool.

Mr. Mann continued to ignore his daughter as he turned the page with a heavy sigh.

"You will have to talk to me at some point," Franceska continued.

"No, I don't," Mr. Mann responded shortly.

"Very mature." Franceska sipped her tea.

"You want to lecture me on propriety?" Mr. Mann offered an irritated glimpse over his paper at his daughter.

"Why don't you come to a performance? Then you can decide for yourself if I'm as indecent as you perceive."

"I would never sully the reputation of this family by entering that horrid establishment." Mr. Mann returned to reading the paper as he added, "And what's worse is that you're using your mother's maiden name, Lola Horowitz, as a stage name."

"I thought that was clever." Franceska smiled proudly to herself. "No one knows mother by that name, and, if I'm successful, my real name will be kept quiet, thus saving you from embarrassment."

"Just promise me that your mother will never know." Mr. Mann looked sternly at Franceska.

"Yes, well, my friends have been reminded that they're supposed to keep a tight lip." Franceska drummed her fingernails against her cup.

Mr. Mann grunted softly as he turned the page with a shake of his head.

"What are the reports?" Franceska asked as she looked at the paper.

"Nothing good." Mr. Mann glanced over at her.

"How bad is it?" Franceska asked, knowing that if the papers were no longer spewing lies of victory, then it was likely worse than she cared to hear.

"The Germans have enjoyed victory after victory," Mr. Mann replied solemnly.

"What does that mean for us?" Franceska asked as she felt her shoulders tightening.

"That we should probably consider heading east." Mr. Mann rubbed his eyes as he put the paper down.

"We only brought mother home yesterday." Franceska glanced nervously in the direction of the bedroom where Mrs. Mann was sleeping.

"I hate seeing her on those horrible painkillers." Mr. Mann scratched his chin. "She didn't say a single bad thing about the apartment when we brought her home yesterday. Did you notice that?"

"Of course I noticed," Franceska scoffed. "I was bracing for her reaction. I hate seeing her so sedated."

"In any case, I'm glad you were able to convince her to come back to the apartment."

"I don't know if anyone can convince mother of something she doesn't want to do." Franceska smirked. "She was ready to leave the hospital."

"That may be, but still, she's home now and that is in thanks to you."

Surprised by her father's praise, Franceska didn't quite know how to respond, other than offering him a quick nod of appreciation.

"Franceska!" a cry came from the bedroom, startling her and nearly dropped her cup.

"I'll see what she needs." Franceska set her cup on the coffee table and walked toward the bedroom.

"Franceska!" the cry came again.

"I'm here," Franceska replied casually, knowing that her mother's pleas were likely overexaggerated.

"Finally!" Mrs. Mann grumbled when Franceska entered the dark bedroom.

"Finally?" Franceska shot her head back in surprise. "I came as soon as I heard your call!"

"I might as well be back in the hospital with how slowly you responded!" Mrs. Mann griped.

"I'd send you back there, but I'd doubt they'd let you in after you treated the nurses and doctors so poorly," Franceska retorted grumpily.

"They have thicker skin than you give them credit for." Mrs. Mann waved to dismiss her daughter's concerns.

"They also have feelings that you're not considering." Franceska raised a brow.

"Hand me my water." Mrs. Mann pointed to a glass on her bedside table.

"That was the emergency?" Franceska remained unimpressed.

"You keep nagging me to hydrate, but now you're complaining when I follow your orders?" Mrs. Mann rolled her hand for Franceska to hurry.

"Did you take your medication?" Franceska asked as she grabbed the water for her mother.

"Why?" Mrs. Mann grew defensive.

"You seem…touchy." Franceska tried to hide her smirk, knowing that her remark would only spark a heated response.

"Touchy?!" Mrs. Mann huffed with incredulity. "You believe *I'm* touchy?! How would you react if your own daughter broke your back by throwing you like livestock into a cart and then abandoning you in some insane asylum?"

"Reality for others is not reality for you, is it, Mother?" Franceska kissed her mother's forehead. "You need to keep taking your medication."

Mrs. Mann scowled at Franceska for a good measure before relenting and opening her hand to her daughter.

"Where are your pills?" Franceska asked as she looked around the room.

"How should I know?" Mrs. Mann shrugged.

"Because they're your pills!"

"Your father gave them to me last." Mrs. Mann looked around the room in a poor attempt to show her concern.

"Papa? Have you seen her medication?" Franceska shouted back into the living room.

No response. Only the quiet voice of a radio announcer coming from the living room.

"Papa?!" Franceska asked.

Still no response.

"What is he up to?" Franceska asked quietly under her breath as she walked back into the living room to find her father listening intently to the radio.

"I was calling you!" Franceska threw her hands onto her hips.

Mr. Mann waved his hand frantically to shush her as he continued to listen attentively to the radio.

"The Soviets have invaded our sacred nation from the east," the announcement began.

Franceska's legs nearly gave out as she listened to the devastating news, and she quickly sat on the couch beside her father.

"Several Polish cities, believing the Red Army was enroute to fight the Germans, have let the invaders in peacefully, only to their detriment," the announcer continued, and Franceska could tell that he was having difficulty remaining calm. "The Soviet government, under Joseph Stalin, has announced that they're acting to protect the Ukrainians and Belarusians living in the eastern part of our glorious nation, citing that our government has collapsed, and we can no longer protect our citizens. Don't be fooled, this is Soviet propaganda. Poland is still united. Poland is still proud."

Static.

Franceska felt the hair on her arm standing on edge.

"There is no hope for us," Mr. Mann spoke gravely.

"We need to evacuate," Franceska began with a growing sense of urgency.

"Where? How?" Mr. Mann looked at his daughter as he became cynical. "Your mother can barely walk to the couch from the bedroom. How is she going to evacuate the city? Also, where would we go? The Nazis control the west, south, and northern parts of Poland. The east, as we've just heard, is falling into Soviet hands. We're surrounded. No, my dear, it is you who should leave."

"I'm not going anywhere without you!" Franceska looked at her father with outrage for the suggestion.

"You're still young." Mr. Mann looked at his daughter with sorrow. "You can still have a life."

"What is my life without you?" Franceska shook her head.

"That's a sad statement in and of itself." Mr. Mann glanced at his daughter.

"I can't…" the words stuck in Franceska's mouth, and she instead stated, "We're not even entertaining this idea. We either all go together, or none of us leave."

"Don't throw away your future on us." Mr. Mann's lips trembled.

"I'm not leaving you." Franceska shook her head.

"Our lives are over!" Mr. Mann stood and towered over Franceska.

"They're not over until I'm standing at your graveside!" Franceska matched her father's rage as she also stood.

"I'm not going to be the reason that you can't escape!" Mr. Mann pointed at the door.

"And I'm not going to be the reason why you both starve to death!" Franceska yelled back. "We can barely scrape by on what I make, and no one else is hiring with the invasion gaining ground, and they're especially not seeking washed up old men."

"Washed up?" Mr. Mann took a small step back, and Franceska knew that she had hurt him severely.

"That's not what I meant." Franceska squeezed her eyes shut, wishing she could take back her words.

"But it's true." Mr. Mann stared at his feet.

"You're not washed up. I didn't mean to—"

"Spare it," Mr. Mann muttered as he brushed by his daughter and toward the bedroom.

"What was that about?" Mrs. Mann asked her husband as he closed the door gently behind him.

I'll be paying for that one for a while, Franceska rubbed her eyes in frustration. *You just had to say he was washed up, didn't you? You know Papa is a proud man. I wish he would just slam the door or something. Closing it quietly like that just twists the knife deeper.*

Realizing that she should likely give her parents some space, and needing some of her own, Franceska snatched her purse and headed toward the door.

Opening the door quickly, Franceska grabbed her chest in fright, surprised to see Stefania standing in the hallway with an ecstatic smile.

"What are you doing here?" Franceska tried to catch her breath.

"I was going to knock, but then I heard shouting, and I—"

"How much of that did you hear?" Franceska grimaced.

"Not much, just—"

"You heard everything, didn't you?"

Stefania nodded reluctantly.

"I'm terribly sorry about that." Franceska grew embarrassed.

"Don't be." Stefania waved to dismiss her concerns. "It pales in comparison to the arguments I would have with my parents."

"In either case, I need some space from them. Care to join me?"

"I'd love to!" Stefania smiled brightly.

"What brings you by this way, anyway?"

"I'm married!" Stefania held up her hand to show that she was wearing a wedding band.

"Married?!" Franceska's eyes flew wide open. "To whom? Jan? I thought he was married? How did he get a divorce so quickly?"

"Goodness no! Jan and I broke it off ages ago. I'll tell you while we walk together." Stefania linked her arm with Franceska's.

"You don't even know where I'm going." Franceska looked at her friend with amusement.

"The destination isn't important; it's the journey that counts," Stefania continued in her undeterred cheerfulness. "His name is Jerzy Jurandot, and he's a poet."

"A poet?" Franceska grew impressed.

"And he's also Jewish, so we have that in common. I met him when Wiera and I came to watch you dance!"

"That's wonderful," Franceska spoke with as much enthusiasm as she could muster, but struggled to display her happiness adequately.

"What's wrong?" Stefania looked at her friend curiously as they left the apartment. "I thought you'd be happy for me?"

"I am, believe me." Franceska squeezed her friend's arm. "But there have been some distressing reports this morning."

"You mean the Soviets?" Stefania asked innocently.

"You knew?" Franceska frowned.

"Everyone knows." Stefania shrugged. "It's all anyone is talking about."

"But…" Franceska narrowed her gaze at Stefania.

"Why am I still so excited?" Stefania smirked.

"The world as we know it is ending." Franceska shook her head in dismay. "I want to be excited for you, but—"

"Even without the invasion, nothing in life is guaranteed," Stefania continued, still full of joy. "What am I going to do? Sit and sulk? No! I'm going to enjoy what time I have left!"

"But the Germans are massacring Jews!" Franceska pressed. "Only yesterday I heard about two hundred Jews who were killed in Dynów. The Germans mowed down one hundred and fifty with machine guns, and then burned another fifty alive in the synagogue!"

"I heard about that, too," Stefania added solemnly.

"Doesn't that worry you?" Franceska felt herself panicking. "If they're not even trying to hide these massacres, what—"

"I'm not worried." Stefania shook her head as tears formed. "You know why?"

"Why?" Franceska looked at her friend intently.

"Because I can't control anything that is about to happen to us, or to you, or to my husband. What I can control is how I respond, and no matter what those monsters do, they will never break my spirit." Stefania declared proudly as her eyes welled.

"Stefania the Stoic." Franceska grinned.

"Don't tease!" Stefania lightly slapped Franceska's arm.

"I'm sorry, I won't. You've inspired me, my friend. Hopefully someday I can have the same outlook as you. When will we be awarded the privilege of being introduced to your wonderful, mystery husband?"

"I'm sure we can arrange an introduction soon." Stefania beamed with pride.

"Have you heard from Wiera lately?" Franceska asked as she grew concerned. "I haven't spoken to her in a while."

"Yes, actually, and it's a bit scandalous," Stefania whispered.

"Oh?" Franceska leaned in, eager for some gossip to distract her from her worries.

"She's been sneaking out of the city to rendezvous with Adam." Stefania fluttered her eyelashes.

"Really?!" Franceska grinned, but then asked, "Why would she have to sneak out of the city? She's free to come and go as she pleases."

"Don't take the fun out of it for me!" Stefania glared at Franceska who laughed liberally.

"You're the joy of my life." Franceska squeezed her friend's arm. "Do you think we're going to be alright? Life will go back to normal?"

"I don't know." Stefania stared off into the distance pensively before adding, "But no matter what happens, I have you as a friend, and that is enough for me."

"And you're happily married!"

"I'm married!" Stefania squealed and then mentioned, "I should get back. I did initially set out to grab groceries, but then thought I should inform you of the good news."

"I'm glad you brightened my day."

"Where are you off to?"

"The club."

"This early?" Stefania asked with concern. "Why?"

"I…" Franceska recalled the fight with her father. "It's complicated."

"Fair enough. We'll speak soon." Stefania blew a kiss to Franceska as they parted ways.

What a woman, Franceska thought with a smile plastered across her face. She was terrified of what was about to happen to her family, but hearing how Stefania was braving the onslaught with a cheerful disposition gave Franceska some much-needed courage.

Drawing a deep breath, Franceska made her way to the tram, offered a polite hello to an apathetic Henryk, and rode the tram to the nightclub. She didn't know why she was going to the club so early and expected that it would still be locked from the previous night. Still, something spurred her onwards, and she trudged forward feeling that something was guiding her.

Arriving at the nightclub, Franceska was surprised to find that the door was unlocked.

I should tell Marek about that, Franceska thought, but then considered the fact that it might be best to avoid him.

She had successfully evaded all contact with him since the night they danced in his office, and Franceska was content to keep him at a distance. She couldn't be bothered at a time like this to entertain even the thought of romance, and was proud that she had blocked him out of her mind entirely. Although, if she were honest, it felt as though he was lingering on the door of her thoughts, ready to barge in if she dared allow it.

Entering the nightclub, Franceska found the empty club to be an eerie sight. It was odd to see the dance floor, the stage, and the bar vacant. It made her feel uncomfortable, and she couldn't wait until the club was bursting with patrons and bubbling with chatter and music.

"Hello?" Franceska called into the club to confirm that she was, in fact, alone.

No response.

Glancing at Marek's office, Franceska creeped closer and slowly opened the door as she peeked inside.

No one, Franceska sighed her relief. But then, when she noticed the empty stage, a thought struck her, and she felt an urge that had long been suppressed.

"Hello?!" Franceska called louder, making sure that she was, without a doubt, alone.

Then, climbing onto the stage, Franceska removed her jacket and set her purse down before taking place in center stage.

Closing her eyes, Franceska recalled the intricate music with delicate yet moving strings that later would crescendo with blaring bass and vibrant drums.

Taking position, Franceska began to dance the same ballet she had performed in Brussels, reliving the pinnacle moment of her career. An immense freedom poured over her as she let herself loose in the dance. She hadn't performed ballet in some time, having focused on tango dancing lately, and felt that her movements were imperfect, rusty.

Again! Franceska convinced herself when she finished and, although growing short on breath, restarted the ballet.

All her worries with the war, the invasion, her parents, and Marek, fell away as she lost herself to dance. This is where she belonged, in these movements she found purpose, strength, and drive. All that mattered, in this very moment, was ensuring her positions and movements were perfect.

I should've stretched first, Franceska thought when she finished the ballet again and began to rub her legs.

A slow clap came from behind the bar, and Franceska clutched her chest in fright as she watched Marek approaching the stage with a proud smirk on his face.

"I thought I was alone!" Franceska wiped the sweat from her forehead. "Why didn't you answer when I called you?"

"I only walked in five minutes ago." Marek pointed over his shoulder with his thumb at the door. "You were so lost in your dance you didn't notice me, and I didn't want to interrupt you."

"Well, I apologize for using the stage without permission. It won't happen again." Franceska grabbed her purse and jacket before quickly stepping down from the stage.

"Why? That was amazing!" Marek seemed genuinely excited.

"I'm not in the mood for your mockery," Franceska replied, not convinced he was sincere.

"I'm not mocking." Marek held his hands up to prove his innocence. "In fact, I have a proposal for you."

"A proposal?" Franceska squinted at him, curious.

"Why don't you perform that routine tonight?"

"Don't be ridiculous." Franceska rolled her eyes.

"I'm serious!" Marek pressed.

"Really?" Franceska remained skeptical, but then shook her head as she stated, "It wouldn't work."

"Why not?" Marek shrugged.

"Well, the musicians don't know the piece, and the other dancers wouldn't be involved, and—"

"Let me worry about those details." Marek urged.

"Even so, tonight is much too soon."

"Alright, fair enough. What if we plan an evening? A special ballet performance?"

"Marek, I'm sure you've heard the news, this isn't the time to be focusing on ballet." Franceska's shoulders slouched.

"Maybe not." Marek looked thoughtfully at Franceska. "But there are some confused people out there, wondering what is going to happen to them. If they witness what I just saw, they will experience some much-needed comfort."

"That's very kind of you to say." Franceska grinned bashfully.

"I'll start the preparations then." Marek winked as he walked toward his office with a purpose in his step that Franceska had never witnessed.

Yet as she watched him walk away, Franceska let her guard down and felt a surge of emotions that she had been desperate to keep at bay. Her heart ached, and her soul urged her to dance with him alone in his office again, feeling his strong hand on her waist, and guiding her through the movements.

But as quickly as she allowed those emotions, she shut them out again, knowing that it would only lead to heart ache. She had to focus on her parents, and that, she knew, was what really mattered. As long as her parents were safe, then she could look to her own interests, but not a minute sooner.

Chapter Seventeen: Surrounded

"Hell is empty and all the devils are here."

William Shakespeare

"I hate this feeling," Wiera complained as she stood with Franceska in the bread line.

"Which feeling, specifically?" Franceska asked while a good measure distracted.

The bread line, which Franceska was grateful for, had swollen over the last while as food became scarce. The produce was beginning to dwindle considerably, and many, even those who had money to purchase food, were now forced to stand in the long line. Most food markets were nearly devoid of anything that wasn't canned goods. And even then, the canned goods were hard to come by.

"The Germans surround the city, but they're not making a further move. They're sitting with their tanks and artillery pointed at us, but I can't tell what they're waiting for." Wiera bit her lip nervously.

"I don't think they're wanting to starve us out." Franceska shook her head. "Most of our army has surrendered."

"My father joined a resistance group." Wiera glanced at Franceska with worry. "Many of the soldiers were unsatisfied with the army's decision to surrender and are recruiting anyone willing to fight."

"Don't let my father hear that." Franceska shared in Wiera's concern. "He'd half-run to the recruitment line with that rifle he's so proud of."

"He should keep that rifle close by for as long as possible." Wiera raised her eyebrows in warning as she continued, "I keep hearing reports of Nazi soldiers gunning down Jews or prisoners of war like they're less than animals."

"The Soviets aren't much kinder to Jews, and they're acquiring more territory in the east."

"Do we have to talk about this around children?!" a mother in front of Franceska and Wiera berated them as she covered her child's ears.

"Sorry, ma'am." Franceska grew embarrassed. "That wasn't very thoughtful of us."

"He won't sleep for another week now thanks to you!" the mother continued in her chastisement.

"We really meant no—"

"If it weren't for you Jews, Hitler might have stayed out of Poland altogether," the mother huffed.

"Clearly you haven't read their literature!" Franceska took her turn to berate the mother. "They don't hold Poles in much higher regard than us Jews! Don't be fooled into thinking that they'll treat you any better."

"Don't you dare—"

Some distinct, yet distant, shouts in German sounded, along with the petrifying rumble of tank tracks.

Franceska, the mother, and Wiera, paused from their heated debate as they looked around with wide eyes, wondering which direction the enemy was approaching from.

Suddenly, and seemingly out of nowhere, about twenty Polish civilians armed with rifles and automatic weapons rushed down the street in the direction that Franceska had heard the German shouting.

"Quickly!" one of the Polish fighters whispered harshly to someone behind Franceska.

Turning to inspect, Franceska spotted a few men wheeling an anti-tank gun into position, and she realized that everyone in the bread line was about to be caught in a deadly crossfire.

"We have to go now!" Franceska grabbed Wiera's hand.

A burst of gunfire echoed in the distance to their left, and then a muffled explosion to their right. Shouts of agony and screams from civilians carried in the air from further in the city behind them, and Franceska knew that the final assault of the enemy was upon them. They were encircled with nowhere to turn to.

"Where?!" Wiera clutched tightly onto Franceska's hand as she scanned around. "We're surrounded!"

"In here!" a shopkeeper called out as he opened his door and looked both ways down the street before waving for people to take shelter in his shop.

Not waiting for a better opportunity to present itself, if one even would, Franceska and Wiera scurried toward the shop, followed by a handful of others, including the Polish woman and her child.

Governed by fear and panic, Franceska and Wiera ran into the shop without so much as thanking the shopkeeper.

Franceska was, however, grateful to find that it was a small furniture store full of modest dining room tables, chairs, and coffee tables.

Running to the back of the store, Franceska turned one of the tables onto its side where she and Wiera took shelter.

Breathing heavily, Franceska felt her heart racing. She was terrified of the prospect of being anywhere near a battle, and the thought of being killed and unable to care or provide for her parents sent her into a horrible fit.

"Try and calm your breathing," Wiera spoke through her own labored breaths, feeling the same rush of anxiety and adrenaline.

Some more shouting in German could be heard from further down the street, and the rumble of the tank grew louder as it shook the earth beneath them.

Poking her head above the edge of the table, Franceska peeked out the store window and spotted resistance fighters taking positions, being as quite as possible in the hopes that they could ambush the approaching Germans.

The anti-tank gun was much closer to the store than Franceska wished as she knew that would be the priority target for the Germans, and she feared those inside the store would be caught in the crossfire.

"Can you see the Germans?" Wiera asked anxiously.

"Not from this vantage point." Franceska shook her head before she returned to taking shelter beside Wiera.

"We're going to be alright?" Wiera looked at Franceska with panic.

"Of course!" Franceska drew upon her courage as she calmed a measure and clasped her friend's hand. "The resistance fighters are going to give the Germans hell."

"Thank you for lying." Wiera stared at the ceiling. "It helps."

Franceska also stared at the ceiling and noticed that it was a horrid shade of green. She didn't know why, but at this moment, while she was about to experience the crucible of combat, all Franceska could focus on was the fact that she wanted to paint the ceiling a different color.

Distracted by shadows cast against the wall in front of her, Franceska discerned that more resistance fighters were joining the ranks, and she took some courage in that fact.

"Did you hear about Stefania?" Wiera asked plainly as she trembled, and Franceska knew she was desperate for any sort of diversion.

"About her marriage?" Franceska asked.

"Yeah."

"I heard."

"I wish she would've asked me to be involved."

"How so?" Franceska studied her friend as she felt her heart pounding in her chest and struggled to focus on the conversation.

"As a witness or something." Wiera's teeth rattled as she shivered. "Feels odd that she suddenly married without involving me, or you, for that matter."

"Have you met him?" Franceska asked as she listened to explosions and gunfire erupting from another part of the city.

"No, have you?"

"I heard that you have been sneaking out of the city to meet with Adam."

"I was wondering when Stefania would tell you." Wiera tried to force a smile, but Franceska watched as her friend grew increasingly pale.

"Why do you have to sneak?" Franceska asked with a frown.

"The soldiers are guarding every entrance to the city." Wiera stared at her feet. "If I was caught, they'd likely think I was a spy. It's a stupid risk, I know, but I have to see him."

"We're going to be alright," Franceska spoke unconvincingly.

"I want to believe you, but—"

"Now!" a shout came from one of the resistance fighters outside the shop, and a sudden volley erupted from rifles and the anti-tank gun.

The noise was so deafening and violent that Franceska grabbed Wiera, and the two girls clung onto each other while squeezing their eyes shut.

Within mere seconds, the Germans retaliated in kind, and the windows of the shop shattered as the wall in front of Franceska and Wiera was peppered with bullets and blood.

Screams of agony and terror from the resistance fighters cut deep into Franceska's heart, and she covered her ears to drown out the horrifying noise.

An explosion, just outside the shattered shop window, sent a cloud of dust into the shop, and Franceska covered her mouth with her scarf as she could scarcely breathe.

Women and children, including the rude mother with them, screamed in terror while others panicked and charged out of the shop in a desperate attempt to escape.

"Don't let them leave!" Franceska shouted, but her voice was drowned out by the gunfire and screams of war.

Franceska could barely see anything through the cloud of dust, but she poked her head over the table and waved at those trying to leave the shop, hoping to get their attention and stop them from making a fatal mistake.

Her attempts, unfortunately, were futile, and Franceska watched with a broken heart as women and children, fleeing into the street, were cut down indiscriminately in the crossfire.

There was nothing Franceska could do to save them, and as she watched their lifeless bodies, all she could do was weep, and her hatred for the Germans only increased. She couldn't understand why they were being so heartless and cruel to attack an innocent city. Franceska couldn't understand what these people had done to warrant losing their lives in this manner.

The skirmish was swiftly over, and as the dust began to settle, Franceska spotted dozens of bodies in the street. Some were resistance fighters, others were innocent civilians, but each one burdened Franceska's heart, and she wept bitterly at the sight.

The sound of tank tracks grew louder, and Franceska knew the armored vehicle was approaching them.

"What do we do?!" Wiera asked in a hushed tone as she again latched onto Franceska.

"Stay down! Stay quiet!" Franceska whispered and looked over at the rude woman with them to find that she and her child were deceased.

A tear fell rolled Franceska's cheek as she looked at their corpses riddled with bullet holes.

Glass shattered from outside in the street, followed by shouting in German, and Franceska feared that they were going door by door while searching for resistance fighters.

"What happens if they find out we're Jews?!" Wiera began to hyperventilate. "I can't die like this!"

Franceska didn't reply, feeling helpless and not knowing what direction to give other than for them to remain hidden.

The tank engine rumbled louder and louder, causing the floor to vibrate, and Franceska feared that they would be discovered.

"Anyone inside?!" a voice called in broken Polish, and Franceska glanced at Wiera as they both knew it was a German.

"I'll shoot!" the voice yelled again.

"Here!" the shopkeeper raised his hand from behind the counter.

"Out!" the German ordered.

"We're civilians," the shopkeeper pressed.

"How many?" the German demanded, and Franceska felt her heart pounding in her chest.

The stories of how the Nazis were massacring civilians, particularly Jews, played in Franceska's mind, and she prayed she would not be another number to that growing list of cruelty.

"A handful," the shopkeeper calmly advised as he slowly left the counter.

"Everyone! Out!" the German screamed, and Franceska could hear a rifle rattling.

"What do we do?!" Wiera whispered.

"I don't know!" Franceska shook with terror.

"Out! Now!" the German screamed before firing a warning shot into the wall just beyond Wiera and Franceska.

"We're coming!" Franceska yelled as she held her hands up.

"I can't move my legs!" Wiera whispered harshly.

"Hold onto me!" Franceska held her hand out to Wiera.

"I'm going to be sick." Wiera returned to hyperventilating.

"Everything is going to be alright," Franceska lied as she helped Wiera to her feet.

Glancing out the shattered store window, Franceska spotted the Germans, with the tank in the middle of the street, going door to door, dragging everyone out of hiding.

"We're going to die, we're going to die," Wiera muttered under her breath.

Slowly, and cautiously, Franceska, Wiera, and the other civilians approached the German who had his rifle raised, ready to shoot any resistance members hiding among the group.

"Faster!" the German commanded as he lowered his rifle, satisfied that it was only women and children hiding in the shop.

Obeying, the civilians began to quickly file toward the door, which Franceska noticed was barely hanging onto its hinges.

"Stand there!" The German pointed to the brick wall outside the shop as a couple other guards came to his assistance.

Huddling together, the civilians did as commanded while awaiting their fate.

The stench of blood, gunpowder, and metal from the battle filled Franceska's nostrils, and she nearly gagged when she realized that, at her feet, was a deceased woman with a bullet threw her eye.

"Line! Make a line!" the German shouted as he waved for them to spread out.

With whimpering and little squeaks of fright, the civilians lined up against the wall, and Franceska feared that they were about to be executed by a firing squad.

Reaching down, Franceska squeezed onto Wiera's hand, and her friend squeezed tightly back.

Franceska was convinced this was the end, and her mind dwelt on her parents. How Franceska wished to tell them that she loved them, to hear her father's dry muttering or her mother's complaints one last time. They were far from perfect people, but Franceska preferred them with their blemishes.

Please let them know how much I love them, and please watch over them, Franceska prayed inwardly. She didn't know who would listen, but she wanted God, the universe, or whatever it was that listened to prayers, to convey that message to them.

The German soldier began going down the line as he inspected each civilian quickly. He seemed to be looking for something specific, but it wasn't evident to Franceska what that might be. But the closer he came down the line to Franceska, the harder she squeezed on Wiera's hand.

"What you have?" the soldier asked Wiera in broken Polish without so much as looking into her eyes.

"Have?" Wiera asked nervously.

"On body!" the soldier lost his patience as he held his hand out.

"On body?" Wiera glanced nervously at Franceska, not understanding the soldier's broken Polish.

"What are you searching for?" Franceska asked in German, and the solider glanced at her with surprise.

Yet in his gaze Franceska only saw coldness. There was no soul behind his eyes, only a vacant and indoctrinated shell, and Franceska knew he would do anything he was commanded.

"Cigarettes," the soldier spoke plainly.

"We don't smoke." Franceska shook her head.

"How do you know German?" the soldier asked as he examined her closely.

"I'm well educated. I've travelled many—"

"That's enough," the soldier interrupted as he lost interest and continued down the line.

Not sure if she could allow herself to relax, Franceska kept her guard high as she watched the other soldiers near the tank. They were interrogating other civilians while screaming in their faces for answers. Most of the soldiers were yelling in German, and the civilians who didn't understand simply stared back in terror.

"You! German speaker," the soldier shouted at Franceska.

"Yes?" Franceska swallowed.

"Come here." He waved as he stood in front of the shopkeeper.

Peeling her hand away from Wiera's, Franceska walked over to the soldier and politely asked, "How can I assist?"

"Ask what his involvement is with the resistance." The soldier pointed to the shopkeeper.

"They want to know your involvement with the resistance," Franceska spoke to the shopkeeper in Polish.

"My involvement?" the shopkeeper chuckled nervously. "I didn't even know there was a resistance group. I stay in my shop all day and night. I don't leave if I don't have to. I'm not concerned with the politics of the world, I just want to make furniture."

"He says he didn't know a resistance group even existed," Franceska relayed the message to the soldier.

"Then why were they using his shop?!" the soldier asked impatiently.

"He stated he only wants to make furniture," Franceska defended the shopkeeper. "I was here when they arrived. Like me, he was clueless about their intentions."

"He's lying." The soldier stood back, raised his rifle, and aimed at the shopkeeper.

"He's telling the truth!" Franceska held up her hand to stop the German.

A shot fired.

Franceska froze in place.

She was too stunned to understand what had just occurred. Her shoulders were tight, her mouth agape, and she felt out-of-body as she watched the shopkeeper fall down at her feet, clutching the wound on his stomach that gushed blood, and moaning in terrible pain.

"The rest are fine," the soldier mentioned to the other Germans, and the tank began to drive further into the city.

Franceska remained in place. Her ears rang from the rifle fired a mere foot away from her head, and she struggled to process what had just happened.

It was so swift and thoughtless. The soldier simply deemed the man guilty, raised his rifle, and shot. There was no time to react. It was so barbaric, cold, and cruel, that Franceska wondered if she had merely imagined it.

"We need to go!" Wiera grabbed Franceska's arm.

"He needs medical attention," Franceska could barely push the words out of her mouth as she stared at the wounded shopkeeper at her feet.

"We need to leave!" Wiera pressed in panic. "We can't be caught in another fight!"

"Help me take him to the hospital." Franceska knelt by the man who was now unconscious.

"It's too late." Wiera pulled Franceska to her feet.

"What did he do?" Franceska felt a lump forming in her throat. "All he cared about was making furniture. Why would they kill him for that? They shot him like he was less than an animal and walked away as if nothing had happened."

"We have to go! Please!" Wiera tugged on Franceska's arm.

“Why would they do that?” Franceska asked again as Wiera began guiding her away from the horrific scene.

Why would they do that? Franceska continued to ask herself, shocked, stunned, and growing a bitterness in her heart towards such depraved and vile men.

Chapter Eighteen: Parade

"Know the enemy and know yourself. In a hundred battles, you will never be in peril."

Sun Tzu

<u>October 5, 1939</u>

"It's a bad idea to stay home." Franceska warned her father as he sat in his chair reading the paper.

"I have to stay and care for your mother." Mr. Mann gestured toward the bedroom.

"Your absence will be noted," Franceska pressed.

"I'm of little concern to them." Mr. Mann huffed. "I doubt anyone would be much concerned by our absence."

"They're watching everyone." Franceska grew worried. "They're killing indiscriminately. Don't give them a reason to—"

"They don't even know I exist!" Mr. Mann waved to dismiss her concerns.

"People talk," Franceska leaned in and whispered. "If you have any enemies, they'll report that you weren't in attendance."

"And I'll tell them I was caring for your mother." Mr. Mann remained convinced of his own logic. "That seems reasonable to me."

"You don't understand," Franceska urged. "I've looked into the eyes of a man who killed a shopkeeper because he didn't believe his story. These German soldiers are not reasonable people. They're indoctrinated and here to murder all of us!"

"That's ridiculous." Mr. Mann shook his head in dismissal.

"I hope I'm wrong, I really do." Franceska looked at her father with concern. "But I don't believe I am."

Mr. Mann looked back into his daughter's eyes intently before stating, "I can't leave her."

"I know." Franceska drew a deep breath. "I know."

"Make an appearance and then leave."

"I'll make more than an appearance." Franceska stood and ran her hands down her dress. "I'll make sure I'm noticed."

"Blend in." Mr. Mann examined his daughter. "Be seen, but no more."

"Mr. Rosenberg is organizing a ballet performance for me." Franceska forced a grin at her father as she changed the subject. "I would love if you attended."

"I wouldn't go anywhere near that degrading establishment." Mr. Mann scrunched his face with disgust.

"The Melody Palace is not what you believe it to be." Franceska tilted her head. "Besides, I've heard that the Germans are treating other famous dancers and performers well. If I can make a name for myself, I can make sure that you and mother are taken care of."

Mr. Mann didn't reply but instead returned to reading the paper.

"Anything of note?" Franceska asked as she nodded to the paper.

"For once, no, which is encouraging." Mr. Mann glanced up at his daughter. "No news is good news, especially these days."

"I'll be back shortly. I'll swing by the club first but then I'll see about buying a few groceries. Maybe we can have a nice supper?"

"Yeah, alright," Mr. Mann spoke in his monotone manner which Franceska was happy to see returning.

In her adolescence, and even before the invasion, Franceska had loathed how unresponsive and passive he was in his nature. But now she understood that he wasn't unattached, but rather, constant. How she needed that in her life right now.

"See you tonight." Franceska kissed her father on his head.

"Yep," he replied dryly, his nose stuck in the newspaper.

With a relieved smile, Franceska exited the apartment. While Warsaw was now under Nazi rule, Franceska felt a sense of calm that the bombing raids had ceased.

She wasn't sure if it was merely the sense of tranquility before the storm, but she hoped beyond hope that the Nazis were merely content with their conquest of western Poland and that the Soviets were pleased with the portion they had taken in the east.

She knew that such wishful thinking was dangerous, and prayed that a solution would show itself soon. Even if they could flee Warsaw, Franceska knew there was nowhere they could go, and her heart was burdened for those who had fled to the east and were now trapped under Soviet rule. She had heard the stories of their labor camps and how brutally the prisoners were treated, or how arbitrarily the Soviets qualified who was an enemy of the state.

Regardless, Franceska was adamant to show that she appeared like an obedient subject. She would attend the parade, make sure that she was noticed, and hopefully the Nazi overlords would ignore her and her family. She didn't know if that was the appropriate course of action, but Franceska knew she had to try.

Spotting the tram car, Franceska paid the fare, greeted Henryk cheerfully, and hopped on board.

Yet as Franceska took her seat, she noticed many gloomy faces. Tens of thousands of soldiers and innocent civilians had perished during the fighting and the bombings, and hundreds, if not thousands more, had been brutally murdered in cold blood during the ground assault.

An elderly woman sat across from Franceska, staring blankly at her handbag that was laid across her lap. Franceska wondered who she had lost during the invasion, and her heart shattered as watched the woman's face.

Much of the city that Franceska saw from the tram was still a heap of rubble or else very close to it. Entire apartment blocks, shops, cafés, churches, synagogues, defensive structures, and landmarks were demolished.

It was heartbreaking to witness, and Franceska didn't believe she would ever become accustomed to the sight. She thought of all the families, couples, and children who had lived in bliss beforehand, and what an awful tragedy they had come to know.

She counted herself fortunate that she had not lost anything permanent. She still had her parents, and she understood that furniture, clothing, and commodities could be replaced.

The tram arrived near her stop, and Franceska noticed that almost everyone was deboarding as well.

After a polite goodbye offered to Henryk, who grunted in acknowledgement, Franceska deboarded the tram and spotted a sight that she knew she wouldn't soon forget.

Thousands of civilians were lined up on either side of a main road, but they remained almost entirely silent. Growing up in Warsaw, Franceska had the pleasure of being exposed to many parades and processions throughout the city. She remembered them fondly with the various treats and bubbling excitement of everyone in attendance.

Yet here, now, as she viewed this crowd of cautious and frightened onlookers, Franceska knew they, like her, were compelled to attend this event, and knew of the consequences if they abstained.

Still, it was unnerving to see the scores of people lining up to view the parade with such a defeated spirit. Not a word was spoken, no children laughed, and apart from the occasional cough or stolen sniffle, the streets were utterly silent.

Further unnerving Franceska's spirits were the bright red Nazi flags with the swastika flapping in the wind on nearly every single streetlamp or post.

Making her way through the crowd, Franceska was adamant to be as close to the street as possible so that her presence would be noticed.

Yet when she arrived closer to the front, Franceska grew disgusted by a handful of citizens that had gathered in excitement for the parade. They were waving Nazi flags eagerly and smiling proudly. Franceska knew that they were Germanic citizens, and they were thrilled by what they perceived as liberation.

"I was wondering if I would spot you here," a familiar voice spoke from behind her, and Franceska turned around to notice Marek squeezing his way to stand beside her.

"I wouldn't miss it for the world," Franceska spoke loudly, hoping those nearby would hear her. She hated lying, but for the sake of her parents she would play the part.

"You've been avoiding me lately," Marek spoke softly as he looked down the street, trying to spot the approaching parade.

"Have I?" Franceska asked rhetorically, stalling for time so that she could fabricate a believable response.

"Don't pretend," Marek pressed.

"I'm not sure it's appropriate to be discussing this right now." Franceska looked at him sternly.

"Then what should we discuss?" Marek asked softly.

Franceska didn't reply as she kept her gaze at the end of the street, hoping to have the parade over and done with so that she could return to her parents before going to the nightclub.

"I understand you want to keep me at a distance," Marek continued, unimpeded by Franceska's cold shoulder, "But when you're ready to talk, I'll be here."

Glancing up at him, Franceska was surprised by his politeness and respect for her boundaries. Her entire life had been plagued by men who didn't seem to understand that the more they pressed the more she wanted to avoid them.

"Thank you," Franceska spoke quickly in her appreciation.

The distant, but distinct, sound of drums began to swell as it approached the street, and some apathetic applause began to circulate throughout the crowd in preparation for the victory parade.

Then, suddenly, a door to one of the buildings across the street opened, and Franceska's heart dropped into her stomach when she spotted Hitler.

The Fuehrer, along with a delegation of about a dozen officials, walked out of the building and stepped up onto a small wooden platform.

Some applause and cheers erupted from the citizens who viewed Hitler as their savior, but Franceska couldn't understand how anyone had been swayed by this madman.

With a wicked yet triumphant smile, Hitler began to talk cheerfully with the other officials with him on stage, pointing at the buildings that were damaged or destroyed. She wondered if he knew about the families that he had murdered, or that his soldiers were massacring people, her people, like they were less than animals.

But looking at his smile as he spoke with the officials, Franceska discerned that he welcomed this destruction. All her suffering, all the suffering of the mothers and fathers who were now without their children, or the children who were now orphaned, could be laid directly at the feet of this monster.

How she hated him! Her anger festered as she imagined taking a gun from a soldier nearby and shooting him in the gut, much like soldier had shot the poor shopkeeper. If anyone deserved to die in a pool of their own blood, it was this devil who was now standing on the stage as a conqueror.

The drums grew louder and more prominent, but Franceska couldn't turn her gaze from Hitler. She abhorred every part of his being, and somehow she wanted him to see that she reviled him.

But she was nothing to him. She was merely another statistic, or a *disease upon the Earth* as Hitler had crudely stated.

The parade proceeded past her with vibrancy as cavalry divisions trotted, columns upon columns of soldiers goosestepped while offering the Nazi salute to Hitler as if he was a demigod, and armored vehicles displayed their military competency and prowess as they shook the ground beneath them.

"They're marching the very instrument of our death before our eyes," Marek muttered.

Franceska looked up at him, and for the first time, since she had known him, caught the look of terror in his gaze. He was sure man, Franceska thought, someone who was rather confident in himself, and to see him appear terrified did not help to improve her outlook on the situation.

The parade ended as anti-climactic as it started. Hitler and his delegation, while seemingly pleased with themselves, retreated into the building. The music ceased, and the soldiers goosestepping, along with the vehicles, disappeared down the street.

The crowd, apart from the handful that were waving Nazi flags, dispersed in a sea of depression. Everyone's gaze was held low at their feet, no one said a word to anyone else, and they walked back to the vehicles or trams waiting to take them to whatever homes still remained.

"I need to collect some food for tonight," Franceska began solemnly as she walked beside Marek.

"I'll accompany you to the market."

"I don't require an escort, but thank you."

"It's not for your sake," Marek replied, and Franceska looked into his eyes and saw that he was likely petrified at the prospect of being alone.

"In that case, sure." Franceska nodded, and the two made their way out of the crowd that was slowly dispersing.

The air around Franceska was thick with tension, and she knew that most who had attended the parade were briming with hate and fear.

Yet as she was leaving the crowd, Franceska spotted Father Kolbe. He was standing at the back of the crowd with a few other priests with him, and they were staring at the building Hitler had retreated to. Franceska wondered if they were trying to put a curse on him. That was not their way, she understood, but at a time like this she wished it was.

A part of her wanted to speak with the priest, but she also knew that she couldn't stomach any theological or spiritual discussions at the moment and thought it best to leave such things for a better time.

Franceska and Marek walked quietly through the city and to the market. Neither of them exchanged words, and Franceska assumed that his thoughts mirrored hers in that anything spoken seemed somehow inappropriate.

All Franceska could think about was the future, and what that parade meant for her people. She assumed that if massacres were happening, with little effort by the Nazis to hide them, then it was only a matter of time before massacres began in Warsaw. She only prayed that she had the strength to endure, and the cunning to survive whatever was coming.

"Feels odd," Marek began when they arrived at the market.

"What does?" Franceska asked as she picked over the produce, or rather, what was left to look over.

"To watch that parade and then go to the market like it was an ordinary experience."

"We have to eat still." Franceska shrugged.

"May I join you?" Marek looked hopefully at Franceska.

"Is it proper to invite yourself?" Franceska studied him warily.

"No." Marek shook his head. "But we don't live in proper times. And, frankly, I'd rather be in the presence of good company."

"What about Piotr?" Franceska suggested, wondering how Marek's loneliness had become her responsibility.

"Like I said, I'd rather be in the presence of good company."

"My mother is bedridden, and my father hates that I work in the nightclub." Franceska tilted her head as she tested Marek.

"My parents are deceased." Marek looked back at her unphased. "It's not right to leave a poor orphan alone and out in the cold."

"You're hardly a poor orphan." Franceska rolled her eyes before adding, "And, given the circumstances, it's in poor taste to even jest about such things."

"Don't worry, I'll be on my best behavior when you introduce me to your parents." Marek grinned.

"I suppose there's no refusing you, is there?" Franceska asked rhetorically.

"Nope."

"You'll be on your best behavior?" Franceska pointed a warning finger at him.

"I promise." Marek held up his right hand as he vowed. "In fact, why don't you give me the address, and I'll bring by a bottle of vodka?"

"My parents abstain from drink."

"That will make it easier for me to explain why I won't be partaking." Marek smiled slightly.

"This doesn't mean that you and I, in any way, are a couple." Franceska offered a warning look to Marek.

"Of course not." Marek again raised his hand in defense. "Purely platonic."

"Purely."

"Just don't be surprised when I ask for your hand in marriage this evening."

"Marek!" Franceska growled, but, if she were honest, was quite pleased with the teasing as it provided a wonderful distraction from the impending doom.

"Sorry, I tend to make light of situations when I'm nervous." Marek chuckled. "It was a silly joke."

What am I doing? Franceska asked herself as she watched Marek closely while trying to keep whatever feelings she had for him tightly locked away.

Chapter Nineteen:
The Last Supper

"To live is to suffer, to survive is to find some meaning in the suffering."

Friedrich Nietzsche

"Father, this is Mr. Rosenberg, my employer," Franceska introduced Marek to Mr. Mann when they arrived back at the apartment.

"Pleased to meet you," Marek spoke politely as he extended his hand in greeting.

"Yep," Mr. Mann shook his hand quickly as he replied with a measure of disdain for both the unannounced visit and for his prejudice against Marek's place of employment.

"Mr. Rosenberg will be dining with us," Franceska continued as she held up a bag containing as much produce as she could scavenge.

"Oh," Mr. Mann spoke slowly as he jutted out his jaw, and Franceska knew he was frantically searching for an excuse to decline.

"I'll start cooking." Franceska brushed past her father.

"Is this such a good idea with your mother still convalescing?" Mr. Mann asked, finally landing on a suitable excuse.

"I'm sure some company would cheer her," Franceska replied with forced cheerfulness.

"You clearly don't know your mother," Mr. Mann muttered as he sat in his chair while Marek sat nearby on the couch.

Entering the kitchen, which was adjacent to the living room, and setting down the groceries on the counter, Franceska strained to hear what the men were discussing.

Again, she found it odd to be having dinner with her family after witnessing the parade of terrors to come, but the alternative was to sit and mope in silence and fear. She refused to partake in such behavior, and wanted to prove to herself that the Nazis could never crush her spirit.

"We attended the victory parade," Marek began respectfully, and Franceska braced for her father's sarcastic response.

"I had to attend to Franceska's mother," Mr. Mann explained his absence.

"Your daughter mentioned that Mrs. Mann had a terrible accident on the day of the invasion."

"Yep," Mr. Mann replied softly, but Franceska could discern the frustration in his voice.

"The doctors were unable to diagnose her properly?" Marek asked, desperately seeking to keep the conversation going.

"They were finally able to get an x-ray that was unfortunately inconclusive. They need to perform some other tests, but we thought it best to bring her home until the equipment is available."

"I'm glad you were you able to secure her discharge from the hospital. I'm sure she's more comfortable at home."

"They were all too happy to part ways with her," Mr. Mann replied with a little chuckle.

"I doubt that was the case."

"I'll let you make up your own mind," Mr. Mann offered another chuckle of anticipation, and Franceska assumed he was hoping that his wife would scare off Marek.

"So, they couldn't complete their diagnoses? Do they at least have an idea?" Marek continued.

"She's had a poor back for as long as I can remember." Mr. Mann shrugged. "The doctors thought that she may have some sort of degenerative disease, but the x-ray report showed otherwise."

"Franceska?!" Mrs. Mann shouted from her room.

"Yes?" Franceska asked as she left the kitchen and entered her mother's room to find her sitting up in the bed and seemingly in better spirits.

"Who's here?" Mrs. Mann asked.

"The manag—the accountant that I work for," Franceska replied with a soft smile.

"Why is he here?"

"I invited him for supper," she lied.

"Why?" Mrs. Mann looked suspiciously at her daughter.

"I...I felt like having company."

"You felt like entertaining?" Mrs. Mann continued in her suspicion. "Are you going to marry this man?"

"What?!" Franceska shot her head back in shock. "Why would you conclude that?"

"You've never brought a man home before." Mrs. Mann shrugged as if the answer was obvious. "And you don't enjoy the company of men, and you—"

"I get it!" Franceska interrupted. "But I promise you that it's purely platonic."

"Alright," Mrs. Mann replied unconvincingly. "If you say so."

"In either case, be nice."

"Bring him in here. I want to meet him."

"In here?" Franceska frowned as she examined her mother in a nightgown and covered in blankets. "That seems rather unconventional."

"I'm not concerned about such drivel," Mrs. Mann replied coldly.

"How fortunate for everyone," Franceska muttered sarcastically under her breath.

"You sound like your father." Mrs. Mann grinned slightly. "You both think I'm deaf and can't hear your underhanded remarks. Anyway, bring this boy in so I can set him straight and make sure that he'd be a suitable husband."

"He's no boy, Mother. Please don't embarrass me." Franceska grimaced.

"I promise you that I will." Mrs. Mann nodded excitedly.

This was such a bad idea letting him come for supper, Franceska squeezed her eyes shut as she marched herself out to the living room.

"Is she awake?" Mr. Mann asked, and Franceska noticed that the two men were sitting in what appeared to be uncomfortable silence.

"She is, and she'd like to speak with Mr. Rosenberg."

"Me?" Marek pointed at his chest.

"Is there another Mr. Rosenberg here?"

"She gets her attitude from her mother," Mr. Mann explained to Marek.

"Hopefully she gets her looks from her as well," Marek replied, but suddenly stopped when he realized how offensive that might have sounded.

After a brief yet tense pause, Mr. Mann burst into laughter, and Franceska sighed her relief.

She understood her father appreciated a witty remark, even if it was at his expense, but also understood that Marek would have a lot more to prove if he intended to pursue a more permanent place in this family.

If that's what he plans, Franceska watched Marek closely, but felt she was too confused by her own repressed feelings to judge his intentions clearly.

He was a kind man, even if at times his impatience got the better of him, but he had difficulty with liquor even though Franceska had never seen him partake. Still, his core was good, and there was a richness beneath the surface that Franceska knew was begging to see the light. She had seen the beautiful books of poetry in his office, and knew he had a soft heart that sought after connection.

Regardless, her spirit warned her to wait.

"Is he coming?" Mrs. Mann yelled from the bedroom.

"Yes!" Franceska yelled back, possibly louder than necessary.

"How do I look?" Marek whispered to Franceska.

"The same as when you asked me before we entered the apartment," Franceska replied quickly as she ushered him over to her mother's bedroom.

"Mrs. Mann?" Marek asked cordially as he entered the room.

"I'm going to start making dinner," Franceska mentioned as she closed the door behind Marek.

Biting her lip in amusement, Franceska could scarcely contain a laugh as she imagined the discomfort Marek was enduring while being left alone in the room with her mother. This was the real test, after all, she thought. If Marek couldn't handle Mrs. Mann, then there was little to no chance that a union between them would be possible.

"That was cruel," Mr. Mann spoke over his shoulder from the safety of his chair. "Good job."

"I should probably save him." Franceska glanced at her mother's closed door.

"The path to Heaven is paved through Hell." Mr. Mann shook his head.

"I'm not sure Mother would appreciate being described as Hell." Franceska smirked.

"That's why I said it while the door was closed."

Franceska chuckled as she began to prepare the dinner.

Taking out the flour and salt, Franceska began mixing the ingredients into a mold. Then, making a well in the center, she cracked an egg and added milk, oil, butter, and cream cheese. Kneading the dough, Franceska set it aside and allowed it to rest.

"Yes, ma'am," Marek spoke timidly as he opened the door and left the room with wide, troubled eyes.

"What did she say?" Franceska whispered after Marek closed the door.

"A lot…she said…a lot…of things." Marek stared at the floor in shock.

"If you need to leave, no one will blame you," Franceska spoke patronizingly.

"No, no, no." Marek swallowed nervously. "I'm not going anywhere."

Franceska tried to contain her grin, but she found his persistence endearing.

"You misunderstand me," Marek began, noticing her grin. "I'm not going there," he pointed toward Mr. Mann, "Or there," he pointed toward Mrs. Mann's closed door. "I'm staying exactly where I am."

"You can help me cook, then." Franceska nodded for him to follow her, which he gladly did.

"Pierogies?" Marek asked as he looked at the ingredients laid out on the counter.

"Have you made them before?" Franceska asked as she organized the kneaded dough.

"I used to make them with my mother every Sunday," Marek replied with a nostalgic smirk.

"Oh?" Franceska looked up at him, remember how he stated that his parents were deceased.

"She raised me alone," Marek continued as he gently, yet firmly, took over preparing the pierogies.

"Where was your father?" Franceska asked as she stood to the side and watched him with mesmerization as he seemed entirely at home in her kitchen.

"I don't know." Marek shook his head. "I never asked, and my mother never told me. She was treated so cruelly because she was a single mother, but she took their scorn in stride. She was a proper woman, and I don't imagine it easy for her to endure the rumors spread about her, but she never complained, at least not to me."

"And when did she pass?"

"A couple of years ago," Marek replied plainly, but Franceska wondered if he was trying to disguise his pain.

"I'm sorry."

Marek didn't reply as he kept himself busy preparing the pierogies, and Franceska was surprised at his speed and efficiency.

"I wonder what she would've thought of our current state," Marek spoke after a moment. "My mother, that is."

"What do you mean?"

"Well, with the Nazis invading and all."

"Do you know if both your parents were Jewish?" Franceska leaned against the counter as she crossed her arms, content to let him cook.

"My mother kept my father's last name, so I know that he likely was Jewish, and my mother was without a doubt one of the tribe."

"Was she religious as well?" Franceska asked.

"Yes, but she was actually a Catholic convert."

"Really?" Franceska frowned.

"Part of me wonders if that is why my father and her split, or maybe he passed away, or…I really have no idea, and I don't care to know either. It was Mother and me against the world."

"What did she think about you managing the nightclub?" Franceska asked, interested to know more about Marek.

"Well," Marek chuckled before continuing, "Much like your mother, she had no idea."

"She knows," Mr. Mann spoke over his shoulder from the living room.

"She does?" Franceska asked in a hushed tone as she glanced at her father.

"Mothers always know these things." Mr. Mann shrugged.

"I sure hope not." Franceska grimaced.

"Perhaps he's right," Marek muttered quietly.

"What are you reading lately?" Franceska asked Marek, shifting the subject to something of a lighter subject.

"Reading?" Marek glanced at her curiously.

"I've seen the books littering your office."

"Ah, yes." Marek cleared his throat before continuing, "I keep that area of my life quite private."

"You invited yourself over for dinner." Franceska looked at him with a warning gaze. "If you occupy my life then I'm going to occupy yours."

"Fair enough." Marek bit his cheek nervously.

"Well?" Franceska pressed.

"I've, um, I've been uh—"

"Why are you so nervous?"

"I've been reading a collection of poems."

"Oh?" Franceska smiled as she examined him, still busily preparing the meal, and found this soft side of him charming. "And what do these poets write about?"

"You should know." Marek paused and looked intently at her and with a gaze she had never seen him offer before.

"What do you mean?" Franceska looked back at him nervously.

"They're writing about you."

Franceska was stunned into silence at the sudden amorous statement, and even Mr. Mann turned around in his chair to look at the two of them.

"Oh." Franceska cleared her throat.

"I don't mean to make you uncomfortable," Marek continued, undeterred by the awkwardness of the moment.

"Not at all," Franceska lied. While she did appreciate the romance, she found it entirely misplaced with her father a few feet behind them. Although, she concurred that if he had said such things to her in private, she would've let her guard down entirely.

"You've infected my thoughts since the day I asked you to dance at the club," Marek persisted affectionately.

"I…really?" Franceska swallowed as her cheeks burned crimson from embarrassment mixed with desire. "I thought you hated me?"

"The only thing I hated is that I couldn't get you out of my head." Marek took a step closer to Franceska.

"I…" Franceska was lost for words, and still very conscious of her father a mere couple feet behind her.

"You're my first thought in the morning, and my last at night." Marek gently touched her chin.

Mr. Mann cleared his throat to call attention to the fact they were not alone.

"I'm…" Franceska remained bewildered as Marek took a step back.

"I would like to marry you."

"I thought you said you were merely teasing about that," Franceska replied, entirely shocked by the turn of events.

"You don't have to reply now, but with the way our world is changing, I would like to spend what time we have left in love and happiness." Marek looked down at her with a bright and hopeful smile.

"I'll…" Franceska again cleared her throat. "I will think about it."

"She agrees," Mr. Mann interjected.

"I do?" Franceska shot her father a heated glare.

"Marrying him would get you out of our hair." Mr. Mann shrugged.

"Excuse me?" Franceska grew indignant. "You would still be living under the stars if it wasn't for me!"

"And we're grateful, we are, but you need to start living your own life."

"You are my life."

"We shouldn't be." Mr. Mann raised a brow.

"In either case, I can't leave you." Franceska shook her head. "You need someone to help around the house and with Mother."

"We would manage."

"How would you manage?" Franceska tilted her head. "When have you ever cooked anything?"

"I could learn." Mr. Mann shrugged.

Franceska scoffed.

"I have some savings," Marek began.

"You have savings? You live at the nightclub!" Franceska remained unconvinced.

"Which means for years I have been saving, and all that money is safely in a bank." Marek grew a cocky grin. "We could get a larger place, your parents included."

"A newly married couple doesn't want some old freeloaders like us tagging along." Mr. Mann waved to dismiss the idea as ridiculous.

"Your family is my family," Marek spoke tenderly as he looked deep into Franceska's eyes before quoting from scripture, "Wherever you go, I will go; wherever you live, I will live. Your people will be my people, and your God will be my God."

"If you don't marry him, I will," Mr. Mann muttered as he returned to reading.

"This all very sweet, but what are we going to do about the fact that we're occupied by a government that hates Jews?" Franceska remained in her wariness.

"There will always be a reason not to get married," Marek spoke softly and with understanding. "I can't promise you a good life, or a life of prosperity or unending happiness, but what I can promise you is my love. You will always have that."

"You're kind, but I need some time to think." Franceska looked at him sheepishly.

"Of course." Marek grinned as he rubbed his hands together while watching the pierogis coming along nicely and stated, "This should be ready shortly. Why don't you sit and relax, and I'll bring this out when its ready?"

This is not at all how I thought the evening was going to go, Franceska thought as she walked back to the couch and sat near her father.

After a few moments, Franceska realized that her father was staring at her with a peculiar grin.

"What?!" Franceska asked, startled by his reaction.

"He's a good person," Mr. Mann whispered.

"I'm happy for him," Franceska whispered back, "But now is not the time to be entertaining such pursuits. I need to focus on you and Mother."

"Don't use us as an excuse," Mr. Mann pressed. "You're scared about what it means to truly love. Don't hide behind your Mother and I, otherwise you'll end up resenting us."

"I'm not hiding." Franceska frowned sharply.

Mr. Mann offered a raised brow of doubt as he examined her closely.

"The food will be ready shortly," Marek spoke cheerfully from the kitchen. "I'll collect Mrs. Mann and we can all eat together."

"What did he say?" Mr. Mann asked as he looked back at the kitchen to see that Marek was walking briskly toward the bedroom.

"If I knew that cooking would've brought out this side in him, I would've asked him over a long time ago," Franceska spoke softly to her father as they both watched with bated breath as Marek knocked softly on the door before entering.

Mrs. Mann could be heard cackling from the room, and Franceska assumed her mother was mocking his suggestion.

Then, and after what seemed like a long few minutes, Franceska watched in shock as Mrs. Mann came out of the room with her arm slung around Marek's shoulder.

"Take your time," Marek spoke tenderly as he guided Mrs. Mann to the couch.

"Careful! Careful!" Mrs. Mann barked as she winced while she fell gently plopped down on the couch.

"There," Marek sighed as he retreated to the kitchen.

"You were right," Mrs. Mann leaned over and whispered to Franceska.

"About what?" Franceska asked as she watched her mother with wide eyes.

"That's no boy." Mrs. Mann cackled.

"He proposed," Mr. Mann leaned over and whispered to Mrs. Mann.

"Good!" Mrs. Mann nodded firmly. "We'll start wedding preparations."

Mr. Mann shook his head in disappointment before pointing at Franceska and adding, "She said that she needs time to think."

"Why would she say something so foolish?" Mrs. Mann glared at Franceska.

"She's worried about—"

"I can speak for myself," Franceska interrupted, and Mr. Mann relented.

"Well, go on," Mrs. Mann prodded. "Speak."

"They're in the oven," Marek spoke cheerfully as he returned to the living room and sat in the chair opposite Mr. Mann. "Shouldn't be too much longer now."

"He's cooking?" Mrs. Mann raised her eyebrows at Franceska. "Do you know what I would give for this useless sack to have cooked for me once? Once?!"

"There's no point in beating around the bush," Franceska began while annoyed. "So, we might as well all discuss it in the open. My final decision is that I need time to think about it."

"She's talking about your proposal," Mr. Mann explained to Marek.

"I gathered as much." Marek nodded.

"Franceska!" Mrs. Mann griped. "If I were you, I would—"

"You're not me," Franceska interrupted coldly. "And the fact of the matter is that this is my life, and I'm entitled to make these decisions."

"Fair enough." Mrs. Mann nodded, and Franceska was almost startled that she wasn't going to pursue the argument.

"I couldn't help but overhearing, but you're into poetry?" Mr. Mann asked with a twinge of excitement.

"I am." Marek nodded, and Franceska noticed his eyes growing bright, hoping that he could have a conversation about a topic he sincerely enjoyed.

"You're familiar then with Adam Mickiewicz?"

"'The nectar of life is sweet only when shared with others.'" Marck quoted proudly.

"He's one of my favorite poets!" Mr. Mann grew excited.

"He's Polish, too."

"Did you read his Crimean Sonnets?" Mr. Mann held up a finger in anticipation.

"Elegant works, to be sure." Marek leaned forward.

Franceska felt a warmth within her spirit as she listened to her father and Marek continue to talk at length about their favorite pieces of work.

She wasn't ignorant enough to believe that nights like these would last, but she was, at least, content to enjoy the moment. She prayed that such beauty and peacefulness would continue forever, but Franceska knew that within the very own city, sinister plans were likely being devised.

Then, and most unexpectedly, Mrs. Mann reached over and took Franceska's hand in hers.

Alarmed, and wondering if something was wrong, Franceska looked over at her mother to find that she was merely being affectionate.

With tears flooding her eyes, Franceska squeezed back on her mother's hand as she returned to watching Marek and her father laughing and enjoying each other's company. With her mother's affection, and Marek's ability to bring her family together in a way that

Franceska had never experienced, her fears began to melt. Drawing a deep breath, Franceska simply allowed herself to enjoy this rare and wonderful moment.

Chapter Twenty: Prima

"Knowing your own darkness is the best method for dealing with the darknesses of other people."

Carl Jung

"Are you sure about this?" Franceska asked as she peeked out the backstage door and noticed a crowd gathering for her debut ballet performance as Lola Horowitz.

"It's too late now," Marek replied as he also peeked out the door, sounding just as nervous as Franceska.

"There are so many Germans." Franceska looked at the officers and soldiers who were swiftly becoming drunk and causing quite a ruckus.

"Let's give them a good performance, then." Marek drew a deep breath to steady his nerves. "Maybe they'll see that this is a respectable establishment, and it'll stay in business."

"But they chased away all the regulars," Franceska replied with worry. "It's become a German nightclub."

"If they keep us in business, who cares who the clientele might be?"

"I care!" Franceska whispered harshly at him. "These men are brutes! They kill without a second thought. If they find out that you and I are, well, you know…they'll kill us."

"They think we're less than animals," Marek replied tenderly. "Show them that you're higher than the angels."

"That's blasphemy," Franceska replied quickly as she returned to staring out at the crowd.

The Polish Tango music was still playing vibrantly and loudly, and Franceska wondered how long the Germans would permit this type of music to continue.

Scanning her eyes through the rowdy German officers and soldiers, Franceska spotted one man who was not joining in the revelry.

She noticed that he was a German policeman, and he wore a green patch with a white swastika on his arm. He was sitting on the edge of the booth with his legs crossed and smiling at the singer.

Yet Franceska found his smile unnerving as his lips were curled in the corners of his mouth pleasantly, but his gaze remained determined as if he was trying to uncover an important truth.

"Something isn't right with that officer," Franceska spoke to Marek.

"I know," Marek replied with concern. "I've been watching him all night. He's been in that exact position the entire evening and hasn't ordered a single drink. He simply sits and stares."

"I don't like this." Franceska closed the backstage door and looked up at Marek with worry.

"Me neither." Marek took Franceska's hands in hers before asking, "Have you decided whether you'd like to marry me?"

"This is not the time!" Franceska growled as she pulled away from him.

"What are you scared of?" Marek threw his hands out in exasperation.

"It's what you're not afraid of that worries me." Franceska looked at him closely.

"What do you mean?"

"We could end up hurt." Franceska relaxed her shoulders a measure. "And I mean really hurt."

"'Better to have loved and lost than not to have loved at all'," Marek quoted.

"That's moving, but I don't know if it's true." Franceska's eyes welled. "If I allow myself to feel for you, and I lose that, it will destroy me."

"Only one way to—"

"And another thing," Franceska interrupted as she threw her hands onto her hips before continuing to berate him, "Chose appropriate times to ask these things! I need to concentrate on my routine, and I can't have you in the back of my mind while I'm up there."

"But that's the problem."

"What is?" Franceska shrugged.

"You can put me to the back of your mind, but I can't do the same with you." Marek offered her a sad smile. "You're always my first thought. When I sit down to eat, I think of you, when I wake up in the morning, you're there, and the minute I say goodbye to you in the evening, I can't wait until we meet again."

"Stop it," Franceska spoke softly as her eyes welled. "How am I supposed to concentrate?"

"Now you know how I feel." Marek offered her a soft kiss on the cheek, and Franceska felt a warmth spreading throughout her chest.

Before he could back away, Franceska threw her arms around his neck and squeezed him tightly.

"Is that a yes, then?"

"I will say yes." Franceska broke off the embrace as she ran her hand along the stubble on his chin, "Just not now."

"When?" Marek pressed.

"I'll know when it's right." Franceska nodded.

"Before I forget, Mrs. Judtowa will be making an appearance tonight."

"Mrs. Judtowa?" Franceska frowned. "The owner of this club? Why now?"

"She fled Warsaw the minute the invasion started, but now that the fighting is over, she's returned," Marek explained.

"Should I be worried about her?" Franceska grew concerned.

"I've never met a more severe woman, and I've already met your mother."

"That is concerning…" Franceska clicked her tongue.

The music stopped, and Franceska listened as the singer spoke in German, "Now ladies and gentleman, we come to the crescendo of the evening. Here it is, the moment you have all been waiting for, Lola Horowitz!"

An ecstatic round of applause erupted, and Franceska felt her heart skip a beat from excitement and nervousness.

"That's my cue." Franceska opened the door.

"You're going to do great!" Marek called after her.

Ignoring him, Franceska closed the door behind her and donned a bright smile as she was welcomed onstage, passing by a disgruntled Celina and Angelica. Franceska wondered if she would ever be on good terms with these two ladies, or if they'd always look at her through a envious lens.

But something happened then that Franceska would never have expected. The minute she walked onstage, the room drew silent. So silent, in fact, that if it weren't for the lights on the stage being dimmed, she would've imagined that the nightclub had suddenly been evacuated. She prayed that she would be able to live up to the crowd's anticipation of her performance.

With an enthusiastic smile, Franceska looked over the crowd, ensuring that she made eye contact with as many as possible.

Yet her enthusiasm almost vanished when she locked eyes with the policeman with the green patch. His smile had faded entirely, and he was looking at her carefully, making her wonder if he knew that she was Jewish.

"You look radiant this evening," Lena began warmly through the microphone.

"Thank you," Franceska replied loudly, returning to her enthusiastic state.

While she didn't want to appear conceited, she was well-aware that she looked amazing. Marek had somehow been able to order her a ballet costume, and this evening she wasn't forced to wear the ill-fitting and faded costume she had become accustomed to. Instead, she sported a gorgeous glittery costume with a layered net skirt that floated every time she moved.

"We have been practicing without cessation for this very special occasion," the singer continued as she returned her attention to the crowd. "Tonight, we will be performing *Swan Lake*."

Another round of applause erupted from the crowd as their anticipation swelled.

The lights shone brighter, focusing on Franceska at center stage, and the patrons drew quiet as they waited anxiously for the performance to begin.

The *Swan Lake* solo was undoubtedly the most difficult to execute correctly, and Franceska was determined to showcase her capabilities.

The cello and violin began softly, and Franceska held her arm up gracefully before bowing it down tenderly like a swan dipping its head into a lake. Her movements were fluid, elegant, and she executed the solo dance routine with a refinement that is birthed from decades of dedicated practice.

Franceska lost herself to the soft music as she performed again in the capacity she so desperately craved. How she missed the limelight of the stage with all eyes on her as she danced. How she missed the beautiful music and the intricate movements.

Not that she despised the dancing she performed during the Polish Tango, but this was where her heart belonged. Ballet made sense to her, and when the world around her was confusing and difficult to navigate, she found peace and meaning in performing.

The music began to crescendo, signifying the end of the solo was approaching, and Franceska spun and spun and spun on her toes, keeping her arms in correct position, and how she wished her parents were in attendance to enjoy the show.

With the final bar of music, Franceska threw her arms up and back with her leg raised and extended behind her, creating the imagery of a swan raising its majestic wings.

The audience burst into ecstatic applause and cheering. With tear-filled eyes, Franceska bowed in thanks for their admiration. Then, turning to the musicians, she bowed to them, thankful that they, although playing an entirely foreign style of music for them, were perfect in their timing and form.

"Lola Horowitz!" Lena announced again through the microphone, promoting Franceska's stage name, and the drunken German officers, policemen, and soldiers who had cruelly taken over the city, applauded a Jewess, and Franceska found that a victory greater than any she could imagine.

"Stunning!" Marek embraced her when she returned to the back of the stage.

"Really?!" Franceska asked as she heartily repaid the embrace.

"I knew you could do it!" Marek beamed with pride as he took a step back.

"I appreciate your faith in me." Franceska smiled shyly at him.

"They'll want more from you," Marek warned. "You teased them with such brilliance, but they'll want to see more!"

"I'll change into my regular costume, then, and join the other two girls on stage." Franceska nodded as she walked toward the dressing room.

Looking behind her, Franceska noticed that Marek was watching her closely, and everything within her wanted to scream *yes!* Still, she knew that her acceptance of his proposal would have to wait for the right timing. She didn't know when that would be, but it would be soon, and she would know when the time was right.

Entering the dressing room, she spotted Celina and Angelica inspecting themselves in front of the mirror, preparing to return to the stage.

"I caught some of your dance," Angelica began sheepishly.

"You did good," Celina added.

"Thank you." Franceska smiled softly at them, wondering if this was some ploy or if they were being sincere.

"Would you be able to teach us some of those moves?" Angelica asked, and Franceska thought she heard a hint of remorse.

"I suppose I could, yeah." Franceska nodded as she sat in front of the mirror.

A knock rattled against the door.

"Give us a couple minutes!" Celina barked.

"I need to speak with Franceska," Piotr began.

"You can't come in while we're changing!" Angelica yelled.

"There's a German police officer here who would like to speak with Franceska," Piotr explained.

"With me?!" Franceska asked as her heart fell into her stomach.

"Yes," Piotr replied.

"What does he want?" Franceska continued in her worry.

"He didn't mention, only that he needed to speak with you."

"What do I do?" Franceska asked the ladies quietly.

"What choice is there?" Celina shrugged, looking equally as worried.

"He says it's urgent," Piotr pressed.

"Tell him I'll be right out," Franceska replied, wondering if her parents were involved, or if she was about to be arrested, or any other scenario that she concocted in a panic.

"I will, but please hurry," Piotr replied before walking away.

"Should I change first?" Franceska asked the ladies again.

"If he says its urgent, I would go now." Angelica gestured to the door.

"You're probably right," Franceska muttered as her mind continued to race with all the horrible scenarios she expected to unfold.

Leaving the dressing room, Franceska felt her heart pounding in her chest as she walked down the to the dance floor.

"Very good performance!" a German soldier exclaimed when she passed by him.

"Thank you," Franceska replied brightly in German, but she kept her eyes firmly on the officer who was watching her with a steely gaze.

Yet now the officer was no longer sitting alone in the booth, which was even more concerning for Franceska. Across from him was a rather plump woman who was wearing a large white hat with fur draped across her shoulders. Franceska assumed she was in her late forties or early fifties, and she wore bright red lipstick and dark eyeshadow.

Neither the officer nor the woman spoke to each other, and Franceska wondered how or why she was being involved in whatever impromptu meeting this was.

"Bravo!" Another soldier held up a drink in honor of Franceska.

Franceska wished that she could revel in the admiration from the many patrons within the nightclub who were heaping praise upon her, but all she could contemplate was what the police officer considered so urgent. He was still sitting with his legs crossed and he watched her closely as she arrived at his table.

"Good evening," Franceska greeted him politely in German, and tried to hide her nervousness by squeezing her hands together in front of her.

The officer didn't reply, but instead stared up at her pensively, and Franceska was wondering what he was trying to decipher.

The woman with the large hat didn't bother to even look in Franceska's direction, and she sat smoking in the booth as if she was sitting alone. It was odd, to say the least, and Franceska grew curious as to who this woman was.

Finally, after a moment, the officer pointed to the seat in the booth beside the woman, and, in a surprisingly pleasant voice, said, "Please sit down."

Glancing behind her, Franceska looked through the nightclub for Marek, hoping that he would realize where she was and who she was speaking with.

"You're in no danger," the officer assured her as he held his hand out for her to sit.

Disappointed that Marek was nowhere to be seen, and understanding she had little choice in what was about to happen next, Franceska sat near the woman in the booth who still hadn't acknowledged her presence.

Again, neither the officer nor the woman said anything. Instead, the officer tilted his head as he studied Franceska, who found him unnerving, and sensed that she was being toyed with.

"May I ask what you wanted to speak with me about?" Franceska began, hoping he would at least reveal his purpose.

"I'm Chief Reinhard Schneider of the State Protection Police," he began as he removed his black leather gloves, revealing that he was missing two fingers on his left hand, and Franceska wondered if he had seen action. He was younger than her father, but not by much, and Franceska assumed he had fought in the Great War.

"This is Regina Judtowa." The officer gestured kindly to the woman. "She's the owner of this nightclub, if you haven't already had the pleasure of making her acquaintance."

The woman puffed her cigarette as she looked stonily over at Franceska whose blood ran cold. She was reminded of Marek's warning of Mrs. Judtowa, and Franceska knew she would need to tread carefully.

"I'm Lola Horowitz," Franceska replied as graciously as she was able.

"And your real name?" the officer's countenance remained stern, and Franceska noticed that Regina seemed to be watching her closely as well.

"Franceska Mann," she replied, seeing no benefit in lying.

"Do you know why I asked to speak with you?"

"No," she responded quickly, hoping he would arrive at the point shortly.

"You're fluent in German." The officer narrowed his gaze as he studied her closely. "I'm surprised."

"I've been fortunate in my education."

Schneider uncrossed his legs as he held up his hand to get Piotr's attention.

"Yes, sir?" Piotr was at once by his side.

"A bottle of vodka and three glasses." Schneider ordered.

"At once," Piotr replied politely as he half ran toward the bar.

"So," Schneider sighed as he stared at Franceska and asked, "Do you know why I'm here?"

"That is a vague question, sir." Franceska shook her head.

"Entertain me with a guess, then."

"That depends if you mean here in this booth, or here in Warsaw."

"I'm in this booth and Warsaw for the same reason. Why am I in Warsaw, Miss Mann?"

"I'm afraid that's a question many of us are asking," Franceska replied boldly, but wondered if her courage would be met with retribution.

"Someday soon I will tell you, because I believe you will play an integral role." Schneider crossed his arms.

"I'm not following." Franceska glanced between the officer and owner who both looked at her with some sort of veiled plan.

"You're an excellent ballerina. One of the best I've ever seen, and the reason I came here tonight."

"I am?"

"I heard there was a prima ballerina making a debut under a new stage name." Schneider took a sip of his vodka. "I had to see for myself if you were worthy."

"Worthy of what?" Franceska felt as though she was going to pass out as her heart continued to race.

"A special project." Schneider leaned forward and looked closely at her, and Franceska thought he was searching her face for secrets.

"Oh?" Franceska's anxiety increased substantially, but, then again, she wondered if this somehow would be her big break.

Maybe this special project meant that she would be involved with dancing in greater establishments than this nightclub. Oddly enough, the very idea of leaving the club, and Marek, made her feel sad. It wasn't too long ago that she had refused to even entertain the idea of working in a club like this, but now that she was here, she felt at home, and had found a romance that she would've never expected.

"Can we trust you?" Regina asked, and her voice was rich and commanding while her gaze carried a harshness that Franceska soon wished to forget.

"Of course," Franceska replied quickly, but hoped she didn't appear too eager.

"In time," Schneider spoke to Regina to caution her before he reached into his satchel and retrieved a pamphlet which he then slid across the table to Franceska.

"What's this?" Franceska asked warily without looking at the pamphlet.

"Read it." Schneider nodded.

Looking down at the pamphlet, Franceska immediately understood what was being asked of her.

The pamphlet was a sickly green color that was rather bare apart from the words *Deutsche Volksliste* printed across the front and the Nazi symbol of the eagle clasping a swastika in its talons.

"The German People's List?" Franceska asked for clarification as she put the pamphlet down and hid her hands under the table to try and conceal her shaking.

"Have you heard of it?" Schneider examined her closely.

Franceska shook her head quickly.

"You're tense." Schneider took notice of her trembling before he added, "There's no need to be nervous around me. I have no intention of being romantic with you. It's forbidden for Germans to have relations with non-Germans. It's seen as race defilement and is punishable by death. That's why the barracks are outside of the city."

In shock mixed with disgust, Franceska simply stared at him in silence, entirely dumfounded and speechless that he could utter such hateful rhetoric so casually, and how he could convince himself that she was in any way shape or form romantically interested in him.

"But…" He held up his finger excitedly before tapping the pamphlet and stated, "If you discover that you have some German heritage, provided you have all the required documentation, you may obtain a level of German citizenship."

"I…"

"I know, I know." Schneider held up his hands as he leaned back. "I understand the honor it would be to have German citizenship, and I can't promise you anything, but I know an Aryan when I see one."

Franceska was at a loss for words as she stared at the pamphlet with mesmerization. She was, however, relieved that her Jewishness was hidden from him, and yet also baffled by how incorrect his assumptions were.

"There are four categories of citizenship that you could be eligible for," Schneider opened the pamphlet as he showed Franceska as if he were a salesman showcasing various models for sale. "I think you would fall under Category II under German descent."

Franceska continued to study the pamphlet in utter disbelief. She couldn't understand how blatant the Nazis were with their categorization of people, and how arbitrary they seemed to have arrived at their designations. If someone had told her that such a document or program existed, she would've never believed them.

"There you are!" Marek spoke cheerfully as he arrived at the table.

"Mr. Rosenberg," Regina addressed him uncaringly, and Franceska recalled that the owner had chastised Marek for her idea of the free drinks for the soldiers.

"Rosenberg?" Schneider asked with suspicion as he glared at Marek, and Franceska didn't require any interpretation for what the chief was considering.

"Yes, sir," Marek replied in poor German, and Franceska marveled at how he didn't appear nervous.

"Jewish?" Schneider asked in Polish as his eyelid twitched, and Franceska marveled that he knew their language.

Marek nodded as he swallowed.

Without another word, Schneider took out a notepad from his breast pocket and began writing.

"If you have no further need of Miss Horowitz, then I will return her to the dressing room. The performance for the evening can't continue without her," Marek spoke softly but in such a manner as to convey the urgency.

"Nonsense! Of course they can proceed without her." Regina waved to dismiss Marek.

At a loss for what to say, Marek remained by the table, and Franceska looked up at him to find that he was desperately searching for another excuse to rescue her.

"You manage the club, Mr. Rosenberg?" Schneider asked as he continued to make his notes.

"Yes," Marek replied quickly.

"I'll need to see the financials." Schneider looked up at Marek.

"Sir?" Marek asked with confusion.

"You keep records I would assume?" Schneider shrugged.

"Yes, sir." Marek nodded.

"Good. I'll return tomorrow to collect them." Schneider closed his book and returned it to his breast pocket as he looked at Marek with disdain. Then, turning to Regina, he asked, "Do you have any further need of Miss Mann?"

Regina glanced away as she shook her head.

"Alright then." Schneider stood and looked pleasantly at Franceska before stating, "I will return tomorrow."

With that, the officer turned and left the nightclub.

"Don't embarrass me with the financials," Regina spoke to Marek as she stumped out her cigarette in the ash tray before retrieving another one.

"Mrs. Judtowa," Marek spoke courteously as he excused Franceska and himself, and they hurried backstage.

"What do we do?!" Franceska asked nervously as she clung tightly to Marek.

"What choice do we have? He'll be back tomorrow."

"Why would he want to look at your books?"

"I don't know." Marek shook his head in worry. "But I don't like it. Something terrible is about to happen. I know it."

Chapter Twenty-One:
Synagogue

"There is a way that seems right to a person, but its end is the way to death."

Proverbs 14:12

"I still don't understand," Marek spoke with confusion as he walked with Franceska through the city the next evening. "What special project was he referring to?"

"He didn't specify." Franceska shook her head. "But my Jewish identity is still hidden, at least for now."

"Maybe you should stop associating with me then."

"Perhaps." Franceska nodded.

Marek shot her a startled glance and Franceska smiled back at him before stating, "Don't fool yourself. Only death itself could separate us."

"And I'm afraid it will come to that." Marek looked back at her solemnly. "He made true on his promise and returned this morning to collect all the financial records for the club. Then he began asking about my own personal records and demanded to confiscate them as well."

"Really?" Franceska frowned. "Why would he focus on your personal finances? That doesn't make sense."

"Something is up." Marek ran his tongue along his teeth as he thought. "He's scheming, and I wish I knew how or why I was involved."

"You mentioned that you have some savings?"

"Quite a bit, yeah." Marek offered her a worried look. "And I plan to use that money to buy us a place."

"You should've withdrawn your funds," Franceska spoke her thoughts out loud.

"If I had known that he was going to be digging through my personal finances, I would've. Maybe he's trying to find something against me?"

"Like what?"

"I don't know." Marek shrugged. "Something illegal?"

"Is there anything I should worry about?" Franceska watched him warily.

"Of course not!" Marek frowned. "I'm simply stating that he might try something…"

"This is so stressful." Franceska rubbed the back of her neck as they continued to walk.

Hand in hand, the two walked through the city until they eventually arrived at the synagogue. It was a grand and spectacular building situated within the very heart of Warsaw. Four great pillars, and two enormous menorahs, flanked a large door.

"I don't see the point of this." Marek looked up at the stunning religious building.

"You don't have to come in." Franceska shook her head.

"A lot of people turn to religion when they're scared, but that doesn't mean—"

"I know," Franceska interrupted. "It's not that I'm trying to find God or save my soul, but I want to connect with my roots before places of worship like this are destroyed forever."

"Franceska," Marek began patronizingly. "They're not about to obliterate everything. This has some cultural significance. I think it's quite a stretch to believe that they'll destroy this. They hate us, sure, but don't you think that if they were going to try and kill us all off they would've done so already?"

"I saw it in his eyes." Franceska squeezed tightly on Marek's hand. "I saw the hatred in his gaze when he looked at you last night. In either case, something is coming, and I want to visit the synagogue while I still can."

"Fair enough." Marek threw his hands up in surrender. "I'll wait for you."

"I won't be long." Franceska patted his chest tenderly.

An engine roared from further up the street, and Franceska watched with unease as a German armored transport vehicle rounded the corner. About a dozen soldiers were in the back of the vehicle with their guns at the ready.

The armored vehicle came to a stop about twenty yards from the entrance of the synagogue, but Franceska found it curious that they simply idled there. The soldiers, with their weapons at the ready, stared menacingly at the handful of worshippers who were entering the house of worship.

Quickly pulling her shawl to cover her face, Franceska hid from the heated and hateful gazes and realized that this was an intimidation tactic.

"We should leave," Marek spoke with worry.

"I'm not going anywhere," Franceska spoke boldly. "They're trying to bully us. I won't back down so easily."

Marek didn't reply but kept his gaze locked on the armored vehicle.

"Are you sure you don't want to come in?" Franceska asked.

"I'll be alright," Marek replied tensely as he clenched his jaw.

"I won't be long," Franceska spoke softly as she squeezed his arm.

Opening the door to the synagogue, Franceska walked inside to find a handful of other men and women sitting in pews.

Unsure of the proper protocol, Franceska sat in the back pew and looked around the synagogue.

It had been years since she had attended a synagogue. She recalled her mother taking her to the wedding of a distant relation, but otherwise her Judaic instruction or education had been entirely neglected.

Still, she found the building beautiful and felt a peacefulness that she had long since forgotten. The natural light from the windows streamed into the synagogue, illuminating the white walls that were etched with beautiful designs.

Drawing a deep breath, Franceska looked down timidly at her hands, feeling rather out of place and a part of her wished that she hadn't forsaken the spiritual roots of her people.

"I'm seeing a lot of new faces darken our doors lately," a man spoke beside Franceska.

Turning, Franceska glanced up to see a rabbi looking at her with a welcome, yet firm, gaze.

"I should've attended many years ago," Franceska replied, understanding his wariness.

"In either case, you're here now," the rabbi replied with a kind smile as he sat in the pew in front of Franceska and turned to look at her.

"To be honest, I'm not sure why I'm here." Franceska looked back at the holy man with wide eyes. "I merely felt compelled."

"You're scared. That's natural." The rabbi nodded encouragingly. "What is your name?"

"Franceska. Franceska Mann."

"What are you afraid of, Franceska?"

"That we will lose everything," Franceska replied honestly. "I'll lose my parents, my friends, the man I love, and our way of life."

"That is always the case," the rabbi spoke tenderly. "There is no guarantee that we will ever see the ones we love again. You could walk out that door and be struck by a vehicle. No amount of time is guaranteed."

"I know, but this threat is rather present, and the Germans hate us for merely existing."

"And you're wondering why this is happening?" The rabbi nodded as he contemplated.

"Why would God allow this? We're the chosen people and we're being murdered like we're less than dogs."

"There is a group within our ranks who believe that when bad things happen, it's a result of God punishing us for our sins," The rabbi paused as he ran his hand through his beard before mentioning, "They're convinced that we've become too secular, and God is punishing us as a way to bring us back into the fold, as you're doing now by visiting the synagogue."

"And what do you believe?" Franceska asked, perceiving that his viewpoints differed.

"It's right that we should firstly look inward and contemplate what we have done to allow this? But then," the rabbi paused as he held his finger in the air. "No evil can come from above, and God does not interfere with the free will of mankind. Whatever may come to pass, I'm convinced that the everlasting spirit of our people will never cease. Whether the Nazi invasion is a punishment, or a cause of man's free will, the only thing that matters now is how we respond."

"And how should we respond?" Franceska watched him closely.

"With kindness to one another, with patience to endure, with joy in the moments that are permitted to us, and with the hope that this too shall pass."

"I appreciate you speaking with me today." Franceska forced a smile.

"I'll allow you a moment of quiet reflection." The rabbi touched her shoulder gently before he stood and began ministering to others in the synagogue.

This too shall pass, Franceska repeated the phrase as she again looked at her hands. *I'm not one for praying, and I'm not sure if you even exist, but could you help me? Whatever happens, if I can keep my parents safe, that's all that matters. I don't care if we live in that one-bedroom apartment for the rest of my days as long as they are safe.*

Some shouting in German came from outside, and Franceska, along with a handful of other worshippers, stood quickly, worried that they were in danger.

Fearing for Marek, Franceska swiftly left the synagogue. Yet as soon as she opened the door, her heart fell into her stomach when she found a group of four German soldiers surrounding Marek, grabbing him by the collar and yelling orders.

The transport truck which was once packed with soldiers now also had a handful of men, women, and children who were crying or staring with wide eyes.

"I don't understand what you're saying!" Marek shouted back in Polish, and Franceska detected that he was trying to remain calm.

"He doesn't speak German!" Franceska yelled in German as she arrived by his side.

"Interpret for this useless rat then!" one of the soldiers shouted at her as the other three restrained Marek.

"What's the problem?" Franceska asked as she placed a hand to her chest, feeling her heart racing.

"We're conscripting every able-bodied man, woman, and child over the age of twelve to repair damaged houses and buildings," the soldier continued with a little more composure.

"He operates The Melody Palace nightclub," Franceska spoke to the soldier as she patted Marek's shoulder. "He's unable to assist."

"I don't care if you're the pope!" the soldier shouted back. "You're both coming with us!"

"What's happening?!" Marek asked Franceska as the soldiers roughly took them to the awaiting transport vehicle and forced them into the back.

"They're taking us to help repair buildings," Franceska replied in Polish as she climbed onto the bench in the back of the transport vehicle.

"The buildings they bombed?!" Marek asked with incredulity. "They want us to repair the damage they dealt?!"

"I don't know much German," an younger woman in the transport vehicle interjected, "But they mentioned that they would provide compensation."

"Did they mention how long we'd be working?" Marek pressed, and Franceska knew he was stressed about the nightclub.

The woman shook her head.

"This is so infuriating." Marek rubbed his tired eyes.

"It's going to be fine." Franceska grabbed Marek's hand.

"We should never have stopped at the synagogue!" Marek barked at Franceska.

"You can't blame me for their actions!" Franceska barked back.

"You know how dangerous it is right now!" Marek continued to berate Franceska. "It was silly to make personal stops. We go from the nightclub and home, nothing else."

"If I may," the woman interjected again before continuing, "There are patrol vehicles going all over Warsaw. It's likely you would've been conscripted no matter where you were."

"That doesn't mean you're off the hook." Marek shot daggers at Franceska.

"Don't take your anger out on me."

"They're probably taking us away to be shot," Marek spoke under his breath, but loud enough that everyone in the truck heard.

"Don't scare him!" A woman covered her son's ears.

"I'm not the only one thinking it," Marek defended.

"They've endured enough cruelty," Franceska spoke sternly to Marek.

Looking intently at the faces of the others in the truck, Marek drew a deep breath and relaxed his shoulders before nodding his apology.

"They're going to make us work for a while, then we'll be free to go. You'll see." Franceska placed a gentle hand on Marek's back.

"I hope you're right." Marek looked solemnly at Franceska before glancing nervously at the other soldiers in the transport vehicle.

"They're all so young," Franceska whispered to Marek.

"That's all for now! Let's go!" the German soldier shouted to the driver.

With a lurch, the vehicle roared to life and began the journey which Franceska hoped would be short. Franceska kept her gaze keenly on the German soldiers, and was content, at least, to find that they appeared bored. They didn't seem at all interested in the civilians they had conscripted, and Franceska welcomed their apathy.

"Do you ever think of me?" Marek asked quietly after a few moments.

"What?" Franceska looked at him curiously, wondering if she had heard him correctly.

"Do you ever think of me?" Marek repeated as he watched her closely.

"Think of you?" Franceska asked as she glanced around the transport vehicle, hoping nobody was listening in on their conversation.

"Do I ever cross your mind?"

"I don't understand what—"

"Humor me…please…" Marek looked intently at her, and Franceska knew he was terrified.

Franceska studied his eyes for a moment before answering, "Constantly."

With a smile, Marek reached out and took her hand in his.

"What about you?" Franceska asked.

"If I planted a flower for every time I thought of you, I could walk in my garden forever," Marek replied as he returned the deep stare into Franceska's eyes.

Franceska smiled as her eyes welled before she stated confidently, "Yes."

"Yes, what?" Marek shook his head in confusion.

"That's my answer."

"Yes?!" Marek sat upright as he looked back at her with hope.

"Yes, I'll marry you." Franceska smiled as she closed her eyes and leaned her head on his shoulder.

"You've made me a happy man, Franceska. A happy man indeed."

"Think about our life together," Franceska whispered to him as they found this moment of intimacy amidst the terror. "That should distract you sufficiently."

"How can I think of anything else?" Marek chuckled quietly. "This is an odd feeling."

"What is?"

"To be so happy and so frightened at the same time."

"You don't have to be afraid of me." Franceska grinned at her own quip.

"Cheeky." Marek kissed her head.

"I was looking forward to making pierogies again tonight before we went to the club." Franceska lamented.

"It was your turn, too."

"My turn?" Franceska squinted at him. "There are no turns in marriage."

"Well, before we do marry, I need to make sure you can make a decent pierogi."

"I promise you, I'm—"

The truck came to an abrupt halt, and soldiers began shouting in German as they arrived at the back of the truck with their weapons trained on the civilians.

"He's ordering us to get out!" Franceska explained as the Germans took no care to clarify their demands.

"Back to reality," Marek muttered as he and Franceska left the truck.

Hundreds of civilians, mostly women and children, had been conscripted to repair the damaged houses and buildings. Franceska thought it was quite possibly the most inhumane example of adding insult to injury by forcing the people who were bombed to repair their own properties.

"You!" a soldier shouted in German as he pointed at Franceska and Marek. He was standing beside a large, well-ordered stack of bricks, and Franceska could already guess the responsibility he was going to assign them.

"Sir?" Franceska asked in German, and the soldier was almost surprised to hear her speak his native tongue.

"Take these bricks to that building." He pointed to a partially destroyed house at the end of the street.

"Do you have a wheelbarrow?" Franceska asked as she looked around for one.

"No!" the soldier shouted angrily.

"May I ask how long our shift is?" Franceska pressed.

"Until all these bricks are over there!" the soldier grew irate as he came close to Franceska and screamed in her face.

"That's enough!" Marek became defensive and stood between the soldier and Franceska.

"You filthy dog!" the soldier raised his rifle and aimed it at Marek's head.

"Stop!" Franceska screamed in German as she held her hand out to try and soothe his temper.

"Don't shoot," Marek spoke softly, but in Polish.

"Please lower your weapon," Franceska spoke as tenderly as she was able.

"He's a dirty dog!" the soldier screamed, and Franceska thought he was almost trying to convince himself that he had been affronted.

His eyes were wild, and Franceska noticed that his pupils were dilated. She wondered if he was even in control of his own actions, and he appeared under some sort of spell or, more likely, under the influence of a drug.

"He's my fiancé," Franceska continued to speak tenderly as she walked slowly toward the soldier.

The soldier didn't reply as he kept his rifle trained on Marek, and Franceska took note of the soldier's trembling arms. She knew he could, and would, pull the trigger at any moment. He was indoctrinated, drugged, and far from home.

"Please, my friend." Franceska placed a gentle hand on the soldier's arm before adding, "You're alright. You're safe. No one here wants to harm you."

Glancing nervously between Franceska and Marek, the soldier began to lower his weapon.

Then, abruptly, the soldier brushed Franceska's hand off his arm and ordered them to get to work.

"What was he saying?" Marek asked with wide eyes, and Franceska knew the exchange had severely shaken him.

"I don't think he even knows." Franceska watched the soldier as he began ordering tasks to other civilians.

"I'm guessing we're taking these to the house that he was pointing to?" Marek kicked one of the bricks.

"Are you alright?" Franceska asked as she looked at him tenderly.

"I'm fine!" Marek barked as he bent down to grab a brick. "Let's get this over with!"

Annoyed, but understanding Marek's reaction, Franceska also grabbed a couple of bricks and followed her fiancé toward the house.

It was a scene of organized chaos, and Franceska passed by many other men, women, and children who had been assigned to various tasks. Some were fixing roads, others were dismantling defensive structures, and some were repairing buildings.

Brick after thankless brick, Franceska and Marek supplied the builders with the necessary materials. They didn't speak much to each other as both Franceska and Marek were concentrating on completing their task in time to get to the nightclub.

"I need a second," Franceska panted while out of breath when they made another pass at the pile of bricks, and she felt as though they had scarcely transported any of them.

"Same." Marek nodded as he sat on the bricks.

"Back to work!" a soldier near them shouted when he took notice of them resting.

"A minute of reprieve. Please!" Franceska pleaded in German, and the soldier looked back at her with discomfort.

"No one is permitted rest." The soldier shook his head, but then walked away without ensuring that Franceska and Marek had followed his orders.

"Have you noticed how much it bothers them when I speak German?" Franceska asked as she watched the soldier leaving.

"It humanizes you," Marek replied as he huffed and puffed. "They think we're less than dogs, but when you speak German, they realize you're the same creature as they are. They can justify killing what they perceive as a pestilence, but speaking their own language shows that we are, essentially, one and the same, and maybe their indoctrination is, as we know it to be, false."

"You're a perceptive man, my fiancé." Franceska grinned as she stood to grab a brick.

"There you are!" a friendly voice called in German, and Franceska looked in the direction to find Chief Schneider waving at them from the back of a police vehicle.

With a cautionary wave of her own, Franceska glanced at Marek, unsure of what to do.

"I went to the club to speak with you," Schneider spoke cheerfully as he left the vehicle and walked toward them as if he was being reunited with old friends.

"We intended to be at the nightclub, but we were detained," Franceska replied, and glanced at Marek who offered a polite smile, but it was clear he didn't understand a word of the German she was speaking.

"I see that," Schneider replied in Polish, noticing that Marek was not following along. "Well, we'll put a swift end to that."

Calling the attention of a guard, Schneider gestured that he was taking both Franceska and Marek away.

"Come with me." Schneider offered a bright smile as he held his hand out toward his police vehicle.

Nervously, Franceska and Marek followed Schneider, and Franceska wondered if they were leaping from the frying pan into the fire.

Chapter Twenty-Two: Schneider

"Whoever fights monsters should see to it that in the process he does not become a monster. And if you gaze long enough into an abyss, the abyss will gaze back into you."

Friedrich Nietzsche

"Are you comfortable?" Schneider asked pleasantly when they were all in the police vehicle, which Franceska found unsettling.

"Yes, thank you," Franceska replied as she and Marek sat in the back.

"Good." Schneider nodded happily and then spoke in German to the driver, "Take us to The Melody Palace nightclub."

The vehicle started for the club while Franceska and Marek remained as quiet as possible. Franceska didn't understand Schneider's intentions with them. He was polite and cordial, yet he was also extreme in his views. She didn't know what to expect from this madman, and kept her guard raised.

"Let's stop here first," Schneider spoke with excitement, and Franceska peeked out the front of the vehicle to try and see what had caused him to become so animated.

"Oh no," Marek spoke quietly.

"What is it?" Franceska asked while still trying to look out the front window.

"Don't look." Marek tried to shield her eyes as the vehicle came to a stop, but it was of no use.

A group of men and women, with their hands tied behind their backs and bags over their heads, were standing with their backs against a wall.

A firing squad was aiming their rifles at these poor souls, and Franceska noticed that many other men, women, and children were in attendance, although she understood their presence was likely mandatory.

"Do you know who they are?" Schneider asked Franceska.

"Civilians," Franceska replied with disdain for this cruelty.

"What sort?" Schneider looked over his shoulder at Franceska. "Do you know?"

Franceska shook her head quickly as her eyes flooded with tears. Looking through the crowd, she spotted many who were crying and helplessly watching what was about to take place.

"Professors, teachers, lawyers, and judges," Schneider spoke casually.

Franceska didn't utter a word as she squeezed her eyes shut and prayed that she could be spared this experience and return to her parents.

"Do you know why they have to die?" Schneider asked casually.

Franceska didn't reply, unnerved by his casual tone. He seemed to believe that this was necessary, but Franceska knew it was simply cruel.

"Miss Mann, I need an answer," Schneider pressed.

"They don't have to die!" Franceska cried.

"They do…I'm the one who ordered their execution." Schneider opened the door and exited the vehicle.

Grabbing Marek's hand, Franceska looked at him with wide, terrified eyes, wondering what sinister plan Schneider was about to deploy.

Opening Franceska's door, Schneider held out his hand before stating politely, "Please join me."

"I'm comfortable where I am." Franceska refused.

Bending over, Schneider looked Franceska intently in the eyes before stating firmly, "You mistook that for a request."

Unsure of how to proceed, Franceska looked back at Marek who appeared just as panicked.

Seeing as she had no choice, Franceska exited the vehicle, but refused to accept his gesture when he moved to assist her.

With Franceska out of the vehicle, Schneider turned to look at the pending execution, which Franceska understood was state-sanctioned murder.

"Look at them closely, who do you see?" Schneider asked as he crossed his arms.

"It's as you said; they're lawyers, teachers—"

"Look closer." Schneider pressed.

"Aim!" the shout came from the commanding officer near the firing squad.

Franceska squeezed her eyes shut and pressed her fingers into her ears.

"Don't you dare!" Schneider grabbed her hands and forced them down by her sides before he yelled, "Open your eyes! You need to see this!"

"I won't!" Franceska refused.

"Let go of her!" Marek exited the vehicle.

"Take one more step and I'll kill you both where you stand!" Schneider shouted at Marek in Polish.

"Why are you doing this?!" Franceska pleaded.

"I need you to understand that your entire way of life is at an end. We're destroying everything Polish. Everything! Your statues will be torn down, your elite will be killed off, your castles raised to the ground, and your people destroyed."

Franceska tried to compose herself as a tear rolled down her cheek.

"I want you to watch." Schneider put his arm around her shoulder and squeezed tight.

"Fire!"

The shots rang out, and Franceska, along with a few others, couldn't help a yelp or a cry from escaping their lips as they watched those executed collapse limply to the ground.

"That wasn't pleasant," Schneider sighed as he rubbed Franceska's back gently. "But it was necessary. Do you understand why?"

Franceska shook her head in dismay as she loathed Schneider.

"We're ushering in a new era, a glorious era for the German people. As I said before, I know a German when I see one, and you have all the features, talents, and aptitude to help with my special project."

Franceska shook as she tried desperately to compose herself. She hated this man with all her heart and wished that she knew what special project he kept referring to.

Maybe I don't want to know, Franceska thought.

Without another word, Schneider, with his arm still around her shoulder, led Franceska back to the vehicle.

"Are you alright?" Marek asked with concern.

Franceska nodded quickly, trying to recover her dignity.

"Were you able to obtain documents?" Schneider asked from the front of the vehicle as he looked at Franceska as though they had done nothing more than run an errand.

Franceska shook her head quickly.

"It's imperative that you do so as soon as possible." Schneider offered a polite smile before ordering the driver to continue the journey to the nightclub. "For your sake, Franceska Mann, make sure you follow through."

"What's he saying?" Marek whispered in Polish.

"He's asking about my documentation," Franceska whispered as she sniffled. "Remember that pamphlet I showed you?"

Marek nodded before glancing at Schneider and offering Franceska a nod that indicated they would discuss the sensitive details later.

As they drove through the city, Franceska's heart grew harder and harder at the level of depravity being levied against her people. Executions were being performed at almost every square or park, and Schneider's words of warning rang in her ears. She knew the Nazis were hellbent on ridding the world of everything Polish or Jewish, but she failed to understand why.

"We're here," Schneider spoke cheerfully when they arrived at the nightclub.

Stepping out of the vehicle, Franceska and Marek warily followed the officer.

"Why doesn't he have an escort?" Marek whispered in Polish.

"Do I need one?" Schneider asked over his shoulder with a gratified smirk that he had overheard them.

"Not when you're with us, sir, no." Marek shook his head.

"I'll tell you a secret." Schneider placed his hands in his pockets as he stood back for Marek to unlock the door. "I'm supposed to have an escort. It's a requirement, really."

"Oh?" Franceska asked warily, wondering what his intentions were with them.

"But there are times, you must understand, when I have to do some difficult tasks, and it's unpleasant to expose some of the younger men to the harsher realities of war." Schneider looked at Franceska sternly, and she felt a cold chill running down her spine.

It was still early in the day, much too early for even Piotr to begin preparing the bar, and Franceska wondered how the officer would behave while alone with her and Marek. He had absolute power over them, and she feared that he would abuse that severely.

"Tell Mr. Rosenberg that I need to see the remaining books of business," Schneider spoke to Franceska in German, and she found it odd that he didn't speak in Polish directly to him.

"He says he needs the remaining books of business," Franceska translated.

"Remaining?" Marek looked confused as he unlocked the door to the empty club.

"Yes," Schneider replied quickly in Polish as he walked toward a booth.

"There are no other books of business," Marek whispered to Franceska.

"There are, Mr. Rosenberg," Schneider began after overhearing them. "I want you to bring them to me."

"I'll help you look." Franceska nodded toward the office.

Following Marek, Franceska grabbed his hand and squeezed it tightly, hoping to stay as close as possible to him.

"Miss Mann," Schneider called, and her heart fell into her stomach.

"Yes?" Franceska stopped in her tracks as she turned towards him.

"Grab us a bottle of vodka and two glasses." Schneider sat in the same booth as the previous night and crossed his legs.

"It'll be alright." Franceska patted Marek's arm. "Grab the books quickly."

"If I can find what he's talking about," Marek muttered as he entered the office.

Not wanting to incite Schneider's impatience, Franceska quickly grabbed the bottle of vodka, two glasses, and sat across from him in the booth.

"You deserve a medal," Schneider spoke softly as he poured their drinks.

"A medal?" Franceska frowned.

"For putting up with that Jew." Schneider nodded toward the office. "I don't understand how you can tolerate him. I'm going to have to wash the car's interior before I can use it again."

Franceska didn't reply as she shot her drink back.

"Dance for me." Schneider gestured at the stage.

"Excuse me?" Franceska asked, wondering if she had heard him correctly.

"Dance," Schneider replied casually as he poured himself another drink.

"I'm not prepared, sir." Franceska shook her head. "I don't have my dance costume, the musicians are absent, and—"

"I won't ask again," Schneider spoke harshly as he glared at Franceska.

"I will change into my costume, and—"

"Dance as you are!" Schneider thundered as he lost his patience.

"Yes, sir," Franceska spoke slowly as she walked toward the stage.

Then, removing her jacket and purse, she placed them on a chair nearby before kicking off her shoes and climbing onto the stage.

Looking back at Schneider, who was watching her closely, Franceska closed her eyes and took a deep breath.

Recalling the music in her head, Franceska began the dance she had performed the other night.

"No, no, no!" Schneider shouted, abruptly stopped Franceska, who wondered how she had offended him. "I know *Swan Lake*. Show me something else."

Something else? Franceska thought as she ran through the different compositions and routines.

"Get on with it!" Schneider yelled, making her flinch.

Drawing a deep breath to compose herself, Franceska began dancing a sequence she had been piecing together privately. It was incomplete, and it had been some time since she had revisited this dance, but she knew it would be something Schneider had never seen before.

Recalling the musical number she had envisioned would accompany the choreography, Franceska danced as best as she was able in her restrictive clothing. She knew that the police chief intended to humiliate her, and display his dominance, but she refused to let him humble her.

Losing herself to the movements and the music she had internalized, Franceska performed admirably, and, if she was honest, it was quite likely one of her best performances to date. She excelled under pressure, and there were few things less intimidating than a Nazi officer forcing her to dance.

"Well done." Schneider clapped when Franceska finished and bowed.

"Here they are!" Marek charged out of his office with some accounting books held high in his hands.

"Take them to the vehicle." Schneider gestured to the door as he poured himself another glass.

"I should prepare for the evening." Franceska began to gather her belongings.

"Nonsense." Schneider took another swig of vodka. "Come join me."

"Sir, I must—"

"You don't understand, do you?" Schneider offered a drunken laugh, and Franceska noticed that he had nearly consumed half of the bottle.

"Understand what, sir?" Franceska asked warily.

"Whatever I order, you must do. There is no questioning, manipulating, or negotiating. I have complete and absolute authority over you." Schneider winced at another shot of vodka burning his throat.

Franceska didn't reply as she slowly walked over to the booth and sat across from him.

"Because I like you, and I enjoy your dancing, I'll tell you how to survive. Find documents, anything that shows your Germanic heritage, and don't associate yourself anymore with the Jew, or any Jew for that matter. Things are about to happen, my sweet ballerina, and they're about to happen quickly. Distance yourself from him as soon as you can, otherwise you'll be dragged down with him."

*He really has no idea that I'm Jewish…*Franceska watched the police officer with disdain for his bias.

"You know what," the officer picked up the bottle and studied it for a second as he grew a mischievous grin before stating, "I'm going to tell you. I'm going to you everything."

"Everything?" Franceska asked as her heart raced in her chest.

"I'm going to tell you why I'm here, and why I'm pestering you."

Franceska heart pounded in her chest as she waited for him to divulge.

"Warsaw is to become a model city for German expansion," Schneider spoke loudly as he took another shot of vodka.

A model for who? Franceska remained wary.

"But between you and I, that is a secret." Schneider poured a glass for both himself and Franceska.

Franceska didn't reply as she felt herself growing increasingly nervous.

"Do you know why telling you this secret?"

Franceska shook her head quickly.

"Because no one will believe you." Schneider smiled, again with just his lips, and Franceska knew she was gazing into the eyes of a madman.

"I don't understand."

"Everything you see in here." Schneider pointed around the nightclub. "Everything outside the club, and, indeed, everything of Warsaw, is going to be destroyed. All your monuments, castles, historic landmarks, gone. In its place we will erect a perfect city for no more than one hundred and thirty thousand people. They will have all their needs met, they will—"

"But over a million people live in Warsaw…" Franceska narrowed her gaze, wondering if she could believe what he was telling her.

Schneider didn't reply, but instead grew a wicked grin in the corner of his mouth.

Franceska's blood ran cold as she looked back at him, and realized how much pleasure he took in drunkenly offering up this information.

"It'll be our little secret." Schneider took another sip before adding, "Or tell as many people as you want. No one will believe a word of it."

"They'll believe me," Franceska challenged, understanding that she would have to warn everyone she knew to get out of the city while they still stood a chance.

"No." Schneider shook his head before continuing, "No one will believe you. If you relay this to anyone, they'll think you're mad. They don't want to believe. They don't want to consider that something so drastic has even entered our minds. They want to believe that we're content with conquering, and that they can return to enjoying their lives. But they don't realize they're about to play a necessary role."

"Necessary?" Franceska asked as she again glanced out the corner of her eye to see if Marek had returned from the vehicle.

"Imagine a world occupied by a perfect race of people." Schneider closed his eyes as he grew emotional. "Imagine that we have disposed of all the impurities in humanity. How wonderful it would be not to worry about crime, corruption, or all the wickedness that accompanies the lesser humans."

Franceska didn't reply as she watched him closely. She had heard Nazi ideology many times before, but she never anticipated that she would see such malevolence put into practice.

"But I understand that you think what we're doing now is evil. I admit, it's not ideal, but there is no other way. Like a surgeon, I must remove the tumor from the body, otherwise all of humanity will become infected,"

Schneider explained, and Franceska knew he was trying to convince himself that he was doing something acceptable. "I must undertake a little evil, cutting open the patient, so that I can remove the growth. It's going to hurt, but in the end, I will be seen as a champion. I will rid the world of all the pain and suffering. Sickness and disease will be eradicated, all the baser elements of man will be removed, and we will finally attain paradise."

"How are you going to relocate millions of people?" Franceska asked warily.

"Relocate?" Schneider replied with a twisted smile.

Chapter Twenty-Three:
General Government

"The dance is a poem of which each movement is a word."

Mata Hari

<u>October 12, 1939</u>

"Must you listen to that racket?" Mrs. Mann barked from her room, annoyed at the music playing on the radio.

"I don't want to miss the news!" Mr. Mann shouted back from his chair.

"What's going on in the city lately anyway?" Mrs. Mann asked sincerely.

"I'll know once the news comes on," Mr. Mann replied with a surprising lack of patience.

"Is everything alright?" Franceska asked as she set her book down beside her on the couch.

"I've been cooped up in here for far too long," Mr. Mann replied with a kinder tone, but Franceska detected his frustration.

"I have a few hours before I'm needed at the club. Why don't you venture out? I can watch Mother." Franceska shrugged.

"He's not going anywhere!" Mrs. Mann yelled from her room.

"How did she hear me?" Franceska whispered.

Mr. Mann shook his head with a fearful expression, and Franceska understood he didn't want to utter a word that would land him in hot water.

"You're fine with me going out though?" Franceska yelled at her mother.

"If I had a choice, no."

"There's nowhere to go out to." Mr. Mann grimaced as he picked up the paper.

"A lot of coffee shops are still operational," Franceska suggested. "More and more are recovering from the initial invasion. Life, to an extent, is getting back to normal."

"For now," Mr. Mann cautioned as he offered a warning glance to Franceska. "As soon as they're ready, they'll take whatever young men we have left for forced labor and God knows what else they have in mind."

Franceska remained silent as she contemplated telling her father what Chief Schneider had admitted to her previously. Although, she wondered if Chief Schneider was merely rambling while drunk. She supposed it could've been his own imaginings and not part of the official Nazi protocol.

It had been a while since she had seen or even heard from Chief Schneider, and she half hoped that some higher authority than him had caught wind of his outrageous ideas and relieved him of his duties. It was a wild hope, she understood, and she prayed that Marek was correct in his assumptions that Chief Schneider was merely mad.

"What are you reading?" Mr. Mann nodded to her book.

"*Jane Eyre.*"

"That's not like you to read romance." Mr. Mann frowned. "I'm not sure I appreciate the influence of Mr. Rosenberg."

"It's hardly a romance," Franceska scoffed.

"In what sense is it not?" Mr. Mann put his paper down.

"Romance plays a key part in the story, sure, but it's used to discuss class, religion, sexuality—"

"Yeah, yeah." Mr. Mann waved to dismiss the conversation, growing uncomfortable at even mentioning the word *sexuality*.

"The point is, she wants to be loved not just in the romantic sense, but also for who she is as a person."

"Good." Mr. Mann nodded as he stuck his nose back into the paper.

Franceska grinned as she watched him growing increasingly uncomfortable all while trying to hide his unease. Before the invasion, Franceska loathed his awkwardness with discussing anything sexual, but now, she relished it as an exceptional quality. How she wished more men were as reserved as he was.

The music on the radio cut out, and both Franceska and Mr. Mann leaned forward, anxious to hear every word of the daily announcement.

"Today, our glorious Fuhrer, Adolf Hitler, has established the General Government in central Poland," the announcement began, and both Franceska and her father shot each other an annoyed glance for the grandiose.

The official Polish radio stations had all been terminated, and the new Nazi stations never failed to deify Hitler.

"Turn it up!" Mrs. Mann yelled.

Groaning, Mr. Mann adjusted the volume.

"The Jewish Council has also been appointed with a committee of twenty-four members, headed by Adam Czerniaków."

"Jewish Council?" Franceska frowned as she glanced at her father for clarification.

"Likely a puppet council for Hitler to orchestrate his orders," Mr. Mann replied solemnly. "Our community will take orders more readily from a Jewish Council than the Nazi government."

"Furthermore, the Prime Minister of England, Neville Chamberlain, has formally replied to Hitler's peace offer by stating that a settlement 'must be a real and settled peace, not an uneasy truce interrupted by constant alarms and repeated threats.' The Prime Minister also reported saying, 'Herr Hitler rejected all suggestions for peace until he had overwhelmed Poland, as he had previously overthrown Czechoslovakia. Peace conditions cannot be acceptable which begin by condoning aggression. The proposals in the German Chancellor's speech are vague and uncertain and contain no suggestion to right the wrongs done to Czechoslovakia and to Poland. Even if Herr Hitler's proposals were more closely defined and contained suggestions to right these wrongs, it would still be necessary to ask by what practical means the German Government intend to convince the world that aggression will cease and that pledges will be kept.' He concluded by stating, 'Past experience has shown that no reliance can be placed upon the promises of the present German Government.'"

"He shouldn't have read that on air." Mr. Mann shook his head.

"The Nazis will take him away for sure." Franceska agreed. "Simply because he was quoting what the English Prime Minister stated."

A knock rattled against the door.

"That's probably Marek," Franceska mentioned as she jumped to her feet.

"Was that the announcement?" Marek asked through the door.

"Yes, actually," Franceska replied as she opened the door.

"I was hoping to make it in time." Marek grew disappointed. "What did they say?"

"The Nazis have established a General Government," Franceska began as she ushered her fiancé inside before closing the door behind him.

"And they also created a Jewish Council," Mr. Mann added.

"Sounds like a puppet council," Marek spoke nervously.

"That's what I said." Mr. Mann looked impressed. "I think they're trying to pacify our concerns by pretending our people have a voice."

"I haven't been able to forget what the police chief told you." Marek looked solemnly back at Franceska as he removed his coat and hung it up.

"And?" Franceska asked quietly, hoping her father wouldn't press for clarification.

"And…" Marek glanced over at Mr. Mann.

"I'll check on your mother." Mr. Mann took the hint and left the living room.

"I know we've discussed this in passing before, but I think its time we make plans to leave," Marek spoke quietly.

"Where are we going to go?" Franceska shrugged. "There is nowhere safe."

"What about America?"

"How in the world would we transport my mother?" Franceska frowned sharply. "She can barely lie in a bed without discomfort, how are we going to get her all the way to some port and then take a ship across the ocean? How would we pay for it?"

"I have some savings," Marek pressed.

With a slight shake of her head, Franceska looked regretfully at Marek before stating, "I'm not leaving without my parents."

"Then what about the documents that the police chief was asking you about?" Marek tilted his head. "Can you forge something?"

"Half of Warsaw knows that I'm Jewish." Franceska paused as she drew a deep breath. "Besides, forging one document would be difficult enough, how are we going to forge some for my parents too? Not to mention I'm not leaving you."

"You can't stay for my sake." Marek shook his head adamantly.

"I'll do as I please." Franceska frowned at him.

"If I'm the reason that you don't make it through this, I'll never forgive myself." Marek placed a hand over his heart as he offered Franceska a pleading look.

"Wherever you go, I will go; wherever you live, I will live. Your people will be my people, and your God will be my God." Franceska offered him a sad smile, quoting to him what he had quoted to her.

"That's not fair." Marek tilted his head.

"There is no way out of this." Franceska took Marek's hand in hers. "The only way is through it. We will get through this together. I promise."

"I still think we should present the police chief with documents."

"There are no documents!" Franceska chuckled ironically. "I can almost trace my Jewish lineage back to Adam."

"They don't have to be legitimate..." Marek raised a brow.

"I imagine that will go over well with the authorities when I'm caught." Franceska raised a brow in return.

"There's a service..." Marek glanced into the apartment to make sure that Mr. Mann wasn't nearby before continuing, "There's a service that is creating false documents. They're allowing many Jews the chance to escape."

"We're staying until my mother can get reasonable care. Traveling would be detrimental to her health. It's too risky."

"You risk her life by staying, too," Marek spoke tenderly to soften the blow.

Franceska sighed as she rubbed her neck, trying to understand what the best course of action would be.

"Has a doctor looked at her?" Marek pressed.

"A doctor has attended the apartment on a couple of occasions." Franceska nodded. "But without the proper equipment, there's nothing they can do."

"And what if we had her looked at, properly that is?" Marek placed his hands on Franceska's shoulders.

"If we can make her healthy, then I would consider leaving." Franceska nodded.

"I will contact the hospital right now and see if they can see her for a proper diagnoses and prescribe a treatment plan."

"I've tried." Franceska looked hopelessly back at her fiancé.

"Let me at least make an attempt."

"It couldn't hurt." Franceska relented.

"I'll be right back." Marek grabbed his jacket.

"Leaving already?" Mr. Mann asked when he returned to the living room.

"Yes, and I'm rather disappointed in your daughter's stubbornness." Marek winked at Franceska.

"Well, no one is forcing you to get involved," Mr. Mann replied quietly, and both Marek and Franceska shot him a surprised yet amused glance.

"Hopefully your wit proves useful in the coming days." Marek grinned at Mr. Mann, but his cheer faded as he was reminded of the gravity of their situation.

"If my wit doesn't prove useful, my rifle may." Mr. Mann glanced at the weapon hidden in the hallway closet.

"Let's hope it doesn't come to that." Marek planted a kiss on Franceska's forehead before pointing a finger at her and warning, "I'll meet you at the club. Be careful. Go straight there. No deviation."

"You won't have to worry about that." Franceska recalled their trip to the synagogue.

"When's the wedding?" Mr. Mann asked casually after Marek closed the door.

"We haven't discussed it that much lately," Franceska replied as she sat back down and picked up her book.

"How come?" Mr. Mann asked as he cleared his throat while he stared at the paper, and Franceska knew he was uncomfortable with the discussion but also anxious to know, which she found rather endearing.

"How could we?" Franceska asked as she tried to read her book, but her mind was held captive by worry.

"Why not a quick and simple wedding?" Mr. Mann glanced at her and then away. "Go to city hall with a couple of your friends. Sign the certificate. Done."

"I'm not sure that's the issue."

"Then what is?"

"How can we think about ourselves at a time like this?" Franceska grew animated.

"Nothing is guaranteed, but if—"

"I've heard that speech so many times before," Franceska interrupted, but the hurt look on her father's face for the interruption made her regret the outburst.

"If your minds made up then." Mr. Mann stood and took the paper with him to the bedroom, leaving Franceska to feel rotten about the interaction.

"Good news!" Marek grew excited when Franceska arrived at the nightclub later that day. "I was able to book your mother in for a proper examination at the hospital!"

"That's excellent!" Franceska shot her head back in shock. "I was certain they were going to give you the same answer they kept giving me. How did you convince them?"

"Somethings are better left unsaid." Marek continued grinning before pinching Franceska's cheek.

"Did someone owe you money?" Franceska narrowed her gaze as she grew suspicious.

"Like I said, somethings are better left unsaid."

"Yes, but, did you—"

"Franky, my dear, all you need to do is say thank you."

"First of all, never call me Franky again," Franceska spoke sternly to Marek, but then melted as she abandoned decorum and wrapped her arms around him while squeezing tightly and stating, "Thank you for helping my mother!"

"You're most welcome." Marek chuckled.

"When is the appointment?"

"Not for another month." Marek looked at her with regret. "November twentieth, to be exact."

"That's better than never."

"True."

"I'll go get ready for the evening." Franceska began to head to the backroom.

"Actually," Marek stopped her.

"Yes?" Franceska looked at him with confusion.

"We have other plans."

"We do?" Franceska narrowed her gaze.

"We're taking the night off."

"Oh?" Franceska remained wary.

"Your friend, Wiera, she's a singer, yes?"

"She is…" Franceska wondered where this was going.

"I thought tonight we could watch her perform and then spend some time with your friends."

"What? Why?" Franceska smiled as she examined him closely, wondering what ulterior motive he possessed.

"Can't a man spoil his fiancé?"

"Should you spoil me?" Franceska asked with concern but immediately changed her mind and smiled before stating, "You definitely should."

"Then let's not waste any more time arguing about it and let me spoil you."

"That sounds lovely." Franceska smiled. "I could use the company of friends, especially now."

"I would like to get to know them better as well."

"Have you heard from Chief Schneider? Has he returned the books of business?"

"No." Marek shook his head as he grew pensive. "I'm sure he's looking for something that he can use to either blackmail me or use against me in some manner. Piotr, for his many faults, is impeccably detailed. Not a single drop of liquor has been unaccounted for, and he helped me with the books. I doubt the chief will be able to find anything worthwhile."

"Glad my father wasn't around to hear you say that." Franceska smirked. "I'm not sure how much longer I'll be able to keep the secret from my mother."

"We'll cross that bridge when we come to it. We should be on our way."

"Where are we meeting them?" Franceska grew excited as she wrapped her arm around his.

"There's a pub called The Sparrow."

"That's close by!" Franceska glanced up at him. "I've wanted to go there for some time."

Leaving the club, Franceska and Marek jumped onto the tram after paying the fair and saying a quick hello to Henryk, which he ignored, and took their seats for the short journey.

"This city used to be so beautiful in the evening." Franceska smiled sorrowfully at Marek as she inspected the German patrols marching through the city.

It was so common to see the patrols within the city, that Franceska almost became accustomed to them. Thankfully, Franceska found that if she left the patrols alone, they usually left her alone. Besides, they were still too busy hunting down any resistance members to pay her much attention.

"At least the restoration is going quickly," Marek added. "Which makes me wonder why they would repair all these buildings only to tear them down to build a model city. Maybe Chief Schneider is delusional?"

"Maybe." Franceska chewed her lip as she grew reflective.

She knew that life was likely going to change, and she was terrified of what that meant for her and Marek or her parents. She doubted Chief Schneider's plans were part of the grander scheme that the Nazis had adopted, but in either case, she knew that life for her people was about to become austere.

But tonight, Franceska agreed, was for friends, and to remember that life had meaning, purpose, and beauty. Tonight was to forget sorrows and enjoy what precious moments she had with those she held so dearly in her heart.

"This is us," Marek spoke quietly and the two exited the tram after thanking Henryk and walked toward the pub.

"This is our first night out on the town." Franceska could scarcely contain a squeal of excitement.

The Sparrow, Franceska thought, was an adorable little pub that was squished into the heart of Warsaw. She had passed by the establishment many times on her ventures and thought it looked appealing.

"It makes me happy to see you like this." Marek opened the door for Franceska, and she was struck by the sound of joyful chatter and music.

The atmosphere was akin to the nightclub, but much less formal. There were numerous booths, tables, and chairs, but they were made cheaply and somehow Franceska found this endearing. There were many photographs of Warsaw and famous people on the wall, and she felt a sense of ease that she so desperately needed.

But what Franceska found the most enjoyable about the nightclub was the mere fact that there were no Nazis. It was well known that The Sparrow was a popular pub for young Jews to congregate, and no Nazi dared to blemish their name by becoming a patron.

"Franceska!" an excited shout came from further within the pub, and she looked in the direction to see Stefania waving emphatically. She was sitting at a table with Wiera, and two gentlemen that Franceska didn't recognize.

"Hello!" Franceska half ran toward her friend and the two embraced.

"Lovely to see you," Wiera spoke with less enthusiasm than Stefania as she offered a light embrace to Franceska.

Franceska, again, found the difference in personality between her friends amusing. They were as contrasting as night and day, and Franceska wouldn't have it any other way.

"This is my husband, Jerzy Jurandot." Stefania beamed with pride.

"Nice to meet you," Franceska spoke cheerfully as she extended her hand in greeting.

"You as well," Jerzy replied kindly, but then immediately turned his attention to Marek and stated, "I hear you enjoy poetry."

"I do." Marek looked pleasantly surprised.

"I've been working on a composition that I would like to run by you."

"Well, by all means." Marek placed his hand on Jerzy's back and the two walked toward the bar.

"That was easy enough," Stefania giggled as Franceska sat across from her and Wiera.

"Go with them," Wiera spoke coldly to the man accompanying her.

"I don't want to talk about poetry," the man whined.

"Then stand outside." Wiera nodded to the door.

"Fine, I'll go with the men," he sighed.

"When's the wedding?" Franceska asked Wiera sarcastically when her date was well out of earshot.

"I'm afraid that's my fault." Stefania looked apologetically at Wiera. "I thought it would be nice to set her up for the evening."

"What about Adam?" Franceska asked with concern.

"That's exactly the point." Wiera shot Stefania a heated glance.

"You haven't heard from him in some time, I thought maybe it would be—"

"Let's change the subject." Wiera grew annoyed.

"I'm here to listen to you sing tonight." Franceska beamed.

"I appreciate that." Wiera grew a bashful grin. "But I'm not merely singing."

"Oh?" Franceska tilted her head. "What do you mean?"

"I'm the star in a play that Stefania's husband helped orchestrate."

"The star hey?!" Franceska glanced at Stefania with a smirk. "Which play?!"

"Have you heard of *Antigone*?" Wiera asked.

"I'm vaguely familiar with her." Franceska narrowed her gaze.

"I think you'll enjoy it." Wiera nodded.

"Attention everyone!" Jerzy called from the small stage, and the patrons of the pub turned to look at him. "Tonight, we have the extraordinary pleasure of showcasing a work that I'm rather proud of. Now, before I discuss the details, we need to address the rumor that the theatrical performances are going to be shut down by the Nazis."

Booing erupted in the pub, but Franceska wasn't certain if it was safe to partake in such behavior. She found it odd that Jerzy would be so bold given that any one of the patrons could harbor Nazi sympathies.

"But not here, at The Sparrow!" Jerzy shouted, and he was met with cheers and applause. "For those of your fretting, don't worry, that is the worst thing I will say tonight about our dearly beloved conquerors."

Everyone in the pub, apart from Franceska, laughed at the jest, and she feared that it was too risky to indulge.

"Tonight, we will be performing, accompanied by the wonderful musical talent of Miss Gran, a play, mixed with some singing, entitled *Antigone*."

Some more applause came from the patrons of the pub as Jerzy took a slight bow for Wiera and a couple others to join him on stage.

"This is for you," Marek whispered when he returned to the table with a glass of vodka for Franceska.

"Thank you," she whispered back.

Holding her drink, Franceska eagerly awaited the play to begin.

The lights dimmed, the crowd grew excited, and Franceska watched with amazement as Wiera began singing and acting with two other men on stage.

The play was set in ancient Greece after a civil war had turned the royal family against itself. Two of the king's nephews died fighting on opposite sides of the war. The king decreed that the body of Polynices (Antigone's brother), who fought against his native city, would not be given burial rites. As a warning to traitors, Polynices' body is left to rot in the elements. The king also decreed that anyone who dared to bury Polynices would be punished with death.

Franceska watched with astonishment as Antigone, played by Wiera, defied the king's orders. Wiera sang a beautiful song of familial duty and responsibility, which resonated with Franceska as she thought of her parents, and, despite the severity of the punishment threatened, Antigone buried her brother. Regardless of the circumstances, Antigone followed what she knew to be right in her heart.

The king was enraged when he discovered what Antigone had done and sentenced her to be entombed alive. Despite the pleas from other family members, the king moved forward with his sentencing, and Franceska held a hand over her mouth in shock as Antigone was entombed.

The lights went dark entirely, and the pub grew deathly quiet as they awaited the next scene. Franceska sat on the edge of her seat as she listened intently, hoping that Antigone would be spared from a terrible death.

A single light onstage turned on, and Franceska watched as a prophet approached the bitter king on his throne, warning him of divine disapproval should he not relent. Moved by the prophet's warning, the king's heart softened, and he decided to release Antigone.

But it was too late. Antigone had perished, and the king realized the tragic consequences of his pride and stubbornness.

The play ended and Franceska noticed that not a dry eye remained in the pub. But when Wiera, Jerzy, and the two other actors returned to the stage for a bow, the pub erupted into uproarious applause, and Franceska was convinced it was the best performance she had ever seen.

"You were amazing!" Franceska embraced Wiera when she returned to their table along with Jerzy.

"Well done love." Stefania kissed her husband on the cheek.

"How was it?" Jerzy asked Stefania nervously.

"Spectacular!" Franceska interjected on Stefania's behalf.

"You're just being kind." Jerzy remained unconvinced.

"No, no, I'm not! Honest!" Franceska insisted. "I think that was one of the best performances I've ever seen! With the intimacy of this pub, there were no distractions from large sets or big actors. It focused on the human condition of pride, fate, and family loyalty. I was very impressed."

"That's a glowing review." Jerzy smiled bashfully.

"Let me get you a drink!" Marek wrapped his arm around Jerzy and the two walked toward the bar.

"You and that manager fellow seem to be serious?" Stefania looked at Franceska hopefully.

"Serious enough to be engaged." Franceska bit her lip in eagerness for their reactions.

"You're lying!" Stefania smacked the table in excitement. "Tell me you're lying!"

Franceska shook her head as she was unable to conceal her grin.

"I love that." Wiera smiled brightly.

"Tell me everything!" Stefania leaned forward, eager for every detail.

"The wedding won't be for a little while yet. We want to have a small reception with family and friends, and we both thought it would be best to wait until things calm down a bit."

"How was he possibly able to turn your opinion around?!" Stefania looked at Franceska curiously.

"He's surprisingly romantic." Franceska grinned bashfully.

"So is my Jerzy." Stefania fluttered her eyelashes. "He recites the sweetest poems to me."

"I never understood you until recently," Franceska admitted.

"What are we drinking to tonight?" Jerzy asked when he and Marek returned to the table.

"To love." Stefania beamed.

"A bottle of vodka should do the trick then," Marek set the bottle down on the table, and Franceska was shocked when he poured himself a drink as well.

"Are you sure?" Franceska asked Marek while trying to be discreet.

"One night will be alright, hey?" Marek shrugged.

"Will it?" Franceska asked. She didn't want to control him or feel that he needed to be controlled, but she had never seen him drink before, and she worried that she might witness a side of him that she seriously disliked.

"We never know how many nights like this we'll get again." Marek shot his vodka back, and Franceska felt a pit forming in her gut, knowing that her opinion of her fiancé was about to shift drastically.

"Oh, Franceska, remember that priest who took you to find your mother?" Stefania asked eagerly.

"Father Kolbe?" Franceska asked but was distracted as Marek and Jerzy returned to the bar.

"That's him!" Stefania grew excited.

"What about him?" Franceska frowned, still preoccupied.

"He was arrested," Wiera added solemnly.

"What for?" Franceska grew concerned.

"They raided the monastery that he had converted into a makeshift hospital," Wiera continued.

"And?!" Franceska pressed, anxious for the details.

"They discovered that he was assisting Jews." Stefania offered a solemn look of her own.

"And they arrested him for that?" Franceska remained confused. "That doesn't sound illegal."

"They arrested him because he was also using the monastery as a publishing house to produce anti-Nazi publications," Wiera explained.

"That was bold." Franceska shook her head, wondering if she would ever have such courage.

"He also refused to sign the papers which would grant him German citizenship." Stefania gratefully accepted the bottle of vodka from the waiter.

"The Deutsche Volksliste?" Franceska tilted her head.

"Correct."

"He could've signed the documents, giving him German Citizenship," Wiera added. "But he refused."

"That's rather brave of him." Franceska stared at the table, wondering if she should tell the girls about the chief of police and his maniacal designs for Warsaw.

"Regardless, tonight is for us to be together again, like old times, enjoying each other's company."

"Agreed." Franceska raised her glass, followed closely by Wiera and Stefania.

"They're asking for an encore!" Jerzy spoke eagerly as he returned to their table.

"I'm glad you two are here for this. I could use your support." Wiera made herself ready. "I'm nervous."

"You just sang!" Stefania looked puzzled. "And don't you sing professionally at the theater?"

"Yes, but I have nothing prepared, and the theater is full of well-respected individuals who conduct themselves properly. This pub is full of drunks, and who knows how they'll behave."

"If anyone steps out of line, I'll tackle them myself," Franceska warned.

"I believe you." Wiera forced a grin before drawing a deep and anxious breath.

"You're going to be superb! I know it!" Stefania encouraged.

Without a further word, Wiera marched up onto the little stage in the corner of the pub and, tapping the mic, captured the attention of the patrons.

"For anyone who doesn't recall, my name is Wiera Gran."

"Sing us a song!" a drunk from the crowd shouted, and Franceska looked over with disgust at the man only to realize that it was Marek.

"Is that your—" Stefania began.

"Yes," Franceska interrupted.

"Sorry." Stefania looked at Franceska but then added with a grin to try and ease the tension, "Aren't you going to tackle him?"

"If only I had a tomb that I could place him in." Franceska grew embarrassed as she watched Marek take another shot of Vodka and continue making a fool of himself.

Some cheers and applause echoed around the pub as the patrons grew excited for Wiera's encore, and Franceska watched her friend's nerves building. Franceska knew that feeling all too well where even the slightest mistake could be disastrous. Everyone was waiting to see if Wiera could lift their spirits out of the mire.

Without the accompaniment of music, without strings or percussion, without anything beyond the purity of her voice, Wiera began singing.

Her voice was so wholesome, so clear, and cut straight to the heart. Not a single person stirred or even dared to move. Everyone, even the drunkest among them, including Marek, knew that they were in the very heart of something special. This was a moment they would remember well as Wiera sang of long-lost hope.

The world about them was about to change, and their ambitions, hopes, dreams, now counted for nothing because a mad man decided they didn't deserve to exist. Whether Chief Schneider was truthful, or he was telling a boldfaced lie, Franceska couldn't decipher.

In any case, as she sat and listened to her friend's beautiful voice, Franceska knew that dark times were coming, and she prayed that she would be able to withstand the terror. And if not her, then at least her parents would be able to survive. All she wanted was to keep her parents safe and without enduring the coming horrors.

Chapter Twenty-Four:
Seizure

"A single act of love makes the soul return to life."

Father Maximilliam Kolbe

"What would you like for dinner this evening?" Franceska asked her mother as she walked into her room.

"Why are you asking about dinner? It's not even noon yet!" Mrs. Mann griped.

"I know, but I have to go to the market this morning, so I need to know what I'm shopping for."

"Ask your father." Mrs. Mann waved to dismiss her obligation.

"I did."

"What did he say?"

"He said I should ask you." Franceska grew annoyed.

"Go ask him again. Tell him he has to make up his mind."

"I'm not your messenger." Franceska crossed her arms.

"Did your husband hear about the results of my tests yet?" Mrs. Mann shifted the subject.

"First, he's not my husband."

"Just a matter of paperwork really."

"Second, we will be the first to know your results, not Mr. Rosenberg."

"Why would we know first? Didn't he make the appointment?"

"Yes, but I assume, and hope, that the doctor would contact the patient first."

"Probably best if they did contact me first, otherwise you'd withhold the information and use it against me." Mrs. Mann scowled at Franceska.

"Do you really think so little of me?" Franceska tilted her head. "Don't you think that I'm eager to see you back to good health?"

"Please, you've shut me away in this room like I'm a terrible inconvenience. You're embarrassed of me, so you hide me away."

"Believe me, if I could get you out of here, I would." Franceska leaned against the wall as she glared at her mother. "Sometimes I wonder if you know how much I've done for you?"

"How much you've done for me?!" Mrs. Mann scoffed. "Who put you through all those dance classes? Who paid for you to travel to competitions? Who put up with your horrible years of adolescence? Who—"

"I was an admirable and well-behaved young woman!" Franceska defended.

"Well don't we have some rose-tinted glassed about ourselves, hey?" Mrs. Mann raised her eyebrows.

"I know my faults, and they are many!" Franceska continued in her defensiveness. "Believe me, being a horrible teenager was not one of them."

"It can be difficult to assess ourselves properly," Mrs. Mann spoke condescendingly.

"Tonight, I'll be cooking whatever I want to, and you're going to eat it and be grateful."

"With your cooking, the only thing I would be grateful for is if I choked."

"I'm a good cook!" Franceska nearly yelled at her mother.

"Don't you take that tone with me!" Mrs. Mann grew indignant. "I deserve more respect than that!"

Franceska shook with rage as she stared at her mother, but bit her tongue from lashing out, knowing that it would only sour their relationship further. But for her part, Franceska struggled to accept her mother's rebuke. She understood that her mother was in considerable pain, but it wounded her deeply to know that she wasn't appreciative of her efforts.

"Help me up." Mrs. Mann gestured as she gingerly threw off her blankets. "I need to relieve myself."

"Don't you think your husband would better be suited in helping with something so intimate?" Franceska contorted her face with disgust.

"That twig?" Mrs. Mann scoffed. "You actually have some muscle on your bones."

"Is that a compliment or an insult?" Franceska asked as she threw her mother's arm around her shoulder.

"Can't it be both?" Mrs. Mann chuckled but then winced with pain and yelped, "Slowly! Slowly!"

"One step at a time," Franceska encouraged her mother.

Steadily, and carefully, mother and daughter walked to the bathroom, and Franceska, although still afflicted in spirit by her mother's words, felt pity. Franceska hated seeing her mother in so much pain and discomfort where even a small walk to relieve herself was an excruciating journey.

Franceska prayed that the results from the tests would lead to some answers and direction for her mother. Lying in bed all day long was no way to live, and Franceska wished that she could see her mother at least shuffling around again, if not simply for the sake of improving her attitude.

"Am I still difficult?" Franceska asked as she assisted her mother back into bed.

"Yes," Mrs. Mann replied quickly while out of breath. "But I prefer it that way. Nothing simple is worth doing."

"I haven't heard from Mr. Rosenberg in a couple of days," Franceska began solemnly.

"Are you worried?" Her mother asked sincerely.

"He's not the sort of man to apologize, so I think he may be avoiding me."

"What did he do?" Mrs. Mann looked at her daughter curiously.

"He has trouble with liquor." Franceska watched her mother closely, wondering how she would respond.

"My grandfather was the same way." Mrs. Mann nodded in her understanding.

"He was?" Franceska frowned. "You spoke so highly of him when I was young."

"I didn't want you to know." Mrs. Mann offered Franceska a slight look of embarrassment.

"Should I stay away from him, then?" Franceska asked.

"Does he hit you when he drinks?"

"No." Franceska shook her head. "I've only witnessed him drinking once, and he ignored me the entire time."

"Then he has two loves: one for you and one for liquor. He can love one or the other, but never both." Her mother looked at her sternly.

"What would you do if you were in my place?"

"I've never seen you smile the way you do when he is around. It's clear that you love him, and if you believe you can handle the burden he brings, then I would proceed. If not, it would be best to sever ties now."

"If only it were that simple."

"Matters of the heart are never simple, and that's why you have to make the decision with your head." Mrs. Mann tapped Franceska's forehead before snapping, "Now grab me some more of that medicine you're forcing me to take."

Rolling her eyes, Franceska provided her mother with more pain medication but couldn't help from wondering if it was doing more harm than good.

Allowing her mother a moment to rest, Franceska left the bedroom and returned to the couch near her father with a heavy sigh.

"Everything alright?" Mr. Mann asked in the manner which indicated he didn't really want to know but was merely being polite.

"Was I challenging to raise?" Franceska asked her father sincerely. She wanted to ask his opinion about Marek but knew that she would need to test his attitude on serious subjects first.

Mr. Mann glanced at her with a smirk, but when he noticed that she was genuine, turned his gaze away and stated, "Not at all."

"How was I difficult?" Franceska asked with confusion. "I thought I was a good child."

"Good, yes, but challenging, also yes."

"How so?"

"Ask your mother." Mr. Mann glanced away as he turned the radio on, and the music filled the room.

"I'm asking you," Franceska stated boldly as she turned the radio off.

"If you must," Mr. Mann began as he stared at his lap before continuing, "You fought with your mother constantly."

"Mother breeds confrontation!" Franceska defended.

"She bred you." Mr. Mann smirked.

"Clever," Franceska replied with annoyance.

A knock rattled against the apartment door.

Neither Franceska nor Mr. Mann moved.

The knock came again.

"Are you going to answer it?" Mr. Mann asked Franceska.

"Why am I the one who always answers the door?" Franceska crossed her arms.

"Because the door is always for you." Mr. Mann shrugged as if the answer was obvious.

With a huff, Franceska stood and walked over to the door.

"If it's Mr. Rosenberg, ask him if he thinks you're difficult," Mr. Mann spoke quietly.

Without taking pains to hide her annoyance, Franceska opened the door and spotted Marek standing in the hallway with a sorrowful expression. He looked pale and offered Franceska a worried glance that indicated he had some troubling news to relate.

"Have you come to apologize?" Franceska leaned against the doorpost.

"That and other pressing news." Marek removed his hat as he held it nervously in front of him.

Franceska didn't reply as she felt a coldness toward him that she wasn't entirely sure was justified. When he had indulged in drink, apart from becoming undignified, he didn't behave terribly. He didn't flirt with other women or start fights, but Franceska hated that he seemed to have forgotten her entirely. It stung to feel unimportant to him.

"I have terrible news," Marek began bleakly and seemed eager to enter the apartment.

"For pity's sake, let him in," Mr. Mann called from the living room.

Relenting, Franceska moved aside so Marek could enter the apartment, and she resumed her position on the couch.

"Sit down, son." Mr. Mann gestured to the couch as he also grew concerned.

"I don't know if I can." Marek squeezed his hands into fists.

"Tell us, then," Franceska urged. "Is this about mother?"

"I doubt the doctor would tell me directly about Mrs. Mann, and I wish I could shed some light on that." Marek's voice wavered, and Franceska grew concerned.

"Go on," Mr. Mann pressed.

"I'm afraid our marriage will have to be postponed indefinitely." Marek looked sorrowfully at Franceska.

"Postponed?" Franceska held her conclusion in reserve. "I know you had one slip-up the other night, but—"

"It's not about that."

Mr. Mann frowned suspiciously as he glanced between the two of them, and Franceska wished that she hadn't raised that subject.

"No?" Franceska frowned.

"Although I'm terribly sorry for my behavior the other night, the reason we cannot wed is because the Nazis have seized all my assets." Marek closed his eyes in disbelief at the words he was uttering.

"I don't understand." Franceska tilted her head.

"Why your assets?" Mr. Mann asked. "What did you do?"

"It's not just myself." Marek shook his head as he continued, "Every Jew with an amount of money over a certain threshold has had their assets seized, and the money confiscated."

"That can't be legal!" Franceska grew irate.

"My life savings have been taken. Everything is gone."

Franceska slunk into the couch as she felt the weight of his statement.

"I now have nothing to my name. Not even a penny. I understand now why the chief was so adamant to see my personal records as well as the ones belonging to the club." Marek stared at his feet dejectedly.

"How much money did you have saved?" Mr. Mann asked as he grew concerned.

"About two years wages." Marek nearly laughed at the absurdity.

"That is substantial," Mr. Mann sighed.

"Miss Mann, it would be best if you married someone of means," Marek spoke formally to Franceska.

"I wasn't marrying you for your money." Franceska looked at him with understanding.

"You should marry a man who can provide for you." Marek pursed his lips to restrain an emotional outburst.

"My dearest Marek," Franceska spoke softly as she stood and embraced him. "I'm so sorry, but you're not getting out of this. You're stuck with me whether you like it or not, for richer or for poorer."

"Think realistically." Marek broke off his embrace as he looked down at her with a heavy heart. "I can't provide for you. We would have nowhere to live."

"You can live here, with us." Franceska shrugged.

"That's a lovely idea, but I'm sure after a day or two you will regret that." Marek shook his head.

"Nonsense." Franceska smiled brightly at him.

"Is there any course of action you can take against the seizure?" Mr. Mann asked, and Franceska knew he was nervous about the prospect of Marek staying with them but too polite to address it directly.

"All the lawyers I know are Jewish, and no gentile is willing to assist a Jew right now." Marek delved further into despair.

"What are we supposed to do without money?" Franceska asked aloud.

"I'll see what I can syphon from the club."

"I'm sure that will only lead to more issues." Franceska offered him a worried look.

"Payments will be in cash from now on." Marek nodded. "We'll have to hide any and all paper trails."

The music from the radio died down, and everyone turned their attention, wondering what horrible announcement was about to be delivered.

"My name is Adam Czerniaków," the announcer began in Polish.

"Isn't he the head of the Jewish Council?" Marek asked.

"Indeed," Mr. Mann replied quickly as he turned the volume up.

"I speak to you on behalf of the eternal Jewish people," Adam continued. "Orders have been issued that require all people of Jewish descent over the age of ten, who did not qualify under the Deutsche Volksliste, to wear a white armband with the Star of David."

"Orders?" Franceska asked warily.

"Please note, that the punishment for refusal is severe, up to, and including, execution," the Jewish Council president continued.

The air escaped Franceska's lungs as she listened to the harrowing announcement, and she knew now, beyond a shadow of a doubt, that Chief Schneider's plans were far from imaginary or the drunken ramblings of a madman.

"I need to sit," Marek spoke with a weak voice as he collapsed onto the couch.

"I would urge you to not resist. My greatest concern is for the safety and well-being of the innocents. Any refusal will be met with severity, and I encourage you to comply," Adam spoke emotionally. "Furthermore, all Jewish businesses and establishments are ordered to display the Jewish star on their doors and windows."

"This is how they intend to control us then?" Marek asked bitterly. "Through the guise of our own Jewish council. They know if the orders come from the Germans, compliance will be much more difficult, but have the head of the Jewish Council urging obedience, and we'll fall in line like sheep."

"The badges will be handed out by police. If you are not required to wear the badge, you must produce the necessary documentation," Adam continued. "We shall show that we are a peaceful people, and not the wickedness that they assume."

The radio went silent, and the only noise in the living room was static. Franceska didn't dare speak a word, understanding that what she had heard was the end of their people, the end of their way of life, and the end of all she held dear.

"Nobody believes that they will stop at badges," Mr. Mann spoke after a moment.

"What will they stop at?" Marek asked, but Franceska detected that he didn't really want to know the answer.

Mr. Mann didn't reply as he sat in the silence while the static continued to play as if the radio itself understood the gravity of what it had just aired.

Eventually, after what felt like a painful minute, the radio began to play soft music, but even the gentle strings sounded insulting.

Stretching over to the radio, Mr. Mann turned it off, and the room once again fell silent.

Franceska didn't dare move, and she wasn't sure if she even could. Her muscles felt stiff, and looking down at her hands she noticed that her knuckles were turning white from clenching her hands into fists.

"Now I understand why Chief Schneider wanted my books of accounting," Marek spoke quietly.

"He was using you as an example," Mr. Mann added.

"I was going to buy us a nice place to live," Marek again spoke softly, and Franceska knew that he was so dejected that he couldn't even bring himself to an angry outburst.

"They're going to force us into bankruptcy," Mr. Mann spoke quietly as well. "If a business has the Jewish star, no one who is not of Jewish descent would dare do business there for fear of reprisal."

"I'm going to the synagogue." Franceska slowly stood.

"Synagogue?" Marek frowned.

"I don't know if it's wise to go out right now." Mr. Mann shook his head.

"Do you think God cares what we're going through?" Marek scoffed. "Why would you go to pray to a deity that has abandoned His people?"

"I don't pretend for a minute to understand why God is allowing this," Franceska spoke softly to her fiancé. "But I know that I need peace. I found it when I was in the synagogue last, and I would like to experience that again, even if it is fleeting."

"Then you're not going alone." Marek also stood.

"I would appreciate if you joined me." Franceska offered Marek a sorrowful gaze.

"I'm not going in." Marek shook his head as he straightened out his jacket. "But I'm not letting you walk alone out there."

"If you do join me in the synagogue, you might find something of impor—"

"Please don't try and convince me," Marek interrupted as he impatiently held up a hand to stop her. "I've never been so angry in my life, and I'm struggling to keep my composure. Please don't force me to go inside."

"I won't." Franceska offered a gentle squeeze on his arm.

"Don't be out late," Mr. Mann spoke nervously.

"We won't. I promise. We'll come straight back."

Franceska watched with a heavy heart as Mr. Mann bounced his leg anxiously before beginning to chew his nails, and she knew how much he hated the idea of her leaving. But Franceska knew that she couldn't stay.

"Are you sure about this?" Marek asked as he closed the door behind them.

"There are few things in life that I'm sure about," Franceska began as she stared at her feet. "But this is one of them."

With a reluctant nod, Marek held his hand out for Franceska to lead the way.

Yet as soon as they left the apartment building, Franceska and Marek could already here orders being shouted in German coming from the streets. Even from a distance, Franceska deciphered that the policemen were busy reviewing documents and confirming identities.

"Are you ready?" Marek asked as he took her hand in his.

Franceska offered a resolute nod, and the two of them left the apartment building to find that many policemen, and even volunteers, were handing out white armbands to anyone who couldn't produce the correct documentation.

"Papers!" a policeman held out his hand to Franceska and Marek.

"We are Jews," Marek replied boldly, and Franceska felt his hand clasping hers tightly.

With a look of disgust, the policeman retrieved two white armbands from his satchel before handing it to them and ordering, "Put them on!"

Taking the armbands, Franceska gestured for Marek to turn so that she could tie his on his arm. Slowly, but with a defiant gaze to the policeman, Marek offered his arm to Franceska.

Tying the armband, Franceska felt as though she were sealing the fate of her fiancé, and hated the sinking pit that was growing in her stomach, wondering what the Nazis had in store next.

Then, when she had finished, Franceska offered her arm to Marek, and he tied the armband around her.

She was no longer a ballerina, she was no longer Franceska, she was no longer a daughter or a friend, she had been reduced in her identity to a single classification. To the people that hated her people, her character didn't matter, her skills or achievements counted for nothing, all she embodied now was the coincidence of birth.

"This isn't right!" a shout came from further up the street, and Franceska watched as an angry man screamed at an officer forcing an armband on him.

"Shut up!" The policeman struck the man in his stomach with the butt of his rifle.

"Let's go," Marek whispered to Franceska as he again took her hand in his.

With their heads down, and walking as briskly as they were able, Franceska and Marek made their way to the tram.

"It's good to see a familiar face," Franceska spoke warmly to Henryk as she handed him the fare.

"I cannot accept it." Henryk refused the fare. Instead of his usual look of indifference, Henryk looked at Franceska with sorrowed etched across his face.

"Is everything alright Henryk?" Franceska asked, wondering if the white armband was souring his attitude toward her.

"It's forbidden," Henryk began as he swallowed.

"What is?" Marek pressed.

"Jews are not permitted to use public transport," Henryk whispered in an attempt to limit the humiliation.

Glancing into the tram, Franceska noticed the glares and stares from the other passengers who looked at them as if they were the cause of all their grief.

"You know me, Henryk." Franceska looked him in the eyes. "You've known me since I was a little girl. I remember the treats you would give me."

"You've always been kind to me," Henryk spoke with regret before turning his gaze away and stating, "But the law is the law, and I can't risk it."

With another glance at the passengers in the tram, Franceska and Marek slowly returned to the sidewalk feeling humiliated and angry at the injustice.

Yet this time, when the tram lurched to a start, Henryk did not ring the bell, and Franceska, for her part, appreciated that he had, at the very least, acknowledged the wrong that was done to them.

Franceska was enraged and shocked to suddenly become so isolated from society. She wondered how much longer they could exist in this condition and began to realize that Chief Schneider's plan may not have been the utterings of a drunkard.

Regardless, Franceska knew that they couldn't run. They now had no money, nowhere to flee to, and her parents wouldn't be able to travel. No matter what, they were forced to endure, and she prayed that they would have the strength to persevere.

"It's a twenty-minute walk," Franceska spoke to Marek. "You don't have to come with me."

"There's no way in hell I'm letting you go by yourself." Marek shook his head.

With a smile, Franceska took Marek's hand in hers and the two walked as briskly as they were able through the city.

The scene throughout Warsaw was one that Franceska had long feared. Only a handful of businesses that had the Jewish star in their window had been spared from vandalism. Jewelry stores had been ransacked, grocers had their produce stolen, and tax or law offices had been painted with graffiti that included horrible slurs.

And as they approached the synagogue, Franceska spotted a group of men outside who were chanting insults at anyone who entered the house of worship.

"Jewish dogs!" one of the men in the group spit in the direction of Franceska and Marek when they had come close enough.

"I swear to God, if—" Marek began with raised fists, but Franceska latched onto his arm to drag him away.

"Keep your dog on a leash!" one of the men yelled and the group laughed.

"I ought to kill them!" Marek gritted his teeth.

"It won't do any good!" Franceska spoke sternly. "They'll use it as an excuse to attack our people."

"I hate this, and I hate them!" Marek fumed.

"Are you sure you don't want to come inside?" Franceska asked.

"Maybe I'll stand in the foyer." Marek nodded, understanding that it was too precarious to be outside, especially with his temper.

Entering the synagogue, Franceska noticed that it was full of people, her people. They were all nervous, anxious, and desperate for reassurance. While she wished that this calamity had never befallen them, Franceska did take courage in seeing her people brought together in a way she had never seen before. Maybe, she pondered, they could endure as long as they were united like this.

"You're going to stay here?" Franceska asked Marek as he stood in the lobby.

Marek nodded quickly and anxiously.

"Sit with me." Franceska placed her hand gently on Marek's chest.

"It will only make me angrier if I come in there with you." Marek warned.

"I understand, I do." Franceska drew a deep breath before she continued, "But I need you to be with me."

Marek watched her for a moment as he shuffled his jaw before shaking his head and refusing.

Without another word, and with a heavy heart, Franceska walked quietly, and alone, into the synagogue where she took a seat in the back pew.

Many within the house of worship were crying, some sat bitterly, and others waited expectantly for direction from the rabbi. But the one thing they all had in common was the white armband.

Glancing back at the lobby, Franceska caught a glimpse of Marek pacing back and forth. She knew he was distressed and angry. She understood his emotions, but she hated that he wasn't with her now. Not to mention, her mother's words of caution about his drunkenness replayed in her mind, and she wasn't sure how to proceed.

"Thank you all for coming," the rabbi began as he stood at the pulpit. "As you may have noticed, I'm speaking to you today in Polish, not Yiddish. The reason for this departure from customs is simple. There are many here who are not familiar with the language, and I want this message to be conveyed clearly and concisely."

Franceska watched as a few harsh whispers were exchanged between those of a more conservative nature who were likely displeased with this change.

"I know why you're here." The rabbi looked out among those gathered. "You want answers, or consolation, but I have none to offer you. This is not going to be a sermon to make you feel better, but it should, at the least, give you some hope."

The rabbi paused as he looked over the congregation, and Franceska waited anxiously to hear the rest of his address.

"Today, we gather to reflect on the profound struggle of maintaining our faith amidst severe persecution and suffering. Throughout history, our people have faced not only physical torment, but also spiritual attacks aimed at extinguishing both our bodies and our souls.

'Emperor Nero, for example, demanded that a statue of himself be placed in Solomon's temple. This, we know, is directly against our Holy laws. Our ancestors refused and rebelled against the greatest empire the world had ever seen. It was David and Goliath on a colossal scale. It's estimated that over eight hundred thousand Jews died during the wars of rebellion against Rome. Still, the Torah, and our people, survived.

'The Greeks also sought to make us forget our Torah and force us to violate God's decrees, attempting to erode our faith through tyranny and torture.

'Yet, it is precisely in these moments of distress that our faith in God and our devotion to His Torah must grow stronger. We must remember that our ancestors faced similar trials and emerged with their faith intact, serving as a testament to the power of unwavering belief."

A finger tapped Franceska's shoulder, and she looked up to see Marek standing beside her, gesturing for her to make room in the pew for him to sit with her.

With a smile, Franceska slid down in the pew, and Marek, while trying to maintain his pride, sat beside her. Then, slowly, Franceska reached over and took his hand in hers. She knew that if anyone had noticed, they would've been chastised for this display of affection in a synagogue, but Franceska took the risk knowing that they needed to be close to each other.

"Now the Jewish faith is alone in its uniqueness in the world. We are bound through our ancestors, and God himself is bound and tied to us. It is the reason why we say in our prayers, Our God, the God of our fathers, God of Abraham, Isaac, and Jacob. The light of God is within us.

'Let us consider the concept of total devotion, which means continuing to believe in God even when He seems hidden from us. The story of Rabbi Akiva, who recited the Shema while being tortured by the Romans, accepting the yoke of Heaven, serves as a powerful example of unwavering faith. Rabbi Akiva's willingness to sacrifice himself for God's love and justice reminds us that our faith must be wholehearted. We must guard against questioning God's actions, as doing so can weaken our faith and distance us from Him.

'Finally, we must understand that our suffering is not a punishment for wrongdoing but a test of our faith. Our persecution is due to our identity as the people of Israel, bound to God and His holy Torah. Let us draw strength from the teachings of our ancestors, who endured similar trials and remained steadfast in their devotion. By doing so, we can reinforce our faith and remain committed to

God, even in the face of unimaginable suffering. As we pray for mercy and an end to our suffering, let us reaffirm our belief that everything we endure is derived from God's love for His people. May our faith grow stronger, and may we continue to stand firm in our devotion to Him. Amen."

Nobody in the congregation moved. Not a soul stirred. Everyone remained seated. It was not a sermon that promised an end to suffering, or the hope of an eternal reward, and Franceska knew it was right for the rabbi to be realistic. These current tribulations they were facing were only the beginning of the horrors about to befall the Jewish people.

Shivering in terror, Franceska leaned her head on Marek's shoulder, taking a small measure of solace in knowing that her ancestors endured previous tribulations. Still, she knew it was not without great suffering and loss of life.

She didn't know what the future held for her and Marek, for her parents or her friends, and how they would possibly survive the hell that was undoubtedly coming.

There was no way to escape, either. The entire west half of her homeland was now controlled by hate filled and indoctrinated Nazis, and the east was under the iron fist of the Soviets.

Regardless, she knew that the only way they would survive would be together, and Franceska clung tightly to Marek. She took to heart the sermon provided so eloquently by the rabbi but feared that she would buckle under the pressure. She did not have the faith that some others in the synagogue carried, but Franceska knew that she would need to bolster her resolve for the coming days.

If the police chief was correct, she knew that Hell awaited them, and she would need ounce of strength within her to survive the approaching storm.

Franceska held Marek's hand firmly, knowing that no matter what the future held, their love and resilience would guide them through the impending turmoil.

End of Book One

9 781738 888283